PRIVATE WALLS

A NOVEL

Kris Heywood

Private Walls

This is a work of fiction. All the characters, names, incidents, organizations, and dialogue in this novel are either the products of the author's imagination or are used fictitiously.

Published in the United States by Siskiyou Press.

Library of Congress cataloging-in-Publication Data

Heywood, Kris

Private Walls/Kris Heywood

2011912669

ISBN: 0615514049 ISBN-13: 978-0615514048

Siskiyou Press

1. Maria and Lucius—Fiction. 2. Munich 1960s—Fiction. 3. Multi-cultural—Fiction. 4. Mixed Race—Fiction. 5. American Occupation—Fiction. 6. Dysfunctional Family—Fiction. 7. Race-Bating—Fiction.

Printed in the United States of America

First Edition

Cover Art by Leanne Zinkand, Silverlining Designs

ALSO BY KRIS HEYWOOD

VOID

MARIA

EM'S WHEEL

For Beautiful Bavaria, Minga, and the Patrona

Munich, June 1961

CHAPTER 1

ON THE DAY OUR HONEYMOON ended Lucius asked me to wear the new skin-tight white pants and clingy green sweater he'd bought me the week before. "I'll take a mental snapshot of you before I turn the corner. Then I'll have a pretty picture in my mind while I'm at work," he said as we descended the stairs together at dawn. I stood on the sidewalk and watched him swagger toward the Kurfürstenplatz, waving to him each time he turned. He always waved back. At the corner he aimed his pretend camera at me and I struck a pose. He clicked the shutter, gave one last wave, and was gone, leaving behind an afterimage of raw male power wearing olive-green US Army fatigues.

I started my first day alone as a new wife by going back to sleep, still wearing the racy outfit. Around eleven I let the rumblings of midmorning traffic pull me out of my dreams and half an hour later I took the streetcar to the *Kaufhaus* (GLOSSARY page. 343) where I bought poster board, glue, and picture frames. Then I sat at the juice bar in the housewares section and drank three hazelnut milkshakes for lunch. They sloshed languidly around inside me on the return trip.

As I carried my purchases up the five flights to our roost I realized I was no longer bothered by the fact that we didn't have running water in our shabby little room. What did it matter? In one month Lucius and I would fly to California to explore our own Promised Land. Meanwhile we were happily exploring each other.

I tossed my unwieldy packages on top of our rumpled daybed, grabbed a couple of shopping nets, and clattered downstairs again to visit the three little shops on our block. At the butcher's I chose a slab of meat for our stew. At the greengrocer's I picked the most flawless potatoes and vegetables I could find to dice into the pot, and at the baker's I bought milk and a loaf of glossy new rye.

Then I climbed up our five flights of stairs for the third time that day. The bulging net bags kept banging against my shins, making me move a bit slower with each flight. Unfortunately it wasn't until I arrived on the top landing that I remembered about the lettuce I was supposed to buy for our salad. Leaning over the banister, I briefly considered navigating the vast distance to the lobby one more time. Then I admitted to myself that I simply didn't have enough energy left for the feat. I consoled myself with polishing our name plate under the bell-button, the one that said, Duncan, *4 rings.*

In the last two weeks the bell hadn't rung for us once.

Back in our room I opened the cookbook my considerate mother had included in my trousseau to an Eintopf (stew) recipe, cubed and braised the meat in my new yellow-enameled stew pot, and added multihued bits of fresh produce. As the colorful meal simmered toward perfection on the two-burner hot plate I tossed in some herbs, permeating the air with the aroma of thyme, marjoram and a bay leaf. And then, at last, I began my afternoon decorating project.

Lying on our narrow daybed with Lucius during our two-week introduction to matrimony it had occurred to me that the walls above us were empty space needing to be filled. And now that our brief honeymoon was over I knew just how to fill it. First I thumbtacked my sky-blue silk scarf above the pillows. Then I penciled a precise X on each side of the scarf at eye level and hammered in tiny nails with my smallest copper bottom saucepan. I matting and framed two enlargements of our black-and-white wedding photos, hung them on the nails, and stepped back to consider the effect.

The Hungarian photographer had done good work. One picture showed the bride and groom emerging arm in arm from the *Standesamt*, blinking into mid-May sunshine. He was wearing a form-fitting winter uniform that looked dark gray but was really forest green. She was floating on clouds of white lace. The second shot showed the joyous couple pausing on the steps leading to the sidewalk. He was bending down, his long arms clasping her slender waist. She was reaching up, her hands around his muscular neck. The contrast of her light hands against his dark skin was startling even in the black-and-white photos.

When the stew bubbled dry I added more water to the spitting pot and turned the heat to its lowest setting. Then I tore all twelve of my honeymoon sketches out of the oversized spiral pad I kept under the bed and tacked them on the long wall above the mattress. I'd drawn my new husband from every conceivable angle as he lay stretched out on the bed in lulls between wedded bliss, his dusky skin shiny with sweat, his muscles and sinews glorious mixtures of light and shade.

Soon a dozen benevolently smiling Luciuses were looking down upon me. With graphite and charcoal and earthy pastels I had transformed my African prince into King of the World.

By the simple act of pinning up the overlapping pages I was claiming the room for us the way he'd claimed the bed mere minutes after he carried me over the threshold.

Turning on my battered transistor radio, permanently tuned to the AFN station, I helped Jim Reeves sing, "Put your sweet lips a little closer to the phone . . ." while I brushed my long, nearly black hair over one shoulder. Then I changed into my yellow gingham shift, which had an efficient zipper instead of clumsy slow buttons. I slapped my cheeks pink, sat, and waited for the musical tinkle of Lucius's keys out on the landing.

Soon the doorbell shrilled once, twice, thrice, four times. I laughed with delight, sure he was trying out the code on our name plate. Skipping through the hall, I flung the landing door wide. A stranger stood before me. He was my height but stocky and short-necked, wearing a cheap blue business suit that did little to hide the beer belly underneath. I stared at him. He stared at me. Then he shifted his feet.

I said, "*Ja?*"

He tapped the *Duncan* label. "I rang four times."

We stared at each other some more. Then I said, "And?"

He spread his beefy hands. "And here I am."

Why would an overweight and utter stranger struggle up five dismal flights of sagging medieval stairs to ring four times for Duncan? Sorting through my meager life experiences for some revelation, I narrowed my eyes. "What are you trying to sell?"

"Sell?" he repeated. "I? But it's you—" He nodded at the label and said slowly, as to an imbecile, "See? It says *Doonkahn* four rings."

Business suit. Black tie. White shirt. "Jehovah's witness!" I sputtered. They would climb to the top of the Matterhorn to save a single soul. In a lapse of good taste Vati had once joined the sect until he realized he was required to convert unwilling non-believers on a regular basis.

Before the missionary had a chance to confess I said coolly, "Sorry. Not interested," shut the door in his astonished face, and turned the lock. An instant later the bell shrilled again, one, two, three, four times. I ignored it.

Ingrid stuck her school-marmish head out of the room next to ours before the last peal had faded. "It must be for you," she said. "I counted four rings."

I muttered, "Someone made a mistake."

She looked at the landing door, then at me, favored me with one of her insufferably superior smiles, and asked, "Do you want *me* to take care of him?"

"Don't let him sell you something you don't want," I advised in my mature married voice and went into my room to arrange china and silverware on our table. Looking out of our only window at the massive buildings across the street I wondered again why Ingrid found Lucius and me so amusing. Was it because she had seen him scoop me up, wedding gown and all, when we arrived fresh from our wedding, or was it because he was the only male actually living at this address?

I turned off the radio, folded three linen napkins into intricate triangles, and strained so hard to hear Ingrid's murmured conversation with the man on the landing that I missed the sound of Lucius's footsteps until he walked into our room.

"This door isn't even locked!" he said, aghast. Behind him I saw Ingrid beckoning the missionary into the hall. Then Lucius firmly closed and locked our door and wrapped his arms around me. "Long time no see. What time did Mutti say she was coming?"

"Around a quarter past five."

"Excellent!" He pulled at his boot laces. "That gives us fifteen minutes." His military belt buckle clicked; he left a trail of fatigues and underwear on his way to the bed.

"Hey—I just made it up," I protested. "And suppose she comes early—"

"Late. Bound to be. Traffic's fierce. Stossverkehr (rush hour)."

I shrugged, reached for my zipper, made it purr down the shift, and stepped clear off the garment as soon as it dropped to my ankles. I was not wearing anything underneath. A Taurus could be quite practical that way.

From his favorite position on our bed Lucius didn't notice the newly transformed walls. From mine I saw how the breeze he was making rippled the silk scarf hanging above me. My last conscious act was to try and keep us centered so that my left knee would not hit against the wall and broadcast our pastime. I failed. Cringing as a rhythmic knocking joined the squeal of worn mattress springs, I hoped the wall was too thick for Ingrid to guess what we were doing.

Then I closed my eyes and shut out the world. When I opened them again the blue scarf billowed out in one fluid motion just before Lucius buried his damp face in my hair. The jury of twelve gazed approvingly at me from above.

And then the doorbell shrilled. Once. Twice. Thrice. Four times.

We froze.

"Told you!" I said.

He scrambled up. "Stall her!"

Smoothly, I stepped into the gingham shift, zipped up and finished tugging my bangs into place while he still hunted for his second sock and his briefs.

"Keep her on the landing till I give the all-clear!" he whispered.

I left the room door ajar and crossed the corridor just as the second volley began, shrieking like an intermittent siren. "Yes!" I cried, "I'm coming!" Opening the landing door a hand's breadth, I saw Mutti standing outside, impatiently tapping a heel. She was wearing her beige secretary ensemble, including spikes and the hat I thought I'd permanently ruined during my misadventure with Spider.

Holding a cone-shaped bag of strawberries to her chest like a shield, she gave a tense smile and asked, "Am I late for our dinner?"

I assured her she wasn't. "What huge berries!" I said, blocking her entrance.

"*Gell?* "she agreed. "I stopped by the *Viktualienmarkt* and couldn't resist that ripe-strawberry smell. They are fresh from Italy." She gave me a measuring glance. "I believe you've grown these past two weeks."

"I *feel* taller," I admitted, turning to see a coffee-brown hand wave from our room-door. Stepping aside to let Mutti pass, I said graciously, "Please come in. We've been expecting you."

Lucius was sitting on the edge of our surprisingly well-made bed. He was dressed in the black slacks and red polo shirt he'd worn the Sunday we met, last July. His long legs were casually crossed and my German cookbook was propped on his lap upside down as he pretended to study the *Eintopf* recipe. He'd found his second sock but not the briefs, which poked out from under the foot end of the bed. "Looks delicious," he said. I plucked the book off his lap, toeing the briefs out of sight at the same time. "*Hallo*, Mother," he beamed, jumping up to pull one of our two chairs out for her. "Wie gehts (how are you)?"

She beamed right back at him and sat, still clutching the berries. "You have had good holidays?" she asked in her stilted English.

"Prima (great)!" He dragged out the other chair for me.

She blushed, remembering what our vacation had been for. Lucius went to sit on the bed. She turned to keep him in sight and found the twelve naked Luciuses tacked to the wall. Suppressing an involuntary gasp, she pulped the strawberries against her beige dress and grimaced as juice stained the fabric.

Following her distressed stare, Lucius finally noticed the artwork. "Maria!" he cried. "How could you!" Then he leaned solicitously toward Mutti. "Are you okay?"

"I believe I've ruined my dress," she murmured.

I pried what was left of our dessert out of her hands and said, "Quick, take it off in the bathroom and rinse it under the faucet."

"But what'll I wear?"

"My pleated wool skirt and a blouse." I pulled my old school outfit out of the wardrobe for her. She accepted it with a long-suffering sigh. I unpacked a brand-new towel from my trousseau and preceded her to the bathroom to make sure it wasn't occupied by one of the other three tenants.

"Really, Maria, you should have left those pictures under the bed," Lucius said when I came back alone. "For a second there I was afraid you gave her a heart attack."

"But you said you liked my sketches!"

"I do. Only — "

"Only what? It's called life-drawing. Artists do it all the time. I bet Anna did it in that fancy art school she went to. Besides, if Mutti weren't so prissy she'd have noticed that nothing really shows."

He chuckled. "God, the look on her face!"

"She'll get over it." I sorted through the soaked paper bag, removing the strawberries she'd crushed. "She's too naïve for her own good. It's about time she wised up. Besides, this is *our* house, you know. Our walls. We can hang any pictures we like."

"True," he said, rescuing a half-crushed berry before I could throw it away. "Only, Maria — don't you think a dozen of me are a bit much?"

Mutti returned looking younger than she had any right to in my old school clothes. She laid her damp dress on our rickety counter and said in German, "I apologize for my prissy attitude. I'm getting quite tired of it myself."

It was my turn to blush; I'd forgotten she understood more English than she could speak.

She reclaimed her seat. "Now that I've spoiled our dessert I'm taking you both out for some Italian ices. In my new car." She leaned back to enjoy the befuddled look on my face.

"What did she say?" Lucius asked, eager for a translation.

I said, "I don't have the faintest idea."

"Herr Adler's blue VW," Mutti explained. "I've been paying him in installments. He didn't ask much for it. He said he was glad to find someone who'd give it a good home. It's so ancient it barely passed inspection. But he's gone over every nut and bolt. And it's clean." Her green eyes shone. "I have more news. But first we eat."

Halfway through the meal she complimented me on the hearty stew and chided me gently about the forgotten salad. "Every day of your life, from the time your baby teeth came in, I've served you lettuce with shredded carrots. That's why your skin is smooth and your hair shiny. Don't stop while you're ahead. It's just as important as the meat on your plate."

I rolled my eyes and scooped up a green bean. "This stew is *full* of vegetables. Didn't you have some more good news for us?"

Mutti rummaged in her purse and held out a document as if it were the first prize in the lottery. "My new driver's license. Entirely without O.F.'s assistance."

"No!" I said, almost envious. "How?"

"I've been studying for months. And the last couple of weekends Herr Adler has been taking me to the country in the blue VW to let me drive it on deserted dirt roads. He's an extremely patient man."

Lucius rapped a spoon against his water glass. It gave a melodious ring. "Clue me in," he said. "Was gibts (what's happening)?" I translated everything for him. He laughed and said wistfully, "I sure wish *I* had a car. Only, it isn't a beat-up old VW *I* want."

"Yes, yes," I told him. "I remember. A red sports car. With black bucket seats. Going down the Autobahn at 150 miles an hour — or was it 200?"

After I translated our conversation for Mutti she said, "But you will fly to America soon. Yes?"

"Next month," we answered together.

"You buy a car there," she told Lucius. Then she asked me, "Have you gone to the police station yet to get your passport changed over to your married name?"

"Not yet," I admitted. "I've been . . . busy."

"Do it tomorrow. The precinct office is in walking distance. You must always keep your documents in order."

She could be so tedious sometimes. "Yes, Mutti," I said. "But I don't think I'll need it in America. They'll give me something called a green card."

She buttered a slice of rye and took an appreciative bite. "Nevertheless. A lot has been happening since you two got married. Horst is moving his studio out of that roach-infested building in the middle of Schwabing. He told me he'd been looking for an affordable place for a couple of years, but what with the housing shortage he's had too much competition. Then he saw a high-rise just starting to go up and put his name on the list. A week ago they gave him the key. He'll keep his private apartment, of course, but after O.F.'s despicable behavior on your wedding day he's decided to let Anna move into the new studio. She's all packed and ready to go. There's hot running water — in the kitchen sink, the bathroom sink, *and* in the tub. Not to mention a real shower."

As I interpreted, Lucius and I glanced at our own sink-less, bathroom-less nest, and then at the woman who'd found it for us and rented it on the spot asking no one's opinion.

"This is nothing," she said with a dismissive wave. "You'll be in your California palace soon enough. But you should see my new place. It's a farmhouse so old it ought to be condemned."

"What?" I asked weakly, wishing I had someone to interpret for *me*.

"Anna is planning to move out before O.F. comes home on Friday. So am I. His stupid curse was the last straw."

"Bitte (what)?" Now I was totally lost. "I have the feeling you've left out a sentence or two."

Her eyes flashed. "Only that, with both of my girls safely gone, I'm finally leaving him. Bei Nacht und bei Nebel (in the dead of night). Without a forwarding address."

Her words gave me a chill. Despotic O.F. would not allow the defection. Things were bound to turn ugly. And soon.

CHAPTER 2

A FEW DAYS LATER, IN LATE AFTERNOON, I stood on the shaded sidewalk in front of our building, chewing on a hunk of dry salami. The aroma of hot rolls was drifting from the bakery shop to my receptive nose, tempting me to run into the shop and buy half a dozen. I only stayed put because I'd promised Mutti to be at the curb precisely at five. She was un-characteristically late.

A pensioner approached, wearing a gray cardigan to match his sparse hair and hugging a loaf of Schwartzwälder rye. He was staring at me from behind thick-lensed glasses, running his eyes up and down the whole length of my body. I pretended not to notice but as soon he passed me I stuck my tongue out at his retreating back.

A staccato of heels announced the approach of a stodgy housewife, her skirt midway to her calves. She was lugging two overstuffed leather shopping bags and glowered at me so fiercely that I yielded the entire sidewalk to her and pressed my back against the building, nervously nibbling on my sausage. She shifted her load, sneered at my bare-toed flat sandals, and inspected the rest of me with frosty eyes.

When I offered her a polite "Grüss Gott (hello)," she sniffed as if the air had gone bad, raised her long nose, and crossed the street to the opposite sidewalk as if she were afraid I might contaminate her in some way.

Furtively, I inspected myself to see if there was anything objectionable about my figure or my clothes. My toes were clean enough. So were my jeans. If they were a bit tight at the buttocks it was only because Lucius liked them that way. And I'd just ironed all the wrinkles out of the cotton shirt I was wearing. I ran my fingers through the unruly hair I'd brushed out of my face only a few minutes before and found it more or less where I had put it. Could it be the salami? Mutti never tired of reminding me it was uncouth to eat in public.

I stuffed the sausage into the trench coat I carried draped over my arm just as a faint *clickety-click* became audible from the direction of the Kurfürstenplatz. And then a roundish shape darted out of traffic and squealed to a stop at the curb, the sidewall of the right front tire scraping cement.

The old blue VW's passenger door no longer opened from the outside, so Mutti leaned across, released the inside latch, and said, "Climb in. Traffic's heavy. We're bound to be late. I hope they started without us."

Before we had finished our memorable dinner on Monday Lucius had volunteered the two of us to help my mother and sister move. Mutti accepted at once. Now I lowered myself on to a spongy seat, slammed the passenger door, and clutched the dashboard handle as the *click-click-click* increased in both volume and speed and the car pulled away from the curb. I marveled at the abrupt right turn Mutti coolly negotiated onto the next side street, and the sharp left turn a block later, this one followed by the sound of screeching brakes and the warning clang of a streetcar. Mutti didn't even blink.

"You've developed nerves of steel," I said.

She laughed. "If I'm polite the other drivers won't let me merge. Did you tell Lucius we would be at the house by five-thirty? Well, now unfortunately it will be closer to six. Herr Neumeyer is going to be upset. He's in a great hurry this afternoon because he foolishly scheduled another move after mine and is afraid he won't be able to finish that job before dark. I only hope he can hold up his side of the couch. He's such a puny man."

"But tough." I remembered how valiantly the skinny mover had struggled up our five flights with my wooden trunks on the eve of my wedding. "Are you sure he'll let Lucius help him? He refused to let me." I pictured him slinging Mutti's green couch over his shoulder, wobbling as he pushed Lucius aside so he wouldn't have to worry about splitting the hauling fee.

Mutti chuckled. "I already told him Lucius will do it for free." She slammed her foot on the brake at the Scheidplatz, narrowly avoiding a small boy darting across the busy street. "Over there," she pointed. "The second high-rise behind the new supermarket. Anna's place is on the sixth floor."

"You mean Horst's place," I corrected, a bit envious of my sister's good luck.

Mutti shrugged. "She's the one moving in, isn't she? Horst helped her bring over most of her clothes yesterday. I'm not exaggerating when I say they filled his BMW to the roof. She had to leave her shoes behind so she locked them in her wardrobe. I'm sure Lucius and Herr Neumeyer won't even notice the additional weight when they carry it out. Anna had to go to Grünwald with Horst this afternoon. She gave me her front door key." Mutti fished it out of the ashtray and held it up for me to admire. It was brassy and as new as the high-rise.

I had something for *her* to admire. As we passed the Schuttberg on our left I pulled out an envelope, removed the check it contained, and held it in front of her nose, obscuring her view of the street. She pushed it away. "What is it?"

"It's called an allotment check. It came in the mail. Made out to Maria Duncan. Two hundred dollars! That's eight hundred *Mark*. Every month, Lucius said. Just for being married."

She said drily, "Where are you planning to cash it? Or have you finally gone to the police-station to have your passport updated?"

"I'm going tomorrow."

She gave an exasperated sigh.

"Besides," I went on. "Lucius says I can cash my check at the American bank inside Warner Kaserne. With my new dependent ID card."

"You'll open a savings account, of course," she said, passing the Harthof bus unloading a slew of passengers at the next corner.

"Of course," I repeated, though my first impulse was to buy two celebratory steaks to mark the occasion. I peered up at the bus windows, wondering if I knew any of the passengers, but the sun reflected from the glass, glaring into my eyes and threatening to blind me. I used to come home on that bus. Most of my old neighbors rode it to and from the city, since cars were still scarce in the Harthof. This time of day the bus was always overloaded, the passengers wedged between armpits and bad breath.

"Your car's nice," I said, grateful for the elbow room. "But somehow I can't quite picture Herr Adler sitting in it. Are you sure it was his?"

"His hobby-car. He claims rebuilding the engine helped him unwind from office politics."

"Did he actually drive it?"

"As little as possible, I'm sure. It's been standing in his garage for years. There isn't a single rust spot anywhere on the chassis. I believe he's as fond of the old wreck as other men are of their wives."

"Maybe more," I said, thinking of Vati and O.F., neither one capable of honest affection.

And then, when we were within a few blocks of the bakery shack that stood in front of the disreputable Alabama Bar, Mutti's new car coughed a few times, jerked, stopped clicking, and rolled to a stop in the middle of the street. A chorus of horns bleated their protests behind us.

She hit the steering wheel, groaning "Verdammt nochmal (dammit)!" Impatient drivers passed left and right, thumping their foreheads, while she pumped the gas pedal with increasing desperation, twisting the key as if it were part of some kind of magic act. The car coughed one final time and continued to block traffic. Mutti sputtered a litany of swear words I had never heard before, concluding with a mild combination I recognized. "*Himmeldonnerwetter,*" she cried. "Now the stupid key won't come out!" She pulled at it until I stayed her hand, afraid something would break.

"Ach Gott (oh God)," she said, cautiously opening the door. "Will you help me push?"

I got out and applied all the force I had in me to the VW's well-rounded behind. Mutti pushed at the door, one hand inside on the steering wheel. When it was safely parked at the curb she closed the windows, snatched up her purse and Anna's key, and walked around the whole car as if she might discover a secret button that would make it go. Finding none, she kicked a tire with the pointy toe of her shoe. The car, used to a more logical driver, gave a discreet shudder. Mutti gasped and hopped on one leg. Her paisley skirt swung in a great arc, exposing the flesh-colored lace on the bottom of her slip and two well-shaped knees. For one instant I saw how pretty she was but then I blinked and she changed back to the dull, everyday mother I expected to see.

"We'll walk," she decided. "It's faster than waiting for the bus." It caught up with us ten minutes later when we were almost across the street from the bakery. We started to run and she cried, "We won!" as we passed the bus stop seconds before the bus squealed to a halt.

After we crossed to the opposite sidewalk I automatically veered toward the bakery. "Not now," she said sharply. "We're quite late." I kept on going anyway. She called after me, "I'm not waiting for you. You'll have to catch up," and walked away, hips and skirt swinging, her heels striking sparks.

I bought the half-dozen rolls I'd missed out on earlier, along with two almond crescents, and had to run a block at top speed before I could fall into step beside her again. I held out one of the crescents as a peace offering but she shook her head and said pointedly, "*I* don't eat on the street!"

In answer I bit off the pastry's crunchy, chocolaty tip. Clouds were gathering overhead. I put on the trench coat, buttoning it up to the chin. I had already pinned a cushion on the inside before leaving home.

"It's not going to rain," she said, looking skyward.

"I know. It's just that I don't want to confuse the neighbors." Thanks to Mutti they still thought I *had* to get married.

We rounded the final corner and saw an old truck parked at the far end of the apartments. "Good thing you gave Lucius your house-key," I said. "Looks like they just about got everything loaded."

As we drew nearer I noticed that Herr Neumeyer was leaning against a fender, smoking one of his expertly rolled cigarettes. "Es tut mir leid (I'm sorry)," Mutti told him. "My car broke down. Are you ready to go?"

He pursed his lips to blow out some smoke. "As soon as the Ami (Yank) comes out with the coffee table." Watching the smoke dissipate, he suggested delicately, "Maybe you ran out of gas."

"That's exactly what I would expect a man to say," Mutti scowled. "For your information, I tanked up a couple of days ago. I'm going to make a quick phone call. If you can wait an extra five minutes."

His face fell. "Now, Frau Hohner, I told you—"

But she was in no mood to listen and walked off, glancing up at the truck-bed in passing. Then she stopped, stricken. "You do know we're unloading the furniture first?"

He nodded. "At the Scheidplatz."

"Then why is the wardrobe at the front end and the couch on the bottom of all my boxes? We'll have to take everything off to get at both pieces."

"Balance," he said sagely. "About the couch—did you want me to put it on *top* of your boxes?"

She huffed and continued toward to the corner, reaching it just as Lucius came around the other side carrying her stately mahogany coffee table. She looked up at him, her frown instantly transforming itself into a smile.

"*Hallo*, Mother," he said. "We're finished, I think."

"Thank you, Lucius. You please sit in the back and make sure nothing fall off. We go in one minute."

"What's up?" he asked me as she hurried passed him. "Something bothering her?"

"The car is kaputt (broke down)."

He whistled. "Bad timing. I'd be upset too."

He stashed the coffee table on the truck-bed and helped the mover spread a canvas tarp over the load. They tied down the front corners but left the back end loose. Lucius sat on it, knees against chest. I couldn't help thinking that his fatigues were more appropriate to the occasion than Mutti's fancy skirt and heels. When she came back I started to climb up the tail-gate to sit next to my husband.

She put a motherly hand on my arm. "The wind will make you look like *Struwelpeter*. You better get in the cab with me."

I hesitated, wishing she'd begin to understand that I no longer had to act the part of obedient daughter. Then, out of habit, I acquiesced anyway and slid to the middle of the bench seat. She sat by the window, rolling it down to lean out an elbow. Herr Neumeyer started the engine, rumbled into the street, and begged my pardon each time his stick shift jammed my leg.

"Frau Forster insisted that I tell her why we're taking away the couch and the wardrobe," Mutti murmured into my ear. "But I didn't." We passed the blue VW, looking cruelly abandoned. She sighed. "I called Herr Adler. He promised to come look at it. If it's not fixed by tomorrow morning I don't know how I'll get to work. The farmhouse isn't near any public transportation."

"Why are you moving so far out? You could have rented a room in our building instead."

She gave a shudder and said quickly, "No, I could not!" Then she blushed and added, "After all, *you'll* be gone in a few weeks!" as if defending her position in an argument I didn't know we were having.

"Your furniture wouldn't fit, anyway," I told her. "How will you get everything out of the apartment? The oaken hutch in the kitchen must weigh a ton." I indulged in my newest daydream. It was about O.F. returning from his sales route late Friday afternoon, unlocking the door, and finding the place completely and totally empty, his footsteps reverberating from bare walls.

"Exactly," Mutti said. "That's why I decided to leave everything behind — except for the pieces Anna wanted."

I thought she'd switched to a foreign language. "Excuse me?"

"I'm letting him keep everything else," she elaborated. "That furniture was hand-built to last several lifetimes. Most of it's too heavy for two men to budge. In truth, the whole set has become a millstone around my neck. Besides, the farmhouse is sort of semi-furnished. And as soon as I get my half of our Bausparvertrag (savings) I'll buy something more modern. Light stuff I can carry on my own. Danish style."

"Too bad," I said. "I've been looking forward to helping you break into O.F.'s locked half of the wardrobe tonight. Why don't you buy a used pickup truck and give the VW back to Herr Adler? Then you can move your new Danish furniture around whenever you like."

For some reason Herr Neumeyer thought that was funny, for he slapped the dashboard and bleated like an elderly goat.

Mutti leaned around me. "Keep both hands on the wheel, if you please."

He complied at once, but turned to face her. "My wife doesn't drive. Never will as long as I have anything to say about it. Leads a woman down the wrong road."

Her eyes became angry slits. "You better look straight ahead so *you* won't go down that wrong road. If you don't mind."

He drew another hand-rolled cigarette out of his shirt pocket, stuck one end between tight lips, and found a lighter among dashboard debris. After he'd taken the first couple of drags, he asked lazily, "May I?"

Cheeks mottled, Mutti rummaged in her purse for her own pack and lighter, releasing a whiff of cloying perfume. It took my breath away. The smoke swirling at me from left and right did little to restore it. I longed for a glimpse of Lucius but the wardrobe blocked my view of the truck-bed so that I could only imagine my fortunate husband relaxing among the load, fresh air licking at his short cap of curls. With all my heart I wished I had ignored Mutti's admonition and finished climbing up the tailgate to sit beside him.

While the truck rumbled toward the Scheidplatz Mutti and Herr Neumeyer puffed on their cigarettes in fuming silence. I tried to return to my daydream about mean-spirited O.F. finding the apartment cleaned out but try as I might I could not imagine him accepting her desertion with any semblance of grace.

I asked, "Will you have a phone?"

She snorted. "There's a two-year wait for installation."

"How close are your nearest neighbors?"

"There are none."

I had suspected as much. "Then you better explain to Herr Neumeyer that he mustn't tell where you've moved to. In case anyone asks."

She looked stricken. "O.F. wouldn't."

"He would." No doubt he'd call every moving business in Munich in order to track his fugitive wife. Worse — most likely nosy Frau Forster had committed both mover and truck to her memory, including the license number. She'd be glad to impart the details to O.F. the minute he asked.

CHAPTER 3

THE HIGH-RISE MUTTI HAD POINTED out to me earlier sat on one side of a big parking lot. A slightly older version of the building sat on the other. Herr Neumeyer stopped as near to the entrance of the new structure as he could, rolled up the tarp, and began to pull at the pile underneath. Lucius handed down the coffee table. We worked in relays until the truck was cleared of the small stuff.

The men slid the couch to the edge and carefully set it on the pavement, followed by the matching easy chair and Anna's wardrobe. Then they lifted Mutti's crates back onto the truck-bed and I took off the trench coat, tested the weight of the coffee table, and decided I could carry it all by myself.

Mutti stuffed Anna's key into the back pocket of my jeans and said, "Six-thirty-two. There is a freight elevator in the lobby."

"Aren't you coming?"

She nodded at the pile at our feet. "And leave my things? Hardly. I'll start reloading while you're gone."

The coffee table, custom-made by the same village carpenter who had built our three solid wardrobes, was growing heavier with each step. At my side, the mover and Lucius were wrestling with the couch. Judging from their pained expressions it was getting heavier with each step too, no doubt because of the cumbersome hide-a-bed. We crammed ourselves and our loads into the boxy freight elevator. When its slow doors finally sealed themselves shut the space inside seemed to shrink. Giving in to an irrational childhood fancy I imagined faulty steel cables snapping strand by strand as we slowly rose up the shaft. I was giddy with relief when we managed to reach the sixth floor intact.

Horst's new studio was more than twice the size of the Duncan honeymoon suite, not counting kitchenette and bathroom. His two easels stood near an enormous plate-glass window. The clothes he'd helped Anna move were spread over a sheet on the floor. The room seemed to become smaller once the men and I set down the furniture.

They staggered out to get the wardrobe and I turned on every faucet to admire the hot water pouring out. But what I admired even more was the half-sized refrigerator I discovered tucked under the kitchen counter. At our place I had to throw out our leftovers after we ate. Whenever I forgot to scrape out the rice pot the white kernels started growing gray fuzz by the following evening.

The men returned with the wardrobe and argued in pantomime about where to put it, as if it weren't obvious that it should stand perpendicular to the couch-bed to double as privacy screen. While they went to bring up the easy chair I sat on the couch and leaned back, listening to the gentle drone of the refrigerator. Then I caught a whiff of some obnoxious O.F. odors—his miracle cure for baldness, his stale early-morning breath, the cigarettes he invariably lighted as Mutti poured him his tea. The smells had been permanently absorbed by the couch fabric.

Nauseated, I fled to the window, opened it, and leaned out for a bird's eye view of the Scheidplatz. I marveled at the never-ending array of streetcars and buses arriving and departing from that terminal. Past the busy intersection I caught a glimpse of the Schuttberg way off to the left and envied Anna some more. Only a short stroll away, it was surrounded by parkland and wide-open fields while our room on Hohenzollernstrasse was boxed in by clumpy old buildings that cast a permanent shade except at high noon.

Lofty black clouds were sailing across the vast sky, and I envied my sister again for being able to sit here and watch storms brewing. Her floor was newly varnished parquet; mine was ancient linoleum scrubbed bare of color and design. Off past the left corner of the high-rise I could just make out the low, flat roof of the supermarket. There Anna could buy in five minutes everything I had to go to four different shops to procure. On the other hand, if anything did happen to one of her elevators it wouldn't be me that was stuck inside when it came crashing down from the sixth floor.

After Lucius and Herr Neumeyer arranged the easy chair to an angle all three of us could agree on I left the sweating men at the freight elevator and dashed down all six flights of stairs, sliding a hand along the banister, hoping to beat them to the ground floor. We arrived at about the same time but only because the freight elevator did everything at an excruciatingly slow pace, including sliding its doors shut and open.

Meanwhile Mutti had restacked her crates around the overseas trunks, which had not only made the journey to Yonkers and back with her when she was half-grown but had served as make-shift benches in our cramped apartment on

Hilde's farm. The trunks had been hibernating in our dim city attic ever since we'd moved to München when I was nine.

Herr Neumeyer studied the darkening sky. A shower seemed imminent. He unrolled the tarp and Lucius once more made himself comfortable on its loose end. I *almost* asked Mutti for permission to join him. But then I took my trench coat and the bag of baked goods out of the truck-cab, calmly informed her that I was riding in back, and climbed over the tailgate to sit with my husband before she could even think of voicing an objection.

Lucius cradled me against his broad chest, draping an arm over my shoulder. I snuggled into his warmth and inhaled the scent of his soap and his aftershave. When the truck began to vibrate beneath us he took off his cap, clamped it onto my head, and said, "So the wind won't knot up your pretty hair."

A big wide-track red American convertible with its white top folded down was slowly cruising on to the lot. The driver was a young, solidly built American with a brown crew cut, wearing U.S. Army fatigues. His passenger, who looked to be about twenty and had long light-blonde hair spilling down her back, could easily have qualified for a BB look-alike contest. It was lucky for me that Lucius loved my hair just as it was and often told me so, though my secret desire was to look in the mirror one morning and find my dark chestnut curls transformed to a gleaming raven-wing-black.

As the car drew level both driver and passenger looked up at Lucius and me and narrowed their eyes. Lucius gave them a reserved nod and I started a knee-jerk, polite little smile. They made a point of turning away. He muttered something I didn't quite catch. She gave a hard, indignant laugh. That's when I noticed she had dark-brown hair roots. It didn't stop Lucius from looking with ill-disguised longing at both girl and car.

He shook himself out of the fascination and muttered, "Nice car. But I've got my heart set on a foreign make. Something sleek and low. Besides, that Pontiac's too big for your narrow cobblestoned streets. What we want is a Porsche or a Triumph or a Ferrari."

The girl's hair undulated enticingly in a sudden stiff breeze. An instant later the cloud directly overhead dipped without warning and burst, dropping a thick sheet of rain upon us. The GI stopped the car and scrambled out, frantically yanking at the folded-back top. She climbed into the backseat to help him. In less than a minute they looked like waterlogged sewer rats. On the girl it was not entirely unbecoming. "Oh-oh. Their roof seems to be stuck," Lucius said smugly from under the tarp he had raised over our heads as soon as the first drop came down.

I put on my trench coat while Herr Neumeyer drove out of the lot and along the winding access road. Then I pulled out my sausage and rattled the bakery bag. "Hungry?" I asked Lucius. "We might as well eat while we can. Supper might be hours away." I reached in the bag for my second almond crescent but it was gone. My well-mannered mother, alone with the truck, had overcome her obsession with social etiquette and claimed it. That left me with the cold lumpy rolls and the hunk of salami. Lucius took it from me, cut it in half with his pocket knife, and presented me with the gnawed piece.

The rain had gentled by the time Herr Neumeyer merged with traffic. Looking up, it seemed to me as if some child-god had penciled a line across the dome of the sky and colored one hemisphere pitch-black, the other a brilliant blue. The receding Schuttberg stood just inside the dark half. Behind it churned an inky storm-wall. Slanting light from the late afternoon sun reached into the dark side and painted the slopes a vivid green. Rainbow fragments shimmered into being on both sides and grew upward until they spanned the entire hill. The patch of azure above the dazzling display was quickly engulfed by the cloud-bank as it spread to our half of the sky.

The wind increased, sweeping Lucius's cap from my hair, which immediately bushed out and stood on end. Lucius caught the cap on reflex, tightened its adjustable band, and stuffed it back on my head. Then he began counting passing sports cars, muttering, "Fiat. Karman Ghia. Triumph . . ." as if chanting a prayer.

Soon the rain returned full force, bringing with it thunder and lightning. We crept under the tarp and sat on its ends, weighing it down. Lucius sang a song called *Itsy bitsy Spider*, walked his fingers up my arm, and wound up tickling me all over. I taught him Alle meine Entchen (all my little ducklings), and in a burst of enthusiasm boldly recited *Swan swims over the sea*. We took turns shouting the verse as fast as we could until Lucius, laughing, tripped over his. My grand finale was a simple ditty I made up on the spot. I fed it to him word by word. It went like this:

>*Ach, du lieber Onkel Franz/ jetzt bist du abgetanzt.*
>*Ach, du lieber Onkel Franz/ du bist abgetanzt.*

After I gave him a literal translation Lucius said what it really meant was *Old Fart exit stage left*. No sooner were the words out of his mouth than a terrific clap from directly overhead made us cower and clutch on to each other. Somebody up there was listening.

Eventually the truck lumbered past the outskirts of Pasing. The rain had eased by the time Herr Neumeyer turned on to a narrow dirt road. It stopped entirely when he came to a stand of old trees. The two-story farmhouse on the other side of the trees was just as ramshackle as Mutti had said it would be—a lonely place on a path to nowhere. Its masonry was cracked, the green shutters were peeling, and the planters outside the windows were warped with age. When Herr Neumeyer stopped the engine we were surrounded by silence. Tender evening light shone through the tree branches, illuminating raindrops clinging to leaves. The air smelled of damp soil.

I breathed it in like perfume. "I like it."

Lucius nodded. "Me, too. A little paint, a few nails . . ."

"Lots of space," I said, envisioning dawn walks through the little forest.

He sighed. "If only we had a car. Can't live in the country without one."

Herr Neumeyer and Mutti climbed out of the cab, both stiff-kneed. She crossed her arms and shivered. "The temperature dropped. Did you manage to stay dry?"

"We managed," I said. "However did you find this place? It's so well hidden."

"Precisely. Herr Adler taught me to drive nearby. One Saturday I was jerking the VW up this particular lane and saw some people outside the house, tidying up. They let me look around and I thought, 'O.F. will never find me here.' It seemed a good idea."

"What did Herr Adler say?"

"Not much," she admitted. "But then I didn't ask his opinion. I'm through with letting men have the last word. More often than not they turn out to be wrong anyway. Besides, it's time I stood on my own two feet. Funny, though, isn't it . . ." She gave an embarrassed laugh. "I fought for years to get off Hilde's primitive farm and now I'm back where I started, outhouse and all."

"Actually," I corrected, "you've gone way beyond. Hilde's house is a mansion compared to this."

Cocking her head, she studied the wreck before us as if she were seeing it for the first time. "It's only temporary. Until O.F. pays out my half of the Bausparvertrag."

"We like it. Lucius is right. A little paint, some nails . . ."

She shook her head. "You haven't seen the inside."

The mover frowned at his watch and gestured for Lucius to help him shake the rain off the tarp. While they folded it Mutti and I grabbed some crates and made our way past immense puddles. "Does the house have electricity?" I asked her. "It looks as if it's been empty since before light bulbs were invented."

One of her spikes sank into mud. She grimaced, pulling it free. "I've learned a thing or two about oil lamps from our village days. But as far as I know the place is wired. At least the kitchen is."

We entered through the stable, which was well scrubbed, though old odors lingered. With its lumpy sofa and oil-cloth covered table, the kitchen reminded me of Hilde's, except that Mutti's wood cook stove was smaller and had a rusty top. "Cozy in winter," she said bravely.

"With a good fire," I agreed. "In fact, you could use one tonight." I put down my crate and looked inside the kindling box. It was empty. "If we didn't have to ride back to the city on the truck Lucius and I could collect a pile of sticks for you."

"Didn't I tell you? Anna and Horst are stopping by. They haven't seen this place yet, either. I'm sure Horst will be glad to drop you off later on his way through town. Come, we better help get the rest of my stuff off the truck before Herr Neumeyer decides to charge double."

The work was easily done. After the mover left Mutti unpacked three boxes and handed the empties to Lucius and me. I followed him along the trail into the woods. Every stick lying on the ground was wet.

"Only on the outside," Lucius said, snapping one across his knee. "See? Still dry on the inside. They'll burn okay once we get a fire going."

"But how can we get one started if everything's wet?"

In answer he reached up and broke dead twigs off a fir trunk. "There you go—the perfect kindling, matchstick thin and dry as bones. Set it on a heap of torn newspapers and the whole thing will explode soon as you touch a match to it."

"You're so smart," I gushed. "I never learned to build a proper fire. Never had to."

"I did. After I took off from Maryland."

"You see? That's what I mean. When *I* ran away from home I just froze all night. It never occurred to me to bring matches. Or a blanket."

He held me close. "Forgetting the matches was the second smartest thing you ever did in your life. If you had made it to sunny Italy I'd still be living on base. No castle, no *Hackerkeller*, no wedding night."

"And what was the first smartest thing I did?"

He kissed my ear. "Bumping into me on the Landstrasse (highway) that day."

My eyes were growing moist with nostalgia when he cupped my chin and turned my face sideway.

"I wonder," he said.

"You wonder what?"

"I wonder what you'd look like as a blonde."

My eyes dried instantly. I pulled away. "Well, give it up. You'll never find out."

He gave a low chuckle. "I was just kidding."

He reached for me again but I evaded his arms. I'd been absolutely sure that all those times he said he loved me just the way I was he had really meant it. Now I knew he had not and it stung.

CHAPTER 4

LUCIUS AND I MADE UP OUR QUARREL almost at once. In the process we forgot our wood-gathering mission until a twig snapped nearby and Mutti gave a tactful cough somewhere behind us. We drew apart. Public displays of affection were a far more serious offense in her eyes than the indiscreet eating of pastries, no matter how delicious both activities were. I prepared for her chastisement and my pithy response but Mutti just shook her head and smiled.

"Newlyweds have been known to lose track of time," she said. "When I think back to my eighteenth year and your Vati I recall similar lapses. But it's getting late. And rapidly cooler." She'd changed into flats and an old dirndl. Picking up one of the empty boxes, she led us deeper into the woods. Lucius pulled dead twigs off the trees and Mutti and I collected debris from the forest floor. When we found a spruce lying across the path we broke off as many seasoned branches as we could comfortably carry and settled on to the trunk, letting a profound hush enfold us.

Eventually Mutti said, "The day birds have gone to sleep. Soon the night birds will be on the prowl. There is the first owl. Hear it?"

We listened to the raptor's eerie *uhu-uhu*, though Lucius claimed it was actually asking, *who? who?* But then he once told me that roosters said *cock-a-doodle-do* when everyone knew they crowed *ku-ku-ru-ku*.

A distant train whistled. Once the sound faded we could hear the putter of an approaching car. "That must be Anna and Horst. Good, he can take us to Herr Adler's house. Maybe he's had a chance to work on the VW. At any rate, he's invited us all over for Brotzeit (a snack)."

My stomach growled. Mutti put a hand on my arm. "*Gell*, the mention of food wakes you right up. Always has. It takes a lot to spoil *your* appetite. Why don't you run ahead? Tell them we'll be there directly. Lucius can manage two boxes, I'm sure."

Horst was standing beside his car, testing the squishy ground to see if it was safe for his city shoes. On the other side of the BMW Anna was keeping a hand on her door and surveying her meager surroundings with obvious distaste. She was wearing the blue-and-white dress she'd bought for my wedding, with immaculate white heels.

"What a wreck!" she said. "Too bad it survived the bombs. I told Mutti to just change the lock on her apartment door. It's *her* home. Why should she give it up to O.F.? He's only there on weekends anyway. Let him find his own place." Anna had suffered through most of our O.F. years with subdued acquiescence, while I, protesting more vociferously, had received the full brunt of his toxic attention.

"She just wants peace," I told her, repeating the words Mutti had sobbed after each confrontation. "And a new beginning. She won't find it with him hammering on the front door, will she? If you ask me this relic is a step up from the endless rows of Marshall Plan housing."

Horst went around the corner of the farmhouse as if hoping to find more redeeming features on the other side. Anna started after him, then peered at the darkening ground. "Pure mud!" she said, lowering herself onto the passenger seat. "Did you manage to get my stuff moved to the new studio? How do you like it?"

"The view's great," I had to admit.

Mutti and Lucius emerged from the gloom. With his brown skin and drab fatigues he was nearly invisible until he flashed Anna a welcoming grin.

"Did Maria tell you my car broke down?" Mutti asked her. "It's at Herr Adler's. He invited us stop by for a snack. Can you come?"

Horst joined us from his exploration. "I could use a bite. After you give us a guided tour of your old Bude (shack)."

"Count me out. I'm not about to ruin my new shoes in those puddles," Anna told him. "I'm staying right here until you're ready to leave." Turning to Mutti, she asked, "What's Herr Adler's house like?"

Mutti gave an uncomfortable shrug. *"Ja mei, vornehm, halt."* A bit fancy.

I revealed our supper plans to Lucius, who had learned to wait patiently for my translated tidbits.

"He'll have a Mercedes kind of house," he predicted.

I, too, wanted to know where Mutti's former boss lived and was eager to see the Adler in his great eagle's nest. The three of us folded ourselves gratefully on to the rear seat. Horst was an impatient driver, bouncing over potholes, taking curves too fast. I was soon queasy and prayed we'd get to our destination before my stomach rebelled. Lucky for me Herr Adler lived in nearby Pasing.

Last year, at the end of my one-day apprenticeship in a print shop, he'd driven Mutti and me home and seen our Marshall plan wonder for the first time. He'd been hard put to keep the pity out of his voice, though it lay heavy in his eyes. That was why I wasn't surprised to find he lived in a more affluent neighborhood. Nor was I shocked to discover that his house was a villa. The smell of old wealth lingered in the night air.

"Thought so," Lucius said when we parked by a wrought-iron gate.

"Gut gesagt (well put)," Horst agreed.

"*Tja,*" Mutti sighed, looking embarrassed. "He inherited it. From his parents."

Anna stepped from the car for a closer look. "Impressive. From the outside at least."

We walked single-file through the gate and along a narrow brick path bordered by well-tended roses. A stout middle-aged woman opened the custom-made front door. The black German shepherd at her side flattened his ears and carefully sifted our scents.

"Ja, guten Abend (good evening), Frau Hohner," she beamed upon recognizing Mutti. "We've been expecting you all." She placed a finger lightly on the dog's head, whereupon his ears went erect. Wagging his tail a couple of times to indicate we'd passed inspection, he preceded us down a hall.

The woman stepped aside. "I'm Frau Farber, Herr Adler's housekeeper. Come in, everybody. We're ready for you." She led us to a Bauerneck (farm-nook) built inside the bay window of a vast kitchen. We slid along wrap-around wooden benches framing a matching pine table. It was covered with platters of various sizes, filled with a large selection of sliced sausages and rare cheeses. I counted four kinds of bread, six goblets, and two bottles of white wine and red wine each. I even spied chocolate pudding and a couple of cakes.

Mutti wrung her hands. "*Ach!* He shouldn't have."

"He didn't," the housekeeper said drily. "Please help yourselves to some coffee while I fetch him from the leisure room."

Anna bumped me, whispering, "*Leisure* room!" As soon as the housekeeper was gone she said, "He always seemed so ordinary to me."

With those far-seeing eyes? Hardly. "Anna?" I said. "Shut up!"

"Please lower your voices," Mutti said, looking pained.

Lucius held the back of his hand out to Alex, who sniffed it politely with his black nose. Uninterested in the bitter brew Mutti poured into our cups, I sat on the floor, running my fingers over the dog's well-muscled neck, tapered back, and long, bushy tail. He reminded me of Snow-white and Rose-red's good-natured, lumbering bear who was really an enchanted prince hoping someone would break the spell that bound him to his beastly form. But although Alex's eyes were disconcertingly human, he seemed quite at ease inside his dog suit, without the slightest wish to discard it.

As the others stirred sugar and cream into their cups with silver spoons, I held out my hand until the dog put his great paw on it. "You're even better than that rainbow," I whispered into his ear.

"Cakes, pudding and strudel!" Anna piped up. "If this is Herr Adler's idea of a Brotzeit I wonder what his dinners are like."

"When do you want to find out?" asked the amused voice of our host from the doorway. Anna had the grace to look flustered as he walked into the light, looking as dashing in his regional dove-gray wool jacket and Bundhosen as he usually did in his work-a-day business suit.

"You really took too much trouble," Mutti protested.

"I didn't," he said, reaching for her hand. "It's all the work of Frau Farber who takes meal times quite seriously." He shook with everyone at the table and then came to help me to my feet. "I see you two have found each other. Alex loves puppies and children. I'll have to watch out that he doesn't follow you home." He claimed the seat next to Mutti.

For some reason I didn't mind that he'd called me a child, nor did I object when Mutti wordlessly handed me a damp napkin for my germ-laden hands. "I'm sure your coffee and wine are delicious, Herr Adler," I said, sitting down directly opposite him. "But do you by any chance happen to have plain milk for Lucius and me?"

His silvery eyes gleamed as he smiled. "Frau Farber will see to it. Pack zu (fall to). I'm counting on you and Lucius to appreciate this little snack. And let me remind you that you agreed to call me Hannes. Come, this time we'll shake on it."

Grinning, I gave him my hand. His was warm and as steady as his fatherly gaze. "It's hard to switch," I confessed.

"But switch you will." He turned his attention to Mutti. "Lotte, dry wine or red?"

She blushed. "The Mosel, Hannes. I didn't see the VW. Is it fixed?"

He concentrated on pouring her wine. Frau Farber brought two frosty white tumblers. Mutti looked at them and opened her mouth, no doubt to ask her to scald the milk first. I stared her down until she changed her mind. Then I heaped a portion of everything except the salami on my plate and concentrated on the satisfying task of eating a swath across every platter before me to and through the desserts.

Hannes, at ease and attentive to each one of us throughout the meal, waited until Mutti finished the last bite of her cake before getting back to her question. "The VW was quite low on gas," he said mildly. "I brought some with me, of course, but unfortunately, when I turned the key, it broke off in the ignition. And then there was the flat tire . . ."

"Low on gas?" she cried, stung. "What do you mean?"

"No doubt the gauge is faulty," he murmured agreeably.

"No doubt," she said, accepting the compromise. "I couldn't pull out the key. Isn't that right, Maria? But there definitely was no flat tire."

I had a vivid glimpse of the right front wheel scraping the curb in front of our address, another of her pointy-toed spike kicking rubber, but all I said was, "Maybe you drove over glass shards."

Hannes smiled again. "The mechanic thinks the tire stem might have scraped against something solid. He fixed the tire, and the car's all tanked up, but I'm afraid he had to keep it overnight to work on the ignition. I told him you'd pick it up tomorrow, Lotte."

"Oh?" she said in a small voice. "But how will I get to the office? From that godforsaken house?"

"My dear Lotte," he replied, refilling her goblet. "No need to fret. We have several guest suites. I was just going to suggest you spend the night in our best one. We do work in the same building. I'll give you a ride in the morning and I promise that you'll have your car in the afternoon. It seems an easy solution."

"Spend the night?" she said in alarm. "But I'm wearing old flats and my worst Dirndl."

He put another sliver of cake on her plate. "Frau Farber will freshen it for you. And you do sit behind a desk all day. No one will notice your shoes."

Anna and Mutti rolled their eyes at his male incomprehension.

"You can borrow my dress," Anna offered on impulse. "I'll wear your clothes home tonight. Your flats, too. Now that my wardrobe's at the studio I'll have lots of high heels to choose from."

Horst managed to stifled his grin until Mutti and Anna had left for the nearest bathroom. Then he took a swallow of wine and said, "Frauen (women)! I'm still trying to convince Anna that jeans and a cotton shirt are more sensible for an apprentice artist at work. I believe the main reason she's started business school is because she likes to play dress-up."

When Anna and Mutti returned I thought for one startled moment that they had merely exchanged heads, so well did they fit into each other's clothes. Although Anna was half a head taller Mutti's borrowed heels made up the difference in height.

As we got ready to leave Hannes said imploringly, "Maria, you must do me the favor of taking the desserts away with you or else Frau Farber will force herself to eat every crumb. She cannot bring herself to throw anything away, you see."

Chuckling comfortably, the housekeeper made up a care-package for me, adding half of the leftovers from every platter. Lucius and I would be set for days. She handed Anna a similar parcel. Alex rose with great dignity to lead us from the room. Mutti and Hannes, still sitting, were switching to burgundy. He held out her ruby-red chalice. She accepted it with some reluctance, then scooted timidly away from him — but only a few inches.

"Oh, Anna?" Hannes said, stopping my sister at the door. "About that dinner — shall we plan it for next month, in honor of our departing newlyweds? What do you think?"

"I think that would be fine, Hannes. Ganz toll (great)," she replied. On the way home she was quiet for a long time. Then she said, "His bathroom was almost as big as Horst's new studio. There was a sunken Roman tub in the middle of it. Oil paintings on the walls and plants in every niche. Sculptures, too. In the bathroom. Can you imagine?"

I tried but could only recall Anna's humble new bathroom cubicle, the older and even more modest Marshall Plan lavatory with its cumbersome wood-burning hot water tank, and the charmless WC down the hall from our fifth-floor walkup. Everything in it was chipped, faded, and bare.

And even though I could not understand Herr Adler's opulent world I liked him just fine. Grimm's fairy tales were full of princes marrying poor but beautiful maidens who seemed to have no trouble getting used to Roman style tubs. Surely Mutti could, too. For even though she had been married to consecutive toads, there was something still maiden-like about her, unseen and untouched. Maybe the phrase "third time good luck" would apply to the rest of her life. If she'd allow it.

Horst delivered Lucius and me to our curb. Watching him pull away, I grew aware of a woman shouting something from somewhere above. Tilting my head, I saw her outline at a third-story window. She was sitting on the sill, her legs dangling carelessly over the edge.

"Hey, you!" she yelled, beckoning to a man barely visible in the bad light. He ducked and crossed over to the opposite sidewalk. "Du Feigling (coward)!" she called after him. "Come back over here. Third floor. Ring twice. Don't be shy. The night is still young."

"Good grief," Lucius said. "Our resident lush is on another binge. I hope somebody reels her in before she falls. They must be having a party up there. Maybe the landlady's gone deaf."

I followed him into the lobby. At the bottom of the stairs I slapped our sack of goodies at his midriff and cried, "Last one up has to iron your fatigues in the morning!" He groaned, grabbing at the sack while I began to leap up the stairs two at a time, hoping to outrun him for once. Laughing, breathing hard, and trying to block him from passing me by, I clattered past a number of couples, the men amused, the women wry. Elbowing my way to narrow victory on the fifth floor landing, I collapsed against the wall in loud mirth.

"No fair," he protested, catching up. "You tricked me."

"Is too fair," I replied. "Your legs are longer than mine. Tomorrow morning you iron your own pants!" I unlocked the landing-door and we stumbled through the unlit hall.

"All right. You win," Lucius said on our threshold. "I've got to take 'em off first, though."

I switched on our light and the room jumped into focus, as threadbare as I remembered it. Lucius wrapped his arms around me. I rested my head against his pounding chest. Then he clicked the light off again. It took with it one of our senses, leaving the remaining four thoroughly heightened.

CHAPTER 5

THE NEXT AFTERNOON I GOT OFF the bus at Warner Kaserne wearing my tight white pants and a scarlet silk blouse. Pausing in a spot of unseasonably warm June sunlight, I could feel myself throbbing with life. I pulled the blouse out of the waistband and lifted my hair off my shoulders to let the air cool my neck. Then I walked purposefully toward the once-forbidding gate, swinging my respectable little purse in rhythm with my steps. Deep inside I could feel myself shouting "Yes!"

I expelled the sentiment in the form of a heart-felt sigh so as not to scare the young freckle-nosed sentry. He offered me a gap-toothed smile when I showed him my new dependent ID card. Glancing from the picture to me, he said, "You look like you're on top of the world," and waved me through.

"I feel like it, too," I agreed in flawless American English, retrieving the ID. "But right now I'm trying to find the bank."

"Oh? You just arrive from stateside? Where you from?"

"Why, sunny California, " I drawled. "Where you can pick oranges right off the trees. And you?"

"D.C. Boy, do I wish I was there now." He pointed across the square. "Bank's thataway. Can't miss it."

And then I walked through the open gate and stood on United States soil, looking like any other American dependent enjoying the privileges to which she was entitled.

The bank was no more than a cubicle behind a thick window with a slot under it. I slid both the magic card and my endorsed allotment check through the gap. I'd practiced signing my married name on paper scraps for ten minutes before I was brave enough to write it on the back of the check. On the other side of the glass, the cashier spread out a money-fan made with six hundred-Mark bills and four fifties. Tapping each bill with a glossy long fingernail, she counted out loud before shuffling them into a stack and pushing it into the recessed metal tray between us. I gathered them up with all the nonchalance I could muster and slipped them inside my new adult-sized leather billfold as if it were an action I performed every day.

And then, with heightened anticipation, I followed a side street, heading in the direction the arrow on the *Library* sign was pointing. Soon I came to a modern building with big windows. Heart singing, I walked in and wandered through the stacks lined with English language books. Overwhelmed at my good fortune I couldn't decide what to pick until at last I recognized one name. Before me were three shelves crammed with Zane Grey Westerns. I scooped off an armload, planning to read one book per day until I was done with the whole lot. By the time Lucius and I landed in Los Angeles I would be an authority on the subject of cowboys and Indians. In the next room I found a whole section of books about Africa. I chose a magnificent coffee-table edition.

The librarian was wearing an astonishingly big stars-and-stripes brooch resplendent with miniature rhinestones. "That's quite a load," she said. "You must be a fast reader."

"Yep," I replied. "Always was. Say, I'm new here. What do I have to do to take these out?"

"Ah! An Army brat fresh off the plane with no TV worth watching. Your dad stationed at Warner?"

"Henry," I supplied, enjoying myself. If these Americans wanted to mistake me for one of their own who was I to stop them? I considered it a compliment about to come true.

"Oh, well," she said. "Henry's a bit on the ugly side, even if it does have a store and the movie theater."

"Store?" I echoed. "Movie theater?" Lucius had been holding out on me.

The librarian chuckled. "You really *are* new. Or maybe your dad's just trying to keep you away from all those young single GIs running around with no one to date. Got your ID with you?"

I produced it with a flourish and watched her prepare my new library card. Floating on my personal happiness-cloud, I waved at the sentry as I passed out of Warner's gate. He saluted smartly and called after me, "Be seeing you, Maria!" No sooner had I reached the bus stop than a bus rolled up. It was that kind of day.

I rode on it only as far as Henry and walked up the access road to the gate with my armload of books. Glancing at the first row of barracks behind the chain link fence, I wondered what a GI like Lucius did every day. Then I passed the yellow phone booth and experienced a fleeting energy slump, recollecting how I'd called him from inside the booth at the start of a blizzard last December and how he'd helped me find shelter for the rest of that awful night.

Without thinking I put a hand on my blouse to find my wedding band. I liked wearing it on a string close to my heart and considered it a secret talisman and good luck charm. Lucius wore a matching band on his dog-tag chain. Neither of us liked having the confining rings on our fingers. An occasional mental glimpse of the bed we shared and his dark face above me, radiant with love, was all I ever needed to remind me that we were married at last.

That love made me feel invincible enough to smile at the sentry standing under the *Henry Kaserne* sign even though I recognized him immediately as a friend of Jim's. Jim was the white soldier in Lucius's company who had ambushed him last year simply for dating me. When the sentry smiled back at me I realized with relief that he didn't remember me, probably because I had been dressed like a boy the day Jim and his buddies warned me to stick to my own kind.

I showed him my dependent ID, proudly holding my head up high. I didn't appreciate the way his gaze traveled from the picture to my hips instead of my face. But feeling particularly charitable today, I decided to see him as just another homesick young soldier far away from his country who wished he could be as lucky in love as Lucius and I.

"I'm looking for the store," I said with almost sisterly affection. "Can you point the way?"

"Sure thing," he said. "New around here, huh? Just follow the road to the bend. You'll see it from there."

And then I rolled off my tongue a phrase I'd heard on the AFN. "Much obliged," I twanged in a broad cowboy dialect, chuckling inside.

The store was of a good size although the cashier told me it was nowhere near as big as the commissary on the other end of the city. Clutching my books, I wandered through the alien landscape of open-topped freezers containing such exotic items as rock-hard T-bone, porterhouse and sirloin steaks, hamburger patties, and bright green peas in plastic bags. I passed displays of canned vegetables and fruit, tinned, pre-ground coffee, boxes of cornflakes and instant mashed potatoes. Unlike the small neighborhood shops on my block, everything in here smelled of stale air and bleach.

Hoping to surprise Lucius with a real American dinner tonight I chose two T-bone steaks, some powdered potatoes, a can of condensed mushroom soup, dehydrated onions, frozen peas, added Lucius's favorite cola, and grabbed a handful of candy bars for our dessert. I hadn't thought to bring a tote, but as it turned out I didn't need one because the cashier piled everything into a crisp brown paper sack.

Arms full, I pushed through the turnstile with the thrust of a hip, looking up in time to see Spider on the other side, in the process of sliding his shades back up the bridge of his nose. "Afternoon, Missus Duncan," he said respectfully, teeth gleaming in an unreadable face. "Thought I saw you sashaying in here by your lonesome. Long time no see."

He looked almost normal in his fatigues so I decided to bestow my joyous-bride smile upon him. "Hello, Spider. Why aren't you working?"

"Out of smokes," he said. "Looked out my barracks window and saw a fine looking young lady floating by on her own little cloud. So I says to myself, that must be Maria, nobody else walk like that. Never did have a chance to congratulate you on getting hitched. You blissful and all? You think it be worth it?"

I shifted my load to give myself time to decipher his words. Although I'd had no trouble understanding the sentries and the librarian, Spider's speech was beyond me. My bag slipped till a jutting hipbone stopped its progress. The sharp corners of the books I was hugging pressed into my diaphragm. Finally, I had to admit defeat. "Sorry, Spider. I don't understand you."

"Joseph . . . treating you right?" he asked as if it were any of his business.

"Of course," I answered, my tone deliberately cool.

"Glad to hear it. Cause if he's not I'll get on his case. Just say the word. You know he listens to me."

Unfortunately, that part was true. I'd told Lucius several times that Spider was a false friend but had been unable to convince him as yet. "We're just fine," I said. "Very snug in our little place. Until we fly stateside. We're short-timers now, you know."

For an instant I thought he was smirking. Then he said in a neighborly tone, "Yessir. He's mentioned it more than once. As a matter of fact, I'm due to rotate out of this god-forsaken country myself. In December. I'll be celebrating the holidays in Compton. Blue skies even on Christmas. Hey, if you guys really fixing to go to California maybe I'll see you both there. In fact, since we're old friends and all, I could hook you up with a nice little house in my little neighborhood."

"Perhaps," I said, suppressing a shudder. "Now if you'll excuse me, I have to rush home to start dinner." Or rather, to thaw out the steaks.

He glanced up at the wall clock. "At one-thirty?"

"Yes. Well. I'm just learning to cook," I said lamely. Then I swept past him, hoping the cigarettes he'd come for would delay him long enough so I wouldn't have to walk at his side part of the way. Hurrying down the street, I wondered how it was possible that he had not guessed yet how much I disliked him. I'd been giving civilized hints to that effect for almost a year but he continued to slither round the edges of propriety whenever we talked. I wasn't sure if he was amused by my put-offs or merely ignoring them for some reason of his own.

When my bus arrived at the Kurfürstenplatz I debated with myself if I should haul my load to the police station with me or to take it home first. But one mental glimpse of an endless staircase receding into the distance gave me all the answer I needed. In truth, I would gladly have skipped the precinct office for another week but this morning I had promised Lucius I would get my passport revised.

"We don't want any last minute mess-ups," he said. "Your mother is right. The sooner the better." It annoyed me when he took her side and she took his as if I were an unruly child to be managed between them.

The police station seemed quite pleasant after the hot sun. While my eyes adjusted to the artificial light I set my load on a bench in the waiting area and took my green passport to the counter. Two policemen were lounging in sagging office chairs on the other side, contemplating their spiraling cigarette smoke.

"And what can we do for you, Fräulein?" the bloated one behind the typewriter asked.

"I need to change the name in my passport. I just got married," I told him, putting the booklet on the counter.

"You've come to the right place." He inserted a form in the machine while keeping his cigarette clamped between two stubby yellowed fingers.

The lanky officer in the nearer chair reached for my passport with a long arm, thumbed through its pages, compared my face to the picture, and whistled through tobacco-stained teeth. "A child-bride. Just turned sixteen. In the family way, are we?"

Typical. They saw me walk in with a flat belly and a waist so narrow a man could span his hands around it but still couldn't resist coming to unwarranted conclusions. Anna was right on my wedding day when she said that people only saw what they wanted to see. Why should policemen be different?

"Name?" the one behind the typewriter asked.

"My new name, you mean? It's on the marriage certificate. Here." Proudly, I pushed it across. "It's Duncan. Maria Duncan."

He studied the certificate. "This says your first name's Marianne."

"It was. I shortened it."

"Can't," he said.

"But I did."

He frowned and said slowly as he typed with one finger, "M-a-r-i-a-n-n-e. D-u-n-c-a-n. Correct?"

"I told you," I tried again. "It's Maria now."

He took a long puff and tapped his blunt fingertips against the desk top. "What does it say on your birth certificate?"

I handed it over.

He grunted. "Just as I thought. If your mother had wanted your name to be Maria it would have been on the birth certificate that way."

I was beginning to feel a touch irritable. "What's my mother got to do with it? I'm married, aren't I? That makes me an adult capable of making my own decisions."

He laid his cigarette on the rim of an ashtray. "Not until you're twenty-one."

"That's ridiculous!" I sputtered, realizing too late that I should have kept my mouth shut. Similar temper flare-ups had gotten me in trouble with O.F. for years. I never could get it through my head that men in power hated to be contradicted. They made you pay for the attempt.

"Address?" he said lazily, shifting the carriage.

As soon as I gave it to him he pulled his fingers off the keys as if they'd touched live coals. Leering at his partner, he smoothed his brush-like mustache. "That address? Are you sure?"

I said, "Of course I'm sure."

"Then I need to see your health certificate." He was no longer smiling.

"My what?"

"All the residents of that building have to carry a current health certificate with them at all times. It's the law."

I gaped and stammered, "Pardon?"

He planted both elbows on the desk before enlightening me. "Although prostitution's not illegal as such all whores must be properly licensed and show proof of the obligatory monthly exam. It's one of the disadvantages of making a living on your back."

"On my what?" I asked with rapidly growing distress.

"We don't want to spread any diseases, now do we?" he said as if I'd turned stupid. "In your line of business there are plenty. Crabs, syphilis, and gonorrhea, to name just a few."

Suddenly everything slipped into place. The landlady's speech on the eve of my wedding. The way Herr Adler had frowned at the address when he dropped Lucius and me off after the ceremony. The supposed Jehovah's Witness at the door, ringing four times for Duncan. The two grocery-shoppers skirting me as if I might be contagious. The woman hanging out of an upstairs window late last night, soliciting a passerby. And my mother's guilty blush when I asked her why she was not moving into our conveniently located building. She had unloaded her virgin daughter and her new son-in-law in a—in a—.

"But I'm not like that!" I protested, tasting bile.

The long-armed partner gave a dry laugh. "That's what they all say, innocent lambs that they are. Always another trick up the sleeve, huh? Well, forget it—we're on to you now!" He tossed my documents into a file basket out of my reach. "Shall I pull out your record? I'm sure you've got one. They all do."

I fished for my trump card and slapped it down on the counter—the ace in the hole, my American Dependent ID Card. "Bitte (there you are)!" I said, standing tall. "Is that enough proof or do you want to call my husband's commanding officer to confirm? I'm sure he's prepared to be helpful." Though not necessarily to me.

The long-armed officer picked up the pretty ID, flicked it a couple of times with a fingernail, then handed it across the desk.

The officer sitting behind the typewriter took it and shrugged. "I'm willing to bet you got this under false pretenses. And even if you actually did fill out one of those endless Ami (yank) questionnaires, remember this: if you lied just once the whole thing is void. Marriage annulled."

On the screen of my mind the freckle-faced sentry at Warner was barring my entrance through his gate; the no-longer-friendly librarian was withdrawing my new library card; the bank clerk's fingers paused at the teller-tray, gathered up the bank-notes she had spread into a fan, and tore my first and only allotment check to shreds. For not only had I been arrested last year but I'd served eleven days in reform school—and had neglected to mention either fact on the long questionnaire. On Mutti's inexpert advice.

What did that make me but a cheat and a liar? The officer was right. It was very likely that I was exactly the kind of girl who deserved to wind up in a whorehouse, making a living on her back. Or else why would Mutti have rented a room for me there?

CHAPTER   6

THE OFFICERS KEPT MY PRETTY PASSPORT
and made me plead for my other IDs one at a time. I thanked
them politely for each, stuffed all three into my purse, picked
up my books and groceries and went out of the door. They
started to guffaw before I'd half-closed it behind me.

Hot with shame, I felt unable to look anyone in the eyes
and stared past my sandals at the cracks in the sidewalk. I
imagined a big H, for Hure (whore), stamped on my forehead
for all to see, and a flaming arrow pointing right at it from up
in the sky. Marianne Edel, the incipient whore who thought
all she had to do to get a new life was to change her name. In
reform school Sister Gertrude had called me a smudged soul
and O. F. had predicted I'd wind up in the gutter. Turned out
they were right.

Stumbling through the mental fog of total humiliation, I
arrived at my abominable address and couldn't make myself
go in. A Hausfrau on her way to the stores who had been

walking a few steps behind me now stopped to see what I would do next. An old man, plodding toward me from the other direction, carrot tops trailing from his tote bag, looked at me with contempt. I bolted past him, averting my face.

I went to the greengrocer's for lettuce and elbow macaroni, to the baker's for Bretzen (pretzels), and to the cheese shop for Emmenthaler, stuffing each purchase into the large paper bag — merely to keep from having to go home. But eventually my bag was full and I had to approach the unholy entrance again. When I tried to go in this time I broke out in cold sweat. Thinking of tidy Ingrid and the Jehovah's Witness, I groaned and fled to the next corner, suddenly realizing that her superior smile had simply meant, "I know something you don't know, and oh, won't you be surprised when you find out!" How could I have misjudged her so badly? She wasn't a kindergarten teacher at all, but a . . . a . . .

And our daybed, with its creaky springs. How many diseased whores, how many drunken strangers on top?

Whatever was I going to tell Lucius?

I found myself crossing the Kurfürstenplatz in my obscenely tight pants, my red blouse the exact shade of the naked bulb glimmering through the dark from the entrance of the squalid Alabama Bar. A glance at my reflection in the nearest shop window showed me that my hair was every bit as unkempt and slovenly as Vati had told me it was.

I fled across the square and managed to walk past three dress shops without looking at myself once. Then the bag ripped, spilling my groceries all over the sidewalk. The can of mushroom soup rolled to and over the curb.

I crouched, clutching my precious library books and staring helplessly at the makings of tonight's American dinner spread at my feet. Tears of chagrin spilled from my eyes, raining on top of the plastic package of freshly thawed peas. I was incapable of picking anything up. The once gifted girl child could not figure out how to re-gather her burdens.

Short-tempered pedestrians in a hurry stepped around the scattered groceries. One disgruntled man yelled, "Pick them up already! Can't you see you're blocking the way?"

I slumped over the heap, resigned to watching the T-bones defrost, when a crone, leaning heavily on her walking stick, stopped to unclasp her purse, extracted a frayed net bag, and pressed it on me. "Here. It'll be good for one more load I expect," she said in a voice brittle with age. "You can keep it, child. I was going to buy a new one anyway." Her face creased with a smile so encouraging that it erased the arrow from the clouds and the H from my forehead. As she hobbled away I called out my thanks, an act that immediately released me from the malignant spell that had bound me. Why should I care what anyone thought of Marianne Edel? She had ceased to exist. I was what Lucius had made me—Maria Duncan, his wife.

I put down the books and salvaged my groceries, including the soup in the gutter. Then I sat on a bench, pulled the string out of my collar, untied my wedding ring from it, and slipped it on its proper finger. On my way home I kept my left hand prominently displayed around the bag, the ring both shield and testimonial. Pausing in front of the whorehouse, I raised the hand so that the sun might sanctify the golden band and its wearer, but the street was already immersed in afternoon shade.

And then a voice I recognized cried breathlessly from behind me, "Maria! Thank goodness you're here!"

Turning, I beheld the spectacle of an almost perfectly groomed business school student. It was Anna, complete with lacquered beehive, manicured nails the same shade of pastel pink as her lipstick, the small beauty mark she had twirled on her cheek a la Marilyn Monroe, a tailored jacket, tight skirt and sun-tan colored nylons. Even with all that secretarial armor she managed to look slightly ridiculous in Mutti's slouchy flat shoes, which were taking the alluring curves out of my sister's calves and left them looking just plain skinny. Her Prussian-blue eye shadow looked as if she'd applied it with a palette knife and the liquid makeup she'd smeared on her face stopped short at her jaw line, leaving her neck an untouched milky white.

"What are *you* doing here?" I asked. It was her first visit.

"I need to see Lucius."

"What about?"

"This!" She pointed to Mutti's flats. "When I unlocked my wardrobe to get out a pair of high heels I discovered that it was entirely empty. Where did he put all my shoes?"

"Maybe they wound up on Mutti's farm, in one of the crates. Did you call her and ask?"

"Yes!" she said, blinking back tears. "She thinks the men must have taken away your wardrobe instead of mine. If it's true Lucius owes me a big favor."

I smiled with relief, realizing that my dilemma was solved—with her at my side I could muster the courage to reclaim my profaned home. "He won't be back for a couple of hours but come upstairs with me anyway," I told her. "Try on my wedding shoes. If they fit you can keep them. Forever."

Her face lightened at once. She charged into the lobby and I followed in her wake, no longer worried that the nearest passerby would consider it an admission of guilt. Anna kept up a steady chatter as we ascended the stairs, recounting her dismay at finding the bottom of her wardrobe bare. "My first thought was to skip school but we had a typing exam I couldn't afford to miss. So I went in Mutti's old flats. Eva and Gisela laughed themselves silly. Even the typing teacher tittered. When I got home from school I called Horst, hoping he'd give me a ride to the Harthof. He didn't answer his phone. Then I decided to take the bus to rescue my shoes. I tried O.F.'s number first just to make sure he was still out of town. But he picked up the receiver. I hung up without speaking." Her eyes filmed. "If he hasn't thrown my shoes out yet he'll get around to it soon enough!"

Before I could unlock our landing-door Ingrid opened it from the inside. She was escorting out a male friend who was still buttoning up. Anna looked puzzled but my involuntary wince told Ingrid that I finally knew what was what. Her answering smile was both ironic and disappointed.

After Anna and I entered my room she seemed about to ask me a question. I distracted her by pulling the white heels out of the closet. They proved a half size too large for her but she cheerfully stuffed the front-ends with tissues, slipped on the shoes, and kicked Mutti's flats into a corner.

With a sigh of relief she sat at the table and studied the honeymoon sketches on the wall next to the daybed. "I guess practice really does make perfect," she conceded grudgingly, which was as close as she'd ever come to admitting I had any artistic talent.

And then she told me exactly what she wanted Lucius to do for her. I refused to pass on the message until she threatened to return in the evening to tell him herself, armed with a German/English dictionary.

"All right!" I said. "Have it your way!" It wasn't the dictionary that decided me, though, but her return visit just as the building's well-rested tenants would start emerging for their sordid employment. So I agreed to bring my husband to her studio instead.

*

THAT NIGHT Lucius and I sat in the back seat of the BMW as it careened toward the Harthof. In response to Anna's request Lucius was wearing his impressive dress uniform. She had supplied the cudgel. He played with it for half our journey.

Then he glanced at me, asking in a low tone, "Tell me, what does Old Fart look like?"

I couldn't think how to describe him.

"No, really," he said. "If we went to the zoo what animal there would you say resembles him most? A jackass?"

Since I hadn't been to the zoo for a couple of years I had to give it some thought. "A vulture," I decided.

"How depressing," he said.

A minute later I changed my mind. "A repulsive red-faced, red-bottomed baboon. Have you seen how they shriek when they get mad? I saw a whole clan last time I was at the monkey-house. One of them bit another in the butt for no reason at all."

He chortled, slapped the club against his palm, and said softly, "He won't be biting anyone tonight!" I stuck my head out of the window, hoping fresh air would calm my nerves. I was sorry we came.

Horst parked next to the wheat field. When he opened his door Anna told him to stay put. "You look too harmless for this operation. Besides, we might need you to make a quick getaway." She climbed out, slinging a couple of canvas sacks over her shoulder. Lucius and I followed. My heart was pounding. The three of us slunk around the old-familiar corner and up the narrow stairs. Waving Lucius and me away from the apartment door's spy-hole, Anna rang the bell.

I could hear footsteps inside. Then O.F. asked, "What do you want?"

Anna gulped and said bravely, "I've come for my shoes."

He forced out a laugh. "According to your Mutti's good-bye note everything left in the apartment is now mine. If you want your shoes back you'll have to buy them from me."

"How much?" she said, her voice tight.

There was a pause while he deliberated. "One month's rent for all the right shoes, another month's for the left."

"That's almost a hundred Mark!" she gasped, outraged. "It's all I have!"

"Take it or leave it. The shoes won't be here anymore after tomorrow."

With an audible sigh she opened her wallet and pulled out two fifties. "All right, then. Here! Take them!"

He opened the door a couple of cautious centimeters. Anna held out the money to him. His hand snaked through the gap to take it. And then Anna gave the door a hard shove. Lucius stepped around the corner and finished the job, slammed it against the inside wall.

Fully exposed, O.F. stood sputtering before us, one hand still outstretched for the ransom. Next to my husband he seemed an utterly insignificant man.

"This isn't even your apartment!" Anna hissed as she swept past him and turned to wave me on. The moment I did some primitive reflex made O.F. ball his hands into fists. An answering reflex triggered my knees to go weak. Old habits, both. Lucius growled, slapping the nightstick against his palm for added emphasis. O.F. let me pass.

The kitchen felt empty, as if all life had drained out of it. Even though every piece of furniture was where it belonged my footsteps sounded hollow when I crossed toward the bedroom. Anna's shoes were still in the wardrobe, though its lock had already been forced. My sister tossed me one of her sacks and together we liberated every pair. Then we marched back to the hall.

O.F. let Anna slip out but this time not even Lucius could prevent him from blocking my way. "Where is she?" he demanded. "Where did she go?" His glittering eyes seemed more recessed than usual, making his head appear skull-like.

I remained silent.

"Never mind," he said after a few perilous seconds. "I'll find her wherever she is. When she least expects it. And I won't give her a divorce. Tell her that."

"She won't come back," I said, astonished to find that sometime, somehow, I had grown taller than him. And then I pushed past him and rushed down the stairs with Lucius close behind me. We ran through the night and climbed in the car. Horst had already made a U-turn. As soon as we slammed the doors he drove away with the lights off. He did not turn them on until we reached Schleissheimerstrasse. No one spoke as we left the Harthof behind us.

As we passed the Scheidplatz I whispered to Lucius, "Did you see? I've outgrown him!" I tried to ignore a nagging sense of guilt but even though math had never been my best subject I knew enough to understand that two wrongs could not possibly make one right. I wouldn't have admitted it to anyone but I felt almost sorry for O.F. His face hadn't turned a furious turkey-neck red this time. Instead, it had gone exceedingly pale.

Then Lucius said, "You were off the mark about him looking like a baboon, Maria. Or even a vulture. The last time I saw eyes like his they belonged to a snake. The whole time I was standing by that door I could hear it rattling its tail someplace inside him. Don't let his size fool you. That little man's full of venom. Watch out for his strike."

I spent the rest of the trip mentally rehearsing different ways of telling my husband exactly why he was the only male resident in our building. But the hour was late and we'd both had enough excitement for one night. Surely the revelation could wait for a more opportune time in the morning. According to a profound American proverb my husband's continuing ignorance was my best chance for prolonging our bliss.

CHAPTER 7

IN THE MORNING I FELT THE MATTRESS sag as Lucius rose to use the bathroom. It sagged again when he returned to pull the quilt up to his face, drifting into a doze. I stared at the lightening ceiling, refining the speech I'd memorized yesterday. Perhaps after breakfast; there was no reason to spoil his appetite with my news.

I climbed over him, dressed, and trudged down the stairs. As I reached the fourth floor landing I saw a young couple climbing up from below. The plump, rosy-cheeked woman was wearing a festive pink dress and hugging an oversized ceramic flower pot that contained a small rubber tree, its dark-green leaves polished to a high gloss. Her left hand, clearly visible, was adorned with a wedding ring. It matched the one her companion was wearing on his finger. From his ill-fitting baggy suit and shorn hair I guessed he was an American soldier in civvies. He was carrying two boxes. The top one held a set of dishes decorated with tiny pink rose buds. The new tenants were struggling for breath after their long climb. I groped for the banister and stared.

"You got the key?" the GI asked the woman. When she looked flustered he set down both boxes and pantomimed unlocking a door.

"Ja, okay!" she said, bringing out a real key and unlocking the landing-door.

"Are you newlyweds?" I asked in English, forgetting to be shy. She looked bewildered. He gave an indifferent nod. Part of me chuckled inwardly with pure delight and another part offered them an Ingrid-like wait-till-you-see-what-you've-got-yourself-into smile. "Congratulations!" I told them. "My husband and I are newlyweds too." Extending my hand to the woman, I added warmly, "Welcome to the building. I'm Maria." She didn't react until I repeated the information in German.

"Ja, und ich bin die Rosa. Aus Rosenheim (I am Rosa from Rosenheim)," she supplied, shaking my hand. Her words described her exactly: from her pumps to the satin bow in her hair she was rosy all over.

"Rosa! Don't dawdle!" her husband said, retrieving his load. "Remember the taxi!"

"*Ach!*" she said. "Se taxi. Schon gut (okay)." She let him pass into the hall and continued in German, "We're in a hurry. Would you like to have tea with me on Monday? After Freddie goes off to work."

Freddie called from somewhere within, "Rosa? Our room door?"

"Sure," I replied eagerly. "I'll bring something good from the bakery. Around ten?"

We smiled at each other then she went to help Freddie and I continued going down, my footsteps more bouncy now that Lucius and I weren't the only young-married fools who lived in a whorehouse. It was even beginning to occur to me that Mutti might have made an honest mistake. In fact, my encounter with the new renters put a different spin on my forthcoming speech, transmuting a heavy-hearted confession into light, fluffy lines such as, "Guess what my mother has gotten us into now. . ."

Outside, I realized Saturday had started without me. I heard the faraway drone of a tram, a cacophony of bleating horns, and the hum of cars and people on the move. A persistent meter ticked through the open window of a black cab idling next to the curb. I bought the four biggest bear claws they had at the bakery and a whole quart of milk. I carried the milk separately to avoid cooling the baked goods. Setting off for home, I shivered in the early morning shade and wondered what it might be like to wake up in an airy high-rise or sit on top of the Schuttberg at dawn when the city roofs, the nearby mountains, and the sky were all gilded. Not that Anna would ever notice; she was no early riser.

On my return Freddie was leaning into the cab, surrounded by suitcases. He was diligently counting the fare onto a hairy, open-palmed hand. Rosa was not with him; no doubt she was busy unpacking and scouring germs off every surface in their room. When I entered the fifth-floor hall and turned on the light something very big quivered and retreated into the faint rectangle of the open door next to the WC. Then a human-sized cricket clicked from the same rectangle towards me. I stood transfixed as the insect metamorphosed into Spider, complete with black derby, shades, and high-heeled patent leather shoes. Drawing level, he touched two gloved fingers to his hat brim.

"Morning, Missus Duncan," he murmured, sounding amused. "You're looking right pretty today. In fact, seems to me you get prettier each time we meet. You-all have yourselves a good weekend now, hear?" He went out to the landing and reached back inside to turn off the hall light, leaving me in the dark.

Almost at once, a mental light bulb illuminated my plodding brain. If Spider had been here visiting his own special "piece," chances were that Lucius *already* knew what kind of place we were renting — and had been deliberately keeping that information from me. I stormed into our room, slammed the bag of goodies onto our counter, and glowered at my sleeping husband. Just two nights ago he had *pretended* the party-girl gyrating from an upstairs window was a normal everyday drunk — even though he must have been well aware of the fact that she was soliciting. Blinking back tears, I squinted at the twelve cocky two-dimensional Luciuses on the wall behind him.

Then I heaved the bottle of milk at the whole dozen, understanding at last the utter vexation that had driven Mutti to model similar behavior for me on several occasions. The sound of shattering glass made me feel marginally better. But I suspected that, also like Mutti, I'd be stuck with the mess I was creating. Milk spattered in every direction. Lucius jerked awake. "I saw Spider!" I hissed. "In our hall! How long ago did you find out that we live in a whorehouse?"

He sat up. "I had my doubts from the get-go," he admitted. "But on the day I started back to work Spider asked where we were staying and when I gave him our address he recognized it right away because of his wh-woman." He rubbed his eyes and yawned. "I've prayed ever since that you'd keep on being blind to the clues."

"So the room next to the bathroom really does belong to the slug!" I choked out, appalled to realize she had been sitting in the same tub as I did, and on the communal toilet before and after me day in and day out for these past three weeks. If I had known at least I could have sprayed on a disinfectant.

He put a consoling hand on my shoulder but I whirled and fled out the door. I was hardly aware of passing Spider on the stairs, tapping his silly cane going down, and Freddie wrestling with four overstuffed suitcases coming up. I dashed through the streets until I couldn't run anymore and then hobbled on, determined to distance myself from the nightmare my so-called bliss had become. Lucius only caught up because I had developed a side-ache and had stopped to rest on a low stone wall.

He sat down beside me and retied his shoe laces. "It's not my fault," he said quietly.

I gave an ambivalent grunt.

"Not your mother's fault, either."

I nodded, remembering how proudly Rosa of Rosenheim had carried the rubber tree to her new home. Then I cried, "We've got to move!"

"We couldn't find anything last time we looked," he said. "Besides, we're short-timers, remember? And you have to admit none of our neighbors have been bothering us. Right?"

I hiccupped a sob. Last year I'd learned what the English word "mortified" meant. Since then my vocabulary had expanded to the point that I could now list the synonyms *humiliated, disgraced, debased, and crushed.*

Even Hannes had recognized the notorious address!

Lucius spread his hands. "Didn't it ever occur to you that maybe whores are just down-and-out women trying to live the best way they can?"

"*You* can stay there if you want — but *I* have to get out," I said. Before their fate became mine.

He rubbed my back. "You do what you must. Listen, I'll help you move in with your mother. Why not? She's got enough room. You can pay for your keep by cleaning her house while she's at work. Collect firewood during the day and have supper ready for her every night. But even if she invited me to move in with you I'd have to say no. It's too far away from Henry Kaserne. I guess that means I'll have to go back to sleeping on base. I could try to visit you guys on Sundays. Hey, how much do you think it'll cost me to take a cab to the farmhouse from the tram station in Pasing ?"

I watched a herd of white fleece drifting by overhead. Eventually I asked in a small voice, "How many days before we fly to America?"

He gave a relieved chuckle. "Twenty-two. On the nose."

Twenty-two days in a whorehouse were more than I could stand but if there was an acceptable alternative I had yet to stumble upon it. "I guess we'll be stuck in our awful little room until then," I conceded. "By the way, Lucius — how come you never told me there's a cinema at Henry?"

He frowned. "I've never been."

"Don't they show Hollywood movies? In English?"

"I suppose."

"On weekend afternoons?"

"Matinees."

"Will you take me tomorrow? It would be a good way for me to learn more English."

"You know too much already."

"Please?"

He gave an exaggerated shrug. "I was going to suggest the zoo. I hear Munich has a good one. But all right — we'll go to the movies. They're playing a Marilyn Monroe film. It's a long walk from the gate, though."

"I like walking!"

He sighed. "Don't I know it." Craning his neck from left to right, he added, "I hope you can guide us back home from here. I have no idea where we are; I was just following you."

Lucius gave me his arm and I led him from one alley to the next until at last we came to a sign bearing a street name I recognized. In the middle of the following block was a floor-to-ceiling display window. Inside it, on a high pedestal, crouched a small red sports car, glowing under a soft spotlight.

Lucius stopped short and cried, "There she is! That's her!"

I could feel his biceps contract and then go slack. His arm dropped away; his mouth literally hung open. But it was his eyes that underwent the biggest change. Reflecting the shiny red paint, they grew wider and wider as he, succumbing to some invisible, highly selective attraction-power, tilted toward the glass until his nose was pressed firmly against it.

"Lucius," I said, tugging his sleeve. "I'm getting hungry. Let's go eat our breakfast."

Keeping his focus on the alluring display he muttered, "You go. I'll catch up later." I forced his face toward me but his eyes stayed locked on his new love.

"You go," he said again, hugging the window. Afraid of losing his body as well as his heart, I stubbornly pried him loose, piloted him home, and put him to bed. He stared at the ceiling with fevered eyes and mumbled something about impossible budgets and unachievable down payments, leaving me to suspect his kind of fever could not be cured by a nap or by aspirin.

Throwing the milk against the wall had definitely been more satisfying than collecting the shards was proving to be. The explosion of white droplets had ruined every drawing except one. Inwardly weeping, I pulled eleven besplashed sketches off the wall and threw them into the trash. The twelfth paper-thin Lucius stared down at me with hooded, reproachful eyes. Deciding I would prefer the wall bare, I pulled him off too, carefully rolled him up, and stored him in the wardrobe for safekeeping. Leaking tears, I ate my share of our breakfast and waited for my flesh-and-blood husband to come to his senses. Deep down I knew the red sports car would soon change our sunny relationship into something murky and cold.

CHAPTER 8

ON SUNDAY MORNING I WOKE UP freezing. The comforter had slipped off the bed while I slept. It was a chilly predawn. The indent from Lucius's head was still on his pillow but his half of the mattress was empty. I curled against the wall, too drowsy to fish for the covers. Then I heard the landing-door open, and a few seconds later our room door. After it shut I heard Lucius undress, spread the comforter over me, and ease himself down beside me. One of his feet grazed mine. His was icy.

I wanted him to explain where he had been but was afraid to find out, so I shivered silently until I felt warm enough to get up and make us some toast and a pot of tea. He ate his breakfast sitting up, the comforter pulled to his chest. Swallowing his last bite, he reached for his notebook and began jotting long columns of numbers. When I was done eating I climbed past his shins, plumped my pillow, and began to read. The blue silk scarf overhead didn't ripple even once that long morning.

For lunch I wordlessly fried another batch of toast, brewed a second pot of tea, and delved into a new chapter. By then Lucius had torn half the pages out of his notebook, balled them, and tossed them to the floor. He'd also drawn several versions of a low-slung red shape on four wheels, using colored pencils from my art kit. Pleased with his final attempt, he rummaged for thumb tacks and pinned the creature to the wall. Then he cleared his throat and asked, "You still want me to take you to the movies? We've missed the early show."

"Sure," I grunted without looking up from my page. Gently, he took the book out of my hands and laid it aside. Then he made the scarf flutter after all. His new love looked on, headlights glaring.

*

A FEW hours later we were following the avenue inside of Henry around the curve and spied Washington on the other side, scurrying along the tarmac at a fast clip. It was he who had brought me a bag of donuts last fall, along with the note Lucius had scribbled during the purgatory of our separation. I clearly recalled how Jim and his football cronies had bullied the freckle-faced messenger for his act of kindness.

"Hey, Wash—wait up!" Lucius called out. "You going to the movies?"

Washington stopped to give us a bright smile. "Yeah. Hi, Mrs. Duncan. I try to catch me a flick every weekend."

As we began walking together I wondered how one caught a flick, and what, if anything, his answer had to do with the question.

"You like Marilyn Monroe?" I asked him.

"What's not to like?" he said, increasing his pace.

We had to lengthen our strides to keep up. "Why are we running?" I finally asked him.

"Bugs Bunny."

I was beginning to wonder what kind of English he was speaking. When I looked at Lucius for enlightenment he explained, "Bugs Bunny's the name of his favorite cartoon. It comes on right after the newsreel, before the show. He's running because he doesn't want to be late for the cartoon."

We passed battalion headquarters, where Lucius's CO had interviewed me in early spring. Then we passed the PX store. Other GIs trickled from the barracks lining the avenue, half in fatigues, half in casual clothes. They were going in the same direction we were.

The theater was located in an unassuming temporary structure. Even before we stepped into the foyer I could hear the sound of trumpets reverberating from the auditorium walls. A stern-voiced announcer spewed words as rapidly as any AFN disc jockey I'd ever heard. Washington's face fell when he saw the long queue of soldiers waiting at the snack counter. Shoulders sagging, he went to stand at the end of the line.

Lucius pushed him aside. "Don't keep Bugs Bunny waiting, Wash. Go on in with Maria. I'll bring you some soda and popcorn." Turning to me, he instructed, "Sit in the back row. I'll find you."

Washington and I went into the darkened auditorium and waited inside the door for our eyes to adjust to the flickering light. On the screen, a helicopter was landing on the deck of a big ship and a row of uniformed sailors saluted the men climbing out who were holding on to their hats.

I followed Washington to the back row. But this was no regular movie house. The floor was flat, the seats collapsible metal chairs standing too close together. No matter where I sat, some hulking GI blocked my view. Then I spied two perfectly good vacant seats in the middle of the theater. Someone had draped a long overcoat across both. I pointed them out to Washington and headed down the aisle. "Maria? Where you going?" he whispered urgently. "Hey — come back here!"

But I was already bending over a sweet-faced GI with surprisingly long lashes, asking, "Pardon me — are those two chairs taken?"

He glanced at them and grinned. "I reckon we'll find out." Leaning to his left, he murmured something to his neighbor, who leaned to the left and murmured something to his neighbor, until the domino effect reached a blonde girl on the other side of the empty chairs. She glared at me and yanked off the coat. The young soldier moved his bony knees aside and said, "They're all yours."

One by one, the seated men pulled in their legs. I squeezed by, sat down next to the girl, and thanked her. She responded with a loud sniff. Soon the rousing tones of the newsreel gave way to tinny cartoon music. The overhead light came on for a few seconds and went off again, and a gray rabbit appeared on the screen, nibbling on a carrot and saying, "Eh — what's up, Doc?" I turned around to watch for Lucius. During a moment when there were no dark tones on the screen I saw him standing behind Washington, both their faces oddly apprehensive.

I gave an extravagant wave, accidentally brushing my shoulder against the bare arm of the blonde.

"Vould you mind!" she snapped.

I proffered a hasty apology and signaled Lucius once more. This time he walked reluctantly toward me. Just as he stooped toward the young soldier and murmured his first "Excuse me," the film broke. Somebody groaned. A couple of GIs laughed. After a chorus of shrill whistles the overhead light came on.

Even though Lucius could now see where he was going it was harder for him to get there, for none of the men in our row were willing to move their legs one inch out of his way. High-stepping over their knees, he sank into the chair at my right, holding out a small paper cup full of water and a larger one filled with white balls. "Popcorn," he muttered, putting it on my lap. Then he whispered, "I thought I told you to sit in the last row!"

"I couldn't see from there. These seats are much better," I whispered back.

The blonde at my left, who had used the interruption to talk to her partner, now turned to gape at Lucius. Then she nudged her companion. Someone behind us drawled, "Sure stinks around here!" The comment was followed by loud guffaws. A boot kicked the back of my chair. I refused to react. The blonde's friend rose, announced, "This row has the cooties! We need some air!" and pushed his way out to the opposite aisle. The blonde held her nose and said "Phew!" before trailing after him.

I blushed as a wave of exaggerated retching traveled across the auditorium. A sea of hostile pale faces were angling toward us. Lucius sat rigidly upright, gripping the edges of his seat. I heard a cane tapping down the aisle. It was Spider. He stopped beside the young soldier, who hastened to jerk his knees aside.

Spider had no trouble slipping past all subsequent knees, including Lucius's and mine. He nodded at the newly vacated chair to my left. "This seat taken, Missus Duncan?" I shook my head. He sat, removed his hat and his shades, and strafed the audience with his naked, terrible eyes until there was absolute silence. Then the light went off and the cartoon resumed.

Lucius stared at the screen, mechanically shoving white balls into his mouth. I touched his arm lightly and was not surprised to find it rigid and hard. The young soldier sitting at the end of the row offered me a tiny, embarrassed smile. And then, to my delight, I saw Rosa ambling down the aisle. I waved and called her name. She stopped, confused. Freddie, who evidently had better night vision than she, took her arm and guided her to the front of the hall, where they folded themselves onto first-row seats, tipping their faces at grotesque angles up at the screen.

I remembered the cup of popcorn on my lap and ate my first-ever kernel. It tasted both salty and sweet. The feature was disappointing. Marilyn Monroe had a soft voice I could hardly decipher. In fact, there wasn't much of the dialogue I could make out, period. I hungered for more action yet did not want to take any myself, even when my bladder insisted I give it my undivided attention. Eventually I mustered the courage to work my way past endless unforgiving knees and stumbled through the foyer in search of the ladies' room. It held one toilet stall and a small sink.

A couple of young women were leaning over the sink to admire themselves in the wall mirror. One of them was the blonde who'd been sitting beside me. She blew a pink bubble while the brunette pouted her mouth to smear on a new coating of lipstick. Neither of them seemed to pay any attention to me as I entered the stall and quietly locked myself in.

Then the blonde loudly complained, "Ve haff a smelly second-class citizen in our midst!"

The brunette unpursed her lips long enough to say, "If she knew what was good for her and her shit-colored friend she wouldn't stay to the end of the film."

My hips froze halfway to the toilet seat. I was unable to pee or unbend my knees until they'd walked out. Afterwards, while washing my hands at the sink, I caught one glimpse of my stricken face in the mirror and made sure not to look into the glass again. Returning to our row of seats, I could not make myself climb over the obstacle-course of male knees and crouched in the aisle, beckoning to Lucius when he glanced in my direction. Without hesitation he rose and staggered toward me, triggering another wave of jeers.

"Can we leave now?" I asked tonelessly.

"I thought you'd never ask," he muttered, preceding me to the foyer, where he dropped our leftover snacks into a waste bin. Then he took my hand and we went outside. Dusk was settling over a wide-track yellow shark-finned car parked in the theater's dirt lot. Two men were lounging in the back seat. Tow-headed Jim was leaning against the hood, smoking. As soon as he saw us emerge he dropped his cigarette to the ground and crushed it with a boot heel. Then he got behind the wheel.

Lucius shepherded me down the avenue. "They won't dare bother us on base. And with any luck there'll be a cab parked outside the gate. If there isn't . . . how fast can you run?"

"Why?"

The yellow car behind us throbbed to life. Lucius tightened his hold on my hand. Rubber tires inched over gravel. He gave a humorless chuckle. "When Jim found out we had the cheek to get married he told me in his neck of the woods people tar and feather couples like us. To teach them a lesson. I have a feeling he means to teach us one now."

I had a quick mental glimpse of two giant black birds without wings being chased down the street by a shark-finned hearse. Then I heard the soft purr of an engine close at our heels. A car pulled even, matching our walking speed. In spite of my best intentions I turned to look — not at Jim's face, but at Spider's, who was leaning out of his green jalopy. He had resumed his man-about-town disguise, complete with the obscure shades, the foolish hat, and an overly jovial grin. A subdued Washington sat hunched on the passenger seat.

Spider put on the brakes and said, "Joseph, my man, you were right to leave early — that movie was so lame it gave me a toothache. I'm aiming to cure it with a few shots of whiskey at the Alabama Bar. Care for a ride?"

Lucius glanced at the yellow rig creeping closer, helped me into the jalopy, climbed in himself, and said, "Drop us off at the bus stop in front of the bakery."

Spider gunned his motor in neutral. That little action made Jim decide to execute a U-turn and return to the parking lot. Nonetheless, Washington kept staring at the rear view mirror and insisted on getting out as close to his barracks as Spider was willing to take him. "Safest place to be on a night like this is in your own bunk," Washington said as he rushed into the evening.

I had only been in Spider's car once, though not in the back seat. I lived to regret it. But as we drove out of Henry I was unashamedly grateful for his prudent rescue, particularly when I saw there wasn't a single cab parked at the curb outside the gate. I silently conceded that Lucius's deviant friend deserved to wear his gentlemanly hat tonight. From that momentary appreciation the first seed of trust for the peculiar little man began to sprout somewhere inside me. Perhaps Lucius had been right about him all along and he was not as bad as I'd thought.

On the bus ride home Lucius's face appeared strained. Once we briefly locked eyes, both sets brimming with unspeakable humiliation tainted by traces of guilt. He didn't talk until we reached our address. Watching me get out the house-key, he said in a tight voice, "You go on. I'm not ready for bed yet. No need to wait up. I might be late." He offered no further explanation—but then, I didn't need one. Nor did I have to follow him through the dark streets to know where he was going—straight to his gaudy mistress waiting for him on her dais behind the plate glass. My last mental image, before sleep claimed me, was of his shadowy form glued to the glass, embraced by a crimson, shimmering light.

CHAPTER 9

When I WENT TO THE BAKERY the next morning Rosa was there, buying two Bienenstiche (pastries). I wished her a cheerful good morning and she blushed a delicate pink. Remembering the way Freddie had steered her away from our row in the cinema I had assumed the invitation she'd issued the day they moved in had been rescinded. But then she said, "These are for our tea. You're still coming, aren't you?"

Could it be that Freddie hadn't seen me and my unpopular seat-mate, after all?

"Sure," I croaked. "I'm bringing fresh Semmeln (crusty rolls)."

She brightened. "I have some home-churned butter and jam. Let's walk back together."

This suited me fine, as I was still ill at ease about our disgraceful address. By the time we arrived on the fourth floor

I had learned that she was born on a farm outside of Rosenheim and that she'd just started a new job in that town when Freddie interrupted her budding shop-girl career to swoop her off her feet.

While she unlocked her landing-door I scanned the labels next to the bell. The first one said, *Bauer 1 X.* The others said, *Kirchner 2 X, Braun 3 X, Huber 4 X.*

"Which one is yours?" I asked, surprised at the absence of an American surname.

She moistened a fingertip and wiped it over the third. "Freddie's grandparents emigrated from Rosenheim to the United States," she explained. "One of his missions, on coming to Bavaria, was to travel to their old home town and choose a bride to take back to Minnesota with him." Her complexion glowed with pride. "He chose me."

While she laid the table and put the kettle on the boil I checked out her room. It was three times the size of my own and had a real sink and a real counter topped with linoleum. Her table was covered by a cross-stitched linen cloth inlaid with lace. On its center stood a slim turquoise vase containing one red rose. The rubber tree she'd solemnly carried up the stairs the first time I saw her now sat on a stool in the darkest corner, its leaves gleaming next to a mahogany sideboard. The shiny floor smelled of new wax. A washboard leaned against the cupboard next to the sink.

"I use it to scrub Freddie's work uniforms," she said. "They take forever to dry."

"Lucius irons his wet fatigues to a crisp every morning." When he put them on afterwards there wasn't a wrinkle anywhere on them

"Oh?" She wrinkled her forehead in astonishment. "Your husband presses his own clothes? Freddie says that's women's work and I agree."

"*Sometimes* he irons," I amended, eager for her continued approval. "He's very considerate that way."

She let it pass and held up two tin canisters. "Peppermint or black?"

Judging her to be a serious tea drinker I picked the black. She busied herself with tea egg and china pot and I studied the room again, realizing that there wasn't a single book standing or lying anywhere. The only wall decoration was a plain wooden cross above the bed's headboard. On a peg next to the sink hung two wrap-around aprons, one blue and one brown. As she arranged pastries and rolls on a gold-rimmed platter I saw that her hands were quite chafed, probably from the harsh all-purpose detergent on her drain board.

While the tea steeped she sat down across from me and continued the story of her courtship. "Freddie's people were delighted with the photo he sent them of me. But in the beginning my father was not at all pleased with our romance. He thinks the Amis are trying to take over the world by corrupting young people with rock and roll and Coca Cola. Then Freddie showed him an album filled with pictures of the Minnesota farm he'll inherit someday. It's unimaginably gigantic, with huge machines that do most of the work. Now Papa can hardly wait for me to fly to America so he can make plans to come for a visit. How about you? You look too young to be married."

I assured her I was older than I looked and sophisticated enough to live in glamorous Los Angeles. She poured our tea, fetched a bowl filled with sugar cubes and a pitcher of cream, and sliced a lemon into wedges for us. The first sip of the dark brew made my mouth pucker. I poured in cream until it turned white. Then I stirred in three lumps of sugar.

"And your father?" she asked, squeezing lemon juice into her cup. "How does he like your Ami husband?"

"*Everyone* who meets Lucius adores him," I bragged. "Especially my mother." I neglected to mention that Vati had refused to meet him. And that he'd telephoned on my wedding day to announce that the instant I married Lucius I would cease to be his daughter. And that I'd heard nothing from him since. Groping for a more neutral topic, I asked, "Do you know any of your neighbors yet?"

"Only to say hello to," she said, splitting the rolls. "This is such a quiet building. I hardly see people on the stairs or hear a peep from behind their doors. They must all go off to work early and come home late. "

"That's what *I* thought at first," I began. But then I couldn't make myself pursue the subject. So I changed it again. "Is Freddie stationed at Henry?"

She opened a jar of blueberry jam. "Warner."

"Warner has a great library," I said, once more scanning in vain for a book. "But Henry has the store and the movie theater. By the way — I thought I saw you there yesterday. At the Marilyn Monroe film." I held my breath, waiting for her response.

She shuddered. "That was Freddie's idea. I didn't understand a single word. And the audience was unbelievably noisy." She lathered farm-churned butter on the split rolls *and* on her Bienenstich.

I put a protective hand over my pastry. "Lucius and I left early." When her face remained pleasantly blank, I ventured, "He's been teaching me a game called gin rummy. Do you play cards? It's fun with four players. Maybe we can get together after dinner some evening and play."

Her eyes lit at once. "Oh, let's! Tonight? Freddie's always so bored after dinner. He misses his favorite television shows. Why don't you bring your husband over — say at seven. And your cards. The only game Freddie and I have played so far is

Mensch, ärgere Dich nicht (Human, don't get angry)! He doesn't like losing."

We picked the platter clean of pastry crumbs and toasted almonds. She accompanied me to the door, resolutely tying the brown apron around her waist. "I'm going to scrub every inch of our communal bathroom," she vowed. "And then I'm taking a nice, leisurely bath. While the other tenants are off working."

"Or sleeping," I said, offering her the slightest of hints.

She gave an incredulous laugh. "People don't sleep during the day. Not even in big cities." She had a lot to learn.

That afternoon I was euphoric. Not only did I have a new friend but with a smidgeon of luck Lucius would have one too. Whenever I closed my eyes I saw the four of us sitting around Rosa's table, laughing together, a fan of cards in our hands. I could hardly wait for Lucius to come home so I could tell him we'd been invited down for the evening.

*

MUTTI dropped by after work, bringing cherries. While I sucked up the last few pages of the book I'd been reading she put them in a bowl and dipped a cup into the water reservoir.

"Empty," she said, her voice tinged with disapproval.

"Hmm?" I replied, busy riding my stallion across a golden sea of undulating prairie grasses, my hands gripping damp mane, the sound of pounding hooves and horse breath blending with the soft squeak of leather.

Shaking her head, she carried the reservoir out of the room and returned with water sloshing over its rim. By the time I snapped the book shut she was done rinsing the cherries and was blotting them dry. And then, with a sheepish smile, she pulled some iceberg lettuce out of her tote bag. "It was on sale. I couldn't resist buying a head for your supper." She glanced at the hot plate, conspicuously bare. As were my pots. She laid the lettuce on the counter, a hand's breadth away from milk-caked glasses and sticky cereal bowls. For a mere instant her eyes widened. She swallowed a critical comment but I knew she'd work in a mildly chiding assessment of my housekeeping skills before her visit was over.

I made room for the cherries on our little table by pushing dirty dishes to one side, books and art supplies to the other. She glanced at yesterday's crumbs, not missing the dollop of butter that had melted onto the table cloth. Her hands twitched toward the soiled dishes. Then her attention wandered to the wall behind the daybed. "Thank God!" she said. "You took down those sketches. How considerate of you!"

I found the praise insulting. As she was peered at the pictures of the red car Lucius had taped up in their stead I asked, "So, did you enjoy your night at Herr Adler's? Did you bathe in his sunken tub?"

"Goodness!" She pulled out a chair. "There wasn't time for that. He kept me up so late talking that I nearly overslept. If Frau Farber hadn't knocked on the guestroom door with a breakfast tray I'd have made both him and me late for work in the morning. Where's Lucius? Isn't he usually home by now? Won't he expect some kind of order? And dinner?"

I had no idea where he was. But I was certainly not going to admit it to her. "Working late," I said loyally. "How was your first weekend at the farmhouse?"

She showed me her chapped hands as if they were badges of honor. "I scrubbed everything clean."

I nodded, knowing that sentence was the most important one in her vocabulary, though it wasn't in mine. "Tea?" I asked, reaching for the kettle. When I held up our only two choices—peppermint and chamomile—I caught her brushing crumbs off the table top onto her palm. Then she closed her fingers around them, hiding the guilty hand on her lap. She continued to proudly recite her weekend activities.

"I scoured every inch of my kitchen. And the pantry. Then I collected a bunch of deadwood for the winter. I've started a neat stack of kindling at the rear of the house, under the eaves."

I'd forgotten how much she loved keeping herself busy. If someone shut her up in a room for the afternoon with a book she'd consider it solitary confinement. "You're all settled then?" I asked, wondering if Lucius would tolerate another bowlful of cereal tonight, swimming in condensed milk.

She snapped open her purse. With uncanny tact, she dropped the contraband crumbs into a side pocket before she pulled out a white linen handkerchief with ironed-in creases. She shook it out and began to wipe down the dresser, pausing just long enough to show me the astounding amount of dust it had picked up. "If you give me your paste wax I'll polish your dresser for you. You'll be surprised at how well wax covers up old scratches." She studied the worn linoleum floor, which gave no sign it had ever been waxed, polished *or* buffed. "I see you haven't gotten around to buying wax yet. No matter — next time I come I'll bring you what's left in my tin. I used most of it on my kitchen floor. It's so porous, it sucked up coat after coat. But now I can see my face in it."

"Goody," I said. If I wanted to see *my* face, I'd look in a mirror.

She gave a gratified sigh. "At last there's no one waiting for me at home, asking to be fed. And I no longer have any arguments to soothe. Truly, knowing that my two girls are on their own and capable of taking care of themselves is the greatest gift. What I have, for the first time, is peace of mind. Except for the elves." She lifted an armload of books off the table and put them on the newly cleaned dresser top, lining them up along the wall.

"What elves?"

"As soon as I woke up on Saturday," she said, kicking off her shoes, "I sensed I wasn't alone in the house. Little eyes were watching me. From under things." She squinted up the window frame, climbed from her chair to the table top in stockinged feet, and pulled the curtain away from the wall. Then she destroyed the delicate spider web I'd admired on my wedding day. Carefully she gathered every last strand along with the desiccated baby fly, which disintegrated on her handkerchief. Climbing back down, she opened the window, shook out the pieces, and rubbed the cloth vigorously to dislodge the last little limb.

"I cut myself a slice of bread for breakfast," she continued, "and found a neat tunnel inside the loaf, stretching from one end to the other." Chuckling, she carried her chair to the wardrobe to tackle its woefully neglected top.

Thanks to her cleaning compulsion I was beginning to feel like an idle bothersome guest in my own house. I got up, filled the dishpan with the hot water left in the kettle, submerged the dirty dishes, added soap flakes, and swooshed the water until it sudsed. Then I dropped in the dirty dishes and plopped back on my chair.

"The bread was locked in my bread box," she continued. "Who but elves could have opened it? They have their magic ways."

I imagined a tribe of tiny people hiding behind the chromed box, carrying miniature lanterns, crowbars, and pickaxes.

"That evening," she said, "I brought home a some potatoes, rinsed and dried them, and put them in a basket on the table. The next morning every last bite was gone, peel and all. I pictured the elves on their beds in their hidey holes, hugging plump bellies, delighted with the new renter."

I was delighted, too. The dilapidated farm, full of ancient shadows, was the perfect haven for fairies and dwarves. Perhaps there was even a secret passage from the farthest dark reaches of the cellar to their underground realm, which must surely lie beneath the roots of the forest. "Last Thursday when we sat on that fallen log," I told her, "I felt eyes trained on me from under the bushes. Didn't you?"

At last I heard the sweet sound of Lucius's footsteps crossing the hall. When he walked in he was exactly one hour late. Mutti, still standing on the chair, stretched to reach a dusty web clinging to the ceiling. The chair began to wobble and Lucius took a gigantic step to steady it, dropping a manila envelope in the process. "Gotcha," he said.

"Grüss dich, Lucius," she replied, coming down to step into her shoes. He picked up the envelope and shoved it under our ersatz counter.

"I haven't had a chance to start dinner yet," I told him, wondering if I'd dare break out the corn flakes while Mutti was here.

"I ate," he said shortly. Then he smiled at her. "*Hallo*, Mother. Was that your Volkswagen I saw at the curb? Is it all fixed?"

"Ja," she replied after I translated his question. "It runs like a clock and sounds like one too."

"Gaskets," he said absently, glancing at the protruding manila envelope. "How's your new house?"

"She has fairies," I put in. "Little people with hooks and ropes, climbing up the table legs in the middle of the night to eat her potatoes."

That got his attention. "Fairies?" he mused. "I don't know much about fairies except that they're about the size of mice."

"*Mäuse,*" she confirmed. "The insides of the walls are alive with them. And there's a sour smell in the kitchen after I fire up the stove."

"Oh yeah," he chuckled. "I remember that smell. You need a cat."

"Blood and guts?" Mutti shivered, wandering to the counter. "On my newly polished floor? I'd rather buy extra bread."

"They'll have babies every couple of weeks who'll have their own, and so on," Lucius told her. "The more food, the more babies."

She sighed and reached for the dish cloth. "How can I let a cat murder mere babies? Can't I just . . . relocate them? To the other side of the woods? I don't dislike mice. Not after Maria's little white Elvis."

"We could build them a starter nests in a hollow stump," I suggested. "Until they learn to fend for themselves."

"You want a live trap? I can make you one," Lucius said. "If you get me a bucket and some cheese I'll do the rest. On second thought, forget the bucket."

Mutti scrubbed out the first milk-coated glass, spread out a dish towel, and placed the dripping, upside down tumbler upon it. Then she glanced sideways at me, raising one penciled-on brow. Good-daughter-meek, I shook out another linen towel and dried the dishes as fast as she could wash them. When we were done she said, "Can you come next Saturday? With the trap?" and started to push my broom across the floor.

Reluctantly, I knelt with dustpan and brush, sweeping up piles of debris. She went for the mop next but I wrestled it out of her hands, muttering, "Are you here to visit or to take over? I don't mean to be ungrateful but next time you come please just put up your feet and relax!"

She glared. "How can I when your house is so messy? No wonder Lucius has started getting home late. If you don't watch out there'll come a day when he won't come home at all."

I glared right back. "I'm not telling you what to do in your house. Don't tell me what to do in mine!"

Lucius looked from my face to hers. "What?" he asked.

"She's giving me directions to the tram station in Pasing," I told him. Softening my expression and tone, I asked her, "What time will you pick us up from the station?"

"Ten-thirty." She raised a hand as if to cup my shoulder but dropped it again. "Mein Gott (my God)," she said, blinking. "In a few weeks you'll be on the other side of the world. Can't we be nice to each other until then? You might never see me again."

I muttered, "Don't do my dishes unless I ask!"

She gathered her purse and the empty tote bag. "Will you at least make him a salad?"

"Not tonight," I said. "You might as well take the lettuce with you before it wilts. We're playing cards at our new neighbors'. An American couple. Like us."

She stuffed it into her bag, looking impressed and relieved. "Why didn't you say so? Don't let me keep you. Till Saturday then." Smiling at Lucius, she said, "I'll get some cheese for the *Mäuse*. And I make you a good hot dinner!"

"Okay, Mother," he said. "It's a deal."

He walked her downstairs. I stayed behind to peek inside the envelope he'd brought. It contained Simca brochures featuring his favorite red sports car. They called her a Plein Ciel, although there was nothing plain about her. I was brushing my hair when he returned. While he changed out of his work clothes I explained about Freddie, gin rummy, and Rosa's invitation.

"A farm boy from Minnesota, huh?" he said with a pleased grin. "Should we tell them the truth about this place or let them find out for themselves?"

We decided to ad lib. In honor of the special occasion Lucius applied fresh deodorant to his arm pits. Then we walked to the fourth floor. As I pressed the bell button three times for Braun I remembered I'd promised to bring down our cards.

Lucius volunteered to fetch them. "We'll wait for you," I called after him. Then Rosa opened the door.

"Lucius went to get our cards," I said, smiling. "He'll be right—"

She stepped out and closed the door behind her. Leaning against it, she had the grace to blush. "I'm sorry," she whispered. "But you can't come in."

I was flabbergasted. "But you invited—"

She shook her head. "Freddie said I should have asked his permission first. He saw you at the movies last night. He said your husband is—he's a . . ." She opened the door just wide enough to squeeze back inside. Then, with one last apologetic grimace, during which she turned tomato-red, she shut the door in my face.

My neck muscles tightened. I was fed up with spineless, blushing women and considered ringing again just to blurt into her inhospitable face, "Oh, by the way, you and your exclusive Alfred are living in an actual whorehouse!" But then I decided they deserved finding out the hard way, clue by small clue.

It was more strenuous to climb up than it had been to run down. I met Lucius half-way. He waved the card deck at me. I shook my head. "Rosa's . . . not feeling well," I told him. "She's getting a migraine. We'll have to do it another day."

But Lucius was nobody's fool. "Right!" he said, narrowing his eyes. Then he shrugged. "Just as well. There's something I want to show you. You'll never guess where I went after work."

"Where?" I asked with dread, feeling the headache I'd predicted for Rosa follow me all the way home.

CHAPTER 10

LATER THAT NIGHT, AFTER LUCIUS had pinned the shiny brochures to the wall and we lay companionably side by side on our narrow bed, I mustered the courage to tell him, "This isn't the right time for us to buy a car. We need to save for my airplane ticket and for our apartment in Los Angeles."

It took him a while to answer. "I know," he finally admitted out loud. "But wouldn't it be something if we could take that pretty car to California with us? She'd be one of a kind. People would watch us drive on those crowded freeways and wonder where they could get a Plein Ciel just like her. Only, they couldn't. We'd be special."

"You hate to be stared at," I reminded him.

"This would be a different kind of staring," he said. "Admiring, like. What you don't understand is that compared to Munich, L.A. has lousy public transportation. We'll need a car to get around. Here's what I'm thinking, Maria — as soon as we land, we'll both get good jobs, and before you know it, we'll have saved enough money so your mother can buy the car for us and have it shipped over. You'll get your license. I drive every Monday, Wednesday and Friday, and you drive on Tuesdays, Thursdays and Saturdays. What do you think?"

"And on Sundays?"

He grinned. "On Sundays we wax and polish. Old T-shirts are good for the job. Afterwards we'll drive to an outdoor theater. They're called drive-ins. You drive in, I drive out." He chuckled at his own wit.

Lucius had his dream, I had mine. "I want to go to college before I start working," I announced.

"Listen," he said. "In California you can do both. As long as we don't have any kids the sky's the limit."

I wondered what opportunities awaited a sixteen-year-old girl who couldn't type and a twenty-year-old boy who never made it past the fifth grade. How long would it take us to accumulate the funds for a car *and* an education?

"Why not buy a used motor scooter instead?" I suggested. "The same shiny red as your Plein Ciel."

"A scooter? In L.A.?" he huffed. "They'd laugh us right off the freeway. Worse, some eighteen-wheeler would crush us flatter than a slice of bologna."

"Bologna?"

"Salami. Liverwurst."

"Eighteen-wheeler?"

"Semi. Huge trucks too big to fit on your roads."

His argument was persuasive. And now that we were talking again I wanted him to explain what had happened to us at the movies and why. But as soon as I broached the subject he yawned and turned onto his side, facing away from me. I got the hint and remained silent — until Friday night.

By then we had recovered our marital equilibrium. The shame glistening in his eyes on our way home from the cinema seemed forgotten. He brought home a bucket to which he had fastened a slanted aluminum collar. "Washington works in the motor pool. He's good with a welding torch," he said, placing the contraption on the table. "Now all I have to do is rig up a mouse-sized ramp from the rim halfway down the inside. I even bought a jar of peanut butter in case some of the little fairies prefer it to Swiss cheese." He showed me how to snap the collar off and on.

I lined the bottom of the bucket with a couple of discolored hand-towels to provide both comfort and seclusion for the future captives and asked, "What does 'tarred and feathered' mean?"

Looking resigned, he said, "I knew you'd get around to that sooner or later." And then he told me about the Mason-Dixon Line. "In most of those southern states they still have race laws on the books!"

Although cohabitation between members of the white and black races was often tolerated, marriage never was. Sometimes the offending couple was merely arrested and jailed. Sometimes both partners were painted with hot tar, covered with feathers, and chased out of town by people like Jim. If it was the husband who was black he might even be lynched.

"What is 'lynched'?" I promptly inquired.

"One of the reasons I went to Vermont," Lucius said. Then he told me the story of a fourteen-year-old Chicago boy named Emmett Till who visited relatives down south during summer vacation and made the mistake of whistling at a young white woman in a store one day. "Or so she claimed," Lucius went on, describing how white men had come to drag young Emmett from his bed late that night to inflict various acts of torture on him for the sake of that innocent whistle.

Lucius talked about ropes and nooses, jeering, picnicking crowds, white hoods and burning crosses. Then he took my face in his hands and said, "Enough with the questions. We'll never live in the South. And it's not like that in California. Especially not in L.A."

I had no pictures to put to his words. But after I fell asleep my mind plunged to a mildewed dungeon where I found myself nude and in chains. The chains were bolted to a big iron ring attached to the wall. A rough stone floor sucked the heat from my body by degrees. All around me eerie voices moaned and dark forms shifted, parting at last for the darkest shape of all—an ink-cloaked wizard with hollow, glittering eyes. As he drew nearer my skin shriveled with terror. His laugh sounded like the ominous hiss of a snake or like some volatile gas about to explode. I knew I must run but strain as I might I could not break loose. Then the cloaked figure hovered over me, removing its hood to reveal O.F.'s skull-like face. The evil living inside the eye sockets dripped acid onto my flesh.

I awoke with a gasp and found myself between two worlds, connected to neither. Touching the wall beside me I felt not the rusty iron ring but the slick paper of Lucius's Simca brochures. Yet the evil apparition continued to loom, the skull now wearing Lucius' face. He reached down my legs, tugged at the duvet which had tightened around my knees, and pulled it up to my chin.

I moaned his name.

"Go back to sleep," he said, his voice curiously flat.

"I dreamed—" I began.

"Yeah. Me, too. I was Emmett Till, dragged from his bed, skinned alive, hung and butchered. Next time don't ask so many questions!" He turned away and put a pillow over his head. We slept back to back, two magnets repelling, until a steely light crept into the room.

Still filled with dread, I eased into my clothes and went for a walk. Gathering the mantle of loneliness around me, I roamed a myriad of gray streets lined with gray walls until I came to the field behind the Schuttberg. The grass drooped with dew. I climbed to the hill-top, following the same path Lucius and I had taken on one of our first dates. I chose "our" bench and sat on "his" side, evoking more congenial times. From there I saw the first rays highlight the crosses atop the city's many church towers. Golden-seamed clouds parted, awaiting the new sun.

Above me a vast flock of swallows plunged and rose at dizzying speeds, each entirely sure of its part in the whole. Soaring and dipping along with the flock, I had to hold onto the bench to keep myself upright. At the horizon, granite mountains clothed in green stood patiently watching the gilded edges of dawn illuminate first the wheeling birds and then my bench, bathing me in a tender, luminous warmth. The city below unfolded out of night-shadows, each structure well planned and reassuringly solid. I stayed on the hill until the flock swooped up and away, the clouds whitened, and a vision of butter-fried bear claws drew me back home.

Soon the aroma of caramelized pastries blended with that of simmering cocoa, waking Lucius more efficiently than I ever had. He took the brochures down from the wall and committed every word on them to memory while we sat at the table and ate. I leafed through my Africa book, admiring the inventiveness of its many tribes. There were a multitude of bangles and rings on arms, necks and around ankles. There were lips stretched around plates, heads elongated until they became ovals, faces covered with intricate beauty-scars. There were round mud huts with thatched roofs blending with Savannah landscapes. Palatial clay mosques sprinkled the Sahel, embedded with great wooden supports.

A crouching bush-girl glanced up from her page, wearing a plain leaf-green wrap that contrasted beautifully with her brown skin. She was more familiar to me than my own sister. In fact, the longer I stared at her the more I found the essence of myself looking out of her eyes. Perhaps I was made for a life like hers, simple and good, full of music and dance in a twilight world of vines, creepers and leaves.

Raising his cup, Lucius asked, "Is there any more cocoa?"

I poured, leaving the pot on the table for easy refills. "Look at this," I said, pushing the book toward him. He pushed it right back. "Don't you want to know where you came from?" I asked. "The first time I saw you I thought you were a Watusi or a Masai. The men of those tribes are unusually tall and long-legged. More than twice the height of Bushniggers, who are the size of midgets and — "

He jumped to his feet. "Bush-what?"

"Bushniggers," I repeated, wondering at his vehement tone.

His nostrils flared. It was not a good sign. Eyes flashing, he picked up the half-filled pot of hot cocoa and emptied it over my head. While it oozed down my neck and over my blouse I marched to the kitchen, chose my heaviest skillet, and whacked him over the head with it. It gave sickening thud.

"Are you nuts?" he cried, sucking in air.

"You started it!" I held the skillet aloft in case of another attack.

"Because you said the n-word! Nobody says that in front of me and gets away with it!"

"What's an n-word?"

"Nigger." He dabbed at his skull and checked his fingers for blood. "You said it. I heard you. Loud and clear."

"I did not!" I protested. "I said 'Bushniggers.' That's the scientific name for the little people who live in the jungle. See, it says so right here!" I found my little green-kilted friend and pointed to the caption under her photo.

Lucius read, modifying his expression from incredulous to merely perplexed. "Scientific, huh?" he said when he was done. "You sure?"

"Of course I'm sure," I replied with righteous indignation. "There are *Bush-Girls* and *Bush-Boys*, and the whole tribe is called *Bushniggers*. Everyone knows that. Besides, I called *you* a Masai!"

He attempted to blot my chocolate-soaked hair with the dishrag. "Sorry," he said, sounding contrite. "False alarm. What a waste of good cocoa! Go dunk your head in the bathroom sink and change into something old. Collecting firewood isn't for sissies."

Following his instructions I wondered why one little word should have the power to change him from a soft-spoken man into a certified lunatic. How odd that the more my English language skills improved the more muddled communication between us became.

As soon as I was presentable we took the streetcar across town to Pasing. Mutti was waiting for us in her blue VW just as she'd promised. Lucius and I hadn't said more than a dozen words to each other on the way. He hadn't smiled once. But as soon as he saw Mutti he waved and gave her a cheerful grin. I followed his cue. She had worked hard to help bring about our wedding. We owed her a thriving marriage—or at least the appearance of one. And thus we embarked on developing the personae we felt she and our ever-attentive public deserved.

She admired the bucket he was carrying and, peering inside, extracted a bag filled with small white cushions. "Mouse pillows?" she asked dubiously, squeezing one through the plastic.

Yielding the passenger seat to me, Lucius climbed to the back of the car and said, "Something I picked up at the PX for our dessert."

Why hadn't he mentioned the purchase when he came home yesterday? "You were hiding it from me," I said, feeling slighted.

"I was afraid you'd finish off the whole bag before bedtime," he confessed, trying to find a comfortable position for his legs. "Besides, I wanted it to be a surprise. Something new, even for you."

*

SINCE the day we helped Mutti move she had acquired a dented wheelbarrow and a wobbly child's wagon. "They're easier to maneuver than boxes—especially for bark and pinecones," she told us, pointing to a couple of mounds she'd started inside the stable. The three of us decided to comb through the forest for the remainder of the day. "The people who own the land are grateful we're clearing out dead stuff, " she explained. "I promised them we wouldn't cut anything living. Limbs big enough to be sawn go in this pile." She pointed to one she had started in the front yard.

Over the course of the next few hours she seemed determined to be everywhere at once. One moment she was scraping the cones I brought into a neater heap, the next she was adding kindling to her stack at the rear of the house. In the woods she briskly gathered anything that could possibly burn and tossed it alongside the path for us to pick up. Lucius called us the gleaners. When he jokingly asked for a broom with which to sweep the forest floor she started to fetch it for him.

"He's kidding!" I called after her. Vacillating, she looked down the path, then at her watch, and said it was time she started cooking our supper. Lucius wanted to know what was on the menu.

"I make a good salad," she told my lettuce-deprived mate. "And cook a big pot of *Sauerkraut mit Wiener.*"

Except for one split-second during which his eyes widened, Lucius did a good job of hiding his distress. "I have an even better idea," he improvised. "Why don't we have a wienie-roast tonight? Let's start a camp fire with the raunchiest wood, toss some potatoes on the coals, and grill your wieners over the flames on long sticks. It'll give you more time to help us collect kindling."

She saw the logic in that, grabbed the wagon handle, and preceded him to the nearest thicket. I went to the kitchen to gather old newspapers, snatched an apple off the cutting board in passing, and nibbled at it on my way to the far side of the woods.

There, I loosely wadded the papers and stuffed them inside a hollow stump for Mutti's unsuspecting mice. I'd often watched my Elvis gnaw paper until it was the texture of silk. An agitated bumble bee flew out of a hole along the side of the stump to investigate. I held still until it grew calm, then I followed in its wake as it spiraled along a sunbeam. Soon I found myself in a pool of light where yellow wasps rose and dipped in and out of the shade, their wings lazily humming. A patch of forget-me-nots bloomed under a bilberry bush. I spread my jacket on some springy moss between the bush and an oak and lay on my back.

With my eyes closed I could hear sounds I hadn't paid attention to while I was walking. High branches stirred in the breeze. A song bird warbled up and down several octaves. Another emitted only one morose note, replicating it at measured intervals. A woodpecker drummed, boring through layers of bark.

Squinting, I noticed an ethereal spider web stretching from an oaken limb to the bush. A slender ray filtering down from the canopy illuminated each filigreed strand. Studying the intricate details of the weave, I looked for its creator, surely as delicate as the work it had spun. But it stayed out of sight—perhaps hiding under an anchoring leaf. I yawned. The sun withdrew its light from the web. Shadows deepened. The one-note bird resumed his dull song. Then I lost track.

When I awoke, or thought that I did, I sensed undefined forms stir and surround me. A giant black spider with scores of pitiless eyes hung in the oak directly above. It paid out a strand as thick as a rope that stretched and stretched. As the spider fell toward me it changed its shape, becoming a waterlogged brown-skinned boy. His neck, caught in a loop of the rope, angled sharply to one side. His bloated cadaver face tightened to take on Lucius's features. Something wet and cold stabbed the back of my hand.

Recoiling, I saw the shaggy silhouette of a black hellhound with slanted yellowish eyes an arm's length away. When he was sure he had my full attention his nose stabbed at my hand again. Then he sat on his haunches, wagging his bushy tail and raising a paw in greeting. It was Alex, Hannes's German shepherd. Ears erect, he turned his big head and listened intently to a faraway sound drifting through the forest. And then I could hear it, too—three faint syllables, repeated once and again.

"Ma-ri-ia! Ma-ri-ia!" Lucius was singing across the distance between us. Alex rose, stepped away, paused, stepped again, and watched me expectantly until I understood that he had come to fetch me back to the farmhouse.

CHAPTER 11

THE FIRST PERSON I SAW UPON COMING out of the trees was Hannes, dressed in worn corduroys, pulling a handsaw through the tree limb he'd laid across make-shift saw horses. Lucius was kneeling on the ground, building a stone circle around the beginnings of a camp fire. "Another reject," Hannes said, tossing him a gnarled branch. Then he saw me and waved. "Servus (hi), Maria! Are you hungry yet?"

"Wow!" Lucius said, looking up. "That's one heck of a dog you've got there, Hannes. All you said was 'Find Maria' and away he went, nose to the ground — and fetched her back lickety-split while I was yelling my head off for nothing. How did you train him to do that?"

"I didn't," Hannes replied. "He was born with unusual talents. I believe he can even read thoughts. And of course we already know he loves to play with Maria. Bring her a stick, Alex."

Alex sniffed through the nearest pile until he found one he liked and laid it gently at my feet. As I picked it up the memory of my bad dream receded. "Shouldn't I be helping you?" I asked Hannes, marveling at how safe I was beginning to feel.

"Playing stick with Alex *is* helping. And as you're about to find out, more strenuous than cutting wood or starting a fire."

Alex proved a hard player, tireless in his retrievals. Not only did he insist that I throw for him again and again but he expected me to offer enthusiastic praise each time he dropped his wooden toy at my feet. I admired his powerful limbs extending and contracting, the huge jaws snapping unerringly down on the stick as it sailed through the air no matter where I aimed it.

Hannes whistled and continued to toil. Lucius kept feeding the flames. Mutti delivered a tray full of sausages and a bowl of well-scrubbed potatoes from the kitchen and sat near the stones, pulling her flowered skirt taut over her knees. Although the sky was clouding, Hannes insisted these were friendly clouds with no thought of bursting to dowse our fire.

But when an extra-long throw of mine took Alex and me close to the brooding forest I imagined not merry elves but sullen goblins or dwarves, brandishing pickaxes while they watched us from the thicket beyond. One by one the birds stopped singing—and as the silence unfolded I recalled that Mutti had no neighbors, telephone, or electricity.

"So," I asked her after stepping back to the welcoming circle of light, "what happens next? Are you really going to divorce O.F.?"

Hannes paused to put a hand on Alex's neck, entwining his fingers in the dog's ruff.

Mutti looked pained that I had broached such a private subject in front of her old boss. But then she said, "I've been asking him for a long time. His answer has always been no.

With his agreement I could be legally free in one year. Without it it'll take much longer. Right now he's still waiting for me to come to my senses." She raised her resolute chin. "But I won't. He may slow me down but he can't stop me. And I'll never go back."

Hannes's fingers relaxed. He gave Alex an affectionate pat and put another branch between the saw-horse. "I'm sure my attorney can recommend a good divorce lawyer," he said casually and began sawing again. He continued over Mutti's protests until it grew too dark for him to see the blade or the wood it was cutting. Then Lucius fished the potatoes out of the coals, passed them around, and handed us the sticks he'd peeled and sharpened. Roasting the wieners was fun. Mutti refused to let us eat them with our fingers, though, insisting we slide them and the baked potatoes on to our dinner plates next to the drooping salad. Lucius waited until I ate my last lettuce leaf, then he stabbed five of his little white pillows on each of our sticks. He called them "marshmallows." They grew puffy in the flames, the outsides turning golden and the insides melting like hot ice-cream.

"I haven't sat at a campfire in years," Hannes said. "I forgot how much fun they can be. The only thing missing is a sing-along." He hummed the first phrase of Abendstille (evening silence). "Round robin," he said, starting his part with a nice baritone and switching to bass as soon as Lucius had learned most of the words. The comforting melody quieted my heart and spread a cloak of peace over us all. After the last note faded Lucius taught us "Michael, row the boat ashore." We sang it with gusto.

"Tell me," I asked Hannes in English after we finished the tune. "How is it you speak such good English? Did you learn it in school?"

He smiled. "I've traveled a bit."

Mutti laughed, switching to German. "I'll say. Hannes has been to the four corners of the earth. His parents sent him out of the country before the war started. And he wound up—"

". . . in Chile," he continued in English. "It's where I finished my education."

Awed, I asked, "You can speak Spanish, too?"

"Fluently," Mutti replied for him, in German. "Like a native."

"Enough about me," Hannes said calmly with a decidedly Bavarian inflection. "I'm sure you all recall that I promised Anna a going-away dinner party for our favorite Duncans. Shall we plan it for next Sunday? Frau Farber is already scanning her recipe files for the occasion. Have you bought your plane tickets yet?"

"We only need one," I replied. "I'm picking it up at the American Express on Monday. Lucius gets to travel for free on a military transport plane." My heart grew weightless as I imagined actually holding the means to my getaway in my own hands.

"What?" Lucius asked. "What did you say?"

"That life is good," I told him, switching back to his language. "And getting better every day."

"Right this minute it's not half-bad," he agreed. Then he looked at Mutti, baffled by her quivering lips. "Was ist los (what's the matter)?" he asked her. "Are you all right?"

She turned from the flickering flames, rubbing her eyes. In a reedy voice, she said, "I guess. It's just that California is so far away. . ."

She sounded as if I were cruelly abandoning her when, in truth, last year she had abandoned me. I watched her stack our dirty plates, her face drawn. I could feel Lucius watch me watching her. Any minute now she'd break down and cry, ruining our good time. Then I remembered the coat I'd left under the oak on the other end of the forest. "I'll be right back," I said, moving uneasily toward the trees.

Behind me, Mutti muttered something about getting her car keys to drive us to the station. Hannes told her not to bother because he'd be delighted to drop us off on his way home. I paused at the first tree. Then I left all semblance of light behind and entered the realm of the miscreant dwarves, reminding myself with each step that the only things I had to fear were my own creepy thoughts.

I was fine until I tripped over the fallen log I'd forgotten was lying across the path. Retreating, I bumped into something soft and yielding that gave a yelp of surprise. I whirled and I saw an inky shadow astir in the gloom.

"Maria? Is that you?" it croaked with a voice that *almost* sounded as if it belonged to Lucius—but just as likely to an evil changeling good at imitating humans. I jumped away. So did the impostor. Then I ran back to the farmhouse as fast my legs allowed, hearing heavy footfalls behind me.

Mutti and Hannes were sitting side by side by the fire. Alex, lying at his master's feet, raised his head and woofed. "Maria," Hannes said, looking in my direction. "A late evening walk?"

"I . . . l-left my coat," I stuttered as someone who *looked* like the real Lucius dashed out of murky brush and slowed to a nonchalant walk. "On the far side of the woods," I went on. "But it's awfully dark in there. It'll be cold on the way home."

"You should have told me when we were in there," Lucius grumbled. "I would have gone with you. Hannes, you wouldn't happen to have a good flashlight handy, would you?"

"No need." Hannes pointed to the path. "Alex, go find Maria's coat."

Tail wagging, the dog bounded away and reappeared short minutes later, placing my red anorak at my feet.

Rubbing his neck in appreciation, I thought he was better protection than my husband could ever be — for, like me, Lucius seemed to be suffering from an overactive imagination.

At the Pasinger station Hannes parked under a streetlamp and walked around the front of the Mercedes to open the passenger door for me. "It's funny," I told him. "I spent my village years playing in the woods and never knew an instant of fear. But Mutti's forest is eerie — especially at night. Whatever will she do in that drafty old house by herself? In that great silence?" Climbing out of the car to stand beside him, I noticed how splendidly the silver threads in his thick dark hair shimmered in the lamp light.

"Do?" he said with an odd little grin. "For the first time ever she gets to do exactly what she wants. And she's learning to live by herself. A wonderful skill to acquire." He cradled Lucius's hand and my own. "Thanks to you both we've had a wonderful evening. I'll see you on Sunday — say around four?"

*

A COUPLE of days later I ran through our lobby, triumphantly swinging my purse. It contained my plane ticket *and* my revised passport. By sheer luck the two offensive policemen had been busy with other supplicants when I stopped by the precinct station. A third officer, absent on my last visit, asked to see some identification, wished me an auspicious journey, and slid the passport across the counter.

And now, feeling jubilant, I clattered up two stairs at a time and almost succeeded in passing the landlady's door when it swung open and she called me to her.

"Ja, Frau Doonkahn," she said, making an unsuccessful effort to soften her stern features. "I meant to stop you this morning on your way out but you were thundering downstairs so fast that you were gone before I could get to my door."

"Sorry," I muttered, suspecting she was about to issue a formal complaint about my unmannerly exit. But she merely attempted a congenial smile and said,

"You may recall the chat we had on the day you moved in. You wanted a bigger room and I told you I'd let you know as soon as something was available. It just so happens that one of my fifth floor tenants has become . . . unclean. Couldn't pass her last physical. Naturally I will have to evict her. You can have her place when I have finished sterilizing it."

Hadn't she read the letter I'd slipped under her door last week, giving her notice of our intention to move? "Which room?" I asked, curious in spite of myself.

"The one next to the WC," she replied promptly. "It's almost as good as having your own bathroom. I ought to charge extra."

I had seen Spider had come out of that room. It was the slug's.

"But — my husband and I are leaving. In thirteen days."

She yanked at an errant strand of her hair and imprisoned it with a bobby pin. "All right then," she sniffed. "I'm only keeping my promise. I'll hold it for you for one week. In case."

"In case of what?"

"Sometimes circumstances unaccountably change. At the last minute."

Sheer blasphemy! "Not this time," I said, fingering the reassuringly solid airplane ticket inside my purse. "But thanks for thinking of us." I climbed half a flight, then asked, "The sick woman — where will she go?"

She tugged at her apron, rattling the keys she kept in its pocket. "Back to her village, I expect. To her people. If they'll let her."

I resumed my climb only to stop on the second floor landing to pull out the plane ticket and scan all the pertinent information just to make certain that it was exactly the same as the last time I looked. It was. Nonetheless I found it necessary to hold it to my heart until I was inside our room. Locking the door, I considered the wardrobe and both of my trunks but decided to hide my treasure under our mattress instead, determined to leave nothing to chance.

"You won't believe it," I told Lucius when he came home. "The landlady had the nerve to offer us a bigger room. As if she didn't know we're leaving."

"Take it," he said gruffly. "We're not."

I managed an incredulous, "Huh?"

He tossed some forms on the table. "After Freddie's little put-down and what happened to us at the movies I started to realize I wasn't as anxious to get back to the States as I thought. In truth, I *like* being over here. With my new family. So I . . . reenlisted." He tapped on a document I couldn't decipher. Nor did I have a clue as to what he was talking about.

"Go on," I said, hoping to figure it out in a minute.

"The CO's been bugging me about it for weeks," he obliged. "Today I made up my mind. At first I was just going to sign up for three extra years—but that would only have given me a five hundred dollar bonus. It was a thousand for six." He pointed to his signature, gracing a dotted line. "So I signed up for the six. Which means I'll have to stay in the unit for at least one extra year. After that, who knows? Maybe Japan. Or Korea."

I was beginning to get the drift of his speech. We weren't short-timers after all. Nothing was going to change. "But you promised!" I wailed, feeling the blood drain from my face. I had staked my whole future on it. Made no alternate plans. "And I already bought my ticket!"

Unmoved, he shuffled his papers. "Take it back for a refund. We're still going to California. In six years. Meanwhile I have to agree with Hannes. Living in foreign countries is the best education in the world. Even if I have to do it wearing a uniform."

His unexpected attitude-shift gave me goose bumps. It was like the time I'd skied across a wintry slope as a child. Though everything had looked fine, suddenly my knees locked, bringing me to a dead stop. A few seconds later the snow field ahead of me collapsed to become a roaring avalanche.

For as long as I had known Lucius he'd hated the Army. Surely that hadn't changed. Once his reenlistment bonus was spent he'd understand the enormity of what he had done. How many captive seconds did six years hold? How many mutinous heart beats? What kind of avalanche was *he* about to trigger? Was it my job to witness the outcome?

And then it came to me—*I* could still leave. Without him. Why not? I had my passport, green card, and ticket. And enough cash left over to finance my first couple of weeks in L.A. Especially if I slept on the beach.

Perhaps my rebellious thoughts showed. "Are you trying to tell me you married me just so you could get to the States?" he asked, glaring.

Outraged, I could only shake my head.

He showed me another form. "I used the whole thousand to make a down-payment. On Red Pepper."

"What's a red pepper?"

"The Plein Ciel. I'm picking her up on Friday. Just in time for the party. Only now we'll be arriving in style."

I hadn't been imagining his shift of affections. He had chosen to trade me in for a car. "Why didn't you ask me first?" I moaned, sounding exactly like Mutti. At her worst. "I'm your wife!"

"I don't need your permission," he snapped, reminding me of my perpetually irritated father. "For anything. Besides, you'd have said no."

He was certainly right about that. "But Hannes is giving the party to celebrate our *departure*," I whimpered. "I better call him and cancel." It would be good to hear a sane, reasonable male voice. Just for contrast.

I cried all the way to the pay phone, passing a grizzled, very thin man tottering along the sidewalk. It wasn't until I shut the booth-door behind me and he rapped on the glass with deformed knuckles that I realized he'd had the same objective. I showed him my back, leaned against the folding door to keep it shut, and dialed Hannes's office, still knowing the number by heart. The new secretary answered. As she put me through I wondered how pretty she was.

"Maria! Wie gehts (how are you)?" he said, sounding more paternal than Vati ever did.

"Gut, danke, " I began automatically, though I didn't feel good at all. "I called to tell you . . . to say . . . I just found out — that is, I don't think you should have that farewell dinner for us. Because Lucius just decided to reenlist. Which means we're not going anywhere for a long time." I put my palm over the receiver so he wouldn't hear me sob.

"Ah," he said. "I see. I know how much you were looking forward to your American adventure. You must be so disappointed. But I don't think your Mutti will be. To tell you the truth, neither will I. And we don't need an occasion for our party. Why don't we call it your special *Trost* dinner? Just between you and me."

A consolation banquet? I couldn't help smiling. "I suppose blue jeans are out?"

"Quite definitely!" he answered firmly. "In fact I believe Lotte and Anna are planning a shopping expedition for the event. Care to join them?"

If there was one thing I disliked more than wearing fancy clothes it was shopping for them. I was just about to tell him so when he said,

"*Moment, bitte.*" His voice grew faint. "What is it, Frau Weiher? Who wants a word with me? Ach wo (you don't say)!" I thought I heard him give an amused little chortle. Then he murmured into the mouth-piece, "Maria? *Hallo*? It appears the enemy has landed. In my outer office. I'll see you on Sunday, yes? Servus (bye)!" He hung up before I had a chance to reply.

I would have liked an extra minute or two to digest all the changes bearing down upon me. Unfortunately the feeble old guy outside the booth began to rattle the glass door. I was pushing against it with all my might but he succeeded in pulling it open halfway — proving what strength fury could lend. I wouldn't have been surprised if he'd reached in to bodily evict me. "All right!" I told him. "I was finished anyhow. But it wouldn't have hurt you to use the next phone, around the corner!"

Flushing, he sputtered, "What did you say, you hussy?" Then he screeched, "Eene solche Frechheit (what nerve)!" Heads turned in our direction from both sidewalks.

"Ja, und (so what)?" I said coolly, which was as daring as my backtalk used to get in bygone days when O.F. chased me around the kitchen table for less. Then I added, "Sau Breiss (Prussian pig)!" *Eene*, indeed!

The Prussian shook his fist at me, struck speechless at my youthful disrespect. I pushed out past him, shutting the folding doors in his face. As far as I could see I owed him no more respect than he thought he owed me. For some reason I found the hostile encounter cheering, though not enough to want to be in the same room with Lucius. Not yet, anyway. First I intended to console myself with the most expensive item on the menu at the Italian Ice Palace, leaving him to stew at home in his misguided juices.

CHAPTER 12

IN THE MIDDLE OF FRIDAY afternoon I heard Lucius's footsteps rushing through the hall. He peeked in and crooked a finger at me, gave me his come-hither look, and said, "She's downstairs. Waiting to give you the ride of your life."

Red Pepper was parked at the curb, as shiny on the street as she'd been in the show room — though something about her seemed to be smirking. Warily, I settled myself on the passenger seat, rolled down the window, and watched Lucius merge with bumper-to-bumper traffic. He drove as if he'd been born behind a steering wheel, assertive yet cautious.

From streetcars, sidewalks, and nearby automobiles, people craned their necks to observe our crimson passing. But they weren't just staring and pointing. They were also smiling and waving at us, and Lucius, who hated to be singled out when he stood on his own feet, was waving right back at them from the driver's seat as if he were Sidney Poitier, Harry

Belafonte, or Sammy Davis, Jr.'s extra tall cousin. I almost expected him to bless his audience with the sign of the cross.

"Now this is more like it," he said as I struggled to keep my hair from sailing away with the updrafts. He took Schleissheimerstrasse all the way to the Harthof where he by-passed the Marshall Plan apartments, though I wouldn't have minded in the least if Heinz or Wolfi or even O.F. had spotted us in our elegant car. Driving toward the Baggersee, Lucius tossed me a Butterfinger. "She's giving us a smooth ride, isn't she?" he said proudly. "Hear that purr?"

I devoured my candy bar, willing to uphold my part of a truce that included both my husband and his new lover. He turned on to a dirt road and came to a stop. Then he got out of the car. "Go on," he said. "Have a turn." When I didn't comprehend the magnanimity of his offer, he added, "We'll have you driving like a trooper by sundown. That way you'll be able to use the car while I'm on maneuvers. No more lugging heavy bags home on the bus—you can fit at least four of them on here." He flipped his seat forward to show me the tiny upholstered bench in the rear.

The instant I slid behind the wheel I forgave Red Pepper every one of her seductive wiles and began to enjoy myself. After the first few bumpy minutes I began to grasp the concept of working the clutch without stalling the engine. Half an hour later my starts and shifts were almost as smooth as Lucius's.

Finally he declared me proficient and reclaimed the driver's seat. Looking off into the distance, he said, "I bet when you arrive at Hannes's house in Pepper tomorrow nobody there will recognize you. Especially if you put on this tonight." He deposited a small, wrinkled paper bag on my lap. I pulled out a packet with the words *Miss Clairol* printed on it over the picture of a radiant blonde.

"Bleach!" I cried, letting it slip through my fingers. "No thanks—I like my hair natural."

He retrieved the packet and jiggled it patiently in front of my nose. "When you step out of this car with golden waves flowing down your back Anna will be so floored she'll forget how to breathe."

What wouldn't I give to see the look on her face? She and Mutti would be so busy trying to guess who I was they'd forget the embarrassing fact that all my bragging about my imminent future in L.A. had come to naught. "All right." I took the packet. "If it doesn't work you're going to have to buy me a wig."

"As long as it's a *blonde* wig," he said. "But I see no reason why anything should go wrong. Every bombshell I've ever seen got there with a little help from her Clairol friend."

I studied the platinum-blonde head on the package. Why not? The glass vials inside were the equivalent of a bottle of cognac. Total oblivion. I'd simply stuff the old me out of sight and become somebody entirely new of Lucius's invention.

It was he who filled the reservoir and my two biggest cooking pots from the bathtub spigot as soon as we got home, he who set the water to boil. Then we sat at the table and waited. I shuffled a deck of cards while he read the hair-care instructions out loud.

Soon my hair was washed, covered with goo, and wrapped in plastic. We played a couple of rounds of gin rummy, keeping our eyes on the minute hand of our alarm-clock. The moment it reached the twelve I jumped up, grabbed a towel, and ran to the bathroom to stick my head under the tub faucet for a thorough rinsing.

But the door was locked from the inside. I knocked. There was no response. I rattled the handle. Still nothing. I put an ear to the key-hole and heard the sound of soft weeping.

"Please," I cried. "I need a bath. Now!" Who would have thought I'd ever admit it out loud?

Still no response. First with disbelief and then in horror I looked around me, wondering how to proceed. That's when I saw that the door to the slug's room was ajar. No doubt it was she who'd barricaded herself in the bathroom. Probably sitting on the toilet having a nervous breakdown. No telling how long that would take. My scalp was beginning to itch. Carefully, I poked it with a finger, testing to see if my hair might already be melting. Then I rushed to explain my predicament to Lucius.

He accompanied me to the bathroom door and rapped, yelling, "Aufmachen, bitte (open up!)" The slug ignored his Gestapo imitation.

We played a third hand of gin rummy, keeping our room door open so we could hear the slightest sound from the hall. There was none. At last Lucius threw down his cards and shut us in. "You better dunk your hair in our slop bucket," he said grimly. "Only thing in there is the water from your shampooing. Slosh your hair around real good. That way the worst of the mess will come off. Then I'll wash out the rest with what's left in our reservoir. No time to heat it. Sorry about that."

I followed his instructions. He rinsed and rinsed until the reservoir was dry and my spine hurt from bending. Then I staggered to the dresser mirror but the ceiling bulb was so weak I couldn't see much except that my hair was several shades lighter, stuck to my skull, and dripping. If felt uncommonly rough when I touched it. I wrapped a towel around the mess.

"This beauty stuff's hard work," Lucius said, rotating his shoulders in an attempt to loosen sore muscles. "I'm worn out. But I can hardly wait to see how gorgeous you'll look once your hair dries." We went to bed and hoped for the best.

Early the next morning I stumbled through the hall with a full bladder. This time the bathroom door was wide open. And blessedly empty. It wasn't until I passed the mirror over the sink that I remembered the bleach. My towel had come off during the night. At first I didn't believe what I was seeing. But a more cautious look showed me a bright orange mop, standing on end. A mop that felt like desiccated straw wherever I touched it. I squatted over the toilet to pee but stopped myself when I remembered whose unclean bottom had been sitting on the seat for half the night. Raising it with the toe of my slipper, I straddled the bowl and peed standing.

Back in our room I tried to work my tortoise-shell comb through the mop. Every tooth broke and what was left of the comb snapped in half. The unwieldy knots even bent the bristles of my trusty old wire brush. My social life was definitely over; I'd never leave this room again. Maybe I could get Lucius to tell everyone at the party I'd flown to America without him. Collapsing on to the bed, I poked through what used to be my best asset. When I pulled my fingers out of the mop a big wad of hair came with them. Frantic, I shook Lucius awake.

He yawned, opened his eyes, and quickly shut them again, as if he had accidentally strayed into a very bad dream. Then he sat bolt-upright, his expression changing from incredulity to glee. "You look like you got struck by lightning," he said without the slightest trace of guilt. As if the entire mishap had been my idea. Grabbing his trousers off a chair, he pulled out his wallet, and asked, "How much for a good wig, do you think? One with very long and very blonde hair?"

"Can't you unravel this stuff for me?" I wailed, kneeling before him and extending the damaged wire brush.

"No way." He rummaged in our utility drawer in search of our scissors and brought them out, snapping the blades. "Not until we've whacked off all the dead stuff, that is." He patted a chair. I sat. He found my damp towel and wrapped it around my shoulders. Then he stooped over me and began cutting. Every snip of the blade was a dagger stabbing my heart. Clumps the color of autumn leaves fell around my feet. Now and then he said, "Ooops," paused, and bravely continued. Once he nicked my ear and had to stop cutting until the blood had a chance to coagulate. At last he stepped away, wearing a dubious expression.

"Are you done?" I asked.

"Almost," he said breezily, putting the scissors down on the table. "Why don't you go to that beauty shop at the Kurfürstenplatz and let them even it out for you? I'd finish the job myself but I have a date with Spider. He found me some fancy duds for the party." He dressed in great haste, slapped a couple of bills on the table, added a third, and said, "After you're done at the hairdresser's, why don't you buy yourself a nice little dress? On me." He rushed to the door, turned for one final look, suggested, "You might want to wear a cap when you go out," and fled.

I didn't have to go to the mirror to know his rescue attempt had failed. But I went anyway—and couldn't decide if I looked like a criminal newly released from a maximum-security prison, a woman with a terminal form of brain cancer, or a female traitor found guilty of consorting with the enemy whose hair had been butchered in retribution. I put a scarf over what was left of mine and hurried toward the Kurfürstenplatz and my salvation.

I'd often walked past the beauty parlor, admiring the way the sun highlighted my long chestnut curls in its broad picture windows, barely aware of the odd drying cones inside that were frying customers' brains. Upon entering I smelled a peculiar mix of hairspray, shampoo, and singed hair. Mutti always reeked of that blend when she came home from getting a perm. She would keep her newly lacquered curls hidden under a scarf until she could heat enough water to rinse off the stiff helmet of fixative. "We can't all have hair like yours," she'd say sourly as I sniggered. "It's the one thing your father passed on to you that's priceless, but only because he couldn't help it."

Well, now even I didn't have hair like mine. Hopefully one of the beauticians had the expertise to salvage the remnants. Behind the counter, on floor-to ceiling shelves, was a display of empty heads covered with fright wigs, most of them blonde. Wearing one of them on a steady basis had to be at least as itchy as a tight woollen cap. An idle operator waved from the station farthest away from the window. I went to sit on the upholstered seat she offered me, looked around to make sure no one was watching, and pulled off the scarf.

"My husband did this to me," I confessed as if I were uncovering life-threatening bruises. The short, buxom beautician ran her fingers through the results of Lucius's handiwork and told me with barely disguised amusement,

"You'd be amazed at the number of customers who say those very words when they come in here. But, honey — *your* hair isn't just suffering from a bad cut — it's deceased. Nothing we have will resurrect it. I'm afraid we'll have to take off most of what's left. There are a couple of patches where his scissors seriously slipped. It'll come out short. Very short."

She tied a large bib around my neck. I resisted only briefly as she tilted my head backward over a sink and turned on a hand-shower. Watching her remove what was left of my hair was so painful to me that I had to keep my eyes shut. For a long time I felt her well-practiced touch all over my scalp, hearing the decisive click of her blades and knowing that each snip of the scissors added another strand to the pile collecting on the floor. My only consolation was that whatever she left would be too short for curlers, pins, and hairspray.

"There," she finally announced with a hint of satisfaction. "We'll have to tint it, of course. What was your natural color?"

"Dark. Very dark."

"Brown or black?"

"Black," I decided. "Raven-wing black."

She said the good news was that she'd managed to cut off all of the damage and that some measure of life still lingered near the roots. "Short hair grows fast," she soothed as tears gathered on my lashes. Half an hour later she rinsed off the tint, pulled off the bib, feathered a soft brush over the nape of my neck to remove minute stubble, and held a mirror up to my face. "Open your eyes!" she said. "You look very nice. Like an Italian street urchin."

My mood lightened at once. I smiled but kept my eyes shut. She took my hand and put it on top of my head. What was left of my hair felt damp and surprisingly soft. I looked in the mirror and saw a sleek, very black cap so short it couldn't even curl. She was right—I looked like a boy. A *pretty* boy. "Put on some big dangling earrings and take off those jeans," she said. "You'll be stunning. Buy yourself the most expensive dress you can find and a glossy new lipstick. Your husband can hardly object, can he?"

After some window shopping I found something posh and pricey that fit me like second skin. Even so, it was cheap at four D-Mark to the dollar. When Mutti rang the bell soon after I returned home I wound a towel around my head before I let her in.

"Oh, good! You've washed your hair," she said. "I'm picking up Anna to go shopping with me. I was hoping you'll want to come with us."

"I hate shopping," I said with a grimace.

"You're not wearing blue jeans tomorrow, are you?"

"Probably not."

"How about that red dress I gave you for your birthday a couple of years ago? It goes so well with your long hair. Makes you look like a Gypsy."

I would be ludicrous in my lucky dress now. "I'll need some dangling earrings," I said. "Amber. Like yours."

She slipped them off without thinking twice, unclasping the matching pendant from around her neck. "You used to love this set. Keep it. To remember me by, in America."

So Hannes hadn't told her the bad news. The man had incredible tact. I thanked her for the gift and she went to the window, scanning the street and looking uneasy. "Will you watch me drive off?" she asked. "I don't mean to sound neurotic but when I got in my car after work I thought a black Opel was following me. All the way here. The man behind the wheel was wearing a black hat and steel-rimmed glasses. I could swear I've never seen him before."

"This town is full of black Opels," I pointed out. "But sure, I'll watch."

She swept up her purse. "What time shall I fetch you and Lucius from the Pasinger station?"

"I don't know yet," I hedged. "Why don't you just go to Hannes's house without us? He has a phone. We can call when we get off the tram." I put on my old sneakers.

"You're not thinking of wearing those with your red dress, are you?" she said in alarm.

As a matter of fact, I hadn't been thinking at all; obviously, I'd have to visit a shoe store for high heels to match my glamorous outfit. Outfit! Heels! Hadn't I promised myself I'd never wear either again? All the fault of Red Pepper, of course. She was the first domino to fall in the inevitable collapse of every plan I had made.

I watched Mutti's VW roll away from the curb. And sure enough, a black Opel pulled out five spaces behind her. She started out slowly and when there was a momentary lull in traffic she did a sharp U-turn and sped off in the opposite direction. Lucius would have said she turned on a dime. The ungainly Opel tried a similar maneuver but wound up straddling both lanes. Cars honked, blocking the pursuit-vehicle from every direction.

The VW was gone. From the next block came the sound of squealing brakes, angry horns, and the warning clang of a street car — but no clashing metal, no shattering glass. It was an astonishing getaway. Like life, my mother was full of surprises.

CHAPTER 13

ON THE DAY OF THE DINNER PARTY Lucius gathered his cleaning supplies, including an old T-shirt, and went to polish Red Pepper to a high gloss. I did the breakfast dishes and took the garbage out to the dirt-packed, barren service yard in back of the building. Heading upstairs, I decided to stop at the landlady's to tell her as diplomatically as I could that her terrible prediction had come true; we were interested in the room she had mentioned after all.

I was standing at her front door, trying to get my finger to push on her doorbell, when I heard light footsteps descending from above. A little girl of six or seven appeared on the stairs, holding on to the banister while carrying a reeking garbage pail. She was a Mischling (bi-racial) with brown wooly curls and honey-bright skin. Her legs were thin, her eyes bambi-soft. Although I hadn't seen her before she evidently lived somewhere in the building.

I made an effort to smile. She gave me a shy, fleeting smile in response but quickly lowered her gaze to her torn sneakers and went past me to the back door. Wrestling it open partway, she squeezed her narrow frame out to the service-yard, which was fit only for storing refuse. My eyes brimmed and I withdrew my hand from the bell-button, cradling my belly and wondering why there was no law against raising an innocent child in this place.

*

IN THE afternoon we were driving to Herr Adler's house with Red Pepper's windows rolled all the way down. I was determined to use this dinner as an excuse to find out once and for all if Hannes was good enough for my mother. Sitting in the driver's seat beside me, Lucius looked superb in the white Italian suit Spider had provided. The red tie coming with it matched the car's paint *and* my berry-scented lipstick. My new spaghetti-strap dress blended with the passenger seat, highlighting the 2-meter-long golden silk scarf I had wound around my head. Its ends, Lucius had to admit, undulated behind me far more enticingly than any blonde wig ever could.

We cruised to an easy stop alongside Hannes's garden wall, right behind Mutti's VW. She was just climbing out, looking at us in utter befuddlement. I slipped off the scarf and sauntering to her side. Speechless, she clung to her door.

"It's me," I assured her. "The handsome man in the white suit is Lucius, and the low slung sports car he's driving is called Red Pepper. Brand-new. "

"Marianne?" she stammered, disoriented. "But . . . but . . ."

I removed my sunglasses, showing off my new improved eyes, dramatically outlined in black and framed by mascara-enhanced lashes. Then I tugged at the amber teardrop earrings she'd given me and wiggled the matching pendant resting in the V of my cleavage. This prompted a more positive identification. "Maria!" she breathed. "I didn't know you could look like that!" She drew a curve through the air that included everything from my much-altered hair to the black patent-leather spikes I was wearing.

Lucius strutted up behind me, tipping his white Italian straw-hat to a sporty angle. "Guess what, Mother," he beamed. "We've decided to stay in Munich for one extra year. Isn't that nice?"

"*Ach*," she said, swaying on knees that had gone feeble. "Ja, mei (I'm speechless)!"

It got even better when Horst's dull-tan BMW pulled up behind us. Anna was out of the passenger seat before the wheels finished rolling. "Maria! Is that you?" she cried. "I didn't know you could look like that," thereby proving that young apples never fall far from the mother tree.

"Like what?" I asked, smug as a feline who'd just licked a rival cat's saucer clean.

"Did you hear? Maria and Lucius are staying," Mutti squeaked.

"Staying where?" Horst asked absently, studying Red Pepper from all angles. And then all three of them closed rank and began talking at once.

Lucius crooked an elbow at me. "Kind of noisy, aren't they? Shall we?" I gave him my arm. We sauntered up the rose-perfumed brick path to the house, my hips rolling as if they'd been oiled. Our admirers buzzed around the red car and I buzzed the bell, flexing my insteps one at a time to marvel at how well the dark nylons were enhancing the shape of my calves.

Hannes, opening his lavishly carved entry before I expected, caught me in the act of self-adoration. His eyes sparkled as they moved from my legs to the rest of me and on to Lucius. "I see neither of you is wearing jeans," he said, turning to pluck a red carnation from a vase in the vestibule.

Snapping the stem, he wove the flower through Lucius's lapel, then stepped away to study the effect. "Good. Now the success of this evening is assured. Did Lotte fetch you from the station, then?"

"No," I said, off-hand. "We came in our new sports car. Do you mind if we use your bathroom?" I was profoundly curious about the reported sculptures and ferns and the sunken tiled tub.

"Please do," Hannes said. "Did you say 'sports car?' I'll be right back." He hurried out to the street. Alex, who had been standing behind him, gave me a friendly follow-me look and preceded us down the long hall to sit in front of the bathroom door.

I could feel Lucius's ribcage humming with glee. "What did I tell you?" he crooned. "We're a hit!" We grinned at each other in utter delight and entered the room to worship our reflections. At first I was overwhelmed by mine. Then I grew aware of a seal peering over my right shoulder, its sleek blackness matching my outfit. White-suited Lucius let go of my arm, shoved his hat to a new angle, and hooked his thumbs into the pockets of his superbly tailored jacket, glancing sideways at his image.

I ran my palms over the smooth ocean-blue mosaic tiles surrounding the double sinks, the gleaming chrome faucets, the matching floor tiles. At the famed Roman tub the blue tiles became interspersed with turquoise and sea-foam green squares. On the right side of the tub was a mermaid, reposing with her silver-scaled tail curving behind her. On the left, balancing atop a marble column, was the seal I'd seen in the mirror—smooth, streamlined, exuberant. Between them stretched the mural of a misty lagoon at dawn. Ferns spilled from surrounding shelves and ledges.

Lucius draped an arm over my bare shoulders, doffed his hat, and cocked one of his blue-black eyebrows at me. "Missus Duncan, I presume?"

"Indeed."

"You're one half of a very interesting couple!"

"Quite!" I pulled the hat over his eyes. "But now this missus needs a private moment, old chap."

"Rather!" he said with a bow before exiting.

Alone, I did a bump and grind in front of the mirror, savoring each exaggerated move. Then I explored the treasures spread before me, recalling the old saying, "Show me a man's house and I'll show you the man." Tonight was my chance to investigate both parts of the axiom. Since Mutti had never been a good judge of the opposite sex she needed someone sharp-eyed and sober-minded like me to guide her before she became mesmerized by Hannes's easy abundance. While it was true that I thought Mutti deserved a prince, sometimes I couldn't help but wonder what could possibly attract a man who seemed to have everything to a woman who had . . . well, nothing. "Remember — all is not gold that glitters," I told the mermaid, trying to ignore her mocking smile and bared breasts.

When I stepped out into the hall it was empty. I followed the murmur of voices to the sitting room. Someone's inexpert hands were walking up and down the keys of a piano. I posed on the threshold but no one inside was awaiting my grand entrance. Horst and Hannes had Lucius cornered. I heard "cylinders" and "horsepower" and "top speed," and tuned out all three of the lay-experts. Nearby, Mutti sat on a brown leather couch, leafing through a photo album. The long sideboard behind her was heaped with desserts, green-stemmed tumblers, and bottles of wine.

The clumsy musical notes I'd been hearing came from the adjoining room, which was streaming with multi-hued light.

Looking for the source I beheld a stained-glass sun topping a pair of French doors that were open to the backyard. The artfully arranged stained-glass shards depicting the dazzling half-orb were surrounded with glass-rays in shades ranging from pale yellow to deep red. Backlit by the real sun shining in from the western sky, the window was bathing the entire room in fragments of color.

Alex came in from the garden and lay down across the threshold, staring out at something I couldn't see. I felt a bit piqued that he seemed to find whatever it was more fascinating than he'd so recently found me. Anna, slouching on the piano bench, continued to torture the ivory keys with a shaky rendition of "Alle meine Entchen (all my little ducklings)."

I sang along.

She said, "Toller Wagen (neat car)."

"Well, yes," I boasted. "Lucius has already taught me to drive. I'm going to get my international driver's license next week. Then I can use the car when he's away on maneuvers."

Anna flared her nostrils as if she could almost smell a sham. "It's a nice consolation, I suppose," she agreed. Then she shook her head with exaggerated pity. "But you must be *so* depressed now that your plans are in ashes."

"In ashes? Von wegen (that's what you think)! Merely postponed for a year — during which we plan to see something of Europe," I said pleasantly, noting a shadow of envy flitting across her face.

Trying to work her expression back toward pity, she needled, "Didn't you have your heart set on Hollywood and Beverly Hills?"

"That was you," I corrected. "I was more interested in orange groves and sandy beaches. But they'll wait. Why, we might go anywhere from here. Even Japan. The Amis have bases all over the globe. It's a good way to see the world." I fingered some of the tall, iridescent plumes standing in a copper pot beside her.

"Peacock feathers," Anna informed me. "Hannes says they fall off the birds whenever they molt. In India, I think. You missed the guided tour." She pointed to an ebony mask mounted on the wall. "The African corner." A row of glass shelves surrounding the mask held small figurines sculpted from uncommonly dark wood. Beneath them stood a large hide-covered drum, well worn, and a three-legged African stool, high-backed and carved out of just two entwining, separate pieces.

Anna took a small object off the piano top and pressed it into my palm. "Thumb piano," she said as I plucked a row of metal strips and listened to the delicate notes they produced. Then she pointed at the other three corners. "Alaska. Amazon. Australia."

But I was still busy with the African display, for I had noticed the enlarged snapshot of two very tall Masai holding long staffs, standing beside a big-horned brown cow and a white adolescent boy wearing a grubby safari suit. "Is that—"

"Yes. Apparently he's been to some parts where the Amis don't have any bases. Yet. You're not planning to stay in that abominable hole you're renting for one whole year, are you?"

Immediately, I remembered the trapped little fawn-eyed girl coming down the whore-house stairs and struggled to keep a sudden and quite overwhelming distress from spilling into my voice. "As a matter of fact, the landlady has just offered us a bigger room."

"Well, forget it. I have a better idea. I *was* going to mention it to Mutti, but I think she should stay just where she is, don't you? Near all of this." She leaned close and whispered, "Wouldn't you just love it if she and Hannes—I mean, this house makes Vati's hill-top mansion look like a shack."

Trust her to fall for the gold. "What idea?" I asked. "What were you going to mention to Mutti?"

She looked around to make sure we were alone. "I was at the high-rise manager's office today when a tenant came in to demand the return of his move-in deposits. He hadn't given any notice—though the contract requires thirty days in advance. The manager was quite upset about it. Said he'd have to put an ad in the paper and the idea of the resulting onslaught was unsettling. Then he asked me if I could think of anyone who might be interested in a bachelorette. I told him I'd let him know by tomorrow. It's in the older building, mind you, and it hasn't been cleaned. He said he'd waive the deposit if the next tenants agreed to clean it themselves."

Anna reached up, touching my hair. "Smooth as silk. Unlike the unruly mop you've always had." She stroked her own and winced. "I'm tempted to change my style too. Throw away the sticky hairspray. Comb out the tangles, put in some platinum highlights, and let my hair flow naturally over my shoulders. Long and loose. What do you think?"

I said with all the sincerity I could muster, "You'll look great! Beehives are becoming old-fashioned."

Her gaze fell to my décolleté. "What kind of bra—"

"Bra?"

She stared. "Oh my God. I couldn't do that."

I gave a lazy stretch and said, "Probably not."

Her cheeks flushed. "You seem . . . rounder. All over. Although you don't look as if you've gained any weight. Do you like being married?"

"Sometimes I do. Sometimes I don't."

She thought about it. "It might be nice to have my sister close by. Listen—you can't afford to let this slide, Maria. Not even a day. What if the manager mentions the vacancy to somebody else? It's fully furnished. Furnished apartments go extra fast. Go tell Lucius right now. If he likes the idea I'll call the manager from here."

I found my husband studying the sideboard in the sitting room. Behind him, on the brown couch, Horst, Hannes and Mutti were discussing New York. Lucius beckoned me over and pointed to a stunted orange-colored cake smelling of cinnamon and nutmeg. "This here looks like a pumpkin pie. Minus the crust. That would make it a pumpkin pudding."

It was the least impressive of the desserts. "Guess what," I said. "Anna's found an apartment for us."

"All right!" he said with interest. "Where?"

"In the old high-rise next to hers. At the Scheidplatz."

His expression darkened. He shook his head. "Bad idea."

"Why?"

"I'm about to go off on maneuvers—"

I couldn't believe my ears. "You'd rather leave me alone in the whorehouse for a month?"

He scratched his head. "Fact is—I'm close to flat broke. Car took it all, you see. By Christmas maybe . . ."

"This chance won't wait until then!"

"Hold on now," he chided. "Let's not be greedy. We can't have everything at once, can we?"

"Oh?" I said. "Isn't that precisely what you're trying to do? Lucius, please! Remember, every one of your dollars is worth four D-Mark."

"Don't crowd me! I said no!" he snapped, softening the stark declarations with, "Broke's broke. We'll find something else. Somewhere else. Later."

Obviously he didn't much care where he lived and with whom now that he had his dream car. Until that final *no* I had intended to give him the refund I had received for the plane ticket. Now I definitely would not. Nor was I going to mention the apartment again—until I'd signed the rental agreement myself and held the keys to the bachelorette in my own hands.

CHAPTER 14

I DIDN'T WANT TO SPOIL THE EVENING by giving way to my irritation with Lucius, so I merely turned my back on him, pretending an interest in a nearby painting on the wall. I could feel him drifting away, leaving a cold spot that settled between my shoulder blades. Anna hovered nearby, watching us both. I put a finger to my lips to signal a need for secrecy and gave her a nod. She nodded back. With my peripheral vision I saw Lucius wander into the sunroom.

Anna cleared her throat and said, "Verzeihung (excuse me), Hannes—may I use your phone?"

"Which one?" he asked amiably from the couch.

The words hung in the air like two helium balloons, plunging the room into stunned silence through which I could hear porcelain clinking all the way from the kitchen. Then Hannes said, with a tinge of amusement, "It's a big house."

"The . . ." Anna cleared her throat again. ". . . nearest."

"Two doors down the hall. To the right," he told her before refocusing his attention on Horst and Mutti, who had started to recall the time her father took her to the top of the Empire State Building.

While I waited for Anna's report I contemplated the sideboard's center piece — a three-layered Black Forest Kirschtorte sitting on an oversized royal-blue platter. It made the torte's whip cream frosting seem even whiter. The confection was topped with sweet red cherries marinated in schnapps. If memory served, inside the frosting was a rich chocolate cake, each tier drenched with Kirschwasser (cherry brandy) and liberally spread with apricot jam. The other cakes paled beside it — especially Lucius's sad little orange-colored mutant, only one layer thick and quite plain.

Frau Farber had placed two identical crystal vases on each side of the blue platter. The graceful long flowers arching from the vases consisted of a multitude of tiny white bells. When I leaned down to inhale their fragrance my knuckles accidentally grazed the cake frosting. I licked them clean, tasting chocolate crumbs, sugared cream, and a strong hint of schnapps. To keep myself from scraping up a second helping I busied my hands with a glass, filled it with red wine, and tossed it back, mercilessly draining it to the last drop.

In a much improved mood I followed Lucius to the African corner and found him surreptitiously trying to push the tusk of a black elephant sculpture back into its socket. "It came out as soon as I touched it," he said, offering me a sheepish I-want-to-make-up grin. He stroked the elephant's smooth polished back. "Interesting wood. Stone hard."

"Have you noticed the photo?" I said with a conciliatory smile of my own, pointing to the snapshot. "Remember when I said you look like a Masai? Check out their long legs. They're cattle herders. I read somewhere that they tap blood from the veins of their cows and drink it raw."

Lucius grimaced. "Someone should introduce them to Coke." Spying a hi-fi between two potted palms, he crouched to rifle through shelves filled with '33s and pulled out an album. "Leadbelly!" he murmured, in awe. "That Hannes is full of surprises!" Reaching for another, he whistled and said, "Satchmo!"

I wanted to invite him for a stroll through the back garden but I could see he'd already tuned me out. So I went by myself. Outside and off to the right, a stand of slim birches served as a privacy screen. Off to the left I found the elusive Alex.

He was sitting in front of a knee-high brick wall that was covered with a profusion of purple flowers. The wall bordered a doll-sized world that was a garden within the garden, complete with miniature trees and an opulent square of hilly lawn. On the lawn was a small, stone-lined pond ringed with flat boulders. Behind it, wild grasses, entwined with weeds, had been allowed to grow unchecked into clusters as tall as a man. From this thicket came a strange chorus of squeaks, half bird and half mouse. Alex licked his muzzle and gave a low moan.

Grass blades shivered. A tiny blunt nose appeared, cautiously sniffing. Black button eyes followed, along with cauliflower ears, a chest pushed out like a dowager queen's, and four naked clawed feet. The oval-shaped creature was covered in wheat-colored fur. From its mouth or its chest or somewhere between rose high-pitched, multi-octave squeals as the little beast began to waddle along a narrow path worn into the lawn. Instead of a tail it had another head attached to its rear end—and another body, which also had a head attached to its rear, followed by another body and another and another, each different from the rest. One had short fur the color of rust, one was a shaggy black and white, a third's silken blonde locks swept the ground as it shuffled along.

I counted six creatures in the row, forming a veritable train of guinea pigs, all of them twittering and chirping like nightingales as they marched over hill and dale to a patch of white sand. Shivering with excitement, Alex raised his head toward the evening sun and gave a short but enthusiastic howl, whipping his tail.

The goose-stepping tribe crossed their white desert to a trough filled with green pellets. There they waited until their leader gave a shrill whistle. Then they fell to. That last whistle broke the dog's tenuous hold on his self-control. Barking, he leaped over the wall scattering guinea pigs in every direction. They scampered for the safety of their grass-jungle. Only one little creature remained — the leader, frozen in fear.

The dog became wolf. Crouching low, he slithered toward his prey, every ounce of him aquiver with greedy anticipation.

"Alex!" I cried. "Alex, don't!"

He puffed his fur and crept on. I kicked off my shoes, raised the hem of my tight dress, and climbed over the barrier while Alex pressed relentlessly forward, maw agape, exposing his impressive canines. I lunged for his tail and with one mighty heave jerked him to a stop — and unleashed a devil.

His head whipped around. Eyes blazing, he snarled, snapping at my offending hand. But just as his terrible canines grazed my skin he forced his mouth shut with a supreme effort of will. My hand went slack with shock. The dog resumed his stalking until, whining softly, he pushed his muzzle against the snout of his victim. Whereupon it bit him on the tip of his nose.

Alex drew back for an instant and then, gently wagging his tail, he ventured a kiss. It was met by a string of guinea pig curses. Sighing with delight, the dog slopped his tongue over the small creature, drenching it in spit — which led to more curses. Then the soaked dowager-queen retreated to reunite with her troops, holding her head up high until she'd disappeared into the thicket.

"Alex, come," I said again. This time, looking fulfilled, he deigned to obey. Sauntering joyfully past me, he sailed over the brick barrier while I still tottered in fright. After retrieving my heels I lowered myself onto the plant-covered bricks and waited for my fingers to stop trembling and my knees to steady, wondering if what I had just witnessed was real or an illusion triggered by wine.

Anna appeared at the French doors, summoning me back to civilization. "Promise me you won't leave this house tonight until you've seen where he keeps his 'nearest' phone," she murmured when I padded to her side in my stocking feet. Then she grinned. "The apartment's as good as yours. I'll get Horst to vouch for you. All you have to do is show up tomorrow morning at nine, looking responsible. Bring cash. And for goodness sake, don't give the manager your current address. Give him Mutti's. Lucius will thank us for this once it's done. He'll have a real parking lot for his car."

"Toll (great)," I whispered, squeezing my feet into the spikes. "We'll practically be neighbors. Mutti will be able to visit us both in one fell swoop."

"Actually," she reminded me, "unlike you I'm quite busy these days. Between taking my business classes and working for Horst I won't have time to sit around sipping tea."

"Of course," I agreed, realizing that for the coming year-long limbo I'd have far too much time and too few tasks with which to fill it. As we passed Lucius, Anna glanced at the stack of albums he'd put aside.

"Good records, Lucius," she said kindly as if trying to make up for the fact that she'd been plotting against him. "I like Yatz."

The fact that she had mispronounced "jazz" might have made me feel superior on another occasion, but because she had so recently offered her help I decided to swallow the correction waiting on the sharp tip of my tongue. We trailed Lucius to the sitting room, where he showed Hannes his picks and asked if he could put them on the turntable. While they hovered over the hi-fi a silver bell rang in the hall and then Frau Farber appeared in the doorway to announce grandly that dinner was served.

On the day of Mutti's historic move the cook had invited us into her kitchen for a lavish snack. This time she led us to a formal dining room. Inside, a massive table was crowded with an array of platters, bowls, and copper pots piled with the delicacies she'd prepared.

"I asked Frau Farber to arrange everything American-style," Hannes said, looking pleased. "And I must say it's quite a spread." He pulled out a chair for Mutti. Since neither Horst nor Lucius seemed about to emulate his considerate move, Anna and I pulled out our own chairs—next to Mutti. Horst quickly took the seat beside Anna's, but my husband, listening to the opening chords of a haunting melody piped into the room via discreetly mounted speakers, was content to sit by himself, waving his fork like a baton. Hannes raised a hand and seemed about to speak, perhaps to reseat us according to some preconceived chart, then changed his mind and sat down beside me.

"Billie," Lucius announced with his head inclined toward the nearest loudspeaker as a thin female voice, sounding orphaned, began a plaintive song.

Each place setting held a steaming soup plate atop a flat dinner plate. "I couldn't resist ladling out the bouillabaisse myself," Frau Farber apologized, "to keep the broth from dripping on my best linen."

I scanned over flower arrangements, fine china, crystal salad bowls and goblets, and a host of casseroles, recognizing none of the dishes before me. Horst turned his soup this way and that, muttering with undisguised suspicion, "Buja-which? Looks pretty." He sniffed at the bowl. "But what's in it, exactly?"

Mutti sought to override his gaff with a compliment. "You worked too hard for us, Frau Farber! Now let me help you with that heavy tureen—"

"Nix (absolutely not)!" Frau Farber said firmly. Mutti, who had already pushed out her chair and was starting to rise, sat back down looking flustered.

"This bouillabaisse is from Frau Farber's extensive French recipe collection," Hannes explained.

"French?" Mutti echoed, rapping a floating black shell with her spoon. "Ach so (Oh. I see)!"

I was hard pressed to find even one of the mysterious ingredients in my soup-plate appealing enough for an exploratory bite. But Lucius enthusiastically inhaled the steam rising from his dish, dipped his spoon, and shoveled the resulting haul into his mouth. Chewing with deep appreciation, he shut his eyes, swallowed, and said cheerfully, "Seafood stew. Reminds me of home." He bowed to Frau Farber. "Wunderbar! Dankeshane! Sehr gut (this is great)!"

She beamed.

I carefully examined my broth, afraid of finding round, gelatinous fish eyes hiding under the surface. Until then the only fish I'd been forced to endure was the rare freshwater trout full of sharp bones, occasional pickled herring with even smaller bones, an endless supply of Catholic-Friday-night dinners featuring the inevitable breaded cod, and the traditional baked carp tasting of mud that Mutti served religiously every New Year's Eve.

With trepidation I took my first sip. It was rich with butter and an array of aromatic herbs and spices I'd not encountered before. I ate my way around the unidentifiable morsels, waiting to see what Lucius would do with his.

Horst stirred his stew with unabashed reluctance. "Isn't it marvelous," he said gloomily. "All these nice fishy parts and it isn't even Friday."

Hannes laughed out loud. "Spoken like a true Bayer (Bavarian)! Bon Appetit!" He ate his soup with such gusto that I was almost tempted to follow suit. Horst, Mutti and Anna kept their spoons at a safe distance from peculiar shells and the bits of flesh that shuddered on the border between the living and dead.

"Is this how you eat *every* day?" Anna asked.

"Frau Farber has a special knack," Hannes replied as soon as the cook had left to fetch yet another dish from the kitchen. "She makes the plainest fare taste simply delicious."

Mutti, looking stressed, said, "Then you're a lucky man, Hannes. I'm sure no mere mortal can compete with a cook who prepares French cuisine. Myself, I am only capable of producing coarse regional fare like pork roast and Reiberdatschi (potato pancakes)."

"Mutti makes the best Reiberdatschi!" I cried, sorry she thought herself second-best anywhere, especially in the kitchen of this house.

"Potato pancakes have always been a favorite of mine," Hannes confessed. "Perhaps someday . . ."

She gave a placated sniff but let his sentence dangle a bit before saying, "Perhaps."

Lucius pushed aside his debris and scooped up the last quivering object on the bottom of his bowl. "Great oysters! The commissary sells them only in cans, tough and salty. Wherever did Frau Farber get all this fresh seafood? We're nowhere near any coast." He helped himself to the rest of my bouillabaisse without asking. I did not protest.

Hannes seemed pleased. "She has connections. I believe she's wasting her considerable talents on me. She would make a wonderful head chef in an international restaurant." He pointed to some of the platters before us. "Stuffed medallions of veal. Pressed duck. Frau Farber was trying to get you a turkey, Lucius, but it was an impossible task. So she baked you another American favorite." He nodded to where Frau Farber had reappeared with a tray holding two silver serving dishes. On one sat a glazed ham covered with pineapple rings as if it were a dessert. With a flourish, she put the platter directly in front of Lucius, adding a yellow casserole. "This, too, I make special for you," she told him. "I hear you like rice."

"You heard right." Lucius said, obviously enjoying the attention. Under his breath, he muttered, "Only — the kind *I* like is white."

Hannes caught the remark. "The yellow tint comes from saffron, Lucius. This dish is called Paella. It comes from Spain, does it not, Frau Farber?"

Bravely, Lucius dished a heap on to his plate and took an exploratory bite. I followed suit, noticing too late that my pile was full of pink worms. "Shrimp!" he marveled. "And tomatoes! Maria, didn't I tell you about shrimp?"

"Is that what these are? Are you sure?" I stared at the pink curls, wondering if they were still capable of wiggling.

Blind to my appalling manners and me, Frau Farber kept her adoring gaze on my husband. "*Ach Gott,*" she cried, clapping her hands. "Isn't he goldig (precious)?"

Hannes's local guests decided to sacrifice their portion of the shrimp-studded rice dish to Lucius who was determined to polish off every curl and kernel. The rest of us concentrated on more conventional fare. At the end of the meal I looked at the heaps of good food still left on the table and asked Anna in an undertone, "Does the bachelorette have a refrigerator?"

"Same as mine," she murmured. "It'll hold enough for a week." It was a pity we weren't living in the bachelorette yet. As hot as it was, I couldn't risk bringing home anything from the party except leftover desserts. Every other dish would begin to spoil in our room after a couple of hours.

I could have sworn I heard Hannes chortle under his breath. But when I glanced at him, his face seemed entirely composed. "There's something I've been meaning to ask you," I said with an onrush of courage. "The other day you mentioned you studied in Chile. Didn't you come back to serve in the war?"

"Maria!" Mutti gasped. Even Horst and Anna looked shocked.

Hannes chuckled into their disapproving silence. "No, I did not. I contrived to avoid every battle from beginning to end. Very unpatriotic of me some would say."

Mutti stared at her plate, keeping her face neutral. Horst glanced sharply at Hannes but said nothing.

"You *avoided* the war?" Anna said. Turning to Horst, she asked, "Did you?"

He hung his head. "I was fourteen when it wound down. The Nazis were beginning to find my age group attractive by then. Luckily I was still too small to fit in their boots. They refused to stay on my feet, you see." She tittered in response to his attempt at gallows humor, then followed it with the scornful observation that he hadn't grown much since. Horst's eyes found mine, looking wounded. Then he addressed Hannes, stammering, "What . . . how . . . did you manage to . . . . stay out of —"

"Really, my dears," Mutti chided. "This isn't exactly polite dinner conversation. Perhaps another time would —"

"No, Lotte," Hannes said. "I don't mind in the least. I never thought pacifism was something to be ashamed of, even then. Let me pour you all a glass of Rieslinger. Then sit back and relax while I give Maria my . . . résumé."

CHAPTER 15

THE ROOM GREW SO QUIET that I could hear Frau Farber humming to herself in the kitchen. Part of me understood the effort Hannes was making on our behalf, for he was a most private man. The rest of me wanted to read him as if he were a large-print open book—for Mutti's sake, of course.

"If you insist," she said, clasping her hands on the table as if to demonstrate her infinite patience, her thumbs rubbing compulsively against the linen cloth.

He told us about the university in England, where he was increasingly unwelcome even after he made it plain he did not agree with Hitler's politics. Then came the day he realized he could not stay. "I was going to come home but my father sent me a large sum of money and suggested some globe-trotting until he could manage to enroll me in a school in Chile, where he had friends. Africa called to me first but the war followed me there. So I sailed to the other side of the world, learned to shear sheep in Australia, and climbed a couple of breathtaking mountains in New Zealand. Almost as good as the Alps. I took the train through the Orient and flew on to North America. Alaska was splendid." He traced the rim of his glass and stared absently into its depth, lost in his thoughts.

Mutti began to twist at the modest black-opal ring she was wearing. "Go on," she said, sounding impatient.

He continued. "After hitchhiking south along the rugged Pacific coast I crossed the equator and made my way down the Amazon to Peru till south became north. And that, finally, was far enough. I thought Chile was the most beautiful place in the world and settled in Santiago. The country was still rebuilding from the big earthquake."

"Oh?" I broke in, "Didn't they just have another?"

"Last year, Maria," he said with an appreciative nod. "But, actually, as I found out, the ground in Chile shakes any time it wants to. And the volcanic peaks are liable to dance right along. The people are a wonderful mixture of Spanish and native Indian. I fell in love with a young poetess, the daughter of a renowned surgeon. Elena was studying to be a teacher. Gave it up to become my wife. Chileans like to call their country *Land's End*, but the fallout from the war finally reached even there. I was not the only one wanting to get out of Europe."

Mutti's eyes grew hooded. "Yes?" she said. "Please do go on."

Hannes pushed his wine glass away and laid his hands flat on either side of his napkin, like a school boy trying to put the teacher at ease. "In '45 my father wanted me home but I procrastinated and postponed until a telegram informed me that my parents' car had slid off a serpentine mountain road. They'd been on their way to Italy." He glanced at an oil portrait on the wall depicting a young couple in old-fashioned attire. Overwhelmed by the feast spread before us, I had not noticed it before.

"Your parents?" I guessed.

"As newlyweds," he confirmed. It was hard to see a resemblance, for his father wore one of those off-putting early-century hair styles, extremely close-cropped on the sides, the top parted in the middle, with ridiculous sideburns. His curled, waxed mustache didn't help, but the blue eyes hiding behind gold-plated granny glasses seemed kind. His wife's eyes were a placid gray rather than Hannes' striking quicksilver.

Our host shook his head. "They lived through the worst bombing just to die in a smashed car. I brought Elena to the funeral, of course. As soon as our train pulled out of Frankfurt my heart came alive. I hadn't even realized I'd been homesick—for fairy-tale forests, secluded villages, Bauernhöfe (farms) . The Bavarian dialect was music to my ears. Suddenly I knew where I belonged. I wanted pork roast and Knödel (dumplings), a decent plate of Sauerkraut; *Apfelstrudel* —"

"Mutti makes the best Apfelstrudel," I interrupted again. "Zwetchgendatschi (prune-plum pie), too."

She gave me a grateful smile. "You always did appreciate my desserts." Turning to Hannes, she asked, "Your . . . wife?"

He shook his head. "Hated it here. Who could blame her? München was ugly in those days. Nothing but ruins. People in rags. No glamour anywhere, when my wife considered it a necessity. She refused to learn German, insisting we return to Chile at once. But I couldn't just please myself anymore. I had inherited everything, you see, and felt obliged to commit myself to the business. Father's loyal employees depended on me."

Now he looked fully at me, his eyes mercury-bright. "She wouldn't leave the house. Had her father send a trunk full of books, in Spanish. Not long after she finished the last one I came home from work one day and found her gone. A year later her father had our marriage annulled. By then I'd stopped waiting for her and had immersed myself in the reconstruction effort. Apparently our new republic needed people like me, untainted by the past."

I unlocked my gaze from his and glanced meaningfully toward Mutti. He addressed her directly. "Since then I've put down sturdy roots, Lotte. I'm a full-out Bavarian, like you — and far less conservative than my business attire and my impersonal office manners might have led you to believe. One can't travel to the far side of the earth and come back unchanged. Perhaps Eskimos and Aborigines consider *us* quaint these days and are displaying Lederhosen and Alpine hats with Gamsbarts (the beards of mountain goats) in their parlors."

"And so they should!" I said. "You didn't mention the United States. You've been there, too, haven't you?"

"Often," he replied promptly. "On business. It's becoming more common these days. Although the German accent is still reviled in New York. Luckily I speak Oxford English. It's a sound the Americans cannot resist." He laughed. "Even though they loathed it a few hundred years ago. Lotte? What are you doing?"

Mutti had begun stacking dirty plates. With a guilty start, she explained in a matter-of-fact tone, "Helping Frau Farber, of course. The poor woman's been on her feet all day — cooking since early morning. Listen to me, Hannes!" She put her hand on his arm. I suspected she'd never dared to touch him before — except for that one lapse in his car on the afternoon of my wedding, when he'd chauffeured Lucius and me to our lamentable honeymoon suite.

"You must tell her to let *us* do the dishes," she pleaded with the same formal inflection she always used when speaking to him. "The exercise will do us good."

Anna and I looked at each other in shared discomfort. It was easy to guess that the "us" was not going to include anyone wearing pants.

Hannes seemed at a loss for words. Then he said, "Frau Farber would take that badly, I'm afraid. She prides herself on her efficiency, you see. And — most unfortunately — she considers the kitchen entirely her domain."

Mutti withdrew her hand. "I see. There's only enough room in your house for one cook. Is that how it is?"

Anna gave an exaggerated groan. "Good grief, Mutti! Why all the fuss? Most of us would be delighted with such an arrangement. It's the last thing I'd ever argue about."

Mutti pressed her crumpled linen napkin to her face and ran from the room. Hannes broke the awkward silence she left behind by calmly raising a new bottle of Rieslinger, looking at Horst. "More wine?"

Horst patted his stomach. "Frankly, Hannes, I think we could all use a shot of your cognac right about now. It cures any number of ills, including hysterics and overindulgence."

Anna brought a tray from the sideboard. It held a silver flask and six shot glasses. "Pour mine first," she said, putting the tray down in front of Hannes. "I feel like a stuffed goose. I have absolutely no room left for dessert."

"Goose is right," I said, upset not only by our mother's embarrassing display but Anna's comment triggering it. "Stuffed or not."

Hannes uncapped the flask, said, "Children! Nicht diese Töne (lighten up)!" and began to pour cognac into the tumblers. "It's customary for dinner guests to stuff themselves. In fact, it's required. Look at Lucius. He appreciates every scrap Frau Farber has prepared for him."

Oblivious to our conversation, Lucius waved his fork-baton and said, "Ethel!"

"You are the ideal guest," Hannes told him in English. "Frau Farber will always love you for this."

"Yeah." Lucius stabbed another piece of ham. "Until she finds out this wasn't a good-bye dinner after all. When were you planning to tell her we'll be around for another whole year?"

Hannes winced. "Tomorrow? Next week?"

"The later the better," Horst advised, taking one of the tumblers.

Mutti came back fully restored, just in time for the first round. She watched Anna and me down our portions and then told us firmly, "That'll do. Neither of you are used to the effects."

I opened my mouth to point out that rationing my alcohol consumption was no longer any of her business, but then I poured myself another glass of wine and told Mutti with a conciliatory chuckle, "That was a great getaway you made on Friday—just like in the movies."

"Maria!" she warned, but it was too late—she'd already become the center of attention.

"Getaway?" Hannes repeated, puzzled.

"It was nothing, Hannes," Mutti said, her eyes shooting sparks at me. "Nothing at all."

I chuckled again. "You escaped around the next corner. Then I heard screeching brakes and clanging streetcars. Ganz toll (it was great)!"

"Escaped?" A hint of unease had crept into our host's voice. "From what or whom, Lotte?"

She blushed. "I don't know. I thought I saw a black Opel follow me from the office, is all. But Maria was right, this city is full of black Opels. No doubt I was mistaken."

"No, you weren't," I said. "I saw one pull out behind you and try to—" I protested. Her admonishing glance stifled the rest of the sentence. "Oh, never mind," I said, jumping up.

"Hannes, if you want me to do justice to your *Kirschtorte* without the help of a digestive cordial,"—here I glowered at Mutti—"I'll need some exercise first. Mind if I investigate your garden?"

"Not at all," he said. "Feel free to explore wherever you like. But wait . . ." He rang a bell that had been hiding behind a flower display. "I've asked Frau Farber to take some photos to help us remember this special evening. While we are still together in one room with every hair in its proper place."

The cook entered with a camera and took several snapshots of us sitting at the table, raising our tumblers in mock salute. Then she asked us to bunch up on the couch. Smoothing my hair and the front of my dress, I settled on Lucius's knees. Mutti sat beside him, Anna and Horst at either armrest. Hannes stood behind us, his arms wide as if to include us all in a friendly bear hug. On Frau Farber's orders we smiled and allowed her to blind us with a succession of exploding flashbulbs.

Then I remembered the telephone Anna had mentioned. Where was it again? Two doors down the hall? To the right? I expected to find it in a snug study on a desk covered with ledgers, but it was in a large domed chamber lined with books.

Hannes owned more volumes than the library in Warner Kaserne, all of them clamoring for my attention at once, making me giddy. I felt my way along the edges of a massive table, upsetting the phone and scattering a stack of Hannes' current favorites. The sonnets of Shakespeare. Goethe's Faust. Rainer Maria Rilke. Hesse's Gedichte (poems) and The Glass-Bead Game. A slim edition of Spanish poems by someone named Neruda. Sinking into a well-worn leather recliner, I eyed a huge desk dictionary nearby, then the endless book-treasures surrounding me on three sides, half of them leather-bound.

A magnificent custom-built Kachelofen (tile stove) made up the fourth wall. It was a bold, continuous sculpture of tiled masonry in cobalt and green. A ceramic-topped, cushioned bench ran from one end to the other. Cost being no object Hannes probably had as many tile stoves as he had phones. This stove spanned two downstairs rooms and most likely two upstairs rooms too. Oriental pottery, jade horses and other small and rare antiques from his travels graced thick-cut glass shelves. If I owned a library like this I'd never come out.

Giving in to temptation, I walked along the three book-crowded walls, reading titles and allowing my hands to graze spine after spine after spine.

A few minutes later I entered the sunroom and saw the stained-glass sun above the French doors glow like a dark jewel. Outside, the real sun was rapidly sinking toward the horizon. Alex was sitting at the barrier surrounding Guinea-Pig-Land. I rubbed his forehead. "They go to bed early, like chickens," I told him. "Why don't you come for a walk with me?" He dithered but came to heel as soon as I added the word, "Stick!"

Beyond the barrier a dry creek bed wound past a grassy incline. Alex veered off while I climbed it—quite a feat in a cripplingly tight skirt and ankle-killer heels. I shed the shoes halfway to the top. He arrived there before me, an arm-sized stick clamped between his teeth. Dropping it at my feet, he sat waiting for the fun to begin. I threw it as high and wide as I could. He was upon it in an instant. I'd hoped to wear him out until he collapsed. But soon it was me who lay on the grass spread-eagled and winded. He dropped the spit-slimed stick onto my stomach. I flung it off, gasping, "Enough!" To my surprise he did not pursue it and lowered himself onto his belly beside me, a grin in his eyes.

The hill we rested upon was surrounded by shrubs and trees growing wild, English Garden style, many in bloom.

Beyond them a meadow stretching to the back of the property, where a colossal hedge wall surrounded the yard, blocking the view of neighboring estates. Across an arched Japanese foot bridge spanning the stone creek lay a tranquil pond, complete with a fountain. Half-hidden in a grove of bamboo stood a small structure too lovely to be called a mere hut. I could just make out a lacquered table inside, so low that cushions doubled as chairs. Turning back to the villa I noticed a plot of herbs framing the brick terrace outside the kitchen. I thought I recognized lavender and thyme. Around the terrace corner, dim in the gathering gloam, were fruit trees and the furrowed black soil of vegetable beds.

I wondered how much work Hannes put into this piece of land and how much of the original design had survived from the time of his parents. It must have been nice to get the keys to a house like this along with the means to support it. With the library thrown in. Along with that opulent bathroom, its half-naked mermaid, the sleek seal.

Looking down upon the garden was like peering into Hannes's soul. He was the god who'd dreamed and created most of the landscape. Not with brush, canvas and oils, but with living things. Instead of bending nature to his will he had merged with it, played with it, molded it. Wherever I looked he'd tucked flowers, domestic and wild. They pulsed with hot, vibrant colors. I could barely recall that just an hour before I wasn't sure he was right for my mother. Now I suspected she couldn't possibly be right for him. She had little enthusiasm for nature *or* reading.

Watching white clouds flow overhead, I yawned, closed my eyes, and hummed the Blue Danube. It helped me glimpse the girl I used to be, wearing her red Gypsy dress, waltzing in the imagined embrace of a certain archangel. In Freidorf. An instant later, the same fantasy-girl sat in a sunken Roman tub, her arms spread on its mosaic rim. She was surrounded by ferns, seal, mermaid, lagoon. Her long hair undulated around her. And just when I remembered that my hair could no longer float the girl became Mutti, her voluptuous body shielded by bubbles. Hannes was scrubbing her back. I wondered if I should picture him discarding his entire suit or merely the jacket. Then I came to my senses. Rousing, I blamed wine and cognac for the lingering daydream. "Tipsy," I explained to Alex, who was watching me gravely, his muzzle on a front paw. I sat up and studied the angle of the slope we were lying upon.

It was . . . seductive. I tossed my spikes to the bottom and proceeded to coil into the classic somersault posture. When we were kids, Gabriel and I used to tumble down similar hills, chin to chest, holding tight to our folded legs. I began the remembered maneuver and stopped, wondering why I had never broken my neck. Surely I'd break it tonight. But there were safer ways to tumble, weren't there? I lay flat with my arms stretched over my head and rolled down the thick grass sideways, shrieking when my rear passed over a bump. I came to a stop near my discarded heels—and vis-à-vis a pair of men's dress shoes, buffed to a high gloss and fully occupied. They seemed to revolve around me.

Through the spinning haze I stared up into Hannes's amused face. Then I struggled to my knees, self-consciously tugging my skimpy black dress down at one end and up at the other. All at once, the expensive garment felt like a thin slip minus lace trimmings.

"Time for dessert?" I squeaked, cheeks burning.

He held out his hand. "Almost. But first, let's talk."

Nervously, I adjusted my spaghetti straps. Then I allowed him to pull me to my feet. When he placed his warm hands on my bare arms I was convinced that I was still in my dream and that he had entered it at my will to show me the most secret parts of his garden.

CHAPTER 16

HE HELD ON TO ME UNTIL the world stopped spinning. But as soon as my legs steadied he stepped away and said, "My father had this somersault-hill built just for me. A birthday present. When I was seven."

Confused by the direction our conversation was taking, I touched my hair, no longer long and luxuriant but short as a boy's. He had not been sharing my dream, after all, but a reality that didn't necessarily conform to my wishes. Nor did I want it to. Because whatever I had so fleetingly imagined between us was as foreign to his nature as it was to mine. I was relieved he had understood that before I did.

"On the back side he let me dig a special 'secret' cave," he continued to reminisce, giving me a chance to compose myself. "I used to sleep in it on hot summer nights—until a particularly wet storm collapsed my tunnel, fortunately not when I was inside it."

"Do you still roll?" I asked, letting him distract me with his casual banter.

"Sometimes Alex and I hold contests," he claimed with a straight face.

"Alex rolls?" I said, incredulous.

As if I'd given a command, the dog, who'd been watching us from the top, plopped on his side, stretched out his front legs in one direction, his hind legs in the other, and began a swift tumble. When he arrived at the bottom he rubbed his back against the lawn with grunts of delight. Then he retrieved my shoes one at a time and dropped them at my feet.

I decided to carry them; the darkening garden was no place for spikes. "He's not an ordinary dog, is he? What else can he do?"

"What can't he?" Hannes said with a chuckle. Then he nodded toward the part of his hedge obscuring the street. "Lucius has taken my other three dinner guests for a spin in his Pepper. They were arguing about who was going to have to sit on whose lap. It reminded me of the Porsche I once had—a wonderful car for one or two. The only trouble was that whenever I drove anywhere at least four people asked for a ride." He took my arm. "Come. The grape arbor is lovely at sundown."

It stood near the deep-green pond, where tiny spotlights illuminated the cascading fountain in the center I'd noticed earlier. There was an upholstered wicker seat inside the arbor, just big enough for two. Alex, an instinctive chaperone, settled himself between Hannes's feet and mine.

"Good dog," Hannes murmured, sounding grateful.

"Not that good. A while ago I saw him go after a guinea pig. I had to pull him back by his tail."

Hannes gave a soft, impressed whistle. "You pulled his tail and lived to tell?"

"Barely," I admitted, recalling the dog's snapping canines.

My host's face grew stern. "You must promise me never to do that again, Maria. It's one of the two things that transform him into a fiend. But as to Pepita—she grew up with him. They slept together, ate together, and sang to each other. A perfect couple. Till I decided guinea pigs were not meant to waddle across Persian rugs and hardwood floors. So I built her an all-weather habitat—the inside half is in the leisure room. Then I bought her a mate to compensate for her loss of freedom. Alas, it was too late—Alex was already deeply in love with his fair little damsel and I'm afraid always will be, even if she did take up with another and raised four youngsters with him."

Hannes scratched behind Alex's ears, which were rotating as if the dog understood every word. "She does her best to ignore her lovelorn first beau who sits and waits for her to recall the enchanted hours they once shared. He loves watching the whole family but his heart definitely belongs to Pepita and melts at her slightest attention. He tries to keep a grip on himself but sooner or later he loses control and gives her a resounding kiss. Sometimes he licks her until she resembles a drowned overweight rat. He can't understand that she is no longer interested in his showers of affection."

"Poor dog," I said. "But that doesn't explain why he looks like the devil when someone jerks his tail."

"In his youth he was combat-trained. And he's done some police work."

"Is he . . . dangerous?"

"He has a superb sense of right and wrong. You and the rest of our friends will always be safe with him."

"What's the second thing that turns him into a fiend?"

Hannes lost his smile. "I hope you never have to find out." He leaned against the wicker, crossing his legs. "I often come here to watch the sun set behind the hedges. It's quite a show." He pointed to our green ceiling. One final sunbeam had pierced through the westernmost hedge to illuminate the huge grape leaves topping the arbor. Finding a gap, the beam poured down upon us, accentuating the silver in Hannes' hair.

I picked a lilac flower growing near my feet and dipped it into this stream of light, watching its petals glow. The beam thrust itself into the pool, revealing moving orange and silver-blue shapes beneath the surface. From there the light dipped past lilies and algae. But it never got to touch the mysterious bottom because the sun, falling off the edge of the world, hastily retrieved it and whisked it away.

The whole garden seemed to be holding its breath. Then all the flowers within sight released their day's worth of stored sunshine at once, shouting their colors into the cooling air. A butterfly or huge moth hovered over a cluster of white flowers, its quivering wings darkening along with the petals. On the pond, two sky-blue damselflies briefly skimmed over pale lilies and disappeared. Hannes sighed with contentment.

Perhaps it was the aftereffect of the alcohol, the abundance of beauty around us, the welcoming nearness of the man beside me—or a combination of all three—that made me brave enough to blurt, "What do you want with my mother?" The dense grape leaves above us softened my strident tone.

Hannes uncrossed his legs. "I've seen that question in your eyes since the night I invited you all over for snacks. It's why we are sitting here, together." He lowered his voice. "Have you noticed that the pond looks greenest right before dark?

That particular hue reminds me of my favorite lake high in the Andes, although *its* waters were far greener still." His focus turned inward. He was getting ready to tell me a story.

"The Incas have a legend, Maria," he began. "They say once upon a time there was an Inca prince who loved a beautiful princess with emerald eyes. He courted her until she loved him back. They were married up in the Andes near a blue lake. But after the ceremony she tripped on her wedding gown while descending an unstable path and fell to her death. The prince gathered her in his arms and carried her to the water, the most fitting grave in that stony wilderness. Weeping, he lowered her into the lake. The moment her body touched it the water turned a deep emerald green. It was her last gift to the prince. He never left the side of the lake again but stayed there in mourning till the end of his life." Hannes looked fully at me but it was too dark in the arbor for me to make out his expression. "Lotte is my Inca princess, Maria."

With that simple sentence he won my heart. Now let him win hers. "She doesn't read, you know," I cautioned. "Not like you and me."

He laughed out loud. "Neither does Lucius, I bet."

It was a fact I'd begun to notice myself.

"We read, they live," Hannes said. "I've become a prisoner of words. Be careful or they'll swallow you too. Lotte reminds me of what life is for. Besides, don't you think it's time *someone* made her happy?"

I nodded even though I wasn't sure he could still see me. A cricket chirped close by. Something small plopped into the pond. The displaced water broke against the shore, where the silhouette of a bird made of iron and glass stood on a rock, balancing on one leg. The longer I stared at it, the more real the bird seemed.

Hannes spoke again, in a voice so low I had to strain to hear him. "I have loved your Mutti from the moment I first saw her. I made a great effort to remain neutral because I was under the impression she was content with her life and her husband. Until the day at the printer's, when I drove the two of you home and saw how she lived.

"The whole time I drove I tried to convince her to take the printer to court. It was obvious she was afraid Herr Hohner would not permit it. After I dropped you both off at the apartment I asked myself what kind of man would forbid his wife to defend their daughter against a molester. That's when I decided to make my first move.

"I arranged for her promotion and transfer to stifle any public scandal I might unwittingly cause—and to make her independent of me so she would feel free to make her own choices. My last qualm was put to rest later that week when Hohner wrestled the phone from your hands to assure me *you* led the printer astray. Not long after that he managed to convince Lotte to have you locked up. When she finally confessed that error of judgment to me I helped her put everything right."

I always wondered what made her change her mind about Lucius.

"I told her you must be allowed to make your own mistakes—or not—just as she and I made ours," Hannes recalled.

"*I* didn't make a mistake," I quickly protested. "But *she* made two big ones. That's why she's afraid to trust herself with you. And why she wants to live alone, in peace, taking care of no one but herself for a change."

"She's doing remarkably well," he said. "And I can certainly understand her caution. Especially after I finally met Hohner face to face when he stormed into my office last week."

"Oh, God," I cried. "What did he want?"

He reached up and snapped off a straggling vine. "These must be pruned. I've never seen anything grow faster."

Alex lifted his nose, scenting the night air.

"O.F. burst in while you and I talked on the phone," Hannes continued. "He demanded I use my influence to order her home. He'd forgotten she's transferred to another office. When I refused to interfere he broke down and wept. Loudly. Asked me to fire her so she could no longer fend for herself and would be forced back into his arms. I said she had never done anything to be fired for. Then he was kind enough to catalogue her liabilities. He is a clever man, your O.F."

"Not *my* O.F."

"Nobody's O.F.," he agreed.

Alex rose and looked toward the hedge running parallel to the street. It had become a looming mass against the night sky. I touched his nape. The fur was rising under my palm. He growled, just once. It was no more than a quiet rumble inside his chest. I shivered. Crossing my arms, I tried to rub goose bumps away.

Hannes removed his jacket and draped it around me, still warm, smelling faintly of lavender soap. He kept one fatherly hand on my shoulder. It was almost as good as a hug.

I whispered, "It was about me, wasn't it? He told lies about me."

"Not lies," he said gently. "Clever machinations. They made me so furious I could not speak. So I rang for security and asked them to escort him from the building. Afterwards I opened my windows but whatever oozed out of him clung to the walls."

"Like a poison," I agreed, remembering how I used to be physically unable to get in the tub after he bathed.

All at once the iron bird lit from within, becoming a lantern. We continued to sit in the shadowy arbor but now I could see Alex putting his chin on his master's knees, giving a nearly inaudible whine. Hannes placed his free hand on the dog's forehead. Thus calming him and calming me he went on,

"I was hoping that would be the end of it. Until you mentioned Lotte's getaway. O.F. must have hired a detective to trace her to her new address. Last Friday was only the beginning."

A moth brushed my cheek, fluttered wildly at my ear, and careened toward the bird. "The detective will take care to stay farther behind in future," Hannes continued. "He'll follow her everywhere."

I pictured the isolated farmhouse at night, nearby trees swallowing moon, stars, and the shadows of men. "Can't you help her get a phone?"

"There is no line to the old house or anywhere near." He was massaging the dog's neck. The ruff was still standing on end. "But—didn't I hear you say that Lucius is going on maneuvers soon?"

Nothing escaped him. He must have exceptional hearing. "Why?"

"Perhaps you could spend some time with Lotte while he's away. Help her get settled in for the winter. Keep an eye on her since she won't let me."

Move in with my mother? When I'd so recently moved out? Did he have any idea what he was asking?

He ran his fingers from the top of Alex's muzzle to under his chin. Man and beast fit together like a hand and its glove. The dog's eyes were fixed on his master's.

"Alex?" Hannes murmured.

The shepherd's eyes slitted. His gruesome teeth split the muzzle in two. He seemed to double in size.

"Los (go)," Hannes finished in a soft whisper.

Noiselessly, the dog shot away, a black missile driving through inky brush. A moment later he threw himself at the hedge that ran along the side-street, snarling, teeth snapping at leaves. The hedge bent; twigs and whole branches broke off with sharp cracks. A man gave an inarticulate cry that broke off an instant after it started. The hedge shook as if it were buffeted by a storm. Then muffled footsteps receded. A car door slammed. An engine gunned; tires squealed away on bare pavement.

No sooner had the noise faded that a quieter engine approached. Headlights swept the hedge and moved on. From the sound of the motor I guessed it was Pepper, returning from her joy-ride. Her tires rolled around the corner toward the front. Two car doors slammed in quick succession. Horst said something funny; Mutti and Anna laughed, their heels striking cement.

Briefly, the hedge rustled again. Alex came out of the shadows, sat at attention, and deposited something at Hannes' feet. I picked it up. It was a rough square of tweed. "I don't understand what a detective would want in your garden," I said. "After dark."

Hannes took the fabric from me and casually slipped it into his pocket. "Gut gemacht," he told Alex, repeating the phrase he'd used at Somersault-Hill. "Now go tell Frau Farber to give you a bone."

Alex bounded toward the house, which was a sooty silhouette against the night sky. The upstairs was pitch-black, but downstairs every window was bright, the lamp light within diffused by lace curtains. Along the stony creek bed an array of discreet twinkling bulbs led us back to the patio.

Hannes said, "Let's keep this . . . episode . . . to ourselves, shall we? It's possible my strong reaction at the office last week has aroused Herr Hohner's suspicion." He took back the jacket, draped it over an arm, and hooked his other to mine. "Come on, Maria. A piece of Kirschtorte and a cup of hot tea laced with a smidgen of cognac will do us both good."

CHAPTER 17

THE AROMA OF BITTER-SWEET chocolate and spiked cream enticed Lucius and me out of bed early the next morning. We polished off our first wedges of leftover *Kirschtorte* before the water for our cocoa had a chance to boil.

"They call this 'hair of the dog' and I have to admit I feel a bit fuzzy," Lucius said, rubbing sleep from his eyes. We ate seconds while he helped me plan out my day. "You can get on the American bus at the quad inside Warner," he explained. "It goes all the way across town to Second Field Hospital. I'll pick you up from there around five. If you're done early go have a bite in the cafeteria. I'll show you the commissary before we get down to brass-tacks."

Brass-tacks was my final driving lesson, which Lucius had kindly offered to provide on our way home--this one in the afternoon traffic jam. He'd sworn he wouldn't give me the key to Pepper until I qualified for my international license even if it meant I could be without wheels when he left for maneuvers.

I had made an appointment at the hospital the month before to get the vaccinations I needed to enter the U.S. Even though the shots were no longer urgent or even necessary, Lucius thought I might as well get them over with. Besides, when the nurse I spoke with over the phone found out I'd never had a checkup she insisted I get one at the same time.

"What *is* a checkup, anyway?" I asked Lucius, placing a mug of hot cocoa before him. "What do they want to check?"

He shrugged. "Blood pressure. Eyes, ears, lungs. And your plumbing, I suppose—now that you're a married woman. Just to make sure you're not rusting out. We wouldn't want any leaks." He laughed but I didn't get the joke; I had no idea what he thought I had in common with copper pipes. Taking the white Italian suit out of the wardrobe, he held it in front of himself and studied the effect in the mirror for the last time. "Spider charges stiff rental fees. By the day. Even to his best buddy. The man has his hand in all kinds of pies. That's why he's never broke."

I followed Lucius downstairs as I did every morning and waved until he and Pepper were swallowed by traffic. Back upstairs, I polished off the rest of the cake. Then I rummaged under the mattress for the plane ticket refund I'd stashed away and counted the cash to make sure I had enough for my errand. Riding the streetcar to the Scheidplatz soon after, I arrived at the office of the high-rise manager promptly at eight.

"Oh yes," said the bespectacled, pinch-faced Herr Pfeifer once I'd introduced myself. "Herr Obdach has already called to vouch for you. The previous tenants promised to move the rest of their stuff out over the weekend. They never did drop off their keys. Come with me. We'll inspect the place together." He led the way to the elevator but passed it, spryly climbing the stairs to the fourth floor armed with the rental application and an inventory list.

The vacant apartment smelled of burnt lard. Its parquet floor hadn't been swept in a long while. In the kitchenette a couple of sacks were overflowing with garbage. Herr Pfeifer found the missing keys on the counter. They seemed to be covered with syrup. He grimaced as he brushed them into his handkerchief, muttering something under his breath. Then he opened and shut cupboards and checked for sticking drawers.

I went to the bathroom to test both hot-water faucets, ignoring the gobs of spit mixed with toothpaste caked to the sink, and the thick film of soap scum ringing the tub. Back in the kitchen, I played with the spigot, watching the manager peer near-sightedly at the stove, lifting burners.

"Saustall (pig-sty)!" he said. "The Americans never clean up after themselves when they move out. This stovetop is filthy with bacon grease. And I don't have the nerve to examine the oven just yet—I might lose my breakfast. As I told your sister, I'm willing to waive the cleaning deposit if you'll scrub the place down yourself." He squinted at the couch, set against the wall at an odd angle.

I helped him pull it clear, exposing a row of badly charred parquet tiles and a large sooty smear on the whitewash above it. The closet door hung open, revealing a floor covered with discarded wire hangers. We put them on the rod with their hooks all facing in the same direction. It made the closet look almost tidy. When Herr Pfeifer shut the door we discovered that someone had given it a tremendous kick, caving in the outside surface.

The manager lowered himself onto the couch, took off his glasses, and pinched the root of his nose. "I'll have to order some major repairs. You won't be able to move in for a couple of weeks. Are you sure you want this place? I'd be glad to put your name on the waiting list for a better unit."

I wandered to the large plate glass window, pretending to think it over. It wouldn't do to show him how desperate I was for *any* change of address. The window overlooked the parking lot, just like Anna's — but from a different angle. I would have a better view of the Schuttberg from mine. The grimy wreck I was standing in was more than twice the rent of the luxurious room the slug had vacated in the whorehouse. The landlady had let me walk through it as soon as she was done scrubbing every inch of it with bleach — thereby proving that cleanliness had nothing whatsoever to do with godliness.

"We'll take this one," I told Herr Pfeifer, extracting the bankroll from my purse. "Where do I sign? I'll pay you right now."

Once our transaction was completed he punched the lift button for me and shook my hand. "Your lovely sister assured me you and your husband are quiet and scrupulously clean. I ask no more than that — as long as you always pay your rent on time. Welcome onboard. "

He disappeared down the stairwell as the elevator pinged to announce its imminent arrival. He could have been trying to lose weight. Or maybe he didn't trust lifts any more than I did. This one was occupied by a diminutive black-haired woman and a beige-haired, very small boy. He watched me step inside, then backed against the woman's thigh and stuffed an overworked thumb in his mouth. She wrapped a protective arm around him and cast her slanted eyes toward the floor. The toddler's eyes were as dark as hers, though more rounded.

I gave him what I thought was an encouraging smile. In response he hid his face in her skirt. The elevator doors slid shut and we began a silent descent, all three of us clutching at the walls. Oddly enough, their obvious terror seemed to cure me of mine. "Hi. I'm Maria," I cheerfully told the woman, the dreaded picture of unraveling cables fading from the screen of my mind. "Your little boy is beautiful. Do you live upstairs?"

"Fifth floor," she lisped with a courteous bow. "Number five-one-two. I Naoko and this Tommy. We please meet you."

I wasn't at all sure that they were.

*

SECOND Field Hospital was a modern white stucco building with big tinted windows. Its pleasantly curved front drive was lined with roses. To me, the hospital was a hallowed piece of U.S. soil. A chubby American nurse wearing her light-brown hair in a pony-tail took my name, handed me some forms, and asked me to fill them out at the desk. "For our records," she drawled.

I thanked her in my best English. Soon I wished she'd given the forms to Mutti. How was I to know which childhood diseases I had at what age? I vaguely remembered crying through a bout of whooping cough but it could just as easily have been chickenpox or mumps or a combination of all three.

When I was done the nurse checked for blank spaces. "Here's one," she said, pointing a well-manicured finger to the section about race. Even though I'd never thought of myself as belonging to any, I'd decided to compromise by checking the *other* squares under our names.

She erased the penciled mark from that square and circled the word *Caucasian*, explaining that it was another word for white people like us. Then she erased Lucius' *other* and handed the pencil to me. After a brief hesitation I circled *Negro*. "No, no," she protested with an easy smile. "You've marked the wrong square." I shook my head and watched her smile harden. With a toss of her ponytail she banished me to the waiting area and proceeded to ignore me.

Half an hour later an older nurse came to the front desk to pick up my forms, which were now in a folder. She called my name and led me to an examining room. It contained the same kind of metal table I'd struggled on in reform school.

Until that moment I'd expected the doctor would merely thump my back, poke his cold stethoscope at my ribs, make my knees jump, and ask me to step on the scale with a thermometer in my mouth. But the nurse pointed to a flimsy open-backed nightgown. Folded neatly next to the gown lay a linen sheet similar to the one that, last year, had been draped over my stubbornly clenched knees. And then I understood Lucius' dumb little plumbing joke—although I still didn't think it was funny.

Before long a handsome young doctor and a young nurse half his size stood framed between my sheet-covered knees, wishing me a good afternoon in a German so perfect I had no doubt they were locals. I made a point of answering them in flawless English. They ignored my preference and insisted on continuing in the language I was determined to shed along with my country.

"Let me see—Maria Duncan, age sixteen," the doctor said, comfortably leafing through the folder. "Hohenzollernstrasse. Hmm . . . why does that address look so familiar? Nurse?"

She peered at my chart and squinted in concentration. "It's that ad in the newspaper. The one that's always there."

They looked at each other, then at me, the doctor's tone pensive. "I've often wondered what kind of place it could possibly be. Considering that every other apartment in the city is taken before the ink in the classifieds has had a chance to dry."

"Old," I said.. "Without running water. No elevator, either. But we're moving. To a modern high-rise." I still could hardly believe it but the two sets of keys the manager had given me were now in my purse, which sat on the nearest chair.

"Lucky you," the doctor said.

The nurse added, "You didn't get this one through the paper, I bet."

"Well, no," I admitted, momentarily forgetting my vulnerable position.

The doctor read on. "Just married, I see. Einen Neger (a Negro). So young!" His eyes searched mine. Then he smiled. "Did you come to ask about birth control?"

"About what?" I asked.

"Look there. She's Catholic," the nurse murmured.

He gave an exasperated sigh. "Uhm — the rhythm method? Surely you've heard of it, Maria?"

"No," I confessed, feeling stupid. "Not yet."

"I'll explain it to you in great detail in just a few minutes. Although, frankly, there are more effective —"

The nurse coughed and repeated, "Catholic!"

He tossed the folder on to a counter. "All right. I give up. Now, Maria, if you'll just scoot your hips down to the edge of the table . . ."

I froze until the nurse put a calming hand on my shoulder. Then I yielded, staring at a smudge on the ceiling and trying to tune them both out while he probed and kneaded. In my opinion God seriously blundered when he made female parts so inaccessible. They ought to be on the outside, like a man's.

The doctor's hands stilled. "Too late," he muttered.

"Bitte (what)?" the nurse asked, and then she said, "Ach (oh)," following the lament with, "Ach so (oh my)!"

The doctor busied himself with his gloves. They made crisp snapping sounds when he pulled off first one, then the other. "I still want to explain the rhythm method to you, Maria," he said quietly. "For when it'll do you some good. But for the next seven months or so you won't need to worry about it. You're pregnant. You must have missed a couple of periods by now. Or haven't you noticed?"

Stunned, I answered, "I've never been regular."

"A mere child!" the nurse said. "A late bloomer at that. Hardly got started."

"I—I'm still trying to get used to being married," I told them, my voice trembling. "I didn't think babies could happen this fast!" But then I realized I wasn't all that surprised. Because lately I'd felt as if someone had turned on a light deep inside me, so warm and bright I'd occasionally seen its reflection shine from my eyes when I studied myself in the mirror.

The doctor went to the sink. Running water over his hands, he said, "I think we'll skip the vaccinations and set you up for OB. You'll have to come in once a month for blood tests, urine samples, the works." He turned toward me, his fingers dripping antiseptic soap. "Speak to us, Maria. Do you think congratulations are in order?"

On the eve of my wedding I had decided that God only gave you a baby when the timing was just right. Therefore, it must be right now. "Oh, yes," I whispered as the first wave of a new kind of joy pulsed through me. I was beginning to understand the beauty of it. Lucius had his car and I would have . . . this. In my mind's eye I saw a picture of Red Pepper cruising the Autobahn, a jaunty Lucius at the wheel. I sat in the passenger seat, my long golden scarf fluttering out behind me. On our way to Augsburg. Or to Italy, even. The baby, grown to toddler size, was sitting in that silly half-seat in back, which, I now understood, had been waiting to be filled by a child. The picture was my very own version of a happy ending.

"Yes!" I said again, grinning at the nurse. She answered with a smile of her own and shrugged at the doctor, who gave a regretful shake of his head.

"A gay little family then. Is that how it is?" Was there a shade of irony in his voice?

"Of course," I replied, calm and sure.

"Well then. Congratulations." Abruptly, he turned his back and rinsed the soap from his hands. The nurse found it necessary to give my shoulder small pats of comfort. Without looking at either of us, the doctor said, "Nurse, call me when Maria is dressed. We'd best have that little chat before she gets away from us. Even if it *is* too late. And too early."

*

AFTER inviting me to sit beside his desk the doctor rolled his chair around until our knees were practically touching. His finely-wrought face was grave as he attempted to explain about thermometers and eggs. I tried to look intelligent so as not to disappoint him, but the whole time he was talking I could feel the seed growing inside me cell by cell and knew at last why I was born—to let the sacred light flow freely through me and to give new life in return for my own.

With pity, I smiled at the poor man before me. No matter how scientific his bent, he would never feel his whole being enfold and embrace another from the inside out.

Soon he gave up his lecture, suspecting I was not in listening mode. Floating across the waiting area, I followed the arrow on the "Cafeteria" sign toward the basement. As I descended the stairs I could have sworn I was walking on air, for it seemed that the lower I got the higher I rose.

Copying the women before me, most with children in tow, I grabbed a tray from a stack next to glass shelves filled with prepared food and slid it along metal rails. A private celebration was called for. I loaded the tray with a cheeseburger and fries, tomato soup, a vanilla milk shake, a wedge of apple pie—*and* a banana split for dessert. Not one of my choices compared favorably to last night's dinner at Hannes's. Nonetheless, I enjoyed every bite. Now and then I laid my hands flat against my belly, wondering if it had grown any bigger. It hadn't but soon enough it would broadcast my glorious condition wherever I went.

Staring dreamily into space, I noticed a woman across the room nodding at me. I didn't recognize Naoko by her blue-black hair or slanted eyes but by the little boy sitting in a high chair beside her. I took my tray to her table and asked for permission to sit. When she gave it I said, "What a coincidence. Nice to see you again."

They were an interesting pair. She was bird-boned and reserved, keeping her head bowed and speaking so softly that I could only understand half of her heavily accented words. Tommy looked much too serious for a toddler. His beige hair seemed lit by a pale moon, though his eyes and lashes were midnight-black. Even here Naoko kept her arm around him as if something terrible might happen to him the moment she let go.

This afternoon I was incapable of subtleties. "Guess what," I began, not waiting for her response. "I'm going to have a baby too. Isn't it wonderful?" Besides being sincere, my sentiment was practice for the good-news speech I must give Lucius at five.

For once Naoko raised her gaze long enough to look fully at me. "I glad," she said. "You love be mother, like me."

I paused before asking my first question. It was, "Are you Japanese?"

Her eyes warmed. "You only person here understand difference between Japanese, Chinese, and Korean. How you know?"

Actually, it had just been a lucky guess. I'd never met a Japanese woman before but Lucius did mention bases on that part of the globe. From her son's other-worldly appearance I deduced that she was not married to a Japanese man. Thus, my second question was, "You're married to an American?"

Nodding, she blushed.

"And your husband's a soldier, like mine?"

She nodded again.

"What are the other people like, in the high-rise? Any more Americans?"

Her face clouded. "Yes."

"Are they . . . nice?"

She went back to bowing her head. "Nice," she repeated unenthusiastically.

"Are you all friends?"

She clutched at her collar. "Very nice. Very fine. Please forgive. I no speak English so good."

I'd already noticed that the more flustered she grew the worse her accent became. My English seemed remarkably polished by comparison. A few minutes of our mostly one-sided conversation convinced me I was as good as any native-speaker. Her painfully shy demeanor made me feel like a born extrovert. "You speak to Tommy in Japanese?" I asked, each syllable rolling easily off my agile tongue.

Immediately she looked guilty. "Only when we alone. My husband, he no like."

I resolved to speak only English with *my* baby but if by some slim chance he wanted to learn German in school one day I would not object. Finally I arrived at the one question Americans invariably asked each other: "Where are you from, in the States?"

"Husband is from Vermont," she supplied, her head sinking so low that her chin disappeared into her collar.

"Really?" I said. "So is mine—at least that's where he lived when he enlisted. They'll have something in common besides babies and wives who are foreigners."

Frowning, she raised her chin and said with great dignity, "In Japan, *he* is foreigner."

I wondered why I seemed to be pushing all the wrong buttons. Perhaps she sensed my bewilderment, for she gentled her features almost at once.

"In Japan," she said, "I no use talk to strangers."

"Ah," I said, thinking that obviously she'd talked to at least one.

*

AT FIVE I stood waiting on the steps outside the hospital until I saw a flash of red in the distance. Then I skipped down the walkway, waving gaily at Lucius as he drove into the rosebush-framed parking lot. He cranked down his window. I ran to his side.

"I see you're eager for your last dose of Drivers' Ed," he chuckled. "How did the checkup go?"

"Fine. I ate a cheeseburger afterwards. And I made a new friend. She lives in the same—" I bit my lip. The news about the apartment was best delivered later. Bit by bit. I tried to steady my thoughts and find a diplomatic way to inform him about the greater event. As usual, I did not succeed. "Guess what?" I blurted. "In seven months we're going to have a baby!"

At first Lucius just stared at the roses in front of the hood. I could hear him grinding his jaws as if he were chewing my words. Then he focused on something far, far away, something that seemed to be receding from him. Finally, he shot me a dark look, growled, "Damn it to hell!" floored the accelerator, and rocketed out of the lot.

Reeling, I watched car and driver disappear down the street. My knees felt as if someone had struck them from behind with an iron bar. I grabbed on to a bush. Thorns raked my arms from elbow to shoulder. Inside, I was going down, down, down on the longest elevator ride I'd ever known. This time the last strand really did snap and I found myself falling out of control toward some unfortunate end.

CHAPTER 18

WHEN LUCIUS RETURNED HIS FACE was ashen. He didn't have one word to say to me, kind or ill. On Hohenzollernstrasse he let me out at the curb and raced off without telling me why or where to. Even though I waited for him half through the night I succumbed to lonely slumber before he slunk home. Continuing the silent treatment the next morning, he'd left earlier than he had to. For the first time.

The following night I went to bed at dusk, determined to rouse the moment he walked in. And I did. He refused to talk to me until I goaded him by confessing we were about to move to a respectable address. Then he found plenty to say — about strained finances, disobedience, and my spoilt attitude.

"If you'll remember I said no to the move, loud and clear. And with good reason, you have to admit. How in the world do you think we can afford an apartment *and* a baby at the same time?"

"By selling a car we don't really need," I countered.

"Over my dead body," he hissed. "It's the one thing I ever got that I really wanted."

Until a month ago *I* had been the one in that little category. Yanking the sheet up to my chin, I hissed back, "I don't care what you say, I won't have my baby in a whore-house." He flinched, staring at my prostrate form as if he'd never really seen it before. Maybe he hadn't.

*

HE REFUSED to come and look at the apartment until a couple of days before he left for maneuvers, and even then I had to drag him. Unerringly, he uncovered the scorched tiles, still unrepaired, the blackened wall, the moldy refrigerator. In addition he pointed out that every vertical surface near the toilet was coated with old urine splatters.

"I won't be here to help you clean and you never learned how," he said, looking nauseated.

"Mutti will help me. We helped her."

"We helped her *move*. She did every bit of the cleaning herself. By all rights you should be doing all *your* cleaning by yourself."

Out of necessity Lucius and I forged a truce. He wouldn't ask me to give up the apartment and I wouldn't ask him to sell Pepper. In appreciation he tossed me the car keys when he left even though he had been unable to find the time or energy to help me get my license. I was to drive the car just once, loaded with our stuff—but only if I promised to leave it sitting in the parking lot thereafter until he returned from maneuvers. It was an easy promise to keep; Pepper refused to cooperate with me when Lucius was not in the car.

By the end of that week the workmen had repaired floor and closet door and repainted the stained wall. When I came back to clean up it looked even worse, the furniture draped with paint-speckled tarps, the parquet powdered with saw-dust. An hour before Mutti was due to come to help me I felt

compelled to provide her with favorable first impression of
my new home. I began by wielding a broom.

She rang just once. I answered the door with the denim at
my knees wet from mopping. Floor and furniture shone. "It
has possibilities," she said, slipping off her shoes and putting
her cleaning kit down by the coat-stand. Advancing into the
living room, she homed in on the closet, opened the newly
installed door, and pointed to a pile of sawdust inside.
"Missed a spot."

"But the door was shut while they sanded!" I protested.

"Sawdust is like that." She preceded me to the bathroom.
"You're lucky. I've never lived anywhere with instant hot
water. Not even in Yonkers."

"I bet Hannes has plenty."

"Then he's lucky too. Now, I've only got a couple of hours
before my dental appointment, so let's get started. You want
to scrub down the bathroom or the kitchen?"

I couldn't decide which would be worse.

"I'll take the kitchen," she decreed, unpacking her
supplies. "You know nothing about grease and grime." She
brandished a roll of steel wool. "For the oven." She handed me
scouring powder and a bottle of white vinegar. "Do the tub
first. The rest will be easy."

My suspicion that I'd got the better half of our deal was
confirmed before I could plug the bathtub drain. I heard
Mutti's quick intake of breath when she opened the
refrigerator. She slammed it shut and decided to tackle stove
top and oven first, working herself into a comfortable rhythm,
humming, then whistling, until I was convinced I'd done her a
favor by accepting her offer of help.

"How's it going with your firewood stash?" I called out.

"I've just about gleaned everything within walking
distance," she replied. "But I can only do it on weekends."

Remembering the promise I'd made, I said, "Hannes

thinks you don't have nearly enough for the whole winter yet. Now that Lucius is gone I could stay with you a week or two. Help you comb the forest floor for dead branches. Some of them are as thick as my arm."

"Hmm," she said. "I'll have to think about that."

I had expected a more eager response. But on second thought, I wouldn't be terribly keen if she offered to stay with me, either. She came in to empty a bucket of foul water into the toilet — and to check my progress.

"You're doing fine," she said. "And even if this place *had* been meticulous, you'd still want to scrub down every surface. It won't feel like yours till you do. You claim it centimeter by centimeter, you see."

I rose and stretched. "I saw Hannes's library, on the night of the dinner party."

She nodded. "I thought you'd be impressed."

"Aren't *you*?"

She discovered a tiny dab of toothpaste on the medicine cabinet mirror I'd missed and scraped it off with a fingernail. "His house is too big for one person. I don't envy Frau Farber. Merely dusting the shelves must be a fulltime occupation. This bachelorette is much more convenient — plenty of hot water and easy to keep clean. You'll have lots of free time to do whatever you want." Discarding the lecturing mode she asked a bit too casually, "Now that you have a whole year ahead of you — what *do* you want to do? Other than reading."

"Why?"

"You could give that business school another try. Anna just loves it."

I rinsed scouring powder off the tub walls with the hand-shower. "But I'm a married woman now."

"You could still learn to type."

"I don't like typing."

Immediately she looked hurt, as if I'd insulted her choice of professions.

"Anyway," I sputtered on. "They wouldn't want me once I show."

She didn't get it. After Lucius's alarming reaction I was almost afraid to clarify my remark. But she had to know sometime. "I'm going to have a baby. You'll be a grandmother soon."

Her hand shot up as if I were a radio she could click off. "*Ach!*" she said, turning away. But I could see her reflection in the mirror; tears were glazing her eyes. A few drops even spilled down her cheeks. What did I expect? As usual, she was on Lucius's wave length, both of them condemning me as if I had wronged them somehow.

"*Tja mei*," she murmured tragically, making everything worse. "*Tja mei.*"

"Thanks for nothing," I said. "You can be sure I'll never let *my* daughter down."

"But you're only sixteen!" she wailed, fleeing to the kitchen.

I turned on the bathroom faucets and flushed the toilet, hoping to drown out her whimpering sobs. At last they quieted. She resumed her labors but not her whistling. Nor did she hum. After a while I came through the kitchen with a dustpan and clean water, ready to tackle the closet. She was kneeling in front of the refrigerator, staring blindly at the black slime inside.

"Careful. It bites," I said. She didn't seem to hear me. I was cramming my entire trousseau of linens on damp-wiped shelves when she came to stand behind me.

"I have to go. Why don't you just empty the trunks on to the couch for now? I'll help you take them to the basement on my way out."

"Don't bother," I told her. "You've worked long enough. And since you refused to invite me to stay at your house I can't think how to repay you."

She gave me a wounded smile. "But I want to help. Those trunks weigh a ton, even empty. In your condition you're not supposed to carry heavy loads. That's how I lost those three little boys—"

"In that case," I said, glaring, "you'd *better* leave the trunks to me. Since you don't want your grandchild anyway." There was no one who could outstare a Taurus, especially one filled with righteous wrath.

She picked up my pretty teapot, the only thing in the entire trousseau I really liked, turned it this way and that, and threw it against the newly painted wall. It left a gash. As the shards tinkled to the parquet she collapsed on to the couch, steadying her trembling knees with clasped hands. "Sit here. With me," she ordered.

I ignored her.

"Verdammt noch mal (dammit). Sit down beside me!" she repeated, her temper escalating.

I gave the couch a wide berth and sat on the edge of the upholstered chair.

"I don't want to fight," she said.

"You started it!"

"I'm sorry about the teapot. I'll buy you another." She gave a rueful laugh. "Do you have any idea how insufferable you've become since you got married? Just now you sounded like the all-time expert of snide remarks—your father. As if I didn't want what's best for you."

I sniggered.

"It's just that you haven't even begun to live yet, Mariandl. You think that's an insult but I speak from experience. Even if you won't understand. For a while."

I crossed my arms and my legs, anchoring one foot behind the other. "Frau Bischof was sure you'd tell me about birth control the night before my wedding. But instead you went on and on about marital duty."

"Birth what?"

"A foolproof way to keep me from becoming pregnant. Why didn't you? And how do you, anyway?"

She opened and closed her mouth several times, finally managing to croak, "Ask Lucius about those little balloons. He's in the Army. He should know."

"He doesn't know anything," I said. "Obviously."

"That book you had then. The one you were hiding in your closet. Surely — "

"The one you burned? Not a word." I shifted, rubbing my arms. "Once I heard Vati tell someone that I was an accident. Was I?"

She gave me a lopsided smile. It stopped short of her eyes. "I thought you were a gift from God."

"Well, so is *my* baby. And it's listening to us right now. Already keeping me company. It wants to be born. And I want to have it. Because it is, you see. It already is. What can I do except love it?"

She gulped. And leaked again. There was no sense in me holding my breath. She wasn't about to congratulate me. At least not today.

*

ONE DAY before the official move-in date Herr Neumeyer and I took my trunks to the new studio apartment. "Almost as high up as you were in the wh—in your old one," he said, untying the ropes he'd looped around them. "But the elevator — now that's an improvement!"

When I got back to Hohenzollernstrasse I filled Lucius's red darling with the odds and ends he and I had accumulated since May. At first light the next morning I walked out of the whorehouse for the last time, the duvet slung over my shoulders still warm from my bed. I prayed the engine would turn over, and it did. After fumbling with all the wrong knobs I managed to find one that clicked on the headlights and compelled Pepper away from the curb. Luckily no one was on the road to witness me bucking the car across the near-empty intersections, nor did I have to worry about incensed drivers tooting their horns behind me whenever I stalled the motor.

The lot at the high-rise was dipped in pre-dawn shade. I parked beside a dented Renault. Turning off engine and lights, I sat and admired the dark silhouette of our new address. Some of building's windows were already lit behind filmy gauze curtains, the occasional shadow passing in front of a lamp, in a rush to get ready for work. As the engine pinged, cooling, I counted up to the fourth floor but couldn't decide which window in that long row was now ours.

Buttoning my jacket, I watched the clouds behind the Schuttberg take on the first hint of color and only noticed the approaching GI when one of his boot-heels scuffed the tarmac. He was carrying a small boy whose head rested on his broad shoulder. In the dim light their hair seemed the same shade of beige, though the man's was shorter and coarser.

Naoko was shuffling behind them, wrapped in an oversized coat. With long strides, the GI reached the Renault, lifted the boy to the sky, lowered him to kiss his baby-round forehead, then put him into the arms of his mother. He said something soft and low I couldn't understand, inserted his key, grasped the handle to open the door—and froze, swearing.

From the edge of the lot near the access road came a malignant laugh, followed by shrill hooting. A two-toned American car rolled away with its lights off. Naoko cowered, pressing Tommy's cheek to her chest. The GI stared at his hand with disgust. I recognized the sticky stuff on his fingers because Lucius always kept a jar of it under our bed. It was petroleum jelly. Grabbing a folded dishtowel from the pile on my passenger seat, I startled the soldier by rolling down my window, holding out the towel, and saying, "Here, use this!"

He looked from the peace offering to my face, his own pinched with suspicion.

"It's only a rag," I lied. "Really. You can throw it away afterwards. — Good morning, Naoko."

"So solly?" she said, giving no sign of recognition.

"It's Maria," I prodded. "Remember me? From the hospital? Well, I'm finally moving in."

"In the dark? Strikes me as odd," the GI said, his voice rough, as if it didn't get much use. He glanced at his watch and decided to accept my offer, wiping first his palms and then the handle. Then he held the cloth out to Naoko by the only corner left unsullied and told me, "My wife will wash it for you. It'll be good as new. Name's Walt."

"I wash," she agreed. "Today."

"Okay," I said. "I'll pick it up this afternoon. We'll have tea. Five-twelve, is it?"

Their eyes locked; he was giving her some kind of signal. Then they both looked at me expectantly until even I realized they were waiting for me to leave. Climbing out of the car, I announced, "I'm going for a walk," careful to keep my bewilderment from showing. "Up the Schuttberg."

*

THE night was turning gray when I crossed the wide, empty street. By the time I gained the hill top and settled on the bench I thought of as "ours," the clouds to the east had started to blush. I glanced back the way I had come for a glimpse of the shuttered supermarket and the silhouettes of the two high-rises directly behind it, a multitude of windows reflecting a dawning sky. Watching the red tints rush in overhead, first in rosy pastels, then in more dazzling shades until they faded to flat-pink and then everyday-white, I knew with every atom of my being that the news I had given Lucius was more precious than any sunrise I'd ever seen.

At the very least it deserved a heartfelt embrace.

I studied the city spread at my feet and the mountains beyond. Why had the scenery looked better last year when I'd shared it with him? When I started to feel the early-morning chill I retraced my route, re-crossed the street, now clogged with early commuters, and entered the just-opening supermarket, buying rye bread, butter, cheese and pears. Unlike the food I was used to buying in the small specialty shops on Hohenzollernstrasse, my supermarket purchases had no aroma. And the little shops definitely had better and friendlier service.

The elevator ride to the fourth floor of the high-rise still made me a bit uncomfortable. Inside the apartment I sat on the window sill and ate the ripest pear, dripping juice on a wad of toilet paper. Peering down, I noticed a ledge running along the outer wall no more than five feet below. A couple of pigeons sat in a precocious sunbeam, one cooing, the other preening a wing. Farther down, Pepper sparkled in the fresh morning light. I tore the bread and tossed the birds a few bits. Then I closed the window and surveyed my new realm.

I had got what I wanted, but my victory felt more much more bitter than sweet.

CHAPTER 19

I SPENT HALF THE DAY READING SHORT stories by Ray Bradbury and Isaac Asimov. "Science Fiction!" the Warner librarian had huffed when I checked them out. "Moon colonies and rockets to Mars. Now *that's* trash."

For me they were a natural progression from the weird tales Frau Keppler used to supply. They transported me to unseen realms. I did not return to earth until the middle of the afternoon. That's when I finally remembered to get my stuff out of the car. Snapping the book shut, I tossed it on the coffee table and headed down to the lot.

An oversized red American car was parked directly in front of the walkway outside the lobby. Its windows were rolled down, its white top folded. It was the same convertible that had been caught in the downpour the day Lucius and I helped Mutti move. I glanced at the seats inside. They were empty. A bucket of suds stood on the curb next to the nearest front tire. I dipped in my finger in passing. The water was hot.

By the time I'd unlocked Pepper and started pulling out bundles, three young women were standing beside the convertible. One was brown-haired and pear-shaped, the second an insipid, lean redhead. Both wore loose shirts and pedal pushers that covered their knees. The third was a blonde built for short-shorts, her legs as noteworthy as Marlene Dietrich's. She dropped a big sponge into the bucket and unbuttoned the lower half of her blouse, tying the loose ends together and tucking them under to expose an excellent midriff. Her hair was done up in a flawless French twist. From far off she looked like a glamorous Hollywood star. She spoiled the effect by shimmying up the immense hood, reclining on one hip to show off her curves, and blowing a lazy pink bubble. The two ladies-in-waiting leaned against the radiator grill, gazing adoringly at their princess.

While I cleared Pepper's passenger seat I noticed all three were looking in my direction. Self-conscious, I relocked the car door, gathered the four pillow cases I'd stuffed with dirty clothes, and labored across the lot. The brown-haired woman began to uncap three Cokes.

To my right I saw Naoko approach from the lawn that separated the supermarket from our high-rise. She was dragging Tommy on one side, a full net bag on the other. The three beauties transferred their attention to her. The moment she realized it Naoko slowed, stumbled, and drew in her head until she resembled a turtle. Since I couldn't free a hand to wave, I lengthened my stride, hoping we'd intersect before she reached the building.

She passed from lawn to sidewalk, keeping her eyes cast down until she reached the red car. Then she glanced up just long enough to offer her audience a subdued hello.

The greeting was met with silence. Then the brown-haired American swung out a foot and kicked over the bucket. The spill was followed by a three-toned chortle as sudsy water poured over Naoko's sandaled feet. Naoko lifted Tommy onto an undersized hip. The blonde on the hood bowed, steepled her hands, and lisped, "So solly."

Naoko turned to flee toward the entrance.

"Naoko, wait," I called, but she continued until she had scuttled out of sight. Now I was in front of her critics, their merciless, combined scrutiny falling upon me. In response one of the pillow cases I was clutching slid and landed in the soapy gutter.

"Oops," the blonde said, flattening well-chewed gum onto a palm.

"No harm done." I retrieved the dripping bundle. "It's just laundry."

"Hey," she said with a conspicuous German accent. "Don't I know you from somewhere? Have we met?"

"I don't think so," I replied, glad my radically altered hair style made me nearly unrecognizable, for I had begun to realize it was she who had been sitting beside me in the movie theater at Henry.

"Is that red sports car with the American plates yours?" she asked, trying to sound gracious.

"My husband's."

"You just move in?"

"Yes, this morning."

"Well then." She saluted me with her bottle. "Welcome to the club." Tapping her noteworthy chest, she went on, "I'm Linda. This is Nancy. And that's Barb."

I shifted my load. "My name is Maria."

She drained half of her bottle and burped. "Care for a Coke, Maria? We have spares."

"No, thank you. I'm still full from lunch."

Linda put the flattened gum in her mouth and blew another bubble. "One thing," she said as I began to move on. "We don't mingle with the Jap. We already told her husband.

In several ways. You want to do yourself a favor you leave her alone."

"We're trying to persuade them to move," brown-haired Nancy explained, scrunching up her freckled button-nose.

"So we won't have to look at them anymore," auburn-haired Barb added with a caustic laugh.

Linda wagged a playful finger at me. "So don't you go encouraging them, you hear? We think whites should stick with whites. Et cetera." She rubbed a finger over her smooth calves as if checking for stubble. "Why, only last month a white girl came to our movie theater with a *Negro*." She shuddered. "God, how he smelled!"

"Linda made them leave," Nancy said. "When they walked out the whole theater started to clap."

It wasn't how *I* remembered the scene, though our exit had been humiliating enough without that little touch.

"Making second-rate citizens uncomfortable is one of my special gifts," Linda confessed modestly, knocking her bottle against those of her friends in a mock victory toast. I inched away. "Hey," she said. "You took that apartment on the fourth floor?"

"Uh — yes."

"It was George and Ellen's. They finally got to the top of the dependent-housing list. Nice enough people but God were they pigs. When are you going to give us a ride in your shiny new car?"

"I promised Lucius to leave it parked until he comes back from the boondocks," I said, dropping another bundle.

Nancy retrieved it and held it out to me. "Oh, neat. Your husband's away on maneuvers, too."

"You call him Lucius?" Linda sniffed as if she'd caught a rare scent. "What kind of name is that?"

I stood tall. "A nice name."

"A bumpkin kind of name," red-haired Barb said. "Straight from the hills."

"Vermont," I supplied.

Barb nudged Linda's knee. "That's French for 'green hills.' Which makes me double-right. But don't mind us, Maria. We're just in a bitchy mood, is all. Must be full moon tonight. I'm in three-o-six. Come on up sometime. Or down, as the case may be. I make a mean pot of coffee."

"Three-o-six?" I repeated. "I'll remember. You'll have to excuse me — my bundles are slipping again. Nice meeting you all."

"Likewise." Linda smiled. It was a harmless smile. Maybe even a friendly smile, signifying *we're on the same side, right?* Then she sat up as if intending to slide off her perch. "Hey — want us to help carry them to your place?"

"Don't trouble yourselves. They're going down to the washing machine in the basement. But thanks for the offer." There wasn't the slightest doubt in my mind that even if I allowed a friendship to blossom between these women and me it would wither the moment Lucius returned from the war games.

While the laundry cycled in the machine I went up to Naoko's apartment and rang her bell. To no avail. I thought I felt a presence on the inside of the door and could have sworn I heard a floorboard creak, but even when I said, "Naoko — it's me, Maria!" the door did not magically swing open to admit me.

For the next hour I hid behind my drapes, looking furtively down upon Princess Linda's dark roots hoping she and her devoted followers would disappear so I could fetch the rest of my things from the car. Then I realized nothing short of a cloudburst would persuade them to give up their post. Clearly reveling in their uncanny ability to make the other tenants squirm as they passed in and out of the building, the trio volunteered rude comments in English, laughing at locals touchy enough to look flustered.

My gaze kept returning to ring-leader Linda. I found her as mesmerizing as a mouse might find a poised adder. Why was she acting like an ugly American when she was no less German than me? The more I watched her the more ashamed I grew of ever having pretended to be something I was not and promised myself I wouldn't do it again.

I kept expecting Herr Pfeifer to come and take the heckling women to task. Surely at least one of their victims had gone to the manager's office to complain. Whatever his reasons, he stayed away. It wasn't until dusk brought a cooling breeze that Linda gave up her tanning aspirations, climbed on the driver's seat, and took her friends for a ride.

Regardless of Walt's unsolicited opinion, the dark *was* a good time for moving. At least for me it was. I finished emptying out Pepper while no one was watching. When I came back to the fourth floor I found a small brown paper bag on my threshold. It contained the dishtowel I'd loaned Walt, washed and ironed. Naoko's accompanying note thanked me again for its use. Why didn't she knock or ring the bell? Was it something I said?

For the rest of that week I planned my days so that I wouldn't have to pass by the threesome. I took my walks before dawn, shopped and did laundry in the early morning. By the time they appeared for a sunbathing session I had my nose in a book and did not take it out again till daylight waned. On Friday the weather finally broke and it rained. I did not see them outside for the entire weekend. There was nothing to do except read.

Since Anna had already told me she could not spare a minute for socializing during school days, I didn't even try to visit her until Sunday. And even then I was unsure of my welcome. I hardly recognized her when she let me in. She was wearing a classy cornflower-blue dress matching her eyes. Her beehive had been transformed into a light-blonde shoulder-length flip. She'd applied a new shade of makeup with skill and discretion, even going so far as to leave off the penciled on beauty mark.

"Are you all settled then?" she asked, leading me to her couch. The coffee table was covered with pieces of mail laid out as if for a game of solitaire. On closer scrutiny I noticed every envelope had been slit open. While she went to the kitchenette to spoon instant coffee into two cups and fill them with barely-hot tap water, I turned over a few of the envelopes to scan the return addresses, but they were just marked with numbers. She plopped my cup in front of me, gathered the letters into a stack, shuffled them, and fanned them out in a generous semi-circle.

Without taking my eyes off her, I took a sip. The coffee was vile. "You've changed your whole look!" I said, stating the obvious.

She tossed her head, making the flip sway from one side to the other. I was envious; I could never have accomplished that nonchalant swing even when my hair was still long.

"I told you I would. At Hannes's. Remember?"

"Yes, but—"

"That night I decided I want a Hannes too. And if Mutti doesn't hurry up and claims hers I may show up on his doorstep one night with a bottle of booze." She was only half joking.

"What about Horst?"

She shuffled the envelopes again, this time laying out the individual letters in a zigzag pattern. "Oh please!" she said. "His idea of fun is hiding his nose behind the newspaper, sucking on sugar cubes. The high point of his evening is opening a fresh pack of cookies to dunk in his tea. He couldn't even make himself give up that grungy atelier in Schwabing.

He spends most of his time there, claiming this apartment is too modern and doesn't inspire him. If you ask me he's sorry he agreed to a move. I guess he considers inch-long roaches a more attractive companions than me."

I braved another sip of my muddy brew. "The last time I saw you together you both seemed content."

"That was before the dinner party. Since then I've done a lot of thinking about the unfortunate trend in our family to get married too young. Obviously it's too late for Mutti and you but at least I'm going to make sure I marry someone who can afford me and who adores me." She shot me a withering look. "As soon as I heard how you got yourself stuck I had my hair done and put a personal ad in the paper. If I do say so myself, I am pleased with both results. And now I'm in the process of interviewing possible life partners. Want to see my ad? I had to keep it short. They charge by the word." She passed me a section of the classifieds, tapping an ad circled in blue.

I read, *Adventurous young natural-blonde with hourglass figure/seeks single companion/ for sailing, dancing, and carefree matrimony. / Good profession a must.* "Hourglass figure?" I said, focusing pointedly on the little fat-roll on her belly.

Anna yanked the page out of my hands. "I'm going to start exercising. Besides, who cares about the middle? It's the top that counts." She held up two envelopes. "My favorites so far. One's a police lieutenant, the other an architect."

"Take the architect," I advised. "At least he'll be creative."

She considered one of the envelopes, then put it down with the rest. "He's too fat." She sniffed at the other envelope. "The lieutenant now—he's a hunk. He'll look good with his clothes on *and* off. And he doesn't want any children, either."

I was beginning to catch on. "The other day, did Mutti rush over here from my place to tell you I'm pregnant?"

"You were planning to keep it a secret? I'm only sorry for Lucius. He bought a sports car, not a family sedan!"

I banged down my cup. "Well, I guess that makes it unanimous! No one wants my baby except me." I swept the letter montage off the coffee table, jumped up from the couch, and stormed out. It wasn't until I'd slammed and locked my own door that I realized I could barely recall the wondrous feeling that had spread through me after the doctor told me the good news. The only three people in the world who cared about me seemed determined to extinguishing my connection to the light within.

I sat on the couch, leafed through Isaac Asimov's book to a story on space exploration, and followed him to distant worlds in the hopes of finding signs of intelligent life elsewhere.

CHAPTER 20

I MANAGED TO AVOID MUTTI AND ANNA for the entire month Lucius was gone. At the same time Naoko was getting ever better at avoiding me. The first couple of weeks I occasionally crossed her path in the store, where she'd meld with the shelves hoping I wouldn't notice her. Occasionally I caught her watching me the same way I watched Linda and friends—from a window above.

Lately Naoko had learned to space her errands so she would not run into me *or* the Americans. Just once, I surprised her in the basement laundry room. I was convinced she was rinsing Tommy's diapers in her kitchen sink every night since and hung them over the tub to dry.

I still couldn't figure out why she didn't like me. Was I too loud? Too young? Too foolish? Or maybe she held it against me that I'd seen her get humiliated in public. Twice. If she could have overcome that loss of face we might have done each other some good. From what I could see her days were even lonelier than mine, friendless as she was in a country neither hers nor her husband's.

Since she spurned an alliance with me I formed one with my apartment instead. First thing in the morning I liked to sit on the window sill, sipping peppermint tea and watching the Schuttberg slowly emerge out of the night. As soon as the pigeons on the ledge started to coo and preen, I broke a slice of bread to pieces and tossed them their share. One day I tenderly shampooed the couch, stroking the upholstery dry with a towel. The next I waxed the parquet and hand-buffed each square until the floor gleamed like a translucent golden-brown sea. Since I had no wine glasses to display I put my growing stack of library books in the glass cupboard of the mahogany hutch. Each dawn I brought home a few field flowers from the meadow behind the Schuttberg and stuck them in a slim vase on the sideboard.

I was roasting a chicken on the day I expected Lucius to come home from maneuvers. It was beginning to smell inviting by the time I saw him crossing the lawn from the direction of the supermarket. He wore rumpled fatigues and had a duffle bag slung over one shoulder. Linda, Nancy and Barb, at their usual station, stopped talking and watched open-mouthed as he nodded politely to them in passing.

I ducked away from the window, fluttered to the bathroom to brush my hair, and ran a spit-dampened finger over my brows. Heart racing, I started his bath, holding a hand under the faucet until my skin turned brick-red just to make sure the water was as hot as he liked it.

I knew he had a key but he rang the bell and stood on the threshold like a stranger, his fatigues giving off a salty, metallic smell. Although I wanted to hug him I didn't quite dare.

"Hi," I said shyly, stepping out of his way, "Dinner's

almost ready. I'll make the gravy while you're taking your bath."

He pitched the duffle bag into a corner and took off his cap. His hair was grungy and much longer than usual. "Put in plenty of suds," he said. "Maybe a good soaking will help get the river-stink off my hide." His gaze wandered over the pristine bathroom walls, then darted away from my eyes in the mirror. He examined the kitchen counter, crumb-free for only an hour, and the newly-dusted living room, finally admitting, "Not bad. Only, it looks sort of like a hotel room, you know? Except for your usual trail of books."

"Why didn't you write?" I asked, trying keep the words from sounding like an accusation.

He shrugged. "Too busy I guess. You make friends with any of the neighbors yet?"

"They keep to themselves. Most of them work."

He went to the window. "Those three below. Americans?"

"Two of them."

His mouth tightened. "I recognized the car."

"I like it here," I said. "Regardless."

"Without regard for anyone but yourself, you mean," he said. Then he looked toward the lot and brightened. "Ah— there's my Red Pepper. Guess your solo trip went okay."

"I haven't driven her since. Just as I promised."

His hair felt cushion-soft after his bath. "I wish you could keep it this long," I said when he emerged damp and squeaky-clean.

"Army won't let me. And like I told you before, the barber doesn't know how to cut naps."

"Why don't you let me try my hand at it first? Since you have nothing to lose."

"I don't know," he said. "You don't have the proper equipment. Best let me think on it while we eat."

After a couple of helpings of under-cooked chicken, lumpy gravy, and tasteless minute rice, all of which he declared an improvement over C-rations, he consented to sit by the window in fading daylight while I sectioned off his hair with a fine-toothed comb, worked the its teeth through his curls, lifted them, and cut across with my curved nail scissors. He watched the tufts land at his feet. Soon he relaxed enough to describe his recent deprivations, which included wrapping himself in a river-soaked wool blanket on the tent floor to wait out a cold night. I would have hated that particular hardship as much as he did. I definitely would not have made a good soldier.

When the gathering dark turned hair, comb and scalp the same shade of dusk, I pronounced my work done. Lucius rushed to the bathroom mirror to check for bald spots as if he expected me to retaliate for the botched cut he had given me. While he was out of the room I swept up his hair, shaped it into a soft cloud, wrapped it in my blue silk scarf, and hid it in the cupboard behind my books.

Lucius reappeared with an appreciative smile and offered to unfold our bed. I changed into my nightgown behind the closed bathroom door. When I returned he lay waiting under the duvet, still smiling. Self-consciously I lifted a corner so I could slide in—and caught him staring at my middle with ill-concealed distaste.

I wanted to tell him that I hadn't changed, that the only thing wrong between us was that we had to get used to each other all over again. Lying down beside him, I put a hand on his shoulder and felt it stiffen under my touch. I couldn't think how to proceed.

He gave an exaggerated yawn. "Man, am I beat! I don't know when I've been this tired. What do you say we get a good night's sleep?" He rolled away from me, putting his back between us, and muttered, "I heard the guys talking about a racetrack near Augsburg. Big event tomorrow. There'll be cars racing all day. Might see some Porsches. And Ferraris." Just when I was beginning to wonder what that bit of news had to do with me he dropped his voice even lower, mumbling, "I'll make a picnic lunch. You can come if you want."

I counted to five, just so he wouldn't think me overeager, said, "Okay, then," and kept my hand on his shoulder throughout the long night so neither of us would get lost in the dark.

*

I AWOKE to urgent knocking. It was just getting light outside. Before I could move Lucius was bounding out of bed to open the front door. Mutti stood outside, uncharacteristically disheveled, wrapped in a rain coat, her eyebrows blurred, wearing her shabbiest flats.

"Oh, Lucius—I didn't know you were back," she cried, obviously relieved to see him.

"Was ist los (what's wrong)?" he asked, escorting her to the table. When she didn't answer him fast enough, he said, "Maria, ask her what's wrong."

Although he wore nothing but wrinkled pajama bottoms his new haircut made him look stylish. He glanced at his bare chest, glowing copper, and at our unmade bed, which seemed to take up half the room. "Where are my street clothes?"

I pulled out a hanger from his half of the closet. It held a sleeveless shirt and cut-offs made from an old pair of pants, both a faded black. He rushed to the bathroom to change while I rummaged for his footwear. Mutti sank on to a chair, staring at a drooping bouquet of wild calendula on our sideboard.

Hastily folding up our mattress, I asked, "What's the matter with you? You're not even wearing stockings!"

"Nor clothes," she said, giving me a glimpse at her nightgown. "I came without thinking—but now that I know

Lucius is here I want you both to come back to the farmhouse with me."

"Right now? What for?"

She took a ragged breath. "I don't know if I'm angry or scared. I got up later than usual. Turned on the light. Counted four mice in the bucket. Slipped on this coat, stepped into my work shoes, and opened the door to take the creatures through the woods to their new home. But *he* was standing right there, on the other side of the jamb. White as a ghoul. He raised his hat, said, 'Good morning, Lottchen,' and walked inside. Carrying his briefcase."

"O.F.?"

"I had my keys in the coat pocket. Without a thought in my head I slammed the door from the outside and locked it, just to give myself time. Then I drove here. First I thought I'd go to the police but I'm sure they wouldn't do anything. After all, I'm still married to him. By now he probably climbed out of a window. Or not. I want you and Lucius to help me secure the house. Room by room."

"What if he's hiding nearby?"

"I wish I could buy a gun," she said, and we both laughed at the impossible notion. "I'll have to make do with a big stick by the door."

"You should go to Hannes," I said. "He'll be glad to help."

"I'd be ashamed. Besides, I don't want O.F. to get any ideas about Hannes and me. He seemed so bizarre, standing there. Let's hope one look at Lucius will give him a heart attack."

Lucius reappeared, his legs shapely in the cut-offs. "Is this all you could find?" he said, rubbing at his knees.

"Want me to get you something less sexy?"

"Never mind. What's the emergency?"

Before I could finish explaining he'd unhooked my trench coat from our coat-stand, pressed it at me, and grabbed his socks and sneakers. Then he herded us out the door, his feet still bare but his eyes already determined. "I believe I'll just lift him by the scruff of his neck and shake him up a bit. If it's all right with your mother."

"Ja, doch (sure)," she said once I'd translated the offer.

I finished tying my belt just as the elevator came down the shaft. Naoko and Walt were inside, neither of them smiling. Lucius nodded at them and stepped in, planning ahead. "Maria, you ride with Mother in the VW. I'll follow in Pepper. That way she won't have to drive us back afterwards." I introduced the dour couple to him and to Mutti. "Nice to meet you all," Lucius said, stooping to put on his socks and shoes.

Naoko glanced at the decrepit slippers I wore, then focused intently on her straw-colored zories. Walt gave a short grunt and tightened his hold on a sleepy Tommy. Mutti ran a hand through her hair as if she was beginning to suspect she wasn't looking her best. The moment the elevator settled on the ground floor Lucius dashed through the lobby. Mutti and I had to jog to keep up with him.

"What did you do with the mice?" I asked her.

"They're in the car."

"In the bucket or out?"

"In it. I hope."

Things got worse when we arrived outside. Linda and her husband were busy folding down the convertible's top. A picnic basket sat on the hood. Close behind the rear bumper stood the yellow shark-finned gas-guzzler I remembered from our aborted movie. Nancy and Barb were sitting on its enormous back seat. Lucius's arch-enemy, Jim, and another, vaguely familiar GI, both in their civvies, were rearranging the trunk. It was loaded with sodas, beer, and blankets. Lucius slowed and I took his hand. It was frigid.

As if someone had pulled an off-switch, all three couples stopped moving. Walt and Naoko bolted past us toward the lot. Not one of the Americans reacted. Mutti blinked, holding her coat shut as if the buttons might pop. But they weren't looking at her. Their focus was solely on Lucius. At last Linda's husband straightened, his fists at the ready. Linda, crossing her arms, said, "My, my, my," as if lobbing a gauntlet.

Then we were past them too. Sweat glistened on Lucius's hairline and on the bridge of his nose. All at once, I fully appreciated the old line, "From the frying pan into the fire." Moving to the high-rise had not been my best idea. Whatever came next would clearly be my fault.

He should have warned me louder and longer. I should have listened.

*

THE VW was parked beside the Renault, which was already rattling to life, coughing and smoking, the faces inside pale featureless orbs.

"We'll wait for Lucius, to make sure his car will start," Mutti said, unlocking the passenger door.

The first time he turned the key in the ignition Pepper sighed as if trying to wake from an endless sleep. Twice more, she merely clicked. He climbed out. "Battery's dead. Don't tell me I forgot to ask you to idle her every few days."

"Then I won't," I said, getting into the rear of the VW to cede him all the leg room the front passenger seat provided. The bucket, sitting beside me, was scrabbling with mice. As soon as Mutti zoomed around the first corner my stomach started to lurch. I grabbed on to the edge of my seat with one hand, on to the teetering bucket with the other. "Didn't you say you caught four mice?"

"Yes. Why?"

"I count only three."

"Oh," she said, sounding glum.

Quickly, I pulled up my feet and sat cross-legged. The first squeal came from Mutti just before the car jerked and stalled. The second came from Lucius. He raised a leg to expose the little brown something surging past his sock onto a bare shin. He cupped it on reflex and dropped it into the bucket in one fluid motion.

"There," he said. "Back home with Mommy, where you belong."

*

A WEEK of uninterrupted sunshine had baked the farmyard, cracking the top layer of clay. O.F.'s car was nowhere in sight. The door was still locked but the kitchen window stood open. A faint trace of O.F.'s miracle cure for baldness lingered in the air.

"Gone," Mutti said with relief. And yet, when we peered first into the clammy, unused parlor, and then, upstairs, into two equally unused bedrooms, she and I shadowed Lucius as if we expected an unpleasant surprise. From the room facing the woods we saw a white patch shimmering through the low branches.

Mutti gasped.

"O.F.!" I whispered.

Lucius bolted out of the room and down the stairs just as the white object started to move. Mutti and I ran to the bedroom overlooking the yard. And then two things happened at once. O.F.'s VW rolled into full view, aiming for the road, and Lucius burst out of the stable door. He was a blur of flashing limbs, well-muscled legs stretching their utmost, churning the yellow clay-dust. For several seconds car and runner were even, the machine shuddering over rocks and potholes, Lucius's sneaker-clad feet barely touching the ground.

Now he was at the driver's door, making a grab for the handle. Long-limbed and slender, black against white, he was the most beautiful piece of art I'd ever seen.

Mutti shook her head. "I had no idea he could run like that."

Neither had I, though I'd known him for more than a year. As the car pulled ahead, gathering speed, and Lucius veered into the field for his return loop, still gliding, I wondered what else I had yet to find out about him.

CHAPTER 21

WHILE LUCIUS WAS ATTENDING TO LOCKS and shutters Mutti and I took the four mice to their new quarters. Our path was strewn with the remains of pinecones harvested by prophetic squirrels. The slanting autumn sun set leaves aglow and lit up the brush with splashes of gold.

"Sometimes I think I'm merely providing some lucky owl with midnight snacks," Mutti said. "And other times I'm sure I hear the mice I just dropped off scurry along behind me, back to the house. One thing I know — the walls still rustle in the dark. The other night I was sitting on the couch with a slice of buttered bread when one lone climber scaled to the top of the armrest and sat, sifting the air. Then he looked right at me so expectantly that I broke off a bite for him before I realized — their eyes, you see, are so — "

"Why did you tell Anna I was pregnant?

Her pace faltered. "I shouldn't have?"

"It's *my* job to tell. Who else have you told?"

She hesitated. "Hannes, of course."

"Hannes! Of course!" I repeated, taken aback. "Well. I'm glad I gave you two something to talk about. What did he say?"

"Say? What could he say except, 'I'm so sorry'?"

Somehow, I hadn't expected that response from him. Could she be . . . misinterpreting his remark? I scooped up a partially stripped cone and ripped off the rest of its scales.

"What about Lucius," she said, watching my busy fingers. "How did *he* take your news?"

I tossed the shredded core over my shoulder. "He'll come around. Once he gets used to the idea."

She looked at me sideways. "He's already had an entire month for that. Hasn't he?"

I shrugged. "They don't exactly give him time to think on maneuvers. And he'll only be home for two weeks before the next one starts. Just long enough to soak the sweat out of his fatigues, he said."

"Tell him to dress warm. It's supposed to snow early this year."

We proceeded along the trail until I caught glimpses of a sun-bleached wheat field on the far side of the forest. Mutti stopped, put a hand to her lips, and tip-toed to the rotting stump I'd stuffed with crushed newspapers. She had covered it with a well-weathered board, serving as roof to the mansion we'd created for rodents reluctant to embrace the wilds.

She removed the board, upended the bucket over the hollow underneath, and stepped away. "They must be knee-deep in there," she whispered. "Sometimes the newcomers refuse to abandon the bucket. I like to wait a few minutes to give them a chance to gather their courage."

She sat on a crumbling log, patting the space by her side. "Lucius seems different today. It's taking a few extra seconds for a smile to spread to his eyes. Is your marriage in trouble already?"

What business was it of hers? "Couldn't be better," I replied firmly. "Why do you ask?"

With a dismissive wave Mutti patted the log again, ready to listen to my side of a sad story. Right there and then I silently vowed she'd *never* hear me complain. I lifted the bucket off the stump. The mice were gone. Replacing the board, I abruptly remembered our long-ago family strolls through Freidorf. "The perfect couple!" passing villagers used to gush as Mutti and Vati continued to walk with linked arms even as their marriage secretly foundered. Like Lucius, their social smiles had trouble reaching up to their eyes.

"Oh!" Mutti said, sitting on her log. "I forgot about Hilde. I also mentioned it to Hilde."

Confused, I asked, "You wrote her a letter?"

"I came by your apartment several times this past month to tell you about it but you were never home. Anna said you wouldn't answer the doorbell for her either."

Small wonder. I'd been in no mood for disagreeable company. "I take a long walk every day," I said vaguely, sitting down a couple of arm-lengths from her and peeling bits of bark off the log's sides. "And I spend a lot of time in the American library."

"No matter," she said. "I'm telling you now. I was eating lunch at the *Kaufhaus* one day when Hilde walked by, stopped, and spoke my name. She looks just as she did all those years ago. Same scrawny bun, same shiny red apple cheeks. She asked about you, so naturally I told her you were pregnant and married."

"In that order?"

"What order?" Mutti scooted closer to imprison my fidgeting hand. "Will you stop picking at things? She's worried about Gabriel. Says he went wild after you left.

Sometimes he's gone for a week. He's had a couple of nasty spills on the motorcycle. She's afraid he'll break his neck one day. Too much dancing and beer. She says she wishes she hadn't sent you off like that."

"Like what?" I scoffed, yanking clear of her grip. "I was ready to leave!" I still recalled the wrenching farewell scene with Gabriel on the stairs. "Did she mention Putzi at all?"

"He . . . stopped eating. And died. The shock of losing you twice, she said."

My eyes burned. It had been good to imagine my cat up on the loft, happily curled in the hay, waiting to lap his next saucer of cream. From now on I would be compelled to envision him sitting outside my cold, empty chamber, waiting in vain and wasting away. Putzi had been my last link to Hilde's farm and my childhood. And now I had none.

"Why didn't she write? I would have gone to get him. I could have kept him safe — "

"Where?" she asked, sounding impatient. "In that pension where you stayed from the time you left Hilde's until you got married? At our apartment at the Harthof, with O.F?"

I closed my eyes and saw a tiny white pink-tailed mouse disappearing down the toilet. "Mutti," I said urgently, "you can't live here anymore now that he's found you. We *really* should tell Hannes."

"Let's leave *him* out of this, shall we? I'll be more careful on weekends. And during the week O.F. has his route to drive. Besides — what can he do to me? Nothing!"

My fingers tore a good-sized hole through the bark and rubbed at the smooth surface beneath. With my eyes wide open I recalled the dead hamster floating in our toilet bowl. He'd been too big to flush.

Nothing? To whom was she lying now?

*

BACK AT the farmhouse the ground-floor shutters were all closed and locked from the inside, even the ones at the kitchen window. Mutti stood in the dusk, shaking her head. "It's a good thing I work such long hours at the office. Now that daylight wanes earlier and earlier my at-home time will be spent in perpetual gloam. To the delight of the mouse population, no doubt."

Lucius showed her the padlock he'd mounted on the basement door. Rattling it to make it strain against its metal strap, he told her, "Not even a ghost can get through this."

"Sehr gut (excellent)," she said. "At least now I won't have to lie awake wondering what might lurk in the cellar, waiting for midnight. I bought the locks weeks ago but installing them didn't seem important until today. Thank God for Lucius." She shook his hand. "You are a big help for me," she said in painstaking English. "I thank you very much. We will have lunch and then I will drive you home, yes?"

"Lunch, yes," Lucius said. "But you don't have to drive us any farther than the station. We'll take the streetcar." Looking down on himself, he added, "That is if I won't cause a riot with these old cut-offs. Germans are particular about their clothes."

Taking stock of my own appearance, I hoped my house shoes would pass public muster. Mutti tugged at her coat. "In all the excitement I forgot to get dressed. Why don't you two set the table? I'll be right back."

Lucius sat and watched me bustle around in the kitchen. Since it was a fair bet that the meal would include potatoes I lit a fire in the stove and put a kettle on to boil.

"What a way to start our morning," he chuckled. "When she came pounding on our door I thought the building was on fire. I got a good look at ugly Old Fart as he was driving off. I wonder what she ever saw in him. But then a lot of people wake up one morning, look at the person they're sharing their bed with, and ask themselves, 'Why on earth did I marry this fool?'"

My heart gave a thud. "They do?"

He stared out the window. "Happens all the time."

"But not to us," I said, testing.

He was just getting ready to answer when Mutti came in with her hair brushed and newly drawn eyebrows, wearing a paisley dress. She leaned a wooden club against the wall just inside the stable door and said, "In case."

"Wait a minute!" Lucius told her. He turned to me, looking serious. "Why don't you stay here tonight? The whole week if she wants. I won't mind. With the mess you got us into at the high-rise I plan to spend as little time at home as I can."

Away from the sun, his pupils and irises were so dark that I could not interpret his expression.

"I already offered," I said, neglecting to mention that it had been the month before. "She said no."

"You want to come and sleep at our house tonight?" he asked her, slowly. "Or at Anna's?"

She laughed. "You have only one bed. Anna, too. And she is busy with her police lieutenant. I would be in the way."

"Police lieutenant? What's that supposed to mean?" he said when I was done translating. I told him about Anna's classified ad while Mutti cooked our lunch. "Anna got rid of her rats' nest?" he chuckled. "Changed her whole style? This I've got to see!"

*

MUTE, Lucius and I sat at the streetcar stop in front of the Pasinger station. His bare legs, slim, long and shapely, were noisily admired by three passing teenage girls. He waited until they were out of sight, their hysterical giggles fading, before trying to tuck his legs under the bench. It only made them more conspicuous.

I repositioned the hem of my coat to hide my slippers and asked, "What are you going to do about the dead battery?"

He shrugged. "I thought maybe I could ask Spider to come give me a jump—"

"No!" I said. "I don't want him to know where we live."

"—until I remembered that he went to the races. Everyone went. Even those three toxic couples we saw at our curb. So, what I'm going to do instead is haul the battery to Washington at the motor pool. He'll charge it up for me."

"Today?"

"Naw. First thing in the morning. That way I can bring it back with me after work tomorrow. Once Pepper's operational I'm aiming to do a lot of driving around. And next time I'm gone—please feel free to start her for me every few days. Let her run for a while."

As we were walking home from the Scheidplatz he decided to spend the remainder of his day cleaning and waxing and polishing her gorgeous red hide. "While the sun keeps on shining," he said, studying the sky, which couldn't seem to make up its mind whether or not to bestow another perfect Indian summer afternoon upon us. "Let's take a look at the battery. See what tools I need to fetch from upstairs to unfasten it. Maybe you can find me something to carry it in. Batteries are heavy." He nodded toward the access road. "We'll cut to the lot from there." He seemed to have forgotten about his unfashionable attire and as soon as we'd crossed the busy street he eagerly lengthened his stride, leaving me to trip along in his wake.

Halfway to the parking lot I saw Anna standing on a strip of grass by the fence that ran alongside the entire length of the road. She was picking a long-stemmed daisy. A tall, barrel-chested youngish man stood beside her, both hands clasped behind his back. In the shy-young-virgin mode she was promoting today, she unbent, casually pushed out her chest to show off her best advantage, added the daisy to the bouquet of look-alikes she was holding, and lowered her pretty nose to the petals, savoring their scent—as if the basest fool didn't know that daisies had none; if anything, they gave off a flat, unpleasant odor. The police lieutenant didn't seem to remember that fact. At least, it did nothing to decrease the approving smile on his face.

Lucius waved just as Anna was getting ready to pluck her next victim. He called her name. She didn't seem to hear him. But the lieutenant sure did. He asked a question, such as, "Do you know that Neger (Negro)?" Anna darted her eyes toward Lucius one second and away the next, shaking her head hard enough to make her flip bounce. She answered something short and succinct like, "I swear I never saw him before in my life." Then she concentrated on the grass by her feet.

Lucius lowered his hand. "That's odd," he said, starting to walk toward them.

I took his arm. "We're not looking our best. And the future Frau Leutnant (Mrs. Lieutenant) is obviously trying to make a favorable impression."

Lucius sniffed. "If you ask me we'll never look good enough to impress a guy like him. What's wrong with Horst all of a sudden?"

"She's decided he'd make an unsatisfactory life partner."

He favored Anna with one last look, said, "I think I liked her better before," and continued toward the lot. The instant the little red sports car came into view we saw that she was ringed by a crowd. Lucius began to jog, getting to them before I did. The crowd parted for him. Pepper was a mess. Her shiny new paint was marred by long smears and streaks that had been drying in the sun all morning. The streaks ran from the roof down over windshield and hood, over the chrome bumpers, the rear windows, and both taillights.

At first all the faces before me appeared equally hostile, but then I recognized the astonishingly high forehead of a man who lived on our floor. I'd shared the elevator with him a few times. He had seemed almost pleasant, in the stand-offish way of someone to whom you have not been introduced. But now, at the car, he ignored my timid greeting and said sternly, "Eine solche Schande (this is a terrible shame)!" as if I'd done him some personal wrong.

The next face turning toward me belonged to Herr Pfeifer. "Wie gesagt, die Amis spinnen doch alle (like I said, the Yanks are all crazy)," he huffed, tapping his forehead. "*Eier soll man essen, nicht herumschmeissen!*"

"*Eier?*" I repeated, uncomprehending.

For once, Lucius was able to translate German into English for me. "Eggs. Your cracker-brained American friends must have decided to splurge—I'd say they tossed at least a couple o' dozen. That's a lot of good pancakes going to waste."

CHAPTER 22

THE CROWD HAD DISPERSED WHEN WE came down with the first pails of water. One stocky German man retreated to a mustard-hued VW in the farthest corner of the lot, where he unwrapped a set of wrenches and slid a bowl under the chassis. At our end, Lucius lovingly cleaned Pepper's marred paint with the many refills I brought him. Each time I delivered two full buckets and picked up the empties I intercepted another intense gaze from our observer.

Somewhere between the endless rinses a black, low-slung Porsche cruised out of the access road from the direction of the Anna's high-rise. She was sitting on the passenger seat, looking away from us as if something on the fence they were passing was of vital importance.

But the lieutenant's cool eyes swept over Lucius and me, taking in every detail. Lucius gave him a cheerful wave, muttering, "Adios, prospective brother-in-law," and watching the Porsche leap toward the street and away. Lucius shook his head. "Must be hard to say no to a guy with a Porsche."

He finished removing every trace of the baked-on eggs, then I helped him apply and polish a coating of wax. At the end he took out the battery, put it in the box I'd found in the basement, and placed it on the floor in front of the passenger seat. "I'll have to leave extra early in the morning to catch up with Washington," he said. "The CO's already warned me about reporting for duty late." He shivered. "I'm drenched and it's getting colder. I believe I'll have a long soak in the tub while you cook us something hot and delicious." He locked the trunk and both doors, rattled the hood to make sure it was properly fastened, and said, "The best thing about this fiasco is that your American friends aren't here to gloat over it."

"Stop calling them *my* American friends," I protested, stacking the buckets and stuffing the top one with spent rags. "You have more in common with them than I do. You come from the same place and can understand what they have done and why they did it. I'm with the other Germans. Throwing good food around is a crime."

The man in the far corner abruptly abandoned his wrenches to march toward us. I watched him warily as he approached, bristling, his face flushed. Had he decided to fling some final disparaging remark at our faces? Standing before us, he made a grab for Lucius's hand, barked "*Feiner Kerl!*" and awkwardly slapped him on the shoulder. Providing his own translation, the secret admirer said "Goot Mann!" Then he pivoted and marched back to his post, where he retrieved the bowl, chose a wrench, lay flat on his back, and scooted under to reinstall the oil-drain plug.

Lucius cupped his shoulder as if trying to preserve the neighborly touch. "Well," he said. "That guy just fixed one heck of a very bad day."

*

MAYBE that was true for him but it wasn't for me. Lucius came out of our bathroom so clean he practically glowed and ate a hearty meal of elbow macaroni fried with melted Swiss cheese. He grew animated enough to dunk chocolate-chip cookies in his after-dinner tea, and I silently welcomed the reappearance of the endearing young man I'd met and married. But his glow became glower once he'd unfolded the couch bed and I stood before him in my chaste cotton nightgown. He claimed the far edge of the mattress, his body language repelling any possible advance. Speechless, I lay down on "my" side, missing the uncomfortable daybed we used to share in the whorehouse. It had been narrow enough to necessitate nightly make-up sessions.

I was as surprised as he when we awakened the next morning in a tangle of limbs. For one sweet moment I studied his sleepy face and watched it grow tense. He bolted out of bed and into his clothes, complaining, "Why didn't you wake me? I'm liable to lose a stripe if I'm late!" Grabbing an apple, he rushed out of the apartment without taking the time to say good-bye. It wasn't until I heard the elevator door ping open and shut that I noticed he'd taken the car keys but forgotten his wallet.

I caught up with him in the poorly lit parking lot. He was standing stock-still behind Pepper. She was swathed in something that looked like white bandages. "What is it?" I asked, pulling at a loose end.

"Gift wrap," he said, walking around Pepper stiff-kneed and suspicious. I stuffed the wallet into one of his back pockets as he inserted his key in the passenger door. He grabbed at the handle and then, with a shout, he jerked his hand clear. It was too late. His fingers weren't covered with grease as Walt's had been, but with something fetid and brown. Gagging, he wiped them on the nearest paper wad, only to discover it had been hiding the same hue of brown, smeared all over Pepper's newly waxed paint. A woman's hard laugh tinkled from one of the dark high-rise windows. For an instant, a hurt little boy stared at me out of Lucius's eyes.

"I'll wash it off. Right away," I promised the child. But it was the man who spoke with Lucius's lips.

"By the time I get done scrubbing my hands I'll be too late to get the battery to Washington," he said. "Which means I'll have to ask Spider to give me a jump after work, like it or not. If I don't move Pepper off the lot before nightfall no telling what those jerks will do to her next."

*

PROPELLED by shame and stoked by dumb rage, I waited only long enough to see him merge with pre-dawn shadows before I began ripping the toilet paper off the car. I lugged countless buckets, used up my store of clean wash rags, tore a brand-new linen sheet into strips, and even sacrificed my dish towels to restore Pepper's luster.

Then it was my turn to soak in the tub, squeezing my eyes shut and praying for rain—not to bless the car with one final rinse, but to keep the Americans indoors for the remainder of the day. Immersing every part of my body in water almost too hot to bear, I thought of the moment, down in the lot, when I'd realized there were a good number of maroon-colored American license plates on the parked cars around us—and a good number of unfamiliar American faces passing by me that early morning who reacted to my polite hello by pinching their lips, assuming guarded expressions and carefully looking away. As if the whole bunch of them had been to some kind of meeting where they decided I did not exist.

That afternoon I had no doubt Lucius and Spider would arrive just about dinner time and that Lucius would invite his friend to eat with us in appreciation for his help. I was keeping one eye on the three breaded pork chops I was frying in my largest pan, the other on Pepper, below. The table was set for three. Sodas were cooling in the refrigerator and a brick of ice cream was slowly softening in the ineffective freezer compartment. Tiny red potatoes simmered in my medium-sized pot. The butter-and-parsley sauce I planned to douse them with was melting in a small pan.

It never occurred to me that Lucius *wouldn't* bring Spider upstairs. I saw his ugly jalopy swaying into the lot, saw Lucius getting out to reinstall the battery. Determined to be a good hostess, I got busy arranging the chops on our plates, seasoning the potatoes, uncapping the Cokes. I completely missed the moment the rusty big car and the shiny little car pulled out of the lot together. Next time I looked the spaces they'd so recently occupied were empty and they were gone.

The greasy chops congealed and the buttered potatoes shriveled, and the little salad I'd concocted wilted before I gave up waiting for the men to return. It got dark. The outside lamps came on. I opened a book, read, and ate all three of the chops merely because I needed something to grind my teeth on. Over the course of the next five hours I slowly licked my way through the thawing ice cream, restlessly moving from novel to novel until I stuck with my favorite book about Africa and reread the chapter about the Rift Valley's Masai. The last thing I did that night was pick up the pot with the stone-cold potatoes and the bowl full of lettuce-sludge and empty them into the garbage pail with all the force I could muster.

Humming myself to sleep with a melody that refused to leave my head, I tried to remember the words I'd sung to it in my childhood. But they didn't come to me until I was in a dream. In it I saw myself sleeping on my half of the mattress, Lucius on his, and slowly, the two halves separated, floating on gentle waves that pushed them farther and farther apart until they came to rest on opposing, distant shores, the lake water churning between them, exposing an insurmountable abyss. Lucius sat on his part of the halved bed. I sat on mine. A rich, melancholy voice sang from the blackness of the abyss,

Es waren zwei Königskinder/ die hatten einander lieb
Sie konnten zusammen nicht kommen/ das Wasser war viel zu
tief . . .

Once there were two royal children who loved one another/
but they could not come together/the water was much too deep . . .

Listening to the rest of the sad stanzas, it seemed to me the lake water was draining on to my pillow. I awoke with a wet, sticky face, alert to a small sound coming from the door. It was Lucius, returning at last to shuffle across the dark room, his back stooped like an old man's. With a tortured sigh, he sat on the mattress.

"Lucius?" I sobbed, fumbling with the lamp.

He muttered, "Don't. The last thing I need right now is your teary eyes on me." He lowered himself gingerly on to the bed, still dressed in his fatigues and his boots, his spine cramped and crooked. When it became obvious he was going to fall asleep on top of the duvet, I crept to the closet, brought out a blanket, and covered him, neck to soles. When I cocooned myself under the duvet on my side he murmured, "Real sleep. For a couple of hours. G' night."

I awoke to the noise of a metal spoon scraping against tin. Lucius was leaning against the sill, an inky silhouette against the beginnings of gray light. "Couldn't find anything worth eating in the fridge," he said, raising a can. "And I'm tired of cakes. So I opened some pork and beans."

His pork chop would have tasted better, even cold.

"Brought you something," he went on, unperturbed by my lack of response. "Over by the door. A fold-up army cot. Way things are now your mother's place will be safer for you than ours."

"Uh-uh," I said. "I'm staying put. Most of the Americans are only here until they get into government housing. We'll outlast them."

He slammed the can against the sill, making the spoon rattle. "Don't be so stubborn! How do you think I'll feel, going off for another month and leaving you in this mess? There's not one reason for you to stay here. Not one. Heck. You never do much of anything here anyway that I can see. Except read." He gestured at the books stacked on every available surface. "And you can do *that* at your mother's."

"If you don't want me to read anymore," I said, stung at the injustice of his remarks, "would you rather I take up drinking and smoking? In some bar?" Or was he implying I should get a job? Who would hire an inexperienced pregnant sixteen-year-old married to an American soldier?

He gave a mirthless laugh. "You, in a bar? Don't make me laugh. By the way — thanks for the Cokes." He raised two empty bottles. "Just *try* the farmhouse, okay? For one week. Give things around here a chance to cool down. Till those people get used to the idea of . . . us."

The word *farmhouse* brought to mind mice and owls, dank rooms, closed shutters. I'd be a virtual prisoner, away from public transportation and stores. "You can't make me go," I said.

He rose. "Well, then. Don't expect to see much of me these next couple of weeks." He limped to the coffee table and picked up his keys and his wallet. "CO seems to think I can't handle the freedom of living off-base. Just because I reported for work late a couple of times. One more mess-up and he'll make me sleep in the barracks. Immature, irresponsible, incapable me." Then he went to the door and was gone.

I threw my soaked pillow across the room and yanked the duvet over my face, hoping to fall asleep again since there was nothing to stay awake for. But an undefined anger kept me tossing and turning. Twenty minutes later Lucius returned, panting.

"Quick, help me!" he gasped. "Do we still have our bicycle pumps?" Neither one of us had found the time or energy to bring our bikes to the high-rise but the pumps had been easy to move.

"They're in the basement," I said, putting on my clothes and the teddy-bear coat and stepping into my shoes. I rummaged through a kitchen drawer for the key to our storage unit, said, "Come on!" and led the way.

In the lift going down he told me how he'd been afraid to leave Pepper on the lot last night. After driving around for a couple of hours he had decided to park on a poorly lit side street several blocks from the high-rise. He had drowsed behind the steering wheel until he was cramped enough and cold enough to fool himself into believing the car would be safe without him for the rest of the night. But when he got to it this morning all four tires were flat.

"I went around the whole car, wondering what to do. An old lady came out of the tiny house I'd parked in front of. She was swinging a broom and her husband came hobbling out behind her, scowling at me. And then three teenage hoodlums in leather jackets rounded the corner armed with metal pipes. I didn't stop to ask if they meant to use them on me or the windshield. You have to go back there with me. Explain the situation. Help me pump some air into the tires. Pepper's got small wheels. It shouldn't take more than half an hour. With any luck the CO will give me one last chance. Heck, I won't object to a couple of hours of heavy KP. You know I can't just leave that poor car sitting there. What if the old lady calls the police and they tow Pepper away?"

At last we were united, him and me against the world. Like old times. I found the pumps, thrust them at him, and followed him at a fast trot down one road and around a curve and another until we came to the car.

We were too late. Our bicycle pumps had become superfluous. The three leather-jacketed hoodlums were pumping away on theirs, one at each wheel. The old man, at the fourth tire, was a bit slow and seemed glad to cede his place to Lucius. I didn't have to do a thing except stand idly by until the old guy took my measure and asked if I spoke German. I admitted I did.

He told me how he and his wife, both insomniacs, had heard the sound of an unfamiliar car. Peeking around the curtains, they saw Lucius, dark as Lucifer, sitting behind the steering wheel. They checked every hour, wondering if they should call the police. But what for? He hadn't done anything — yet. Finally he got out and limped away.

Light sleepers, they were roused again no more than an hour later by the sound of a big idling engine and murmuring voices. They saw a huge American car double-parked beside Pepper and then several shadows emerging from it to crouch over Pepper's tires, slyly laughing. As soon as the car sped away the couple hobbled outside. By that time a light had come on in the neighboring house, where three brothers were getting ready for their factory shift.

"I knocked on their door," the old man said. "They helped us figure things out. We all felt sorry for the black Ami. Es war ja gemein (it was a mean thing to do). So was tut man doch nicht (it's not acceptable). And so we decided to make things right again. We all have bicycle pumps, nicht wahr (don't we)?"

While I explained the story to Lucius the old woman came out of the little house with a tray. On it were mugs of hot coffee. Black. "*Für Zucker und Sahne reicht es halt nicht,*" she said with an apologetic smile. I translated that, too, and drank my cupful of the bitter brew as if it were the rarest elixir.

"No money for sugar and cream, huh?" Lucius said, testing his tire for firmness. "Most likely they used up their last bit of coffee on us, too."

One by one, the three brothers screwed caps onto tire stems, drank their portions, and vigorously shook Lucius's hand. Then they pulled the last four cigarettes out of a pack, offered Lucius one, lit a match to theirs when he declined, and got on the bicycles that had been leaning against their house wall.

"Wait," Lucius said, turning to me. "Tell them I'll be back tonight with a couple of cartons of American cigarettes." The moment the last two words were out of his mouth, the boys nodded, grinning, and pedaled away. Lucius set his empty cup on the tray. "Vielen Dank (thanks a lot)," he told the couple. "I buy you American coffee?"

The wife clapped her hands together and said, "Ach! Ja, gut (that would be great)!"

"And sugar?"

Her husband looked as if they'd just won the jackpot, stroked Lucius on the back with approval, and helped the old woman inside.

I thought I saw their curtains flutter when Lucius squeezed himself into the car. He rolled down the window. "If my luck holds I won't be late for work after all. This time. I'm driving across town to the commissary before I come home tonight. That's where they carry industrial sizes of everything. The old folks will be drinking free coffee for the next couple of years. Including sugar and cream." He waved and drove off, leaving me to stare after Pepper's jaunty tail lights until they were out of sight.

CHAPTER 23

PRETENDED TO BE FAST ASLEEP when Lucius crawled into bed late that night. In the process of lifting the covers he let out my entire cache of downy-warm air. He groaned softly, lying down. Once the cover was back in place his icy feet kept me from generating enough body heat to replace what we'd lost. Both of us shivered silently toward morning.

Around five he clicked on his lamp. "Is it my imagination or is it getting colder?" He pulled the duvet off my face. "Your lips have turned blue!" He went to feel the radiator and fiddled with a knob. "No sign of life. How do you turn that thing on anyway?" Peeling off his wrinkled fatigues, he quickly exchanged them for a crisp, ironed set and slipped into a lined pea-jacket. "It was raining till around midnight. Then the temperature dropped. Fast." He put on a fur-lined cap with ear flaps. "Everybody will be scraping ice off their windshields on their way to work. Except me. Brought you some grub from the commissary." He went to a box standing by the front door and deposited it on the table. "Save you a trip to the PX while I'm gone." Unpacking, he triumphantly held up each item before placing it on the nearby counter. There were four industrial-size tins of soup, large cartons of Saltines and Graham crackers, an enormous jar of peanut butter, another of grape jelly, and a huge container of Ovaltine. "Last but not least," he said, hefting the final item, "a couple of weeks' worth of canned orange juice. With Vitamin C. In case you need extra." His gaze slid to my belly and away.

At last we were making some progress—he was almost ready to admit I wasn't merely getting fat. "That's all I could carry in one load. If you want the cookies I left in the car you'll have to come with me to get them."

He led our way through dark streets. "I'm starting to like these pre-dawn hikes," he said valiantly, zipping his jacket up to the chin. "I can see why you're always roaming around early. Seems like the whole world is ours."

"We might be the only two people awake," I said, freezing inside his beige camel-hair coat. I could no longer fit into my own. What would I wrap myself in once I outgrew his? A tent?

This time Pepper was parked even farther away from the high-rise. I would have walked right past her if Lucius hadn't stopped me. "I splurged on a canvas cover," he explained with satisfaction. "Best disguise I could think of. Frost-proof, too. Though it didn't keep out the cold." He started to pull off a gray tarp so stiff with ice that it retained its shape when we put it on the sidewalk. "See?" he said, rubbing his fingertips across Pepper's windshield. "Clean and clear." He made a half-hearted attempt to fold the tarp before pushing the frigid shape in my direction. "Try stomping it flat while I warm up the engine."

I pointed to a piece of paper someone had stuck under one of the wiper blades. "What's that?"

He pulled it loose and unfolded it, exposing the primitive pencil sketch of a stick figure hanging from a rope, its head to one side, the crude printing underneath spelling two words:

UPPITY NIGGER

Lucius gasped as if somebody had punched him in the stomach.

"Well," I said, breaching his stunned silence. "They managed to find her again, didn't they?"

He balled the paper and flung it at my feet. "This settles it, Maria! No more backtalk—I want you packed and ready to go when I get home from work this afternoon. I'm taking you to your mother's." He rummaged in Pepper's interior and thrust a filled grocery sack at me before folding himself behind the steering wheel. I picked up the crushed note and stuffed it in my coat while the starter motor labored and caught. He pulled the choke and pumped the accelerator until white smoke billowed from the exhaust pipe.

"Hannes and Mutti are hiking around the Ammersee today," I said, raising my voice to compete with the rough sound of the engine. "No telling how late she'll come home tonight. Or if. Their last outing before the weather turns."

He scraped at a spot on the windshield where the fog was beginning to etch on some frost flowers. "Don't look now, but I think it already has. Let's hope she's wearing her winter coat."

I said what had been on my mind a lot lately: "The Americans wouldn't be able to bother us half as much if you hadn't bought Pepper."

"They wouldn't bother us at all if we hadn't moved in that blasted high-rise," he countered as if the words had been waiting on the tip of his tongue.

"Well, we did." It was as close to apologizing for something that wasn't my fault as I wanted to get. With more bravado than I really felt I added, "And I don't care what you say, I'm not about to let them chase me out of our little apartment."

"Yeah. Well. What does that make you except a big fat fool?" He slammed the car door.

I clawed it open. "Why are you so ugly to me? We used to be friends!"

His eyes raked over me, top to bottom. "It's you who've turned ugly. Or haven't you noticed?" He yanked the door out of my hands, slammed it again, pushed the car into gear, and floored the pedal. Since the engine was still cold Pepper jerked forward in fits and starts, bucking to and around the next corner.

I kicked the gray tarp to the ground and stomped on it, shattering ice crystals. By the time I'd managed to roll the stiff canvas my hands had turned purple and the fog, rising from iced lawns, was shimmering with the promise of daylight.

Ten minutes later I crossed the dim parking lot and saw Walt tie a floppy mattress to the roof of the Renault. The rear of the car was crammed full of bundles. I stopped, stricken. "You're moving!"

He paused, looking irate. "Yep. We finally found a room somewhere else. Mind you, it's even smaller—but then, anything's better than what we've been going through since we moved into this place."

"Where is your new room?" I asked, suddenly suspicious. "What's the address?"

With an incredulous laugh, he stepped back and said roughly, "You'll never hear it from me." His gaze shifted to

Naoko who was emerging from of the lobby door carrying Tommy. Walt tightened the ropes around the mattress. "Look," he said, his voice mellowing. "I wish you luck. But tell your husband if he cares anything about you — and himself — he'll get you out, too."

"We'll be fine!" I stammered. "Just fine!"

"Yeah, right," he drawled, tying a vicious knot. "That's what I used to tell Naoko!"

Knowing I'd been dismissed I went on, stopping in front of Naoko. With a polite bow, I said, "I'm sorry you're leaving but I hope you'll be happier in your new place."

A shadow passed over her face. "Is very small. But peaceful, I think."

While the elevator was laboring to the fourth floor I realized some part of me considered their move a surrender. If we stuck it out why couldn't they?

Upstairs, I put the grocery sack on the counter, dropped the wet tarp on the bathroom linoleum, and took a hot shower. When I was done I tossed the tarp into the tub, wondering if I could get it to fit in the downstairs dryer. Then I stared at myself in the bathroom mirror from every angle, deciding I was every bit as ugly as Lucius had claimed. I dressed myself in loose layers of cotton and wool and knelt by the wall radiator trying to figure out how to raise the indoor temperature. I was still fiddling with a dial when someone rang the doorbell.

It was Hannes, wearing green suede Bundhosen with matching woollen knee-socks and a Trachtenjacke the same shade of gray as his eyes.

"I didn't know you had our address," I said, dumbfounded.

"I asked the manager, of course," he answered, rushing past me before I had a chance to invite him in. He paced around the living room, making me glad I'd helped Lucius fold up the couch before we left the apartment. Then he stopped and said, "Something is wrong with your Mutti. When was the last time you talked to her?"

I pulled out a chair for him at the table. "A couple of days ago. She told me you were taking her to the Ammersee today."

"Exactly!" He sat and fiddled with our salt and pepper shakers. "I have to fly to London tomorrow. I wanted us to enjoy the end of Indian summer together. It'll be gone when I get back. Oh." He reached inside his jacket for a packet of photos, depositing it in front of me. "From our dinner party." His fingers drummed on the table. With visible effort he forced them to lie still. "We planned an early start this morning. Frau Farber packed us a basket of goodies for the occasion. But when I got to the farmhouse Lotte wouldn't let me in. Both doors were locked and every shutter latched from the inside. When I put an ear to the one at the kitchen window I distinctly heard her crying inside." His mouth tightened. Then he asked, "Any idea why she was weeping?"

As far as I knew she had never needed much of a reason. "None," I said diplomatically. "Maybe Anna . . ." No point mentioning she and I were not on speaking terms these days.

"Anna. Of Course," he said. "Your Mutti told me yesterday morning that they were planning to meet for lunch." He jumped up. "Come. Let's go."

I made a move toward the packet of photos. He took my arm and propelled me out the door. I didn't realize he knew Anna's address too but after we entered her building he found the right floor and the right apartment with no trouble. He leaned on her bell without getting a response, then began knocking loud enough for the sound to reverberate up and down the long corridor. Any moment I expected scowling, disheveled faces to appear at the other doors to protest the unholy ruckus.

Soon Anna capitulated and croaked from within, "Ja, Augenblick, bitte (just a second)!" Then she stood before us, squinting at the hall light. And what a spectacle she was, her brows worn off, her eyes puffy and ringed with yesterday's smeary blue shadow, her expensive flip hanging greasy and limp. Even her robe was decidedly unglamorous, especially since the two top buttons were missing.

"Hannes!" she grunted, shielding her face with one hand while tightening her grip on the upper part of the robe with the other.

He hardly gave her a glance but preceded her into the living room and paced back and forth, coming to rest at the window, where he rocked on the balls of his feet and stared out at traffic. "Your Mutti has barricaded herself inside the old farmhouse. I could hear her crying. You saw her yesterday. Any idea what it's about?"

"Ja, doch (oh yes)," Anna said, barely polite. "I know what it's about. Mutti lost her job and it's all *her* fault!" She stabbed her finger at me and though it didn't make contact I felt the keen edge of her anger.

Hannes looked from my face to hers. "Explain. What do you know?"

She ran a stealthy hand over her eyes, searching for the two missing brows. "Only that O.F. crashed into the inner office of her boss just before noon and made such a scene that Mutti couldn't bring herself to stay on. She told me she *had* to quit because she'd lost the respect of the entire office staff. And we all know why, don't we?"

Hannes actually blinked. Then he said sharply, "Nonsense! She should have come to me. I'd soon have smoothed everything out."

"Oh, really? What's to smooth out?" Anna's tone had grown belligerent. "Her reputation is ruined. She *said* you wouldn't understand. She needs to be alone for a while. I don't want to be rude, Hannes, but I think she's starting to hate men. *All* men."

"Then her *daughters* will have to comfort her. Come, Anna, get dressed. I'm taking you both —"

She backed away. "Not me! But by all means, take Maria. She has nothing better to do. I've made other plans for today. Plans I can't cancel on such short notice."

Hannes stared at her as if he'd never seen her before. "Keeping late hours these days?" he said. "Enjoying yourself?"

She stuck out her chin, a mannerism unconsciously borrowed from our mother's repertoire. "I learned long ago that when Mutti cries we best leave her to it. She'll stop when she's done and not a second before."

"I'll go, Hannes," I said, eager to leave Anna's inhospitable presence. "If you'll give me a few minutes to pack. I did promise you I'd stay with her, at your party."

His face relaxed, erasing the vertical worry line from his forehead. "You remembered! Five minutes?"

"Ten," I said, trying to be realistic.

He looked at his watch. "We'll start the count-down when we get to your lobby. I'll wait for you there." He strode toward the door, then turned, pulled out another packet of photos, and slapped them on Anna's dusty coffee table.

While he sat in the lobby I took the lift upstairs, tossed some clothes and my toothbrush into a carry-all, added a tin of cookies from the grocery sack, and pulled the Army cot out of the closet. Then I left Lucius a terse note. "Hannes came to get me. Don't know when I'll be back." There. That would show him.

With a couple of minutes to spare I spread out the photos Frau Farber had taken. We were on the green couch, laughing together, shot glasses in hand. I was sitting on Lucius's lap, his arms around me. Both of us full of ourselves. His red silk tie. My sleek cap of hair. His white Italian suit. My polished lips.

His blinding smile. My narrow waist in the slinky black dress. The scrumptious Black Forest Cherry cake behind us. Just last month I'd been gorgeous. Now all I had left to prove it were a few glossy pictures. Who would have guessed? I left them on the counter and walked away; a second look might have moved me to tears.

"It was a splendid evening," I told Hannes as he drove us through the city. "I must thank you again."

"It was fine," he said. "I especially enjoyed watching your exuberant roll down Somersault-Hill."

"And Alex's," I added, fighting a quick surge of envy because the dog could be at home there in a way I'd never be.

Upon hearing his name Alex rose from the back seat, thrust his big muzzle into the space between the two front seats, and blew at my ear.

"It was Lucius who latched the shutters for Mutti," I explained, stroking his massive head. "After O.F. showed up at her doorstep last week." I went on to describe that morning's events, including Lucius's spectacular race with the white VW.

"She never mentioned a thing," Hannes said, clearly on edge. "I was right—the detective did follow her home. He must have passed on the address to O.F. who lost no time stopping by for a joyous reunion. When that didn't work he went to Phase Two: getting her fired so she'd have no income. Now he'll let her stew in her Angst for a few days. Then he'll reappear to magnanimously forgive her brief try at freedom— offering her lifelong financial dependence instead." He pulled into the farmyard. "Before you climb out you have to promise me you'll stay with Lotte until this crisis is over. Remind her that she has . . . options."

He held out his hand and I solemnly shook it. He unloaded his picnic basket and my cot, set them both down in front of her door, and knocked. There was no response. He called her name, sounding forlorn. That effort, too, proved in vain.

When he returned to the car I asked, "What if she won't open up for me either?"

"Of course she will," he said firmly. "The moment I'm gone. You're her daughter. She loves you. I might as well start my trip today. That way I can wrap up the meetings early."

"What options *does* she have, Hannes? What do I tell her?"

"That I'll help her find a better job. I have many connections." He looked off into the distance as if weighing two conflicting thoughts. Then he unlocked the trunk, removing a brown leather leash, a plaid horse blanket, and a thick glass bowl. "Frau Farber has decided to visit her sister while I'm away. I *was* going to take Alex to his favorite kennel tonight—but on second thought, I'll feel more comfortable leaving him here."

Astounded, I asked, "You're lending Mutti your dog? For how long?"

"For as long as it takes. You've seen Alex in action. He's more useful than an entire police squadron."

I recalled the phenomenal rapport I'd witnessed between man and dog at the garden pond. "What commands do we give him? How will he know what we want?"

Alex jumped out of the Mercedes and sat down in front of me, calmly meeting my eyes. He already knew.

Hannes rummaged in the glove compartment and pulled out an envelope. Opening it, he showed me a key and stuffed a couple of large DM bills in beside it. "Alex eats mostly raw meat and bones, though yogurt and fruit are his passion. Tell Lotte to go to my butcher for our standing order." He lowered his voice. "I asked Frau Farber to tidy your Mutti's favorite guest room—in case she needs to get away. But don't mention the key until she's in a more receptive mood or she'll fling it into the bushes."

I laughed in spite of myself and marveled at how well he already knew her.

He gave my shoulder a squeeze. "Trust me. Everything will turn out all right." Putting a light finger between the dog's eyes, he said to him, softly, "This place will suit you, my friend. You can roam the fields and guard the house. Your best line of work. Alex?"

The black dog sat erect, his ears rotating forward.

"Gib acht (watch out)!" Hannes told him. And then he left us.

CHAPTER 24

ALEX CONTINUED TO SIT, listening to the receding engine noise. I went to the door without him. Mutti
opened it before I had a chance to knock, her eyebrows intact.
Red-eyed and wet-cheeked, she craned her head toward the
road. "Was that Hannes I heard driving away?"

"He thought you needed some daughterly company," I
said. "Anna would have come too but she has a previous
engagement."

Mutti nodded. "Her new friend Rupert wants to make
sure she's from reputable stock—so she's taking him to Vati's
for dinner. It seems the rest of us don't qualify."

"Good thinking," I said. "I have a feeling he and Vati are
cut from the same cloth. Does she realize that?"

Mutti's lips stretched to a fleeting smile. "Not in the least.
She has become blind and dull-witted. A common affliction of
the women in this family."

Since I was neither, she couldn't possibly be hinting I was on that very short list. I showed her the basket. "From Hannes. Breakfast and lunch for two."

She sighed. "We were going to Andechs for dinner."

"The beer-brewing monastery?"

"The monks have a fine restaurant. You should take Lucius there while the weather still holds." She burst into tears. "Ach, die Männer (oh, men)! They're all the same. Everywhere."

"Including Lucius?"

She blew her nose then gingerly dabbed at her inflamed cheeks. "He won me over too fast. With his sunny smile. I should have asked him some hard questions right at the start. Or so Anna said. Rupert spent a year in New York and he knows—"

"—about Lucius and me?"

"Not exactly. And Anna hopes he never will. He has a very low opinion of—ach Gott (good God), is that Alex?"

The dog had trailed after me and stood wagging his tail.

She looked around wildly. "Are you helping Hannes play some kind of trick to get me to unlock the door? Where is he hiding?"

"Oh, please!" I protested. "You know as well as I do that Hannes doesn't play tricks. Since you canceled the hike he's decided to fly out a day early. He thought Alex would be good company for you, is all. It's Lucius who asked me to spend some time with you. That's why he bought me this folding bed. Mind if I try it out? Here? Tonight?"

I picked up the cot, slapped my thigh, and said, "Come inside, Alex."

"But I just mopped my floor!" she said, blocking his access. "I bet he's got muddy paws!" The two of them measured each other. It was clear he would not venture another step unless he was invited.

"He can play with your mice," I told her, lightly snapping my fingers the way I'd seen Hannes do.

Ignoring me, Alex continued to sit outside the threshold, his gaze only on Mutti. At last he offered his paw as if to show her that it was clean.

She ignored it. "And what am I supposed to feed him? He eats like a horse and I doubt he'll be interested in boiled potatoes — which is all I have on hand."

At the edge of the clearing the sun was tearing a hole through the mantle of fog. "Oh, look," I said. "It'll be beautiful at the Ammersee. You should have gone."

She squinted skyward. "The light hurts my eyes. And I'm getting miserably cold. I suppose you might as well tell Alex to come in."

Even though the sun tried to squeeze a pencil-thin emissary through the shutter slats the kitchen remained shrouded in gloom. The bedding on the couch was in disarray. She pushed her covers aside and sat. Alex put his great head on her knees. Mutti reached out to touch him but stifled the impulse. "Why isn't Frau Farber taking care of him?"

I slid the table toward her and unpacked an array of breakfast pastries, sandwich wedges, fruit, and a large thermos with two cups. "She decided to take a vacation. That's why Hannes is relying on you."

She gave a decisive grunt. "I'm sure it's only because he couldn't find anyone else on such short notice. Why didn't he *ask* me first? He's always trying to manage things. In that he's no different from the men I married. I admired his strength as a boss — but sometimes I suspect he'd make a very pushy husband. Thank God I'll never have to find out. I'm done with romance, even if I wind up in the poorhouse. Which I probably will."

I chose an almond-studded tart filled with poppy-seed paste and savored the first bite. Keeping my voice low in an effort to model reasonableness, I said, "How could he have asked you to watch Alex when you refused to speak to him? The tarts are delicious. You should try one."

"I have absolutely no appetite," she said, crushing her handkerchief. "But don't let that stop you. I know you like Frau Farber's cooking better than mine."

I pushed her pillow aside and sat in the space it had occupied on the sheet. The linens were soaked with her tears. So was the couch fabric underneath. Scrambling onto the armrest, I offered Alex a liverwurst sandwich. He averted his muzzle and whined.

"Spoiled dog!" Mutti huffed. "There's nothing I have he'll want to eat."

I took the money out of the envelope. "Hannes left you some cash for the butcher. Now tell me — what have you got against Lucius all of a sudden? He adores you. And I thought you liked him."

"That was before."

"Before what?"

"Before Rupert told Anna how despised Negroes are in America. He's seen them living in paper-thin shacks, on dirt floors. He says our cattle have better shelter. No running water. No toilets."

"So we'll have an outhouse. Like on Hilde's farm. And here."

"Rats and roaches, Rupert said."

"Horst has roaches and you have mice. They're related to rats, aren't they?"

"Mice are harmless. Rats jump into bassinets and gnaw babies' necks," she corrected, absently stroking the dog's back. "They live in clumps."

"The rats?"

"The Negroes. You'll be the only white woman for miles. Surrounded by heroin addicts, prostitutes, and thugs. Rupert said most of them are alcoholics. "

I bit into a croissant, dropping crumbs all over the sheet. "Just like in München. Only here they get drunk on beer. As for prostitutes—I've already *been* surrounded by those. Remember?"

She shook her soggy handkerchief at me. "You have an answer for everything. What about the baby then? You want him in the middle of that?"

I shrugged. "Lucius and I won't be living in America for a long time. For the next six years we'll be stationed far away from there and from here. Longer, if he makes a career in the Army. Have one of these. They're still warm." I held out a croissant but she pushed it away, keeping a hand on Alex, who gazed at her with such affection that she offered him another liverwurst sandwich. He accepted it with great dignity.

I said, "See? He likes you better than me!"

"He's known me longer," she said, not even trying to demur. Then she took a shaky breath. "You must get a divorce, Maria. An annulment would be even better. If you weren't pregnant we could fix everything." She wept into her hands. "After O.F. disrupted the office yesterday my new boss looked me right in the eyes and said in front of everybody, 'Children like that are abominations. They should never be born. There's no place for them in this world.'" She bent double, sobbing. "And then he said I ought to be ashamed for helping you ruin your life. And I am!"

Something inside me buzzed to signal we'd arrived at a low point in our relationship. I ceased to belong in the same room with her—or on the same planet. Having borne all the abuse I possibly could I stepped outside for some fresh air, pacing the farm yard.

I'd trusted her. Worse, Lucius had trusted her. Because she seemed to love him, I knew he was lovable. Because she valued his good qualities, I was proud I'd chosen a man who possessed them. With her encouragement I'd grown into my new identity as a woman, ready to leave my daughter-role behind. Now I knew that any identity separate from hers was a thin-walled soap bubble easily pricked and exploded — leaving only hot air. A collapsing illusion just like my marriage. Without it, what did I have to fall back on? Nothing but a clinging, ambivalent mother who would soon consider me a millstone-child. *With* child. A nightmarish cipher.

I ached for Lucius because I understood how important Mutti had been to him. He'd already lost Anna's good will through no fault of his own. Mutti's betrayal would cut much deeper. Sure, I'd been a bit envious of the bond between them — but secretly pleased just the same. Now he had no one but me and I knew I wasn't enough.

Following an anger-fueled impulse I decided to desert my carry-all, the cot, and Alex, and stomped off toward the rail station and home. It was a long walk on a narrow road meandering past open fields and patches of woods. Halfway to Pasing, I heard a faraway locomotive whistle — and came to my senses. I listened to the train rumble somewhere near the horizon. It would take me an hour to reach the tracks, a couple more to get to the station.

Unexpectedly, I felt ashamed. Hadn't I promised Hannes I'd stay no matter what? Even the dog had more integrity than I did; he would never desert his post.

And then I stopped walking. It was true her ravings had driven me away from the farmhouse, but it was also true that Lucius's insulting behavior made me reluctant to return to the city. And yet I had only those two choices. So I walked on, preferring whatever awaited me in the high-rise to the harping from my out-of-work mother. Considering what the word "options" meant for her and for me, I understood she had a better selection than I would ever have.

*

THE NOTE I had left for Lucius was still lying on the table, undisturbed. I threw it into the trash. Scanning the wall calendar, I saw I had scheduled an OB appointment at the Second Field Hospital for tomorrow. I'd return to the farmhouse from there. An extra day of stewing would give Mutti a chance to calm down and start counting her blessings.

No sooner had I settled on the couch with my latest book than someone rang the bell, keeping a finger on it until I ran to open the door. Anna was scowled at me from the corridor. She was dressed in a bewitching new trench coat resplendent with a rainbow-like shimmer, a pale-blue scarf at her throat. Her eyebrows and hair were at their best.

"I was hoping I'd find you here," she said, sounding grim. "Is Lucius in?"

"Well—no. Not yet."

"I'm not surprised," she said, pushing past me for a quick tour around the bachelorette. "He isn't home much these days, is he? In fact, I haven't seen his little red car in the lot for ages. Has he grown tired of you now that you're losing your figure?"

"Of course not," I said. "He's working late."

Anna snorted. "Is that what he told you? Well, guess again." She gave a nasty laugh, reminiscent of Vati's. "Rupert just drove me home—by way of Hohenzollernstrasse. And what do you think I saw parked in front of the whorehouse? A bright red Simca Plein Ciel with American license plates."

The empty space inside me became weighted by the heaviest stone, forcing me to sit. "I'm sure there's a good reason," I mumbled, feeling faint.

"No doubt," she said coldly. "Although you might be the last to know it. Have you any idea what he's capable of?"

I hid my hands behind my back so she wouldn't see that my fingers were trembling. "You liked him well enough before you met your Nazi police lieutenant," I pointed out.

She yanked off her scarf and coat to display a long-sleeved velveteen dirndl, virgin-pink *and* low-cut, and sat down across from me, glaring. "Not *my* police lieutenant. Not anymore. Thanks to you."

It seemed to me I'd been hearing that phrase a lot lately. Digging my fingers into the upholstery behind me, I asked, "Oh? What did I do now?"

She concentrated on folding her scarf, starting out almost mildly. "Do you know *why* I couldn't take Hannes up on his kind offer to take me to Mutti's?"

I risked a nod.

"I suppose she mentioned Rupert was getting serious and wanted to meet my family? My family! What a laugh! I'd already told him *you* were at a boarding school in Switzerland. And I couldn't very well take him to Mutti's hole-in-the-wall. So, being desperate, I asked Vati to invite us to dinner, thinking he was at least capable of giving a good first impression, big house and all. Mensch (man), was I wrong! Gitta still has candles on every sill. She insists on keeping them lit in the middle of the day. She told Rupert, in a crazy sing-song voice, that if she lets even one candle go out her next baby will die."

A flutter stirred in my belly, escaping through my mouth as a sigh.

"Vati was sourer than ever," she continued after a censoring look. "Either the price of candles was ruining his appetite or he's coming down with the flu. His face was all yellow and when he started to eat it actually turned green. He took one look at the soup — liver dumpling — and ran to the bathroom, gagging."

Unbidden, the memory of a long-ago Sunday found the three-year-old me hiding under the table, hopelessly chewing a big mouthful of braised liver while above me Vati predicted that if no one forced to swallow the evil wad I would grow up to be insufferably spoiled.

Now he knew what it was like.

"Gitta assumed he was insulting her cooking again," Anna went on, "so she decided to retaliate while he was safely out of the room—by mentioning the black sheep of the family, her even blacker husband, and the fact that they *had* to get married."

My knees twitched. "Did not," I protested. Her sneer was answer enough. An invisible tremor ran down the entire length of my legs. I desperately wanted to kick something—preferably her. Instead I pinched myself and watched her face inflate with a mixture of pity and scorn.

"Pillow or not, you still had to get married," she said. "As you well know."

By pushing my toes against the parquet I managed to keep them grounded while the rest of me fought the compulsion to claw her face.

"Rupert politely finished his soup," she continued, hardhearted, "wiped his lips and his hands on Gitta's best linen napkin, said he didn't believe in wasting his time on bad prospects, and quoted the old stand-by, 'Show me your family and I'll show you who you are.' Then he insisted on taking me home before Vati had a chance to return from the bathroom. On the long drive Rupert lectured me on how you had forever destroyed the family reputation. Because of *your* bad choices no decent man could ever marry *me*, even if he wanted to. Seems I have become an outcast merely by being related to you."

She stood up, shook out her scarf, and wrapped it around her white throat. "That's why I came—to thank you for making me a pariah. In case you were wondering what kind of future I have, the answer is *none*." She brought the scarf's ends to her eyes, blotting furiously.

Incredulous, I said, "And you believed him? If you ask me you ought to be glad you found out what a shit he is before you put on his ring! *Horst* doesn't think being my sister makes you an outcast." I was amazed that my mouth still worked even though the rest of me, part after part, seemed to be shutting down.

"Horst doesn't like dancing," she said. "He has no muscles to speak of and when he bows his head I can see a bald patch on top."

"And Rupert is perfect, I suppose. Full head of hair, fat wallet and all."

"He has a superb body," she hissed. "And a very discerning mind!"

"And I'm sure he told you so. Repeatedly." I rubbed my numb shins. "In my opinion we did you a favor by scaring him off."

"Don't do me any more favors," she snapped, borrowing Vati's most sarcastic tone. "I'll try the architect next, but — " She narrowed her eyes. " — as far as he's concerned I have no sister and my mother is on an extended vacation. Maybe I'll give the whole bunch of you a Canadian address. Near the North Pole."

Now my hands had gone dead. When I rubbed them together it was like touching a corpse. "I have a better idea," I said. "Why don't you move there yourself and save us the trouble? Take your fancy ball gowns and matching slippers and go dance with Santa Claus."

She blinked. "Who's that?"

"An old man who lives at the Pole."

She raised her chin. The added stretch erased her incipient jowls. "I wouldn't dream of moving away," she said, looking down at me past Vati's classic Roman nose. "Unlike you, ich bin eine echte Münchnerin (I was born in Munich)!"

This back-handed way of reminding me that I was born on a godforsaken farm in the middle of nowhere was the worst insult she could think of. Retrieving her shimmering coat, she slipped her arms into the sleeves. The entire inside was lined with blue-plaid, finely spun wool. "Promise me something," she said when her hand was on the door handle. "If you see me out walking with someone, don't wave. And don't come to my place uninvited."

A fine punch-line, I had to admit. As she marched out I shouted defiantly at her back: "Horst's place, you mean. It isn't even yours!"

In revenge, she slammed my front door against the wall and left it that way, clicking her furious heels toward the elevator until the sound grew faint and fainter. After it was entirely gone I lost the use of my mouth and sat petrified, staring helplessly out into the empty corridor.

CHAPTER 25

SOMEWHERE IN MY DREAMS I FELT the warmth of a face, bending over mine. But when I opened my eyes in the morning I was alone. Even though I could hear low rumblings coming from the radiator the room was so cold that I stumbled to the window just to make sure it was properly shut. Below, the city was pewter and ice. Wearing Lucius's coat, I took the city bus to Warner and caught the American bus to the other end of town.

In the hospital a nurse weighed, measured, pricked and poked me. Afterwards I timidly delivered a cup of warm pee to the lab window. Then I settled on a lounge chair in the lobby, waiting for my doctor to be free. I watched Americans come, mill, and go through the wide glass entrance. The children were loud, the women cat-eyed and snub-nosed with white bobby-socks, mohair sweater sets, and skirts that went midway to their calves. Unlike me they seemed comfortable inside their own skins.

I sat gazing at the cotton ball taped to the inside of my elbow, the immaculate whiteness marred by a small spot of blood. All at once the light in the waiting room seemed to grow noticeably brighter. A young couple had paused just outside the glass doors, holding hands, their arms bare. They seemed to be bathed in a golden glow. Something about the fond gaze they exchanged, or the yellow buttercups printed on her loose blouse, made me think of spring time and rainbows.

He opened the door for her. She took a step in then waited for him to catch up. On their way to the desk her blonde pigtails swayed, brushing her shoulders. The receptionist checked them in, then they chose seats right across from me, facing away from the glass doors. I smelled honeysuckle and tried not to stare, though they wouldn't have noticed since they had eyes only for each other.

Before she even started to sit he was already plumping the sofa cushions for her. As she lowered herself, he quickly thrust a pillow behind her back, then sat down so close beside her that their thighs touched. She wore something called a maternity outfit. I'd seen similar costumes at the PX but had found the belly-sized hole cut in front of the skirt so hilarious that I couldn't stop giggling. The girl's yellow-flowered top was long and ample, with plenty of spare room. The buttercups on it were surrounded by little green leaves. There was a ruffle of white lace on her collar. Her nose was upturned, too, but on her it looked pretty.

They beamed at each other, whispering. He took her small hands in both of his, making them look like little birds safe in the nest. After a while he massaged the back of her neck. She arched, leaning trustingly into his kneading hands. I heard him say in an awed tone, "Gosh, you're beautiful!"

I marveled at her matching yellow socks with lace trimmings, the pink, narrow sneakers, the way her cheeks bloomed afresh each time she smiled.

An older woman was crossing the lobby behind them, heading for the exit. She was wearing a mock sailor suit that reminded me of my least favorite childhood dress. Glancing toward the young couple, she stopped and called out, "Helen? John?" Sitting cheek to cheek, they remained oblivious until she put a gloved hand on the girl's shoulder, repeating their names.

They turned at the same time. The girl said, "Oh! Mrs. Fisher!"

"I thought it was you," the woman chuckled, sitting at Helen's free side. "I heard the good news. Congratulations! Harry and I think it's simply marvelous. Helen will make such a good mother, won't she, John? When are you due?"

"In April," Helen said, and I wanted to shout, "Me too, me too!"

"Wonderful. You must come see us. It's been ages since you baby-sat the kids. They still talk about the bedtime stories you used to tell them. Here, let's make a date. Why, I believe I'll organize a shower."

"But Mrs. Fisher . . ." Helen said.

"No, no, I insist. Besides, we have lots of baby stuff from the last one. Hope you haven't bought anything yet. You can even borrow the crib." She rummaged through her purse for a little black book and proceeded to leaf through the pages. "Sunday after next?" she asked, pencil poised.

"Well, you see, Mrs. Fisher—"

She wrote down a word and snapped the book shut. "Plan on spending the afternoon. We'll be delighted to have you. Oh, golly. Is that snow?" Beyond the glass, huge flakes danced to the ground, melting on the surface of puddles.

Helen turned. "Look, John," she breathed. "Aren't they pretty?"

"Reminds me of that glass jar on our dresser," he said. "The kind you shake," he elaborated for Mrs. Fisher.

She hooked her arm through her purse straps. "Thank goodness the ground's too wet for it to stick!" She hugged the girl, depositing a red stain on her cheek. "Your parents must be so thrilled. Their first grandchild. What an occasion. Well, I have to run. Good-bye, darlings. I'll see you in two weeks."

"Good-bye, Mrs. Fisher," they said in unison. Now it was John's turn to receive a motherly kiss. They watched her walk out, then each of them raised a hand to wipe lipstick smears from the other one's cheek.

"Good old Mrs. Fisher," John said.

Helen covered her mouth and giggled. "Six kids and she's letting us *borrow* the crib."

He put his lips to her ear and whispered something that made her blush. When she replied everyone sitting nearby leaned forward, hoping to hear.

I thought he'd said, "Do you think we can ever top her?"

She'd murmured, "Let's shoot for seven. It's always been my lucky number." She wove her fingers through his. "If she'd have let me get in a word edgewise I could have told her we've already got everything we need."

From far away, a nurse was shouting my name. I was so busy watching John's lips grazing Helen's plump, glowing cheek — and the approving smiles the gesture brought to the faces of their charmed audience — that it took me a few seconds to understand that the nurse was waiting for me to follow her. She was standing impatiently at the start of a corridor, holding a clipboard. I waved to let her know I was coming but she looked right through me. By the time I reached the spot on which she had been standing she was walking rapidly to the other end of the hall, leafing through my chart and shaking her head.

"Nurse?" I called. My voice couldn't span the distance between us. When I ran to catch up I realized my feet had gone numb.

Once my exam was over I lingered on the hospital's driveway, staring up at the swirling snow. My tennis shoes were already soaked from puddles hiding under a cover of slush. Shivering, I decided not to return to the farmhouse today. After I boarded the dependent bus I replayed every move the young couple had made, every look they'd exchanged, every touch they had shared in full view of their rapt onlookers.

I could never have what came so easily to Helen and John.

Yet I wanted nothing else.

Just to be fair I'd give Lucius one last chance. I would wait for him until eight. If he didn't come home by then I'd lock myself in our bathroom, open the medicine cabinet, take out his stack of used double-edged razor blades, and slit both my wrists. I could only hope that whichever one of my loved ones eventually found my remains would always remember the sight.

By the time I arrived at the high-rise I was so numb that I hardly noticed someone had painted the outside of our apartment door with excrement during my absence. Bolting the door behind me, I kicked off my wet shoes and socks and curled up on the couch, waiting for the hours to pass. They seemed in no hurry. At eight-fifteen I sat down at our table and wrote Lucius a short farewell note. Five minutes later I studied my doomed face in the medicine cabinet's mirror, picked up the top razor blade, and, wincing, began the first cut, wishing I had access to a bottle of sleeping pills instead. It would have been so much more convenient to swallow a couple of dozen, lie down, and close my eyes. Forever.

I had to make do with material on hand. After a few minutes of steady sawing I realized there must be some kind of trick to successful wrist-slashing I knew nothing about. The blue veins I was after were actually rolling away from the slippery blade, and even though the cuts I was inflicting did hurt, my wrists seemed uninterested in bleeding. The best I could get was a meager trickle running down each arm. At eight-thirty I unlocked the bathroom door, opened the living room window, and sat on the sill, determined to jump. The thought of what I was about to do was making me dizzy. Afraid of heights, I turned over to lie on my stomach and slid slowly out over the sill, gripping its rim until my bare feet found the pigeon-ledge, gooey with droppings. Was I high enough for a fall to kill me outright or would I simply shatter my bones on the cement sidewalk and live out the rest of my life confined to a wheelchair? Would I pulp my face on the concrete and be horrendously ugly forevermore? Would I even dare to let go of the sill?

Down below, a woman wearing a dark-green Loden cape was crossing the parking lot. Idly, she looked up and saw me clinging to the wall. She stopped and stared. A man in a black greatcoat, exiting the lobby, wondered what she was staring at, traced her line of vision, and noticed me too. In a matter of minutes the sidewalk was packed with curious bystander waiting for the big event. The woman who had seen me first said, in German," Someone should call the police."

The man in the black coat asked, "You think she's serious? She looks awfully young."

Someone shouted at me, "Get back inside, fool!"

Then a hateful voice shrilled in English, "Hey! If she wants to jump, let her!" It was Linda of course, flanked by her two lackeys. They immediately created a catchy refrain, shouting, "Jump, fool, jump!"

I closed my eyes and pretended no one was there while I tried to gather some courage. My fingers were beginning to slip to the edge of the sill.

"Go ahead, jump," Linda yelled up at me. "Don't make us stand out here in the cold for nothing!"

A few windows to the left on my floor, the Swiss with the high forehead leaned out and shouted back in guttural English, "Have you not done enough damage tonight? I saw what you did to her door!" Then he addressed the rest of the crowd in his hard-to-decipher Swiss-German. "Anyone got a telephone? We should request a fire engine. She'll never climb back in by herself."

Then I saw Anna hurrying along the sidewalk, followed by the manager. Passing the spectators she glanced briefly in my direction and ran toward the entrance. Herr Pfeifer slowed to yell at the crowd, "You should all be ashamed of yourselves! Go home at once!"

If I wanted to execute my plan this was the moment to get on with it. But my fingers insisted on renewing their precarious hold. Part of me was relieved. Part of me was ashamed of the base cowardice I couldn't seem to overcome.

And then Herr Pfeifer and Anna were in the window above me, looking down. "Here," Anna said, reaching. "We'll help you back up."

The manager grasped my other hand. If either of them had let go I would have tumbled off the ledge backwards. But they held on, slowly reeling me in. The bump in my belly blocked me from passing smoothly over the sill. They kept at it until the three of us sat on the parquet floor, panting.

"Who smeared your door?" Herr Pfeifer asked. "The Americans?"

I nodded, feeling bereft because I had been cheated out of an honorable demise. The truth was I couldn't get anything right. Not even this. Making fists and pummeling my belly, I moaned, "I don't want to be here anymore!"

"That's absurd," Anna snapped. "Here's where you belong. You *and* the baby."

"Why?" I asked. "Nobody wants us. Not even Mutti. Or you."

"You don't have to believe everything you hear. It's entirely possible he'll grow up to be somebody important. So might you—if only you'll let yourself. Come, you need a doctor to see to your wrists."

She helped me get into some warm clothes and boots and then we followed the manager to his office. He let Anna use his phone to call Horst. While we waited for him to drive over from the atelier Herr Pfeifer took the phone as far as the cord would stretch and engaged in a couple of low-toned angry conversations.

I was sure Anna meant to come to the hospital with me but she decided to leave before Horst could get here. The last thing she said was that she intended to mop up every drop of blood I'd spilled before tackling my apartment door.

The manager held up his hand. "Don't touch the door, Fräulein Edel. I am arranging for the perpetrators to clean it themselves. As part of a package deal." His smile was grim. "Unless they'd rather move out."

*

HORST ran every red light we encountered on our way across town. I was impressed with his sense of urgency since my wrists, resting on folded hand-towels, had almost stopped bleeding. He took me to the Second Field Hospital emergency room, where he browsed through an old National Geographic while the doctor on call tended my wounds, gave me a tetanus shot, and expertly applied twin bandages. When he was done he made me wait in his office cubicle for a psychiatrist from upstairs.

The psychiatrist, a short, rotund man wrapped in an over-sized lab coat, sank onto the chair vis-à-vis and crossed his legs. His shoes were immense. Opening a notebook, he clicked the end of a ballpoint pen. "You must have been pretty mad at someone to go to all this trouble," he said, sounding weary.

I was astonished. "Mad? Me? I never get mad."

He made a notation. "Hormones, maybe. Sometimes women get kind of odd when they're pregnant. You have a marital spat?"

"I'm not odd," I said coolly. "And what's a spat?"

He put the pen on the inside crease of the notebook and lowered it on to his lap. His eyes, magnified by horn-rimmed glasses, were not unkind. "I'm supposed to write up a report about your . . . mishap. If I say you're mentally unbalanced it'll go in your file. They may not allow you into the States. A spat is a misunderstanding. Let me ask you a question. Did you really mean to kill yourself?"

I gave an elaborate shrug, wondering how to explain something I hadn't thought out for myself. It wasn't that I had wanted to die, exactly, but that I didn't want to go on living. There was a big difference. Finally I said, "I just wanted the bad stuff to stop."

"How juvenile of you." He picked up the pen. "Precisely what you'd expect from a sixteen-year-old. Next time try *talking* things out — or else someone will deliver you to the unit upstairs where every window and door is barred."

"Why?" I asked, shocked.

He shifted, tapping the notebook against unpolished shoe leather. "By law, attempted suicides get locked up until they change their minds."

I was dumfounded. Surely what I did with my life was nobody's business but my own. But I didn't say it out loud. What I said was, "No. I do not want to die."

"Atta girl!" He patted my knee. "You'll be all right. I'll just have a short word with your husband. Then you can go."

Once I explained that Horst was merely a kind-hearted neighbor the psychiatrist made another notation in his book, shut it, and waved me out anyway.

"So," Horst said a few minutes later as we settled ourselves on the car seats in the dark lot. "You've had a bad day. I know what that's like. If you let them things will get better. For you. Do you want me to drive you back home?"

Another night alone in the high-rise was more than I could bear. Especially after my debut as local clown. I tugged the cuffs of my sleeves over my wrists and bent my arms to make sure the white gauze remained covered. "Take me to Mutti's," I said. "I believe she's expecting me." She was so busy with her own unfortunate life she wouldn't even notice something was amiss with mine.

As Horst drove away from the hospital I had a vivid image of a limp alternate-me sprawling across my convertible sofa, sinking into a sleeping-pill-induced coma right about now. What a tidy way to slip toward that final oblivion undisturbed. Seductively easy — although perhaps a bit premature.

I rubbed Horst's slumped shoulders. "Don't give up on Anna. She volunteered to clean up my blood. There's hope for her yet."

And maybe even for me.

CHAPTER 26

THE THIN LAYER OF ACCUMULATED SNOW was no problem on our tarred, well-traveled city streets. But as soon as Horst veered on to the lonesome dirt track leading to the farmhouse the BMW's tires started to spin. Cautiously, he applied the brakes and said, "I can't risk getting stuck so far away from a phone. We'll have to walk from here."

"Not you," I said, climbing out. "You're wearing city shoes." I pointed to my winter boots. "I'll be all right on my own."

I stood in front of the car and watched Horst roll down his window, peer at the pink snow behind his tail-lights, and reverse until the tires gripped tarmac. Bathed fleetingly in twin beams, I waved as the BMW turned and waited until it disappeared from view. Then I began to feel quite alone. The night seemed to crouch all around me. I recalled my childhood fear of the dark.

The shimmering snow lit the ground under my feet as I hastened past the black forest toward the end of the lane. When I finally reached the farmhouse it looked deserted. Shrouded by shutters, the crumbling structure gave off no light. I tried the door to the stable but it was locked. I went around to the rear and knocked on a kitchen shutter, calling Mutti's name. When that brought no results I appealed to Alex who was no doubt a lighter sleeper than she, with superior hearing. Immediately, he gave a joyful yelp from inside the window and followed it with a couple of woofs from the other end of the room.

Mutti responded with a garbled, uncomplimentary phrase. Half a minute later she unlocked the outside door to the stable, wrapped in an ankle-length terry robe. "You didn't have to come back, you know," she said, bleary-eyed. "I really don't need you here."

It wasn't the welcome I'd expected or thought I deserved. My resolve to be patient and understanding with her left me. "All right," I said with a cool nod. "Then I'll just leave again. Good-bye." I managed to cross the entire front yard before she and Alex caught up with me.

"Where do you think you are going?" she cried, breathless.

"Back to München," I said, still walking.

She grasped the loose end of my coat. "Wait!"

I yanked the fabric out of her hand and said bitterly, "What for? I know when I'm not wanted."

"I never said I didn't *want* you," she said with an exasperated sigh. "Only that I don't *need* you. And since you're already here why don't we drink something hot before I drive you back to the station? I don't mean to hurt your feelings but I *did* tell you yesterday I'm not in the mood for company."

"Well, neither am I!" I resumed my march until I ran into a knee-high wall. It was Alex who had decided he'd had enough of our theatrics. He stared up at me and I stared down at him until there was no doubt about which one of us was in command. He gave a single bark, then pointed his muzzle toward the house. "All right, then," I said meekly, turning. "I could use a cup of strong peppermint tea."

Once we arrived in the dusky, freezing-cold kitchen, Mutti glanced briefly at me before she went to the sink. "You seem a bit pale. Are you okay?"

"Why wouldn't I be?" I said, covertly checking my sleeves to make sure the bandages weren't showing.

She filled her kettle at the sink. "I'm almost grateful you made me get up. I went to bed early, trying to save on firewood, but it got so cold I couldn't fall asleep. I spent the last couple of hours chattering my teeth and fretting. If the couch were a few centimeters wider I'd have invited Alex under my covers."

She didn't sound like the same woman who'd refused to allow the dog in the house yesterday morning. He was standing close by her side, completely at ease, watching her put the kettle on the cook stove, stir the coarse ashes inside the firebox, and stuff in a bundle of twigs. "Sit!" she said, pointing to the head of the couch. I thought she meant me and obeyed even faster than Alex did, plopping on to the cushions a moment before he could reach his blankets at my feet. Pleased with our hasty response, she continued in a more conciliatory tone, "I saved some of Frau Farber's sandwiches and pastries. Which do you prefer?"

"Both."

"Thought so." Squatting, she blew at bits of reddening coal until the dry twigs burst into flame, adding several pieces of deadfall before closing the firebox door. Then she kicked off her rubber boots to step into a pair of worn felt slippers, went out to the stable, and returned with the picnic hamper, shivering. "It's like a refrigerator out there." She lifted the hamper onto the table and, pressing both palms against the top, leaned forward to look fully at me for the first time since I came. "I'm perfectly all right, you know," she said with quiet conviction. "If O.F. comes back I'll tell him we're absolutely and definitely through and that I never want to see him again. What can he possibly threaten me with now that he's had me fired?"

"Not a thing!" I replied, admiring her spunk. "But will he believe you actually mean it?"

She stood on tiptoes to pull two cups off a high shelf. "He'd better!"

Brave words out of a mouth that used to moan "Franz, bitte nicht (please don't)!" every time he chased me around the kitchen table. How desperately she had wrung her hands the few times he caught me! By contrast, her fingers, now measuring crushed peppermint leaves into the tea egg, seemed steady and sure.

I slumped against the sofa's backrest, relieved. "You really *don't* need me, do you?"

She shook her head. "I ran out of tears hours ago. And then I got angry. Just bring him on. I'll give him an earful he won't soon forget!"

"A long-overdue earful," I said. Although I could never have admitted it to Hannes the mere idea of "saving" my mother from O.F. had made me quake deep inside; my stepfather's habit of bullying me throughout my formative years had made me an unspeakable coward. There was no way I could prevail against his maliciousness.

The kettle whistled. Mutti poured boiling water into her white china pot and put on the lid. "Have you heard from Anna? How did the dinner at Vati's go? Is she engaged yet?"

I grinned, reaching for a stale croissant. "That plan misfired. Vati and Gitta made such an unfavorable impression on Rupert that he insisted on dragging Anna out of their house right after the soup."

Her eyes filled with glee. "What was wrong with Gitta's soup?"

"It wasn't her soup. It was her mouth." I described the scene to her exactly the way Anna had described it to me, and concluded with, "So now Anna's interviewing the architect."

Mutti carried tea pot and empty cups to the table, sliding one toward me. "She's always had a good head on her shoulders," she said admiringly. "Unlike you and me she was born with a healthy dose of selfishness."

I laughed. "She must have inherited it from Vati."

"His is entirely *un*healthy. It's like salting broth. A little bit is good; too much spoils the whole pot. And poisons it, too."

One thing hadn't changed — she had no intention of giving up the habit of raging against Vati, not if she lived a hundred more years.

I dropped a sugar cube into my cup. "If you want to practice increasing *your* selfishness, start by asking Hannes to find you a new job."

She bristled. "What for? So that O.F. can get me fired again?"

She had a point.

"Why don't you demand your *old* job back, in his front office? Then you won't have to worry about O.F. coming around. Hannes will toss him out in a minute. Just like he did before."

She sat motionless. "Before what?"

Oops. He hadn't told her yet. Had I promised him I'd keep it a secret forever? Maybe it was high time someone told her the truth. So I did.

Her eyes grew round. "He threw O.F. out of his office?"

"Ordered the security guards to escort him out of the building."

"Oh," she said, looking impressed.

For good measure, I mentioned the detective who'd breached Hannes's hedge and Alex's reaction to the intruder. "That's why Hannes wanted his dog here with you—he's a trained Schutzhund (guard dog)."

"Oh," she said again, studying Alex with growing respect. He seemed to be dozing but his ears remained erect, ceaselessly sorting the airwaves for unusual sounds. "I'm afraid O.F. holds certain . . . unfounded suspicions. About Hannes and me. I don't suppose you've noticed how insanely jealous he is. Always has been—though I've never given him the slightest cause."

I chuckled. "I don't know about the jealous part, but I did notice that he's insane." The heat from the stove was beginning to warm the room. I unbuttoned my coat. "Remember the gnarled tree roots Lucius and I found in the forest for you? If you put a couple of those in the fire it won't go out till morning."

"An excellent idea. There should be enough in the stable to fill up the wood box. Here, this flashlight will help." She pressed it into my hand.

"B-But—" I said, unwilling to confess my reluctance to step into the dark all by myself. "Alex, want to come?"

He yawned at me from his blanket and shifted to a more comfortable position. I went to the stable without him. The flashlight beam played over the tidy hoard of cut branches lining the two long walls, then found a cache of unwieldy rejects in a corner. I sorted through the heap and put the toughest pieces into the wood box. When the flashlight beam brushed across the stable window I realized it was not shuttered. An oversight? I angled the flashlight shaft outside. No one had ever bothered to install shutters for this window; perhaps the cows had insisted on unfiltered light.

I played the light shaft over the pallid yard and saw that it had snowed again, the new layer obliterating all our foot prints. Did Mutti really expect her rickety Volkswagen to navigate where Horst's BMW could not? The trees on the far side of the clearing looked sugar-coated. Their glittering branches made the surrounding darkness seem denser. From high up in one of the conifers, the resident owl gave a desolate hoot. A faraway train whistled in response. After the sound died away I heard a car somewhere across the fields. Its engine was soon drowned out by the metallic chugging of the locomotive's wheels, crossing the nightscape. Once the train passed out of range the car's hum was gone too.

The owl hooted again. Then a big pale blur dove into the clearing. Talons outstretched, it seized something small from the shadows, flapped upward, and sailed out of sight. There was no doubt in my mind that the owl had murdered one of our mice.

I tripped on a stray piece of wood, dropping the flashlight. It landed on the hard cement floor and went dead at once. At first the dark was total and I fought a rising panic. Then I blinked until my eyes adjusted. I saw just enough to make my way to the box of firewood and then the door to the kitchen. By the time I put the box down at the stove my cut wrists were throbbing. I rushed back to the door and quickly slid the big bolt home.

"You're getting carried away," Mutti laughed. "It's only the stable's *outside* door we need to worry about. And I've already locked that." In my absence she had unfolded the Army cot and was now covering the canvas frame with a wool blanket.

"You mean I can stay?" I asked, returning the kindling box to its rightful place.

"As long as you understand it's not necessary," she said, smoothing a quilt over the blanket.

"I only came for the food."

"I suspected as much. I hope the tea is still hot." She cradled the pot between her hands. "I've sprinkled the pastries with water. A few minutes in sizzling butter will make them taste fresh-baked. Let's play a hand of cards after we eat. Or a game of *Mensch ärgere dich nicht*—if you've outgrown your childish tendency to throw the board against the wall whenever you lose."

"Don't worry. I've gotten used to losing since the last time we played." I sat down beside her and pushed my cup under the spout. "There's one more thing," I said, hoping she was finally in the right frame of mind to appreciate the key Hannes had entrusted to me. I held it out to her. "Frau Farber got your favorite guestroom ready for you. You're welcome to use it. Anytime."

Her smile quivered. Then she opened her hand and I pressed the key neatly on to her palm.

Without warning, something hard and unyielding smashed against the outside of the kitchen shutters. A voice we both loathed shrilled, "*Lottchen!* Open the door!"

Mutti jerked her hand away as if she'd been scalded. The key dropped to the floor, skidding from sight. For good measure, her elbow swept the tea pot off the table. It shattered on the linoleum, leaving a cascade of splashes and shards. I looked for Alex, wondering how he could have missed O.F.'s stealthy approach. The dog was no longer on his blanket; he was standing right next to the window, his nose wrinkled, his lips drawn back to expose every tooth. His very silence seemed to demand my own.

All at once I felt an overwhelming urge to pee—proof that I was as afraid of O.F. now as I had been in the days before I got married. The panic engulfing me was like a scratch on a worn vinyl record, so deep that the needle couldn't keep from sliding into the damaged groove. I stared at the shards at my feet, big enough to be glued back together by someone with more patience than I'd ever possessed, and scissored my legs in an effort to seal my bladder. Then I placed a protective hand over the child growing inside me.

"Lottchen!" he cried through the slats. "I know you're in there! Open up at once!"

Mutti's throat worked. Her stricken eyes met mine and flicked to the naked bulb at the ceiling. I crept to the wall switch and turned it. Immediately, the world disappeared. I crouched for the poker Mutti kept tucked under the stove. In a few seconds my vision adjusted enough so that I could make out a diffuse glow from the stove top. Then I grew aware of the faintest gray at the window. I guessed, more than saw, my mother's shadowy outline between these two poor sources of light, and groped my way toward her.

"Aren't you going to tell him to leave?" I whispered. "Your car's parked in front. He knows you're here."

She grabbed my arm as if I might save her and I clutched hers. Together, we crept to the fortified glass behind which O.F. stood poised with whatever club he'd used on the shutters. Mutti fumbled with the window latch. The German shepherd wound himself around our legs and tried to herd us away.

"Should I make Alex go out now?" I whispered with profound regret.

"Don't!" she hissed. "If he gets hurt I'll never forgive myself. You know how much Franz hates animals."

Ignoring the pressure of the dog's muzzle, she gapped the windows and croaked, "Go away. If you have something to say contact the lawyer I've hired to sue for my divorce and for my share of our Bausparvertrag (savings account). Leave me in peace." Her words were more plea than demand.

In answer, he pried at the shutters. They held.

"I'll never give you a divorce," he snarled. "And the only way you'll ever get your half of our savings is if you come home with me now. I'm prepared to forgive you."

"Forgive me?" she sputtered. "For what?"

"I have received written reports. Signed by my investigator. I know who you've been with. But you can never belong to him. You'll always be mine."

She kneed Alex aside and pushed her face to the slats, forgetting all caution. "You've lost your mind!"

"If I have it's your fault," he replied. "And you'll have to bear the consequences. Let me in or you'll regret it. This time I've come prepared and I know you're alone. I even know your friend is out of town this weekend. You have no telephone and I've disabled your car."

I steadied myself with the poker, demoting it from weapon to crutch. O.F.'s stick raked the shutters again. They continued to hold. The paint on them might have become blistered after countless rough seasons, but the wood underneath was still strong enough to keep out the riff raff. And Lucius, whatever else he might be *in*capable of, had done a good job of fixing the locks.

"I don't belong to you or anyone else," Mutti announced. "*This* is my home now. And you'll never be welcome here. You better leave before you get frostbite."

"Hure (whore)!" he screeched in reply. Judging by the pitch I guessed his face had flushed to the shade of a rooster's wattle. "Mother of whores! Do not disobey me!"

Anger burned through my fear, tempting me to shout, "You shut up and leave my mother alone!" But then I decided to follow Alex's advice. He was right. Surprise was our best weapon. A lesser dog would have signaled his presence, barked his threats, and lost the advantage. A lesser daughter might have matched insult with insult. Instead, I merely reached past Mutti's cheek to latch the window an instant before something heavy crashed against the shutters. They groaned but held.

"I am your lord and husband! I have the law on my side!" he shrieked. Mutti made no response. "All right," he said, suddenly calm. "I'll find my own way in."

Alex gave the mildest of whimpers and, firmly pressing his shoulder against our legs, pushed us toward the couch. We sat. He stationed himself in front of our knees. We clutched at his ruff. He was the only one of us not trembling.

"You told him off!" I murmured, in awe.

She whispered, "For all the good it did. What made me think he'd leave just because I asked him to? I only hope he didn't think to bring that derelict world war two pistol of his."

Astonished, I asked, "He has a gun?"

"A collector's item. Completely illegal. He claimed it would make us rich one day. It's been buried in his half of the wardrobe for years."

Now I was glad she'd insisted on keeping Alex with us. What use was a dog against guns? Then, from the stable, I heard the muffled explosion of breaking glass. We sat frozen until someone yanked on the outside of the big metal door.

CHAPTER 27

WE SCRAMBLED OVER THE COUCH, winding up in the same corner, our backs pressed against the wall, staring at the stable door. When it refused to yield to O.F.'s efforts he hit it with his club, howling with frustration.

For a minute, all was quiet. Then I heard a muffled scraping noise.

Mutti clutched my arm. "He found the ladder!"

"What ladder?"

She swallowed. "The one on the stable wall. It's been hanging there so long I forgot all about it. What could he possibly want with it? It's in the last stages of decay. Half the rungs are missing."

I had a mental glimpse of the farmhouse façade. "You didn't ask Lucius to work on your *upstairs* windows. Are they shuttered too?"

"No," she whispered. "Not all of them. I never thought —"

"Which ones are not?"

"At the rear . . ."

"Quick," I said. "We've got to see what he's up to."

Feeling my way through the dark, I opened the door leading from the kitchen to the long, pitch-black corridor. Mutti stayed close by my side until Alex pushed between us. I rested one hand on his head, brushing along the wall with the other. He led us past the padlocked and barricaded front door and stopped at the first chamber facing the rear of the house.

I inched its door open. Stale air rushed past my cheeks. The clammy room gave off a sad feeling, as if someone had died in it and hovered there still. Then came the same kind of scraping I'd heard from the stable. We followed Alex to the window.

"Stay back," I whispered to Mutti. "I'm taking a look." Trembling with fright, I eased windows and shutters apart. There was the ladder, swaying in O.F.'s grasp as he attempted to lean it against an upstairs balcony. The beam of the flashlight he was clutching crisscrossed the backyard. It illuminated a mixture of raindrops and sleet, his hat, and the soaked trench coat he was wearing. Shoving and heaving, he wrestled the top of the ladder higher and higher. There was a stick poking out of his collar. It would make short shrift of any unprotected glass panes he found on the balcony.

With excruciating caution, I pushed the windows wide and put my mouth to the dog's attentive ear. "Alex," I whispered, counting on speed and surprise, "*los!*"

He jumped into the night, aiming point-blank for the ladder. His next leap brought it clattering to the ground, O.F. teetering beside it. The flashlight rolled but stayed lit. O.F. pulled out his stick and clubbed a circling torpedo of muscles and fur. The dog whimpered in pain and outrage, retreated a few meters, then surged forward, clamping his jaw around O.F.'s bony wrist. The man moaned. The stick dropped. Slowly, O.F. sank to his knees.

"Help!" he bawled. "Call him off!"

Neither Mutti nor I moved so much as a finger.

Cloth ripped. Something thudded from a torn pocket and lay dully gleaming. O.F. made the mistake of reaching for it. The shepherd's teeth closed upon his good arm. And then Alex and O.F. were moving off, side by side, the dog slightly ahead. His arm imprisoned in an ivory vice, O.F. crawled and sprawled and lurched past the woodpile to the corner of the house.

Without a doubt, guns were the second thing that turned Alex into a fiend.

Mutti and I ran to the decrepit front parlor to continue our spying. O.F. was limping away across the front yard with Alex right behind him, nipping at his heels, herding his enemy up the lane and out of sight. The yelping and snarling diminished. After a while I heard a car door slam. A motor roared, speeding away.

"Quick, let's go get the ladder!" I said. We ran back to the rear chamber. I climbed over the sill. The flashlight, still on the ground, was already dimming. In its waning light I could just make out the pistol. But before I got near it Alex was upon it, scooping it up and trotting toward the woods, his head high and proud.

I aimed the flashlight at him. "Alex! Bring the gun back!" He ignored the command and disappeared between the trees.

"He's going to hide it!" Mutti said.

"Bury it, more likely," I told her, dragging the ladder to the sill and helping her slide it inside.

"He could have gone for O.F.'s throat," Mutti said. "Instead, he chased him off. Just as I wanted."

I peered into the night. "What do we do when he comes back?"

"Let him in, of course. He's earned a big treat. I have some moldy cheese he might like. Do you think he got hurt?"

"Who?" I asked, confused.

"Alex, who else? Didn't you hear him cry out?"

I locked the shutters. "I meant O.F. If he has sabotaged your car we'll have to walk out of here and take the first cab we run across to Hannes' house."

"And abandon the dog?" she said, incensed. "Besides, how do you know Franz won't be waiting somewhere down the lane? Or follow us to the villa? If he's looking for windows to break he'll find plenty there."

"We'll call the police. Hannes has phones."

"A squad car, on that fancy street? Flashing lights? A siren? What would his neighbors say?"

Not that old song. Not now. Not ever again.

"He wouldn't care," I insisted. "It's one of the things I like most about him."

She locked the window. Decisively. "I'm not going anywhere. At least not tonight. Franz can't chase me off. This is my place, such as it is. I gave him the other."

The ailing flashlight beam died on our way to the kitchen, plunging us into darkness again. Mutti stopped to grope for the wall and said, "I should have kept my mouth shut right from the start. You know how he gets once something riles him."

"He must have had some kind of plan. He did bring the gun," I pointed out, putting a hand on her back to move her along.

She started forward. "You know what he used to say whenever I tried to reason with him? Ich gedulde keine Widerrede (I won't tolerate back-talk). As if I was an obstinate child. And Vati's favorite expression used to be *Women have no rights, only obligations.* I wonder what Hannes' favorite husband-like dictum might be."

"*Just tell me what you want,*" I quipped. "*So I can give it to you.*"

She gave a dry laugh. "He's certainly addled *your* brain."

In the kitchen I helped her find Hannes's key. The ceiling bulb seemed brighter than it had when I first arrived. Its cheerful light contrasted sharply with the inky blackness I groped through as I roamed the entire first floor, checking every window. I was hoping to prove to myself that we were secure so that I could allow myself to go to sleep tonight. When I returned to the kitchen Mutti was just coming in from the stable.

"I called and called," she said, frown lines crossing her forehead. "I could sense Alex's eyes on me from the bushes. But he refused to come."

"He's keeping watch," I guessed. "In case O.F. is planning another visit."

She gave a contemptuous snort. "Without his gun or a ladder? A fierce guard dog on the loose? Hardly. He'll want to take his wrists to the nearest emergency room to get them disinfected, stitched up, and bandaged."

I tugged my sleeves down. "Wrists aren't as fragile as you might think. He wasn't seriously mauled. Alex only intended to scare him away."

I lay down on the cot fully clothed, keeping my boots on. Just in case. Mutti turned off the light. I heard her kick off her slippers. For an hour I tried to unclench my muscles and relax into sleep. Then I opened the window and whistled for Alex, to no effect. Sleet had become steady rain, turning the snow into slush. Tiptoeing to the foot of the couch, I gathered Alex's blankets and took them outside. Without speaking a word Mutti trailed me with his water dish and the promised cheese. We laid our offerings under the wide overhang in back of the house, directly below the balcony. Although both Mutti and I needed to empty our bladders, neither of us had the slightest inclination to visit the distant outhouse. So we squatted side by side in the yard, each loathe to let the other out of her sight.

Then we stumbled back to our beds in the kitchen, breathing in a blend of sweet pine resin and sour mouse droppings. With all the hungry creatures inside and out, there was no reason to think Alex's cheese would stay on his plush blankets for long.

Eventually Mutti gave a loud yawn and said, "I'm so glad you came."

"Me too."

Minutes later she asked, "Do you really think Hannes is different?"

"I don't think so. I know so." I recalled how his voice had gentled when he talked about his Inca princess.

"Just as you knew that *Lucius* was different?"

"You leave him out of it," I blurted with more vehemence than her comment deserved.

"Sorry." She yanked her covers up to her chin. "I won't say another word." She kept her resolve. Soon her breathing grew measured and deep.

But I, having no pillow and finding the army cot un-compromisingly hard, shifted incessantly from side to side, staring dry-eyed into the dark. An eternity later I rose and eased open the door to the corridor. Peering out of the rear window again I saw that the dog blanket was still unoccupied. The cheese had disappeared. I gave a tentative whistle, with no results, returned to the kitchen, and pulled the cookies Lucius had bought for me out of my carry-all. I sat on the cot and ate every last one, though they were overly sweet, had gone soft, and were nearly tasteless. Then I stoked the fire and stretched out on the cot, counting my worries.

The night was full of small sounds—firewood popping in the stove; tiny feet scurrying over Mutti's polished linoleum. One mouse scaled my quilt to sit on my belly, sniffing for crumbs. Something about its tender weight, throbbing with life, reminded me of little Elvis. I held still until the mouse decided to forage elsewhere. Ceiling beams pinged. The walls sighed and settled.

Between clearing and forest some unfortunate creature screamed its death cry, cornered by something hungry and big. I rushed to the window, compelled to launch a rescue attempt, but the cry ceased before I had finished undoing the latches. I peered out at dark things skidding from shadow to shade. The rain had stopped. Clouds shimmered in front of the moon. There was no sign of the dog. I wondered if it had been a squirrel who died—after spending months hording food for the winter. Countless acorns collected, cones peeled and split, all in vain.

I crawled under the quilt, thoroughly chilled, wrapped myself up like a parcel, and switched from counting worries to counting bolts and locks. And just when logic told me we were still safe I realized I'd forgotten to check the door to the cellar. But already I was losing my focus and could only manage a moment's regret at the careless mistake before finding myself in the midst of a basement dream—complete with eerie damp blackness; the indistinct glitter of malevolent eyes; a packed dirt floor anyone could burrow through. Wasn't there something, somewhere, about sinister dwarves, a tunnel dug long ago from the far end of the cellar to the densest part of the woods? The rest of the dream flickered and unrolled like a film:

> O.F., roaming the midnight forest, is inexorably drawn to the tunnel's hidden entrance, wiggles in, and crawls along the cramped tube to the belly of the house. He pushes aside a trap door camouflaged by layers of dust and climbs out onto the dirt floor. Lighting the basement with nothing but the moldering green of his evil intent, he sneaks up the stairs, picks up the rusty lumberjack axe sitting on the top step, and tries the basement door. It opens. Holding the axe aloft, he creeps toward the kitchen.

The door squeaks — or is it a mouse? I wake up for the very last time. Imprisoned by the quilt, I watch his shadowed eyes reflect red from the stove's burner rings. I struggle with my confining shroud, scattering mice. The axe swings in a wide, unstoppable arc. I feel its blade biting through my neck. Mutti is next. He drags our limp bodies down to the cellar while somewhere outside Alex is frantically barking.

A Volkswagen motor putt-putts and the glow of headlights sweeps across the shutters. O.F.'s white car speeds to the rear of the farmhouse, scraping Mutti's towering stack of deadwood. It collapses onto Alex's blankets. At the last second the dog leaps over rolling logs into the darkness beyond. The car veers after him, accelerating. Something limp plops onto the ground. Then the car returns to the front yard where it idles and idles, finally moving on and away. Red pinpricks reflect from a long row of puddles and wink out.

How much was nightmare, how much real?

The next time I opened my eyes — or dreamed that I did — gray light was squeezing through the shutters. Another motor, this one quiet and sure, approached the front yard. Did I hear a car door? A man's voice? Suddenly there was an anguished howl from the tree line. Somebody ran, calling Alex's name.

Struggling out of paralyzing sleep, I tore open one door and then another to see Hannes at the edge of the woods, kneeling by his injured dog, one hand gently stroking a flank and coming up covered with blood.

Mutti swayed in the door frame beside me, disheveled, her eyes blurred with incomprehension. "Is that Hannes?" she asked. "You said he was out of town!" It was not a complaint.

I ran to Hannes, hardly aware that Mutti had chosen to stay behind. "O.F. showed up with a gun," I told him. "Alex chased him off and carried the gun to the woods. He wouldn't come when we called."

Hannes looked unbearably grim. "Last night when I was falling asleep in London I had a compelling vision of Alex in trouble, surrounded by terror. Today I finished my most pressing business and took the next flight." He picked up the slab of raw meat lying near the dog's feet.

"He didn't get that from us," I said. "O.F. must have thrown it to him. You don't suppose—?"

Hannes wrapped his handkerchief around the slab and hoisted the shepherd into his arms. "Alex is trained not to eat tainted meat. But I want the vet to examine it anyway."

I rushed to get the dog's blankets, spread them on the rear seat, and watched Hannes lower the dog gently upon them. "We shouldn't have let him out," I said. "But O.F. found a ladder, you see, and he was about to climb—"

Hannes made an effort to smile. "You did what you had to do. Tell Lotte I'll be back as soon as I can. Then we'll talk." Walking around to the driver's side of the Mercedes, he spied a piece of paper stuck to the blue Volkswagen's windshield. He pulled it free of a wiper blade, unfolded it, glanced at the message, and passed it to me. "Herr Hohner has a lot to answer for," he said, briefly examining all four of the VW's slashed tires. "Whether Lotte likes it or not I'm about to get myself thoroughly involved in her life. Enough is enough."

Mutti must have heard him drive off, for she hurried around the corner clutching an eyebrow pencil and a tube of lipstick, though she needed a comb more than either. I held the note out to her and we read it together.

Liebes Lottchen!
I'm still ready to forgive you, but I meant what I said—you'll never see a single Pfennig of the Bausparvertrag unless you break off all contact with Adler at once. He's led you astray and must suffer the consequences, as will his dog.
Dein Dich-liebender Franz

"That does it!" she said, crushing the letter. "To hell with that wretched savings account. And to hell with Hannes' neighbors. Help me pack so I can take him up on his offer. I'm moving into his best guest room today." She lobbed the wad as far as she could and stormed inside.

I retrieved it, brushed off wet snow, smoothed the paper, and carefully slipped the evidence into my most secure coat pocket.

CHAPTER 28

I STAYED IN THE SECOND-BEST guestroom until Alex recovered enough to start limping around the house. Then Hannes and I took him back to the forest. After a persuasive command from his master the shepherd led us to some moss-covered rocks and sat in front of an outcropping. Hannes put on a glove and pulled the pistol out of the small cave underneath, held it almost worshipfully toward the light and said, "Now we've got him where we want him!"

I gave him the note I'd salvaged but he refused to reveal his intentions. I didn't hear the rest of the story until the next time I saw Anna.

Meanwhile I realized that my presence in Hannes's house did little to enhance the romance trying to unfold between him and Mutti. I decided to go back where I belonged despite his protestations, asking him to drop the cot off at the high-rise next time he had any business in my part of Munich.

The paint on the apartment door was still fresh enough to smell of enamel. Inside, the parquet was spotless. The bathroom sparkled. I had no idea how much of the improvement was due to Anna, how much to Lucius. For it was obvious he had recently been there. The message I had left him was gone from the table and one of the living room walls was lined with boxes that certainly hadn't been there on the night I'd sawed through my wrists. But the photos of our dinner party were still spread on the counter like a deck of cards, untouched. Next to this display of happier times was a note from Lucius, written on the reverse side of mine, explaining that the boxes contained C-rations that had been free for the hauling.

I brought you all our favorites. And the gallon-sized can of milk powder will give you the extra calcium you'll need for you-know-who. Get yourself a big stack of books and hole up till I come back. There's one little favor I need you to do for me, though. I finally located a good place to park Pepper—in front of our old address. It's kind of far but since you like long walks anyway maybe you can go in that direction every few days to run the engine for five or ten minutes. I'll be thinking of you.

XXX
Lucius

So much for Anna's triumphant "revelation" about his clandestine return to the whorehouse. I emptied out one of the boxes, took the next bus to Warner, and stuffed it full of science fiction, earning another censorious sniff from the librarian. Back at the apartments, the Swiss with the high forehead stepped into the corridor the exact moment I carried my library finds past his door. He turned red, pivoted, and dove back through his doorway so he wouldn't have to speak to me. I couldn't blame him; I had become a scandal-prone pariah among people who prided themselves in being discreet.

Deciding to follow the rest of Lucius's advice, I kept the curtains drawn and the lights on, spent my days reading, eating, and napping in no particular order, and ignored the occasional doorbell and sporadic, insistent knocking. I took my first walk to Hohenzollernstrasse at daybreak several mornings later, before the hoity tenants of the high-rise and the self-employed working girls at our old address were likely to be up and about.

Lucius had given up on Pepper's unwieldy canvas cover after it started to mildew. The undressed Pepper had no objections to me climbing inside her to start the engine. Nothing could have tempted me to drive that day, for the night had ended with a freezing fog and slippery roads. A rusty old Renault was parked behind me, confirming my suspicions that Walt, Naoko and Tommy had taken up residence on one of the upper floors of the bleach-scrubbed whorehouse.

I was shivering on the clammy seat, listening to the AFN while the motor coughed and stuttered, when a set of brown fingertips scratched at the thick sheet of ice covering the windshield. They belonged to Spider who was leaning on his ebony cane, dressed all in black with a long wool coat, a felt beret, one hand encased in a fine leather glove.

I rolled the window down a crack. "What are *you* doing here?"

He brushed ice off his nails, rubbed his palm briskly against the wool coat, and with a quick grin wiggled his damp fingers into the second glove. "Bronchitis attack. Happens in foul weather. I do better in a dry climate."

"I was sure you weren't about to dirty your hands with war games," I said. "But I thought, since your girl-friend had to leave town . . ."

The grin slackened. He gave a dismissive wave. "Oh, that. Me and Ingrid started a little arrangement. You fixing to take the car for a spin?"

"Not on this slick road! I'm walking."

He nodded. "There's an art to driving on ice. Tell you what. You finish warming up your car and I'll warm up mine. Then what do you say I give you a ride? I'm going right by the Scheidplatz. I could let you out in front of the store."

It *was* an exceptionally cold morning and Spider offered a smile as hearty and sincere as someone like him could possibly make it. I hadn't conversed in English since the last time I saw Lucius and needed to practice the language every chance I could get. Besides, wasn't I married *and* pregnant? It made me doubly taboo.

"All right," I said, trying to sound matronly. "We appreciate your kind offer."

*

SPIDER drove at an unhurried pace. Once the car slid but he managed to abort the subsequent spin by a clever maneuver with the steering wheel. True to his word he let me out at the supermarket. A few minutes later I was sitting at my table, sipping hot tea, and wondering if Spider might have welcomed a cup.

The following week I decided to start Pepper again but this time I overslept. It had snowed during the night and I thought with pity of Lucius, curled up in a rickety tent. The snowplow was in the process of clearing the streets I was walking along, but the sidewalks were still covered. By the time I arrived at the car my thighs were quivering from exertion. When Spider appeared and repeated his offer I was grateful enough to propose peppermint tea.

He grimaced. "Herbs are for rabbits. Make that coffee and we have a deal."

When we were passing the supermarket some unlucky driver, who had just shoveled his car out of the snow bank in front of the store, was pulling away from the curb. "Bingo," Spider said and maneuvered easily into the newly cleared spot. Cutting across to the lawn and the high-rise, I was relieved when we encountered no one on the sidewalk or on the elevator.

Compared to the outdoors my little bachelorette was positively balmy. I prepared a cup of Nescafé for Spider and brewed myself a pot of the inevitable peppermint tea while he propped his cane carelessly against the side of the couch and pulled off his hat and gloves. His coat and a long woollen scarf followed soon after. He tossed the garments on the easy chair, crossed his legs, and studied the room. "Any word from Joseph?"

"Not this time," I confessed.

He raised his brows. "Honeymoon over?"

I put a hand on my belly. "I guess."

"I thought so," he chortled, lighting a cigarette without asking if I'd mind. Then he spied the C-rations I had stacked behind the couch. "Jeeze," he said. "The platoon's been trying to give that out-dated trash away for months. Looks like Joseph saved the supply sergeant a trip to the dump."

The whole time I was growing up the only cans Mutti ever brought home contained rarefied items like condensed milk, tomato paste, pineapple rings and sardines. Surely the U.S. Army's ready-made soups and stews were the height of modern technology. "What do you think is wrong with them, then?" I asked Spider.

"They're pig slop," he said.

The doorbell rang before I could think of a clever reply. As usual, I ignore it.

"Want *me* to get the door?" Spider asked, uncrossing his legs.

It was then I wondered what the odd little man was doing in my apartment, at proprietary leisure, his stuff strewn all over the room. "It's *my* door," I said. "I'll go."

It was Anna, of course. Standing there in her shimmering coat. "At long last!" she said. "I've been trying to reach you for days."

"Sorry you missed me," I said coolly. "Don't you have school this morning?"

"I'm skipping first period for this little talk," she said, hanging her coat on the coat-stand. Turning, she saw Spider lounging on the couch and cried, "Lucius has shrunk."

"Don't be stupid," I snapped. "He's away at maneuvers. This is his friend, Spider. He's been ill." As if that could explain the man's unseemly visit.

Her gaze went to his cane and softened. I introduced them. She gave his hand a firm shake and wished him a good morning, in English.

He eyed the form-fitting gray knit suit she was wearing. "She don't look like you," he said, smiling past me at her. "Not much, anyway."

"Less every day," I conceded, feeling frumpy in my pregnancy tent. "Anna, do sit down!"

She glanced at the easy chair, occupied by his garments, and went to sit on the far end of the couch, chastely pulling at the seam of her dress to cover her knees.

"Tea?" I asked.

"Yes, please. You wouldn't by any chance have something good to eat? I skipped breakfast so I could tell you my news."

I sacrificed a package of chocolate-chip cookies for the occasion and carried them to her, along with one of the dinette-chairs. "How's it going with the architect?" I asked, sitting across from my guests and placing the cookie platter on the coffee table between them.

"Actually, it isn't. Turns out his stomach's is even bigger than yours. Quite a let-down after Rupert. If only . . ." She sighed, helped herself to a cookie, and dunked it into her tea.

As she delicately chewed her way through two more, Spider muttered, "You been holding out on me, Maria. I had no idea you had such a good-looking sister. Does she understand English?"

"Only a couple of words."

"She spoken for?"

"Spoken? For what?"

"She free, like? Unoccupied?"

I was shocked at his nerve.

Watching us intently, she asked, "What?"

"He thinks you're attractive," I told her, taking liberties with the translation.

Flustered, she rewarded him with a half-smile.

Thus encouraged, Spider showed her his treasured gold tooth. "Fine day," he said slowly.

"Yes it is," she answered in English. Then she asked in German, sotto voce, "Why is he wearing sunglasses in winter? They make him look like a gangster."

"Maybe the snow hurts his eyes," I improvised. "He's from South California. They don't have any snow there."

"He's not in the snow now," she pointed out. "But never mind him. How come you didn't tell me that O.F.'s tried to break into the farmhouse? If Mutti hadn't stopped by last week I still wouldn't know that she's moved in with Hannes. She assumed I had heard it from you."

"As I recall," I said with remarkable equanimity, "you asked me not to darken your doorstep again unless I was invited."

"Oh, that. A silly mistake. I was angry. With good reason, you have to admit."

"Huh!"

"Okay, okay—I was mean and I've been sorry ever since. Satisfied? Aren't you thrilled about Mutti and Hannes?"

"Is that what you wanted to talk to me about?"

"No. My news is even better than that." She chuckled. "I used to think Hannes was quiet and boring. I've had to change my opinion of him several times since he had Mutti transferred last year. And after what Frau Forster told me in the Kaufhaus yesterday he's become my idol."

"What did Frau Forster ever pass on that wasn't malicious gossip?"

Anna stubbornly shook her head. "This time it's not," she insisted. "Last Saturday when she was waxing the landing two men came up the stairs and stopped in front of O.F.'s door. Both wore expensive suits and one of them looked like Hannes. The other carried a spiffy briefcase. Frau Forster said he was the lawyerly type."

"Are you sure?" I cried, getting caught up in the tale in spite of myself.

"It gets even better," Anna said with undisguised relish. "Hannes stayed clear of the spy hole while the other one knocked. The moment O.F. cracked the door open both men pushed their way in. Poor Frau Forster couldn't hear a word of the conference going on inside but it lasted almost an hour.

"The next morning O.F. started to pack the VW with all his clothes and household effects. First thing on Monday he took the front door key to the housing office and told them he was relocating to Bremen to live with his sister. Didn't even give them a forwarding address. Frau Forster said he abandoned every stick of furniture that was in the apartment. She wants me to ask Mutti if she can have the blonde-oak hutch in the kitchen, and the table and chairs."

At first I was stunned. Then I found myself on my feet, bouncing up and down and laughing hysterically. Anna joined in. The next thing I knew we were hugging—for what might well have been the first time in our lives. I mussed her hair and she patted my belly. When we managed to curb our enthusiasm enough to sit back down, still giggling, Spider said drily,

"Don't mind me. Pretend I'm not even here."

The bell rang again. This time it was Hannes with Alex sitting beside him. "Maria, grüss dich (hello)," he said. "I just happened to be in the neighborhood, tying up loose ends. I'm taking Lotte to Italy for the rest of this winter."

I stared at him, trying to digest the fact that my mother, who'd never voiced the slightest desire to travel to my second-favorite country, should get what I'd always wanted.

"I'm returning your cot." He gestured to where he had leaned it against the corridor wall.

"Oh," I said, feeling wounded. "I don't suppose you have time for some tea?"

"One cup? With pleasure. May we come in?"

Chagrined at my poor hostess-skills, I pushed the door wide. "Please do!"

He brought in the cot, sliding it neatly between coat-stand and wall. While he unbuttoned his overcoat I wrapped my arms around the dog's neck. "Are you leaving him with Frau Farber?"

"That was my intention," Hannes said. "But Lotte refused to consider the trip unless Alex comes along with us. Luckily I was able to rent a villa in the Tuscan hills. A marvelous region for romantic walks. As to Frau Farber . . ." He rubbed his hands together and turned, smiling at my other two guests. Opening his arms, he walked toward Anna. "I'm so pleased to see you here. Now I can say a proper good-bye to you too — and wish you both cheerful holidays." He shook her well-manicured hand.

She looked up at him, naked reverence exuding from every one of her visible pores. "You! Here!" she stammered, stating the obvious.

"But not for long," he said. Then he glanced questioningly at my other guest, who sat scrunched against his corner of the sofa, knees to his chest as if he were expecting a flood.

"That one of them police dogs?" Spider asked, his voice holding a hysterical note. "He bite?"

"Only on special occasions," I said. "He and my husband are great friends. Buddies."

Gingerly, Spider lowered his feet to the floor. "That a fact?" He stretched out a hand and snapped his fingers to attract Alex's attention. The dog gave a cautious sniff, flattened his ears, and retreated, flashing his teeth. A low rumble came from his chest.

Spider withdrew his hand and lifted his feet high off the parquet.

"Lass das (leave it)," Hannes murmured. The growl ceased, but the dog's lips remained curled as he watched Spider's every move.

"I'm sorry," Hannes said in his cultured Oxford English. "I believe it's the sunglasses. And the fact that we have yet to be introduced."

With a groan, I corrected my second hostess-mistake, adding the bit about Spider's bronchitis attack. As the two men shook hands across the coffee table I saw how flimsy Spider's suit sleeve looked next to Hannes's. I also noticed that he made no attempt to take off his shades. Then Hannes blithely sat in the middle of the couch and Spider hugged the armrest to accommodate him.

Anna gazed at her hero, too overcome to speak.

"I'm surprised you can get away from the office long enough to take an extended vacation," I told him.

Hannes shrugged. "I haven't had one in years. And I'm good at rearranging my schedule. Especially in winter." I poured him a cup of lukewarm peppermint tea. He consulted his inconspicuous wrist watch and took a long sip. "Lotte is wrapping your Christmas presents as we speak. That was another thing she insisted on before she would agree to come with me. She asked Frau Farber to give them to you on Holy Night. Please stop by."

"Your housekeeper will have nothing to do when you're gone," Anna said. "No cooking. No Alex to watch."

"On the contrary," Hannes replied, pausing briefly to ask "Gestatten (may I)?" before he helped himself to a cookie. While my face flamed at my latest hostess-blunder, he smoothly went on, "Frau Farber will have plenty of planning to do while we're gone. You see, Lotte decided to run the whole household by herself once we return."

"Say you won't let her!" Anna cried.

"Why not?" Hannes asked. "As long as she'll allow the gardeners to stay. I'm particularly looking forward to frequent intimate suppers featuring Lotte's *Reiberdatschi* with applesauce. Frau Farber always considered potato pancakes beneath her. Which is why I've made her a proposition — München needs more international cuisine. Frau Farber's considerable talents are wasted on me so I've offered to become her silent partner in a business venture next spring. In exchange she's agreed to cater every one of our dinner parties thereafter — and to keep a special table in her new restaurant reserved just for *us*." He pronounced the last word with great relish. "Meanwhile — get ready for a deluge of postcards from Italy."

"I suppose you'll take lots of photos," Anna said. "Like Vati."

He laughed. "Not at all. I prefer living in a scene to recording it."

Spider's head spun from face to face like a well-oiled swivel chair. Every now and then he glanced quickly at Alex just to see if the dog's focus was still on him. It always was. When Hannes finished his last drop of tea and decisively put the cup on its saucer, Spider said with evident relief, "Leaving already?"

"Leaving. Already," Hannes repeated, sounding amused. "With my ill-mannered dog." He got up and pressed Spider's slack fingers. "I hope you'll feel better soon. Our winters can be quite nasty."

"I'm about to cut this one short," Spider replied. "I'm getting out of the Army next month. With any luck I'll be celebrating my Christmas in sunny L.A."

"Sounds like a good plan," Hannes said. Then he got up and bowed over Anna's milky-white hand. Her eyes grew wide with delight.

"It's been an honor to drink tea with you," she gushed. "I hope you and Mutti have a wonderful trip."

"No doubt we will," Hannes said. "Maria, if you would walk me to the door?" I held his coat for him and he slipped his arms into the sleeves. We stepped out of the apartment together. His eyes were shining. "It seems the ogre has had a change of heart," he murmured. "He's giving my Inca princess a divorce, after all. Along with every cent she paid into the Bausparvertrag. Isn't that considerate of him?"

I knew without a shadow of doubt that if O.F. ever gave up anything it was only because someone had made him a better offer — perhaps one he couldn't refuse.

Hannes held out an envelope. "My secretary took this telephone message for you. She said it was urgent. And — listen — feel free to use our second-best guestroom. Any time. I'm sure Frau Farber would be delighted with the arrangement."

I wished he'd invited me to accompany him to Tuscany instead, with or without Mutti. Such was my envy at her good fortune. I stuffed the sealed envelope into my cardigan pocket, gave Alex one final pat, and went back inside to continue playing hostess for my remaining guests. Now that Hannes was no longer occupying the center of the couch Spider felt free to scoot several feet closer to Anna. She jumped up and went to the window, saying, "I want to watch Hannes leave."

I joined her in time to see man and dog exit the lobby and leisurely cross the parking lot.

"What you all looking at?" Spider said, getting between us. She tilted out of his way.

"Hannes was my mother's old boss," I explained, fervently wishing I'd never invited Spider up for instant coffee. "They are getting married next year." After a short pause, I added firmly, "Anna will, too," hoping that was a broad enough hint even for him.

"Well now," he said, sounding bitter. "You sure are one marrying family. I see I've been wasting my time." He watched Hannes open the back door of his Mercedes, watched Alex jump in. "Your mother's seems to be better at picking husbands than some people I know."

I knew it was an old cliché, but I couldn't resist quipping, "Yes, she does. Which proves that practice really does make perfect!"

Hannes drove toward the access road and stopped to wait for an incoming vehicle, which pulled to the front of the lot and parked at the curb.

"Isn't that an American jeep?" Anna asked. "The Military Police?"

Indeed, two white-helmeted MPs were climbing out, consulting a clipboard.

Suddenly Spider's armpits began to reek. Sweat pearled on his forehead. He slid his shades to the tip of his nose to gape at the MPs, and as one of them pointed to our lobby, he pushed them up again, glanced at his large imitation-Swiss wrist watch, and said, "Shoot, it's getting late. I best get a move on. Don't bother seeing me out." With one single swipe he gathered his hat, gloves and coat and hurried off, trailing the scarf behind him.

An instant later I saw that he'd forgotten his cane and followed him out to the corridor with it. It was empty. I ran to the elevator only to find it was parked on the lobby floor. It started to rise. For a moment I stood there, mesmerized, then I ran into my apartment, shut the door, and hid Spider's cane behind the coat-stand. But as the doorbell rang for the third and final time that fateful morning I knew it wasn't Spider the MPs were looking for.

They had come to find me.

CHAPTER 29

THE TWO YOUNG MILITARY POLICE officers were tall, muscular, and excruciatingly polite even as they thoroughly scanned the entire living room over my shoulder. I could not have been more afraid if they had been Gestapo agents snooping for hidden Jews, though I took great care not to show it.

"Mrs. Duncan?" the taller one asked, looking from me to the window, where Anna was standing, pale and wide-eyed.

"Yes?" I said.

"*You're* Mrs. Duncan?" he said with an air of incredulity

I wished I could deny it. I wished I had not opened the door. And more than anything I wished Anna were not there, witnessing my shame.

"I am. What is it?" Whatever it was, it couldn't be good. From everything I'd ever overheard or read the police only came to a house to impart bad news or to drag someone away, and yet I wasn't aware that I had done anything wrong.

"We are here to see your husband," he said.

I couldn't have been more surprised. "But he's not here."

It was obvious that they didn't believe me. "Can you tell us where he is?" the other one said, still scanning over my shoulder.

"On maneuvers. Isn't he?"

They glanced at each other, keeping their faces deliberately blank. The shorter MP said without the slighted hint of emotion, "We really couldn't say, ma'am. But the battalion commander would like to talk to you this morning. If you don't mind we'll take you to him right now."

That was it, then. It really *was* me they had come to drag away. I did my best to keep a stiff upper lip. "They need me at Henry Kaserne," I told Anna as if being made to ride in their jeep was an entirely normal, everyday procedure. "I've got to go." I exchanged my bulky cardigan for the teddy-bear coat, grabbed mittens and scarf, and left the building between the two guards—just like any other prisoner. No doubt gossip would soon have it that I was dragged off in chains.

The ride across town in the open vehicle was cold and drafty, and if it had not been for the gnawing fear in my belly it might even have been exhilarating. I had been in battalion headquarters once before, in the early spring, when Lucius's CO had had the onerous task of deciding whether or not I deserved to marry a man he considered to be one of the lowliest of American citizens. The MPs walked me to a different office, this one farther down a hall that smelled of cheesy socks. They knocked, opened the door, and stood at attention, announcing my arrival.

The man sitting on the other side of the desk was much older than the CO. His sparse brown hair, longer than the usual regulation buzz, was parted on the left, the thickest strand wet-combed across a lined forehead. Gravely, he introduced himself as Major Wright and asked me a number of questions about the last time I saw Lucius, what his mood had been, what we had said to each other. He wrote my answers down word for word.

It seemed that two nights ago Lucius started a fight and then disappeared. He had been AWOL ever since. It meant *absent without leave*, the Major explained. The longer Lucius stayed gone the worse it would be for him. "I'm sure there's some logical explanation for his actions," he said. "And I'd like to hear it—from him. What we have to do now is to keep Private Duncan from compounding his mistakes. For his own good. Here's my number. I want you to promise you'll call me the minute he walks in your door so we can help him out of the hole he's digging for himself." He made it sound like the best thing I could possibly do for Lucius was to turn him in as fast as possible.

"What if he won't come home?"

"The weatherman's predicting a real cold snap. He'll need shelter. And remember, your cooperation will go in his favor."

The MPs were not waiting for me in the hall. I guessed I was expected to make my own way back home. I considered myself lucky that I'd thought to bring my purse. The walk to the gate was fraught with old, bittersweet memories. On a wintry day like this, about a year ago, I'd come to see Lucius after escaping the nuns. Back then he was the only person in the world I still trusted. He spent the better part of that night trying to help me find a refuge.

He would never have turned *me* in.

I stopped at the PX for some candy bars to tide me over till lunch. Unable to decide between a Butterfinger and a Baby Ruth, I bought both. Spider walked into the store while I was paying for them at the register. Looking small and insignificant in his fatigues, he passed me without speaking, but after he'd walked to the end of the aisle he beckoned me to follow him to the rear of the shelves.

"Word is Joseph's on the run," he murmured, his expression unreadable. "I don't know what the commander told you but according to my sources a bunch of crackers jumped him in the boonies. Only this time they knew he could box. He's lucky to be alive. He won't get out of this jam anytime soon, Maria. If I was him I'd head for the East German border. I hear tell they treat American defectors real good on the other side."

I blocked my ears. "We'll work it out. Major Wright wants to help him."

"I wouldn't be so sure about that. Did he tell you that Duncan is hurt? There's a review happening in a couple of weeks, about the battalion's treatment of colored soldiers. Big brass coming through. I think the Major's worried Duncan's story might spoil our image."

I couldn't process the information. "You forgot your cane," I said, apropos nothing.

"Keep it for me. I'll pick it up next time I'm in the neighborhood."

Another good reason not to answer the doorbell.

On the bus trip back to the high-rise I munched the two candy bars and tried to puzzle out Spider's report, unsure if his version of events could be trusted. He looked shifty even in broad daylight, while the commander had seemed wise and sincere. As I licked my chocolate-smudged fingers I felt my stomach clench shut. No matter what Lucius did or didn't do, life would different from now on because of it.

Once I was home I changed into slippers and reached for the cardigan. Then I remembered about the envelope Hannes had given me. I pulled it out of the cardigan's pocket and ripped it open.

"A woman named Gitta Edel called," Hannes's secretary had written. "She says your father is in the hospital, dying. You are to go see him at once."

I grabbed the directions supplied on a separate piece of paper, jammed my feet back into the boots, unhooked my coat from the coat-stand, and dashed out.

He asked for me! a voice inside kept chanting on the long streetcar ride to the hospital. Not Anna but me. Maybe — although I hardly dared think it — maybe he meant to tell me he was sorry for cutting me out of his life. I would smile magnanimously or even beatifically and take his hand to tell him all was forgiven. The final, righteous communion between a father and the true child of his heart. *He asked for me! For me!*

*

IT MIGHT have been because it was old, built in a time when long, cloistral windows were considered a virtue, that the outside of the hospital seemed to radiate subdued despair. My footsteps echoed in the antiseptic front hall. I showed the receptionist my note. She called for someone to relieve her and took me through a labyrinth of corridors to stop at a closed door. "You wait here," she said and went in.

She came back out a few moments later. "Herr Edel has agreed to see you, but only if you leave your husband outside," she said, looking as puzzled as I felt.

I tiptoed into a sick room reeking of unsavory body-fluids. Vati lay with his head propped on a couple of pillows. His eye sockets were hollow, the skin underneath them a blotched greenish-yellow. His normally well-tended curls plumed like an exotic bird's. He waved me to him with a limp wrist.

I sat on the edge of his bed. "I came as soon as I heard. What's wrong with you?"

He chuckled mirthlessly. "Remember those little white pills I've been taking for my rheumatism since the war? Turns out they have the unsuspected side effect of quietly destroying the liver. The doctor says I'm dying of something called *cirrhosis*. Like a common drunk."

"I'm sorry," I whispered, fighting tears.

He raised his hand as if to stay them. "*I* never asked you to come. It was Gitta. She called Adler's office without my permission, knowing if she could get you to come here with your husband it would be the end of me." His yellow-tinged eyes slid to and away from my belly.

I hunched, hoping Lucius's oversized coat was hiding my condition. But then the full import of Vati's words hit me and I jumped up, wanting only to leave. I had to use every ounce of will-power I could muster to make myself stay in the room. I went to the window and stood with my back to him, looking out at the bleak landscape, seeing nothing. I had no desire to add to his pain. Nor was I eager to carry around with me, for the rest of my life, the guilt of having been cruel to my father on his deathbed. And yet I could no longer swallow his insults in silent submission.

When I returned to his side I was utterly calm. "I have loved you since I was born," I said, keeping my tone flat to match his expression. "All my life I've been waiting for you to give some kind of sign that you loved me back. There was none. Not once." I sat down on the bed, feeling his legs shift to the other side of the mattress. "One time I heard you tell Mutti that the reason you can't show affection is because no one ever touched you when you were a boy. Well, you stopped being a boy long ago. And that life-time's worth of love you've kept locked away in your heart—you can either take it with you to your grave where it will do no one any good—or you can spend it while you're still here. But even if you do survive, you'll never get to see me again unless my husband is included." I rose, ignoring the trapped look in his eyes, brushed a fingertip across his fevered cheek, and walked out.

It was my profound belief and best expectation that no matter what his doctor predicted my father was too nasty to die.

*

FROM THE moment the battalion commander had revealed Lucius' plight some kind of stop watch started to tick inside me. He needed me. I had to be where he could find me. During the endless ride home from the hospital the day darkened and the streetcar's interior lights came on. By the time I arrived at the Scheidplatz the only thing I could see in the tram window was my own anxious face. Crossing the parking lot, I looked up at the high-rise and thought I saw a lamp flicking off inside our fourth-story window. A reflection of the nearest street light?

On entering the apartment I could have sworn that someone had just been there, leaving behind the small, bitter breeze of his parting. The emptiness in the living room hit me like a physical blow.

"Hello?" I said, my voice strained. "Lucius?"

Nothing seemed out of place. I went into the bathroom. It was as I'd left it, except—was that a drop of fresh blood in the sink? In the kitchen, the silverware drawer was ajar. The top teaspoon inside it was damp. And even though the trashcan under the sink had been too full to properly close in the morning, now the garbage was squashed down, a C-ration can *I* had not opened on top of the pile.

The mosaic of photos I had left on the counter was missing one piece. It was the picture of me sitting on Lucius's lap at the dinner party, dapper white Italian suit, slinky spaghetti strap dress. Gone, too, was the double-sided note we'd left for each other. In its place was a new sheet of paper covered with his hasty scrawl.

Hey, Maria! Are you all right?

I'm sorry I let Jim and his buddies get to me again. Played right into their hands. And I'm tired now. Of everything. So I'm taking Pepper for one final joy ride—into the thickest brick wall we come across. I know I've let you down. I guess you should never have married me. You and the rest of the world will be much better off without me.

XXX

Lucius

I ran to the elevator and then through the streets. Three distinct sounds accompanied my charge along the snow-shoveled sidewalks: labored breathing, a rapidly thumping heart, the slap of boots on salted concrete. For some reason I thought if only I raced fast enough I could catch Lucius while he was still warming up the car. I'd wrestle the key out of his hand. Swallow it if I had to. Smuggle him home and stuff him into the closet the next time they came looking for him. But the only hiding place he'd fit was also the first one they would want to search.

I ran until the ground under me swayed and the street-lights grew dim, but I got to the whorehouse too late. Pepper's spot was empty. She and Lucius were gone.

*

I BORE two nights and days of agony. The baby inside me seemed to have turned to cement. I couldn't eat. I couldn't sleep. Worst of all, I couldn't read. I sat and rocked and paced, dry-eyed. In my darkest moment I unrolled the only surviving honeymoon drawing of Lucius I had left and pinned it to the wall. He looked lonely up there. I rummaged in the hutch cupboard for his hair-trimmings and sat directly below the drawing for hours, holding the small curly cloud to my heart.

Once I even found myself in front of Anna's apartment with the vague notion of telling her about Vati's expected demise. I was relieved when she didn't answer and propped a note against her door. But the next time *my* doorbell rang, it wasn't she who was standing out in the hall. It was the two MPs with their officious clipboard.

"Mrs. Duncan?" the taller one said.

I nodded, aware that my hair was uncombed, the white terry robe I'd wrapped around me unwashed.

"The battalion commander wants to see you again, ma'am."

"Why?" Had he somehow guessed about Lucius's letter? Was he angry because I hadn't shown it to him?

His answer was flat and entirely predictable. "We really couldn't say. Ma'am."

*

MY INTERVIEW with Major Wright was blessedly short. Afterward I walked to Warner and waited in the library until the dependent bus was due. It was only on the ride to Second Field Hospital, lulled by the clattering engine and the dull conversation of the passengers around me, that I really took in what the Major had said.

In a wooded suburb far from the heart of Munich a passerby had discovered Lucius in his car late yesterday evening. He was unconscious. A garden hose, connected to the exhaust, had been piped into the interior. The Major promised I would find him much improved, upstairs in the psyche ward. And any confessions he might impart to me, needless to say, should be quickly passed on.

Lucius's face was gray, his hair snagged. One of his arms was bandaged. Unsmiling, he looked past my head as if hoping I'd disappear. I felt clumsy, sitting in a chair by his bedside. The most cheerful remark I could squeeze past my tight throat was, "Hi!" After an awkward pause I followed it with, "I'm glad you're still alive."

When the silence between us became unbearable even to him, he said, "Push came to shove, I just couldn't smash Pepper against any wall."

I was glad he'd spared her, even though he hadn't exactly spared me. I wanted to explain that a woman incubating a fetus needs lots of consistent, tender care. Not sudden shocks.

Not two days of utter despair. Or else the baby might come out crooked somehow. No one told me that; it had become self-evident — though probably not to him.

"Where's Pepper now?"

With a laconic shrug, he said, "Impounded somewhere on base. Undamaged." He attempted a smile. "Unlike us."

My face burned. "Did Anna tell you . . ."

"About your acrobatics on the ledge? No. It was Jim. He told everybody in the boonies that my smutty child-bride was a certified over-the-edge lunatic. Funny, considering that I'm the one they locked in the psyche ward. I guess we both flunked our suicide tests. The shrink claims we're bad for each other."

We might have failed at death, but not at life — at least not completely, not yet. And where there was even the smallest amount of life there was hope, wasn't there? Although I didn't see a spark of either one in his eyes.

"If you don't mind — I'm real tired," he said. "Feeling puky, too. And I don't want to talk. Can you come back in a few days? I'm not going anywhere. Not anytime soon."

But he was wrong about that. When I returned three days later I was not allowed into the psyche ward. The harried psychiatrist, meeting me downstairs in the lobby, said the MPs had taken him away.

"Where to?" I cried, stricken.

He said with unexpected compassion, "To the stockade."

"Stockade?" Hadn't I heard that word once before?

"The military detention facility. Jail. At Dachau."

It might as well have been to the moon.

CHAPTER 30

THE COLD SNAP PREDICTED BY THE battalion commander began with a few voluptuous flakes. I sat at the window, watching them waltz from the cloud-laden sky, each the size of a fluffy cotton ball. As the wind rose the slow dance became an increasingly frenzied flurry of feathery down. Soon I was surrounded by a wall of white bits flinging themselves at the glass and on the sill, where they grew into mounds. Dazed by the incessant spinning, I sat with my eyes wide and listened to the wind cutting across ledges and howling around corners.

I'd found a reason to be grateful for Lucius' arrest: he was not out in that gale.

I slept through the rest of the storm and awakened into silence. Peering down to the ground, I saw it was covered with a thick blanket of snow. The cars in the lot were swathed in it. A plow droned on one of the streets. For a long time it was the only sound I could hear. Eventually trams clanged around the circular Scheidplatz. Cars trickled past on cleared roads with hastily scraped portholes on iced windshields, hoods and roofs still showing the marks left by push brooms.

I stomped to the nearest phone booth, called Major Wright, and asked him what he intended to do about Lucius.

"We're going to keep Duncan locked up for a while," he said, sounding jovial. "His CO thinks it might teach him a thing or two—though I'm not convinced. Whether he really attempted a suicide or merely staged one, he's becoming too much of a liability for us. I'm seriously considering suggesting an undesirable discharge. If you think you can talk some sense into him, go ahead. You can catch a ride out to Dachau tomorrow, with our chaplain. Nine o'clock? I'll have a jeep waiting for you in front of headquarters."

*

THE JEEP was already idling when I arrived. Two obviously bored GIs, lounging in front, straightened when I approached. But then Lucius' CO stepped out of the headquarters entrance as if he'd been watching for me from inside the door.

"We'll only be a minute," he called to the driver before asking me to follow him into the building. He led me into the first vacant room and didn't offer me a seat. "I made you a promise the day you came for you prenuptial interview," he said in his peculiar drawl, keeping his voice low. "I'm aiming to keep that promise. The battalion commander wants to kick Duncan out of the Army. I'm going to recommend against it. For your sake and that of your baby. All Duncan has to do in return is to admit his mistakes and apologize to the men he assaulted. Tell him to write it all down. You bring it to me. That's all there is to it. But make it today. They've already started the discharge procedure."

"He says the men jumped him."

"That's not what they told me."

As if they would. "What about the wound on his arm?"

"Self-inflicted."

I stared at him.

"If you recall," he said, his tone oddly intimate. "Last spring I mentioned that the only jobs Duncan is likely to get in the States are gardener or shoeshine boy. With an undesirable discharge he won't even get those. I can't let him do that to you. He's welcome to stew behind bars until he understands his obligations. He owes you. *And* us. Six more years, to be exact. Remind him he did sign a contract, never mind that he has spent every cent of the reenlistment bonus. And tell him I'm not letting him off the hook."

He walked me outside and watched the lanky driver jump out to guide me up and into the rear of the jeep. The black-coated man occupying the other end of the back seat was wearing a hand-knitted scarf that all but obscured his stiff clerical collar. He nodded at me and scooted closer to his window, giving me plenty of room. I was relieved he seemed mild-mannered, his scanty hair a nondescript brown, his cheeks rosy—not at all like the fierce, bushy-browed parish priest who had crippled my childhood. "Hello, Mr. Priest," I said with all the respect I could muster.

"You may call me Father," the chaplain said with a civil smile. "If you're Catholic, that is."

I politely wished him a plain good morning, no label attached.

The driver turned, popping gum. "Mrs. Duncan. Father," he said. "I'm glad you're dressed warm. It's going to get a bit chilly."

"Go extra slow," the priest advised. "The roads will be treacherous."

"We're both crack drivers," the acne-scarred soldier on the passenger seat volunteered.

"Your reputation precedes you," the priest said. "No racing, okay? Four-wheel drive notwithstanding. I'm sure young Mrs. Duncan wants to get to Dachau in one piece. As do I."

"Yes Sir, Father," the driver said, his features arranging themselves along sober lines though his eyes sparkled.

The priest studied me. "You might want to tie that shawl over your ears," he suggested. "Raise your collar and tuck that fine nose of yours inside it." As soon as the jeep started to roll he leaned back and closed his eyes, his features relaxing. Every now and then his lips twitched. It wasn't until we were well on our way that I saw the rosary on his lap, two of his fingers slowly shifting from bead to bead. He was praying for lost souls.

We passed through a frozen black-and-white landscape. The streets were bordered with snow barricades raised by diligent plows. I soon followed the priest's advice, hunching against a numbing draft that cut effortlessly through every opening in the teddy bear coat. It wasn't until we rolled into the parking lot of the stockade that the priest spoke to me again.

"I trust you've given some thought as to where and when you'll baptize your baby," he said in a conversational tone.

Actually, I hadn't.

He read as much in my expression. "Were you married in the Church?" he asked gently.

"Uhm—no," I stammered. "We went to the *Standesamt*."

He put his rosary away and said quietly and matter-of-factly, "Then in the eyes of God you are living in sin. You are not a wife but a harlot. The child will be born a bastard, I'm sorry to say."

Slack-jawed and unable to think of a fitting reply, I watched him climb out at the passenger side and stride away.

The driver helped me onto firm ground. "I'm afraid the good father is quite particular about who he'll let into his heaven, ma'am. But no doubt he'll include you in his prayers tonight. We sinners *are* his bread and butter, you know."

"Is he going to drive back with us?"

"Once he's done taking confessions. You best stay in the waiting room till then. I'll come get you when we're ready to leave."

Hopefully, on the return trip to Henry I would be inspired to some polite but stinging anti-religious remark I could use to bedevil the priest.

*

THE SWELLING on Lucius' face had already gone down. His color was better too, although he had the beginnings of a rough, curly beard. "They won't give me any razor blades," he complained.

"How are you?" I asked, nervously considering the iron bars on the windows and the guard stationed at the cubicle's door, jiggling a bundle of keys. Although he wasn't looking directly at us he could hear everything we were saying.

Lucius shifted in his chair, stretching his long legs halfway across the cell. "This place isn't as bad as you'd think. Better than maneuvers any day. Only weird thing about it is the location. I try not to look across the street. Place gives me the creeps. You keeping snug up in your castle? Got plenty to eat?"

"Thanks to you I'm licking my way through the instant milk one teaspoonful at a time. Most of the powder winds up sticking to my teeth and to the roof of my mouth."

He laughed. "Worse than peanut butter. How's Mother?"

I told him about O.F.'s siege and the felicitous outcome. He marveled at Alex's part in the adventure. Then he turned serious.

"You talked to the battalion commander? He wants me out of his hair. Give me a discharge. Can't be soon enough to suit me."

"What happens afterwards?"

"They ship me to the States."

"And me?"

"I'll send for you. Pepper, too. Once I get a job and an apartment. And enough money for your transportation."

I'd done some growing up since the last time we discussed that subject. "How soon will that be?" I insisted. "I don't know if they let very pregnant women on planes. Or newborns."

He shrugged. "I'm not sure." It was obvious that he hadn't bothered to work out the details. Perhaps he never would.

"Your CO doesn't want to let you go," I said. "He says you owe the Army six more years. Since you already spent the entire bonus."

Lucius's eyes blazed. "After what I've been through? He's got to be kidding. Thinks he's got me over a barrel, huh? Watch this!" He stormed up to the guard. "I need to write a letter. Pen, paper, an envelope." When the guard showed him two empty hands, he added, "For my confession."

Not only did that remark earn him the writing material he had requested but also a clipboard, which he put on his lap, furiously scribbling. When he was done he folded the paper, sealed it into its envelope, and gave it to me. "Don't hand it to my CO. Take it direct to the Major. Promise?"

"Okay."

The guard rattled his keys. Lucius rose. "Next time you come can you bring my socks and some underwear? I'm undersupplied." He put a finger under my chin. "Do me a favor? Check up on Pepper. Make sure she's okay."

I told him I would. The guard opened the door to the waiting room and watched me walk to a seat. Then he closed it again, grating a key in its lock from the other side.

I contemplated the envelope, wondering what Lucius had written. But if he had wanted me to know he would have told me. The messenger was not necessarily entitled to see the content of the message that had been entrusted to her. I stuffed it into my purse, picked up an old Readers' Digest, and leafed through the pages for jokes to lighten my mood.

When the driver finally stuck his head in the door I was more than ready to go. The priest was already sitting on the back seat. As the driver coasted out of the parking lot the priest asked him to stop and then addressed me, pointing across the street. "Look," he said. "Do you know what that place is?"

The two soldiers in the front glanced at each other and groaned. "Father. Please," the driver protested.

"No," the priest said, frowning at him. "It's a guilt she must carry." He turned to me. "See the gate? The barbed wire fence? That's the infamous concentration camp where your people killed six million Jews. Take a good look."

But I couldn't. A thick mist had descended in front of my face. In it materialized a pile of corpses with a young girl on top, shaved bald, with hollow, accusing eyes. The image had burnt itself into my mind one day last year, when I accidentally watched a foreign documentary on TV. It had haunted my unguarded moments ever since.

"I bet Mrs. Duncan wasn't even born then," the driver muttered.

"Nonetheless," the priest said.

The driver gunned the motor and took a sharp right. We drove in silence, my cheeks on fire, my lids squeezed shut. After a while I said, my voice shaking, "I'm sorry." The words blew away on the wind.

*

THE BATTALION commander was not in his office. I stood in the doorway, envelope in hand, wondering if I should simply put it on his desk. Then the CO came in, standing so close behind me that I could smell his mouthwash, and asked, "How did it go?"

I stepped into the room, trying to distance myself from him. "My husband doesn't want to be a soldier anymore."

He followed me inside. "Can't say I'm surprised. What have you got there? The apology?"

"It's for the Major."

The CO pulled the message out of my hand. "Fine. I'll give it to him." Examining both sides of the envelope, he muttered, "It's not even addressed to anyone." He rummaged in the top desk drawer for a letter opener. Slicing it along the crease, he extracted the note and scanned it.

"Sit down, Mrs. Duncan," he said when he was through.

I sat. He contemplated the wall behind me. Then he shut the door and asked, "He showed you the letter?"

I shook my head. He dropped it on to my lap. I read:

> Sir,
> I can't keep my secret any longer. I have always been and will always be a homosexual. I've tried to change but I am what I am. So sorry.
> Sincerely,
> Private Joseph Maddis L. Duncan

I longed for my dictionary. "What's a homosexual?" I asked, feeling faint.

The CO examined my face. "You never heard the term?"

"Not until now."

He expelled an uneasy breath and fidgeted with a jacket button. "That's what they call a man who lusts after men."

At first I didn't understand. Then I did, although I could form no mental picture of likely details. But even without illustrations the meaning was plain—if Lucius was a man who loved men what did that make me? Worse, what did it make the baby?

"If the Major gets this note we're duty bound to expedite that discharge." the CO said with his broad Southern inflection, so like that of Jim and his crew. "Whether or not the confession is true. Is that what you want?"

They would ship him out and leave me to fend for myself. Minus the dependent-allowance. "No!"

"Well, then," he said. "I suggest you put it on the desk and leave. If it gets lost it certainly won't be your fault. Or mine."

Our eyes locked. The hard glint in his showed me that he liked me no better than I liked him. He merely considered me a convenient pawn. Yet I did what he asked, lowering the note on to the desktop as if it were a live grenade. In the war between Lucius and his tormentors I had deliberately broken the promise I made him and gone over to the enemy's side.

CHAPTER 31

I WAS HALFWAY BETWEEN HENRY Kaserne
and the bus stop when an old Ford wagon slowed to a crawl
beside me. The GI behind the wheel took off his cap and rolled
down his window. His tight black curls were full of silvery
threads, and his dusky face, though unwrinkled, looked
decidedly weathered.

"Mrs. Duncan?" he said, his voice cordial, his eyes kind.
"I'm Master Sergeant Sid Murphy—an old friend of your
husband's. I believe you and I are going in the same general
direction. Mind if I take you home?"

"If you are a friend of my husband's how come he's never
mentioned you to me?" I asked, feeling suspicious.

"Ah!" he said. "I guess I should have said, 'A well-meaning
acquaintance.' Ready with a word of advice but only when
asked. Joe's not good about asking."

My trip to Dachau had been so tiring that the idea of
exchanging a lumbering bus ride across town for a few

minutes of comfort in a weather-tight car was quite appealing. "Do you go anywhere near the Scheidplatz?" I asked as if he were driving a cab.

"It just so happens I do. Today," he said.

I sank gratefully onto a seat covered in soft lamb's wool, unbuttoned the top of my coat, and untied the shawl from under my chin. "Do you know where he is?"

He chuckled. "Yes. But that's not half as important as where he's going to be. Young men are bound to mess up. You should have seen me at his age. If it hadn't been for the sensible woman I married I'd probably still be stumbling around clueless." He lowered his sun-visor and tapped on a photo affixed to its back. It showed a middle-aged clear-eyed blonde surrounded by three milk-coffee-brown, curly-haired teenagers, the oldest a boy. "He's in his last year of high school. He'll go to college next fall. In Burlington, Vermont. That's where the wife and I are planning to settle when I retire."

"Where is she from?"

"Here. München. We met at the end of the war. This is my fourth tour of duty in your country. I like to please her. That's why we'll live in Vermont. It reminds her of home."

I looked at him sideways. "Then why not stay here?"

He grinned. "She's become a dedicated American. Besides, we'd never see our kids. But no doubt we'll come back to visit Munich every couple of years."

From the time I was small Mutti had drilled into me that it was impolite to ask nosy questions. But for once my longing to know could not be squelched. "What was it like for you? When you got married?"

He stroked the photo. "Hard. Very hard. I had to rethink my attitude not only toward white people but to black people too. And learn to develop certain . . . social strategies. Our marriage was pretty rocky at first. Seems there wasn't one individual anywhere willing to see beyond our skin color and be on our side. But in the end we were both too stubborn to let the opinions of outsiders control our lives. And too stubborn to give up on each other."

"Oh," I said, with the merest inkling of what he meant. "So. Are you happy now?"

He looked at me. "Are you?"

"We are *very* happy," I said quickly, sitting tall.

His eyes twinkled. And then he laughed. "I remember giving that answer myself. Way back. Let me tell you something I learned since — you're not nearly as happy as you have the right to be. Provided you allow it, that is."

It was obvious he had no idea what Lucius and I had endured. I stared at my overlong fingernails. Lately, they and my hair had been growing like weeds. "Thanks for the ride," I said, although we were only halfway to my destination.

"Sure thing." He snapped on the radio, tuning in a Bavarian folk ensemble playing a boring Landler (a folk dance).

I made a face.

Chuckling, he switched to AFN, where Elvis Presley was singing "Jailhouse Rock." I could never hear that particular song without remembering my own little dancing Elvis.

"Sorry. Bad timing," Murphy said, clicking the radio off. At the Scheidplatz he let the engine idle while he searched for a scrap of paper. "We don't have a phone at the apartment but you can leave a message for me at work. Anytime you need some advice. Okay?" He scrawled down a number and passed it to me.

I stashed it carelessly in a pocket as soon as I got out of his car. What kind of advice could an old man like him possibly have to offer someone like me? Even his eyebrows were turning gray.

*

THERE WAS a large brown paper grocery bag waiting for me in front of my door. The top was folded over and carefully creased so that it would stay shut. Thinking Anna had left it for me, I took it into the apartment and put it up on the counter, wondering why it felt so heavy and limp. Then I looked inside. A curled up, very dead cat looked back at me, its eyes popped out of their sockets. On top of the bloody tiger-striped carcass lay a note, the handwriting on it somewhat familiar. I read,

THIS CAT WASN'T WATCHING ITS STEP. YOU BETTER WATCH YOURS!

With a gulp, I whisked the bag off the counter and returned it to the doorway, extracting the note before locking myself in. I remembered the other note, the one Lucius and I had found on Pepper's windshield that frosty morning. He had thrown it away but I had retrieved it, not wanting to leave that shameful piece of trash on the street. Where did I put it? I'd worn the teddy bear coat then too. I searched every pocket, finding Mr. Murphy's phone number first, and then the original note, balled and squashed deep into the breast pocket. I put Murphy's number in my wallet, smoothed the note as best I could, and placed it next to its mate. Same handwriting. Maybe I should show them to someone. The cat, too. But to whom?

Exhausted, I sat on the couch, placed my hands atop my protruding belly, and waited until the baby gave me a good kick. Lately, it was the only way I had of feeling alive. After I got tired of staring at nothing I opened a science fiction anthology. The print swam in front of my eyes. I was grievously hungry but had absolutely no appetite. And I was too anxious to sleep. So I turned on the radio, permanently tuned to the AFN station, and listened to Gene Pitney wail *A Town Without Pity*. It struck me that the high-rise was very much like a heartless small town. A depressing thought.

For the first time since I got married I moved the tuner — and stumbled across the ever-lurking *Bayrischen Rundfunk*. Classical music. To my dismay, a cultured male voice calmly announced a boring Mozart concerto. Before I could touch the dial again the first chords of a flute piped into the room. Immediately, everything around me was transformed. Colors grew brighter, the furniture more substantial. Something like peace began to enfold me. I lay back and closed my eyes.

The layout of Hannes's exquisite garden instantly appeared on the screen of my mind, complete with his somersault-hill. The flute painted in one detailed memory after another. Flowers unfurled. Bushes bloomed. I followed the stone-covered creek bed to a curved wooden bridge. One musical brush-stroke tempted dowager-chested Pepita out of her lair. She swayed on her naked clawed feet and chirped along. Soon there were blossoms everywhere, in riotous colors. On my way to the pungent herb plot, sound and color faded until I became oblivious to both—and to everything else.

I resurfaced to the rich, creamy tones of a horn breezing through my imagined garden. It swept in and out of the Japanese tea hut, over the bridge and up the grassy knoll. From the top the buttery sound escaped over the tall hedge-wall and flowed across the Bavarian landscape. And wherever it went, white changed to an opulent green. Caressing spring meadows and fields, the melody flew arrow-straight toward the heart of Bavaria—the village of Freidorf. To where a flaxen-haired boy sat on his unmade bed, a golden horn at his lips, shaping my world.

The doorbell rang. Halfway between dream and reality, I answered it to find Spider peering into the grocery bag.

"That your cat?" he said. "Must have been *some* accident!"

I retrieved the ebony cane from behind the coat-stand and gave it to him. "Not my cat. Someone put it there for me to find."

"Say what?" he said, tossing the cane it from one hand to the other. Then he casually sauntered into the living room although I had not invited him in. "Why on earth would somebody give you a dead cat that isn't even yours?" he said, looking all around.

"I don't know. But they left this." I showed him the crude notes and explained where I had found the first one. "Maybe I should take them to the CO tomorrow. The cat, too."

Astonished, he said, "Whatever for?"

"Justice! The notes will show him that he's been listening to lies."

Spider shook his head. "That man will thinks what he wants to think. Nothing you can do about that."

"Okay. I'll take them to the battalion commander then."

He stared at me over the rims of his shades. "Not if you want Joseph to get out. For that he has to act crazy or claim he's a queer. Which is what I advised him to do."

I should have guessed Spider had his hand in this mess somewhere. "Why?" I said, incensed. "If they discharge him he will fly to America and I'll be here all alone."

He shook a finger at me. "You're listening to some mighty lame music there. Mind if I turn it off?" He did just that before I had a chance to reply. Then he said, "I've been meaning to talk to you about . . . *things*. You know I'm going home next week. Being that Joseph and you are headed in my direction I thought you-all could stay in Compton with me for a while. At one of my cousins', that is. Till you get on your feet."

Last time he made a similar offer I had haughtily declined. "I don't have enough money right now for an airplane ticket!" I confessed, my voice thick with humiliation and regret.

Clearly amused, he threw back his head and showed me his molars. The sound of unmitigated mirth, exploding from his pulsing wet gullet, raised goose bumps on my arms. "Of course you don't," he said, chortling. "But you will as soon as you can get Joseph to sign over his little red Simca to me. It'll be no loss to him. Once he gets hisself thrown out he'll have to dump her anyway. If they don't repossess her first. And since I'm getting an *honorable* discharge, the Army's going to ship that pretty car stateside for me. For free. I'll be the only man in America with a Plein Ciel."

He let his words linger between us. Then he leaned closer. "Soon as you give me the signed pink slip I'm heading to the American Express for your ticket. I'll get the paperwork done before I ship out, catch me a military plane to New York and pick up the car on the dock. Mosey her cross-country on the open road. When your plane lands at LAX I'll be waiting for you at the gate. With an apartment and everything. All you have to do is show up." He slapped his hands on the two notes. "These things are useless to you. And if you take them to the battalion commander now — with the general coming and all — he'll just lose them so he can tell the general out-and-out lies about how honky-dory everything on base is for the colored soldiers. You can bet he'll make sure Joseph stays put in the brig till the general is gone. Then he'll give the crackers another go at him. They've already got his number. Any way you look at it Joseph's best bet is the confession he wrote. The one you took to headquarters this morning."

Guilt at my bungled assignment washed through me. "The Major wasn't in his office. The CO told me to put it down on the desk."

Spider collapsed on to the couch and groaned, "Girl, you ought to know by now that Joseph is his favorite whipping boy. And you might have realized that your husband's too obstinate to keep hisself out of trouble. They bait him and he falls for it, every time." He twirled the cane, lost his grip, and watched it clatter to the parquet. Then he lowered his voice. "You should have stuck with *me* last year, Maria. Didn't I try to warn you about what that young Blood might be getting his self into?"

He was right about the confession — I should have kept it in my purse, browsed through the store till the lunch hour was over, and returned to headquarters after one o'clock. "I made a mistake with the note," I admitted. "How can I fix it?"

With an exasperated sigh Spider bent to retrieve his cane. "Try again. Tomorrow. Take Joseph some writing paper and tell him to start over. Convince him to sign the pink slip at the same time. Hand it to me. Then I'll drive you to Henry where you'll put the new confession in the battalion commander's hands before twelve. And in the afternoon I'll run to Warner and buy you that plane ticket. Which I will deliver to you in person tomorrow evening. Right around dark."

He was spinning out ideas faster than I could think. "Did you and my husband talk this over?" I asked, feeling a headache coming on.

"Naw. Just a couple of snatches here and there. But I'm a good guesser. And I don't mind helping out friends. Yep, I do believe my bronchitis is going to act up tomorrow morning. I'll get the CO to give me a pass to the hospital. You wait for me inside that bus shelter at Warner."

I told him I would. He left soon after.

Since I was little I had suffered from a severe case of homesickness for a country I had never seen. If I couldn't get to America now I would be condemned to live the rest of my days in Germany as a permanent exile in the land of my birth.

Maybe it was time I asked myself a few questions. Was I simply getting lost in an obsession or was I pursuing an obtainable dream? What or whom was I willing to trade in order to get what I wanted? And how reliable a savior might Spider turn out to be?

I didn't realize he'd taken the notes with him until I opened a can of over-salted beef stew on the counter for supper that night. When I checked outside the door I discovered that the dead cat was gone too.

*

"WHY aren't you taking your own car to America with you?" I asked Spider as we pulled into the stockade's parking lot the next morning.

"What, this old jalopy? It ain't worth more than twenty-five bucks. On a good day. Naw, I got my heart set on Joseph's perfect little Pepper. Besides, I like a great bargain. As long as I'm the one comes out ahead." He parked between two jeeps. "I'll stay in the car. Got everything you need?"

"In here," I said, tapping my purse before shouldering Lucius's duffle bag. The roads had been cleared and the sky was an arctic blue. The morning sun, although powerless to warm the wintry air, made the snow sparkle like diamonds.

I was afraid I might not be able to see Lucius without the Major's written permission, but the soldier behind the desk recognized me from my previous visit. "I brought my husband some clothes," I said, handing over the duffle filled with socks and underwear. He emptied it on to the desk, sorted through the contents, stuffed them back in, and held the bag out to me. "Purse, too. Regulations," he said, pawing through it as if I were attempting to smuggle in a weapon.

Soon the door to the cubicle opened and the guard from yesterday beckoned me in. Lucius was already sitting on one of the two chairs, an extra day's worth of new wiry fuzz on his face.

"I brought you the stuff you wanted," I began, putting the duffle bag on his knees.

He dropped it to the floor at his feet. "How did it go? What did the battalion commander have to say about my letter?"

I swallowed and sat close beside him. "That's why I came back so soon. I'm afraid it got lost. Spider says you better give me another one. I'll get it right this time."

He made a dissing sound, which I knew I deserved.

I brought out the stationery and watched him rewrite the note — this time without visible passion. Once he'd sealed the envelope I slipped it inside my purse, exchanging it for the car-ownership document I'd found on the bottom of his sock drawer. My fingers trembled when I put it before him. "Spider says you'll be out in no time. After you sign this over to him he'll buy me a ticket to Los Angeles. Maybe I'll get there before you do."

"Spider says," he echoed, turning the document over to read the printed instructions on the back side. But then he put down the pen he'd been holding and stared at me. Hard. "As I recall, you never trusted the guy. Why do you care what he says all of a sudden? Is it because he can give you what you've always wanted when I can't?"

"You should talk," I spit, mindful of the watching guard. "You were planning to leave me behind!"

Lucius glared. "I figured you could stay with your mother and Hannes until I send for you. Instead of sleeping under a bridge with me in L.A. And being a drag."

"I belong with you, not with them," I said in a fierce whisper. "Spider said we can stay with his cousin till you find a job."

I saw that his fingernails were chewed to the quick. He dropped his hands to the cleft between his thighs, muttering, "Which one? According to him he's got dozens. We don't even know what these so-called relatives are like. But I bet he hasn't asked any of them if they're itching for two extra mouths to feed. Or three." He hesitated. "I was kind of hoping to leave Pepper with your mother for a while."

"She'll be in Italy until spring."

"Or Anna," he said, shifting around on his chair.

"She can't drive. And God knows what the Americans in our high-rise would do to it when nobody's watching. At least this way the car will wind up in the states. Maybe Spider will let you buy it back—for the price of my ticket."

"Then you don't know Spider."

"What it comes right down to," I said, no longer caring who overheard, "is that you finally have to choose between your wife and your car."

For a second I thought he was going to cry. Then he picked up the pen and scrawled down his name. I eased the document out from under his slack hands. "Or," I said, taking the false confession out of my purse, "you could tear this up and stay here with Pepper *and* me. In the Army."

"Never!" he said, rising and turning away.

Frowning, the guard preceded me to the door. As I stepped into the waiting room, I told Lucius, "I'll come again just before I fly out. To bring you my new address. So we won't lose touch."

"If I'm still here." His voice had grown cold. He kept his back toward me, waiting for the guard to shut the door between us. I felt the beginnings of a headache tighten around my head like a vice.

*

"THAT WAS short 'n sweet," Spider said as I climbed on to the passenger seat. "You got what we came for?"

Since when was *I* part of his *we*? "Yes," I admitted with some reluctance.

He held out his hand. "Pink slip?"

"He signed it," I said, feeling as if I were betraying Pepper. "It's yours the instant *after* you give me the ticket."

His eyebrows shot up. "Say what?!"

I raised my chin, though I was quaking inside. "I wasn't born yesterday."

"Course not," he said, driving out of the lot. "You were born the day *before* yesterday."

I kept my head down as we sped past the fence enclosing the concentration camp.

"How'd he take it?" Spider asked a few minutes later.

"How do you think?" I snapped. "You know he worships that car."

"He was going to lose it anyway," he reminded me. "Time he realized his life won't be all cherries."

Nothing about what we were doing felt right and yet it was the only logical and reasonable solution to my predicament. I only wished I could have said a proper good-bye to Mutti, but thanks to Hannes, at least we had celebrated our departure together. And also thanks to him she would never need me. For anything. First chance I had I would send her a postcard from L.A., the center of the known universe. The only thing I really regretted was that she would be too far away to play the role of doting grandmother.

When we arrived at Henry Kaserne Spider said, "He gave you the car keys, I hope."

"I believe it was towed. The CO—"

"I don't want him in my business. No keys, no ticket. Don't you have spares?"

"I know where to find them. If you take me to where Pepper is parked."

He frowned at his watch. "All right. It's only eleven. And by the way—I'm changing her name. To . . . Cherry." Grinning, he slapped his thigh. "Cherries are red, too—and much sweeter than peppers."

The barracks had come alive. Trucks and jeeps passed in and out of the gate. GIs walked on the side of the road. From behind one of the ugly long buildings men were yelling as if they were at a soccer match until one commanding voice overrode them with, '*ten-TION!* A group of soldiers, smoking outside the PX, watched us cruise past, their mouths tight until Spider rolled down his window and called, "Hey guys— you-all have a good workout in the boonies? This place sure was lonesome without you!"

They shook their heads and laughed.

"I know how to play 'em," Spider said, driving on. "If they towed my sweet little Cherry on to this base she's probably sitting behind the motor pool."

I saw her as soon as we got there. No other foreign sports car had her style or her spiffy shade of red. Spider parked close beside her, got out, and tried her door. It was locked. I felt around on the inside of Pepper's rear bumper until I found a small metal tin. I dropped it into my purse.

"Aw, come on," Spider said. "Might as well see if you can start the engine. We'll do a few loops around this empty lot. You drive."

It was a reasonable request. While I unlocked the door he went to the passenger side. Then he gave a horrified gasp. I ran up behind him and saw it too—the passenger door was crushed; something big and heavy had scraped a groove from the dent to the right headlight, shattering it in its socket.

I said, "Jim."

Spider's face hardened. "The mother's gonna pay for this. Big."

I thought I'd misheard him. "What does your mother have to do with it?"

He tore off his shades. His eyes were filled with rage. "You're a kick!" he yelled. "You know that? A real kick!" Circling Pepper, then walking away from her, he gawked at the squashed passenger side. At last he stuffed the shades in his coat and raised his face to the sky, twisting it into an agonized grimace. Then he stamped his feet, yelling, "Our deal's off! I'm not buying no busted car! Everybody in Compton be laughing at me! I hate people laughing at me!" He threw himself into the jalopy. "Jim done messed with the wrong man. Don't *nobody* make a fool out of me!" Peeling rubber, he reversed out of his parking space and careened away.

My best guess was that he was *not* headed to the American Express for my plane ticket. For some reason this did not worry me. I relocked Pepper — as if anyone would want to steal a grossly disfigured sports car — and pushed the keys into the zippered mirror-pocket inside my purse. Then I walked down the lane toward headquarters. When I arrived there I fished for Lucius's envelope but I couldn't make my legs go inside.

"You promised to get it right this time!" a voice within me complained.

"Tomorrow," I said, feeling my headache recede. "Maybe I'll do it tomorrow."

*

ANNA had pushed a message under my front door. "Come see me right away. Very important!"

I went to her apartment. She answered my knock wearing no make-up except for lightly penciled-on eyebrows. It made her look soft and pretty. Her hair was drawn back and held in place with a plain rubber band. I recognized the paint-speckled jeans and plaid flannel shirt she was wearing as belonging to Horst.

He was dressed in similar clothes, standing by the window in front of an easel. "Oh, good. We're done and here you are," he said with a warm smile. "We were *hoping* you'd give us enough time to finish our project. I'll drop it off in Grünwald on our way out of town."

Anna cleared her throat. "Sit down," she told me, pulling a chair away from her table. It was the first time she'd ever been solicitous toward me.

"What's wrong?" I asked, immediately suspicious.

She picked up an old newspaper. "I was covering the floor around the easels with a bunch of these. I just happened to glance at this one. Look, I've made a circle around what I found." She held a page in front of my nose. "Read it. Go on."

The ink she used to mark the report had bled into the rough paper. I read:

> MOTORCYCLE ACCIDENT IN MIESBACH. A group of inebriated young men, leaving a dance on their BMWs late yesterday night, encountered an icy stretch of highway and lost control of their cycles. One of the revelers flipped, breaking his neck in the process. Gabriel Bauer was rushed to the hospital but is not expected to recover.

I sat. My hands shook. "How old is this newspaper?" I asked, afraid of what Anna might say next.

"At least a month. Hilde doesn't have a phone, of course. So we called Freidorf's inn for more information. Gabriel's paralyzed but alive. And he's been asking for you." She put a coat on over her borrowed work clothes—a completely unprecedented move. "Since Lucius is still on maneuvers Horst has offered to take us."

The only thing I could think of, on the long drive, was that the three most important men in my life were falling like bowling pins, though they were far less likely to rebound.

CHAPTER 32

THE CLOSER WE CAME TO MIESBACH the taller the mountains loomed before us, their snow-covered peaks coldly majestic under a frail afternoon sun. Once we reached the outskirts of town Horst followed some scribbled instructions and soon got us to the hospital. He charged down several hallways ahead of Anna and me, then stopped at a closed door and said, "Maria, you better go in by yourself first. I saw a Wirtschaft (inn) across the street. Anna and I could use a quick bite." He took her arm and steered her back the way we had come.

I wished I could have gone with them. The last thing in the world I wanted was to walk into that room and find out how hurt Gabriel was. But then I realized that the door wasn't shut all the way. When I nudged it a bit I could hear a murmuring female voice. Slowly, I pushed the gap wider. I saw a white metal bed, white sheets, a white body-cast. Imprisoned in it, Gabriel lay trussed to the mattress, his sky-blue eyes resting upon the rosy face of the girl reading to him from a chair at the foot of his bed. She wore a pin-striped apron and looked a lot like me except that her hair was hazelnut-brown and in braids and her silhouette was enviably slender. Her head was bent earnestly over a book. I knocked while she was turning a page.

Gabriel's eyes found mine. "Maria!" he said.

The girl blushed, jumped to her feet, and slammed the book shut. "My goodness, it's late," she stammered. "I've stayed much too long!"

As she rushed past me, Gabriel called, "Come back soon. I don't know what I'd do without you!" When she was gone he said, "Sabine keeps me company twice a day. We usually plow through one chapter per visit. But since she loves to read as much as I love to listen time does fly. While she is here, that is." Then he just looked at me, not missing a bulge or strained button. "When Hilde couldn't find you I was sure you'd gone to America. For good."

I sat on the vacated chair. "We just found out what happened to you. From an old newspaper. I'm sorry."

With a wistful smile he said, "Don't be. I've learned a lot, lying here. About how I've been throwing my life away. Soon as the hubbub died down and it became clear I'd be in here for a very long time, my drinking buddies deserted me, one by one. Now nobody comes to see me anymore except for Sabine — and Hilde who visits on Sunday afternoons."

"It's not easy to get here from Freidorf without a car."

"Easy enough by motorcycle," he amended. "But I no longer mind. Being alone gives me plenty of time to think. About my mistakes. And everything. "

"Everything?" I whispered.

His eyes glistened. "Mom shouldn't have agreed so easily to let you go. I should have stopped you. Be honest with me —

on the morning you left, if I'd said I wanted you with me for the rest of our lives—would you have stayed?"

He saw the answer in my eyes and asked, "But are you happy now?"

It was impossible to hide the truth from the boy who used to be like a twin. So I modified it. "My husband and I are working on it. Besides—I've made my bed and all."

"You love him?"

I thought about it for a few seconds. Then I nodded.

"More than me?"

I shook my head. And modified again. "Not more. Just differently. You were right last year. I *was* too young to get married. So were you. Lucius too. He's only twenty. Like you."

He stared at my belly. "If it weren't for the baby in there I'd tell you everything I've saved up to tell. But now I can't. Except—" His gaze fastened to mine. "Any friend of yours is a friend of mine. Forever. Even if he is your husband. Understand? Once I'm—"

The intensity of our moment was lost when Anna gave a tactful cough from the doorway. She was holding a small bouquet of white carnations, sure to blend with the decor. "Ouch!" she said cheerfully. "You look like you've been hit by a truck! Mind if we come in?"

He grinned. "Bitte (please do)! It's not as bad as it looks. See—I can wiggle my toes." He demonstrated. We clapped and he said, "According to my doctor that's a good sign. He thinks there's every chance I'll be as I was. Once everything heals."

Horst had a knack for chatting and putting the rest of us at ease. Soon we were laughing over old memories—the time Anna and Gabriel had talked me into sticking a pin into an electric socket when I was too small to know better. The time a hive of bees chased Gabriel across the farmyard. The time we feasted on green plums and all three of us were stricken afterwards with the same intestinal symptoms. The time I got lost in the woods and Gabriel was the only one who could find me. The flying ants, swarming all over our pretend-tea party.

We talked until it grew dark outside. Then Horst looked at his watch. "That was fun. I hope you'll let us come back next weekend. But now we better leave before the roads become icy. Anna, let's go to the inn, see if they're willing to fill my thermos with fresh coffee. Maria — we'll wait for you in the car. Take your time."

"He's nice," Gabriel told me after they left. "Ein echter Bayer (a true Bavarian)." It was the highest praise one genuine Bavarian was capable of giving another.

"Not like O.F.," I said. "Did anyone tell you he moved away?" In a rush, I related his last stand and the resulting defeat.

Gabriel waited until I ran out of steam. Then he said, "What I meant to say, before — Mom and I want you to bring your husband to the farm. The baby, too. In the summer. When I'm all better. Promise?"

"Do you think Freidorf is ready for Lucius and me?"

He grinned. "I'll make sure it is. A visit from the three of you will enlighten the rest of us. Drag us more fully into this century."

Carefully, I sat on the edge of the bed and put my cheek to his, savoring the warmth of his skin. "I will if you do me a favor first."

"What favor?"

"As soon as you can sit up and hold a book I want you to read to Sabine."

He blushed. "Hey — you know what I'm thinking."

"Not really," I said. "But I know what you're feeling. And always will."

On the drive back to Munich Anna sat astonishingly close to Horst. They talked companionably back and forth. I stared out into the night. A month ago Gabriel had been a wild boy on a collision course with disaster. The crisis he was being forced to work through had already served to transform him into a man. Was it possible that Lucius might emerge from *his* crisis equally whole?

*

HIS CONFESSION, though in my purse and thus out of sight, was never far from my mind. Every evening I was determined to take it to the battalion commander the next day. But I could never make myself go. After wavering for a week I tore the thing to shreds and stuffed them down my garbage pail. Then I dialed Murphy's number and asked him to take me to Dachau. To my relief, he readily agreed. Nonetheless, I felt guilty for taking up the time of an almost total stranger toward my own selfish ends.

"How are things in the battalion?" I asked after I got into his car.

With a big grin he said, "Never a dull moment, these past few days. You'd be surprised."

"About what?"

He laughed. "Things. Mighty *big* things. Now that the general's arrived."

"Is Spider still here?"

"No. He left yesterday. Took his entire collection of canes but gave away his jalopy. To the unfortunate Washington. Probably means it's about to break down. Good thing Washington works in the motor pool."

"Is Compton really at a long beach, like Spider said?"

"Huh?" Murphy looked startled. "You're talking about the Compton on the south side of L.A.? No beach within shouting distance. Far as I know."

I wasn't surprised. "You've been to California?"

"Wife liked it fine at first. But after a couple of years of nothing but merciless blue skies without so much as a snowflake for Christmas my Wanda got antsy. Said she needed more clouds, less heat, and four honest seasons. Which is why we agreed on Vermont." He chuckled fondly. "We've got a bunch of books on the subject. Wanda likes to do research. Lots of pictures too. Come to our house next Sunday and check it out. Bring Joe, if you can."

I sighed. "He may not be around long enough to accept your invitation."

Murphy gave me an enigmatic smile. "Then again, he might."

We arrived at the stockade just as a convoy of military vehicles was leaving the lot. One of the jeeps stopped close beside us. An aging soldier with shaggy white brows rolled down his window. He was wearing a full dress uniform crowded with decorations. Murphy executed a sharp salute. The soldier returned it, less snappy, and beckoned to him.

"Go on inside," Murphy told me, getting out of his car. "While I say good-bye to a friend."

Both men watched me walk away. I could feel their benevolent eyes on my back until I entered the waiting room. The place looked as if it had been scrubbed and polished all night. I smelled floor wax and lemon oil. The door to the cubicle was already open. Lucius was standing inside, by himself. His freshly shaved face lit up the cell, shining as if he'd just been in the presence of God's special messenger. I got ready to confess my most recent sin.

"Guess what," he said, holding up a sheaf of papers. "The general was here. He said he wanted to apologize on behalf of a few very misguided souls. He called me 'son.'" He collapsed on a chair. "Sat right beside me and helped me work out this plan." He showed me what looked like a map, full of bold diagrams and underlined words. "Career goals, he called them." Lucius touched the chart with reverence. "He told me I'm about to get a new CO. The old one's been reassigned. To Korea." He dimpled. "It means I'll make PFC back before you know it. This time I'm keeping the stripe. The general says my promotion is long overdue. Spec 4 will be next. Then Spec 5, which is the same as sergeant. More pay with each step. Only thing is — that letter I gave you — "

My heart thudded. The hour of reckoning had arrived. "That's why I came. To tell you I couldn't bring myself . . . that is, I tore it up. Even though I promised — "

"Oh, good," he said with a huge sigh of relief.

"Good?"

"Yeah. It would have spoiled everything." He struggled for some emotional distance. "So. You're still leaving?"

I shook my head. "I'm not if you're not."

His face relaxed into a smile. "Then I guess we're both staying. Pepper's cramped little rear bench is just big enough to hold a baby's car seat and a diaper bag, did you notice?"

"I noticed."

He looked toward the waiting room, absently trying to nibble a finger nail that was already chewed to the quick. "Say, who gave you a ride?" he asked. "Spider?"

"No, he's gone." I sat beside him and pulled his hand down to my lap, where I cradled it between both of mine. "It was an old guy named Murphy."

He grinned. "Good old master sergeant Sid Murphy. I used to call him 'preacher' because he was always trying to give me advice. Till I told him I didn't need any. Boy, was I wrong."

I said, "We're going to his house for coffee next week. When are you getting out of here?"

"The general wants me to wait for the paperwork to catch up with his orders. Tomorrow, he said. And the minute I'm released I'm heading for home."

I decided not to mention Pepper's little mishap, afraid the news might dampen his glow.

*

"DON'T even *try* to be perfect," Murphy preached while driving me back to the city. "And don't expect Joe to be. At least not for the next twenty years or so. And listen—don't be surprised if black women won't like you any better than white men like him."

Now there was a thought that hadn't occurred to me. Mainly because I had yet to *meet* any. Until Murphy's dire prediction I'd assumed they would treat me like a long-lost sister.

"Learn to appreciate him the way he is now," he counseled. "Nurture what you two have going between you — and let it grow."

"Yessir," I said, biting my tongue.

"Really, if you think about it, we're social pioneers. Bound to change the life of everyone we meet." I could tell this wasn't the first time he'd mused on the subject. And he was right; that was exactly what we were.

"Good-will ambassadors and ice-breakers!" he went on. "Especially our babies."

Those had been fleeting thoughts of mine on my first real date with Lucius, without the baby part.

"But nobody's an island," Murphy embellished. "What you need is to hang out more with people like us." He stopped just before the Scheidplatz and looked at the high-rise. "Might as well take you to your front door." Spotting the access road, he cruised toward the lot, parking in the hinter-most row. "You'll like my kids. If I'm not mistaken you're the same age as my boy."

"Was that the general we saw driving out of the lot at the stockade?" I asked, buttoning my coat.

"He and I go way back. In fact, he came to Henry because I asked him to," Murphy acknowledged, all at once serious. "I wouldn't be telling you this without his okay. He thought you should know that *someone* passed him a couple of nasty notes along with a dead cat and a hot tip about a hit-and-run. We found red paint chips on the bumper of Jim's car. Everyone involved in the harassment is being transferred to the four corners of the earth. And Jim is paying for some mighty expensive repairs. The little Simca will be out of the body-shop by tomorrow."

"That *someone* was Spider?"

"Not at liberty to say. But since you mentioned his name — he asked me to give this to Joe. With his best wishes." He took a bundle from the back seat and planted it on my lap.

I opened it and saw a beloved white suit of the finest Italian linen, carefully folded, a red tie coiled in the upended white hat resting on top.

"That outfit mean anything to you?" Murphy asked.

"A lot," I said. I started to climb out. He grabbed my wrist.

"Not now. Look." He nodded toward the curb in front of the lobby, where three over-sized American cars stood in a row, their trunks open. The car in front was red and had a white convertible top. The one in the middle was yellow with murderous shark fins. The third was a nondescript faded green, shaped like a bullet. A much subdued Linda was stumbling out of the lobby, lugging two hefty suitcases.

"I don't understand why she's so mean. She can't be from the American south like her friends; she has a German accent. Where does her arrogance come from?"

"She's trying too hard to pass," Murphy guessed. "Fit in with the wrong crowd."

"They made her their queen bee," I said, still bitter. "She's the worst of the lot."

Dowdy Nancy and spindly Barb appeared next, dragging large suitcases of their own. The three husbands brought up the rear, carrying an array of bags. They stashed them in the yawning trunks. The women went into a huddle and hugged. The men punched each other on their biceps. Then they all got into their cars and the three vehicles pulled away from the curb in a funereal procession.

"The general said the transfers would be swift," Murphy grinned. "I can see he wasn't kidding." Then his voice grew official. "The high-rise is now secure. Go up in peace. There won't be any more dead cats. I guarantee it." We shook good-bye. He pressed a greeting card-sized envelope at me. "Don't open it till you're inside your front door." As I climbed out I heard him mutter, "No more'n sixteen! Like my Lewis, for crying out loud!"

On the lift I wondered why Spider had stuck out his neck and gone to the general. Revenge? Altruism? For friendship's sake? As soon as I entered the apartment, I tore open the envelope and read,

> SAY MARIA
> I forGoT tO mEntION thaT I boughT yOuR pLAnE tickET WAY aHeaD of TimE. IT's uSeLeSS to ME NOw. YOu cAn DO with iT whaT you wAnT But iF you aSk ME YOu sHOuld START A LiTTle fAMILY EmERGency funD. BecAuSe NO cHild Should cOME intO thiS World wiTH nothing. EspeciaLLy oNe borN to A crazy couple name of MARIA and JoSeph.
>   TAKE gOOd caRe of <u>both</u> youR bAbies.
> LoTS Of luck—
> SPIDER

Under the letter was a ticket for the twenty-fourth of December. I suspected Spider had intended it to be somebody's Christmas present — though I wasn't sure whose.

There wasn't the slightest doubt in my mind that I would ask for a cash refund in the morning. Touching American soil was no longer an urgent necessity. I was beginning to suspect there were decent people like Hannes *and* misguided people like Linda's bunch on every part of the globe. As far as lush scenery was concerned, it would be hard to meet Bavaria's equal anywhere. Besides, there were plenty of good things waiting to tumble into my life right where I was if only I could muster the patience to wait for them to unroll.

*

THE FIRST good thing happened the next afternoon. I was hanging out of the window for the hundredth time, checking the access road for a small red sports car when a cheerful voice called, "Well, hello!" It belonged to a chubby young woman sticking her nose out of the window next door. "I'm Fanny. My husband and I just moved in yesterday. I hear you and I have something in common. I'm pregnant, too."

"If you heard that then you probably already know my name's Maria," I said dubiously. "Are you sure you can afford to be seen talking to me?"

She blinked in confusion. And then she laughed. "Oh, that. Some of the more cliquish Americans around here warned me not to speak to you but I told them right quick I wasn't about to play their stupid games. Listen — I've got the kettle on. Come on over for tea. I'll show you my baby's layette if you show me yours."

Before I could say yes I saw something red with my peripheral vision. It was a triumphant Pepper, returning to her favorite roost. "There's my husband!" I told Fanny. "At last!"

"With my Charlie close behind him," she said. Charlie parked a black Studebaker next to Pepper just as Lucius began unfolding himself from the driver's seat. When he reached his full height I noticed with relief that his hair was newly shorn. He looked just as handsome as he had the day we first met. Charlie got out of the Studebaker and walked around its rear end toward Lucius. I could see he was at least one head shorter. He said something, holding out his hand. Lucius took it. They shook. Then they both glanced in our direction. Fanny and I waved, recklessly hanging out of our neighboring windows.

"Or Coke," Fanny said as we watched the two men walk toward the entrance together. "Charlie loves Cokes. I keep a couple of bottles chilled in the fridge. Oh do say you'll come."

"Of course," I said with great satisfaction. "We'll be right over."

EPILOGUE

WE FINISHED GITTA'S Kaffee und Kuchen (coffee and cake) on a glorious Indian summer afternoon of the following year. Although the village church bell was tolling four o'clock, daylight was still warm and golden, even when we drew close to the lake. Vati and Gitta took turns pushing the stroller; he because his legs were still a bit wobbly and he needed something to hold on to, she because her advanced pregnancy was giving her a constant backache and she appreciated the extra support.

Arm in arm, Lucius and I walked through the village beside them. Our shadows melted into each other on the road stretching before us. He looked quite spiffy in his white suit and I was wearing a sunday-sedate but form-fitting dress that met Vati's stringent approval, though my chestnut hair was as loose and long as it had been on my wedding day. The entire population of *Eichensee* seemed to be afoot, promenading. They passed by us in twos and threes, keeping Vati busy tipping his new hat. I suspected he'd bought it especially for the momentous occasion. As for the Duncans, our recent, successful family outing to Freidorf had been an apt rehearsal for us three roving ambassadors.

Even the corpulent Eichensee mayor, *mit Frau*, wanted a glimpse of our baby. As he waddled importantly closer, Vati lifted his hat with aplomb. "Fine day for a walk, isn't it, *Herr Bürgermeister?* Have you met my grandson Christopher? A strapping boy. Only six months, can you believe it? They grow them big these days."

Bareheaded Lucius gave a dignified bow and offered an amiable "*Guten Tag.*"

The mayor insisted on shaking his hand. "*Ein sympatischer Typ,*" he told his cooing wife. Even Lucius knew by now the phrase meant "a congenial fellow."

"My American son-in-law," Vati explained for the umpteenth time. "And my daughter, Maria. Now which of us do you think the baby resembles?"

The mayor stroked both his chins, musing. "Christopher has his father's eyes," he finally declared. "And Maria's hair and jaw line."

"Nonsense!" Vati huffed. "Can't you see the boy has my nose? As for the hair—if he has Maria's it's only because she has mine. It's all in the family, you see. All in the family." Then he clamped the hat back on his head, grabbed the stroller handle, and pushed on. Above us, a lark trilled, rising straight up into the fleece-dappled Bavarian skies. And little Christopher, snug in the stroller, gave an answering squeal of pure delight, waving his small hands through the gilded air as if bestowing a blessing.

PRIVATE WALLS—Glossary

Abendstille   the stillness of evening
Ach die Männer   Men!
Ach so   is that so! . . . oh, really?
Ach Gott   Oh God!
Ach, schon gut   all right then
Ach wo!   Oh, come on now!
Alle meine Entchen   all my little ducklings
Also   all right then
Ami   American (American soldiers)
Aufmachen, bitte   open up (the door)
Aus Rosenheim   from Rosenheim
Bauerneck   similar to breakfast nook, with Bavarian decorations
Bauernhöfe   farmsteads
Bausparvertrag   a savings account toward buying a house in cash
Bayrischer Rundfunk state-owned Bavarian broadcasting
Bei Nacht und bei Nebel   (literally) bei night and bei fog i.e. come what may, no matter what
Bienenstiche   little rectangular pastry with cream filling topped with nuts and sweet frosting
Bretzen   soft, full-sized Pretzels, fresh baked
Brotzeit   informal meal, mostly with rolls and an assortment of sausages

Bude   shack

Bürgermeister   mayor   **mit Frau**   with wife

Dein dichliebender Franz   your loving Franz

Eene (eine) solche Frechheit   what nerve!

Ein echter Bayer   a true Bavarian, a Bavarian native

Eine solche Schande   what a disgrace!

Einen Neger   a Negro

Eintopf   stew with lots of vegetables

Ersatz   an inferior substitute

Es tut mir leid   I'm so sorry

Es wahr ja gemein . . . It was mean. It's not okay to do that to somebody.

Frauen   women

Frau Leutnant   Mrs. Lieutenant

Franz, bitte nicht   Franz, please don't

Für Zucker und Sahne . . .   there's not enough in our budget for sugar and cream

Gamsbart   beard of the elusive mountain goat

Ganz toll   great!

Gell   an affirmative, such as… *isn't it? don't you? hmm?*

Gestatten   may I?

Gib acht   watch out, watch it

Goldig   cute

Grüss Gott   God's greetings!

Guten Abend   good evening

Hackerkeller   a well-known inn, which is an outlet for the house brand beer

Hallo   hello

Himmeldonnerwetter!   A combination of *heavens!* and *thunder-weather!*

Hure   whore

Ich bin eine Münchnerin   unlike you, I'm a true citizen of Munich

Ich gedulde keine Widerrede   I'll tolerate no backtalk

Ja, Augenblick   just a minute   a moment, please
Ja mei, vornehm halt   a bit elegant   somewhat refined
Kachelofen   custom-built tile stove
Kaufhaus   big department door in center of Munich
Kirsch   cherries **Kirschtorte**   a very rich, fancy cake
Kirschwasser   cherry brandy
Knödel   dumplings
Lass das   leave it   stop it
Lederhosen   leather pants, usually shorts
Liebes Lottchen   dear Lottchen
Mäuse   mice
Mein Gott   my God!
Mensch, ärgere dich nicht   a form of the board game like "Aggravation"   lit., Human, don't get mad—often an impossible feat
Mischling   racially mixed person . . . mulatto
Mit Frau   with wife
Münchner   a native of Munich
Neger   Negro
Nicht diese Töne   watch your tone, lighten up
Nicht wahr   isn't that right?
Nix   absolutely not!
Pack zu   **(Back zua)** help yourself,   eat up
Prima   great, fine, swell
Reiberdatschi   latkes, potato pancakes
Sau Breiss (Preusse)   Prussian pig   (a reaction to the more aggressive Prussian personality)
Schutzhund   guard dog , a dog with police-dog training
Sehr gut   very good
Servus   local greeting, means both *hello* and *good-bye*
Standesamt   a place where civil weddings are performed
Stossverkehr   bumper to bumper traffic
Struwelpeter   wild-haired character in an ever-popular children's picture book

Tja   oh, well
Tja Mei   not as corny as *oh woe,* but similar sentiment
Toll   fantastic, great
Trost   consolation
Und?   so   so what?
Und ich bin Rosa aus Rosenheim   and I am Rosa from Rosenheim
Verdammt noch mal   dammit!
Verzeihung   excuse me, pardon me
Viktualienmarkt   a big, well-known outdoors produce market in the center of Munich
Von wegen   that's what you think!   Indeed!
Was gibts?   what's happening?
Was ist los?   what's up?
Wie gehts?   how are you?
Wie gesagt, die Amis . . .   Like I said, the Americans are all crazy! Eggs are for eating, not for throwing around!
Wirtschaft   an inn
Zwetschgendatschi   a sweet pizza-like dough, baked on a cookie sheet, topped with prune-plums, cinnamon and sugar

www.ingramcontent.com/pod-product-compliance
Lightning Source LLC
Chambersburg PA
CBHW020327180626
46812CB00001B/87